THE

ARSH

BEN SEARA

I am your pen, the one you imagine with. I am the writer, Ben Saree, and I still believe that a person's relationship with the books, stories, and legends they love—and the people with whom they share unforgettable moments—is rarely the result of planning. More often, it's a beautiful coincidence, one we all wish would repeat itself, each time with the same soul-enchanting beauty.

And here, that same coincidence repeats itself with you, the moment your eyes fell upon this book: The Book of Archie and the Fairy of Love Maya, where the playful mermaid Ella weaves through the tale, alongside the love of Archie's life, Charlotte. You will meet the hybrid monster Radenback, who will haunt them through most of the chapters until his dark story is revealed. There is also Isabella and her Book of Destinies, the Magic Pitcher and the desperate attempt to reclaim it before the curse completes its hold. And, finally, the legend of the Healing Ghost, whose appearance will turn the scales in ways both mysterious and terrifying, at a moment you least expect.

Here, do not expect complexity or ambiguity to burden your imagination; Instead, this is a paradise of pure fantasy, its doors wide open to you now. If you cross its threshold, you may never want to leave, for within its pages you will find that same eternal coincidence—an immersive world that you will never want to escape.

This version is polished and ready to set the tone for an exciting and imaginative journey!

Your beloved Archie awaits you.

TABLE OF CONTENTS

INTRODUCTION

When the boy (Archie) leaves his small, secluded village, travelling to the kingdom to meet the letter of his uncle, Mr Albert, to fulfil his dream of joining the Royal Knights Tournament, which he had dreamed of since childhood.

He could not have imagined at worst that the days would turn until he finds himself in a malicious encounter with creatures he had never heard of in the most pervasive myths and never before seen in his nightmares.

When he found the inhabitants of the kingdom calling him the little devil after he came to warn them of a great evil he discovered on his journey until he found them stoning him and chasing him and shouting at him and the evilest people in the kingdom led a campaign against the miserable boy.

And they say: "Expel this devil who wants to enter you into paradise."

Then he decided to escape from their tyranny, until he found himself in the darkness of a deep-sea wrestling with its crazy and angry waves of human evil.

And at an unexpected moment, a whale appeared from the bottom of the darkness of the sea to swallow the poor boy and plunge him into infinite depths, and all traces of the boy vanished.

Chapter 1

KINGDOM NIGHTMARE

The king (The Moses) woke up and his breath raced together with a dreadful feeling as if his soul were taken away, as he realised his life had changed forever after this moment.

The king felt the inner whirlwind of cold nights as if the palace had slipped away before its feet felt it. Holding his eyebrows, like the one facing the ghost of frightening death, he attributed his back to the vast head of the bed more like the throne in its form, and his eyes spin in the roof of the high room, which looked like it wasn't the same bright room he slept in every day.

He said in a strangled voice: why is this dream repeated with me! It's, it's, the third time I have the same nightmare?

But this time it's like I came out of a sleepover, and the fire burnt my bedding, and I mauled my body with a tusk, like a predator's tusk, in my flesh on each side, and I look on, but I don't move on!

The situation did not cool down there, but it seems that the nightmare is the beginning of a reality that has been dosed like poison mixed with boiling lava. Screaming, loud howling, demolition and ruin rose, the walls of the palace shook, as if Judgment Day had come from no prejudices.

Even a light that comes and goes ranges from the window of his dark room to the top of the majestic six-tower palace towers, punctuated by a huge roar that came from afar but was closer to any ear.

Until he made the decision to wade into his fear and walked towards the windows overlooking the balcony like the one that leads to death with heavy steps and he is sure that he will see his dream nightmare before his eyes.

Meanwhile the walls around him were violently shaken and the ceiling cracked until his face covered the rolling dirt from among the fallen roof cracks, the king said, and his hands are trembling "Lord have mercy on me, what's happening?" The curse of heaven is upon us after what did we do to the boy "Archie?" Or is this just a warning message that shakes us up about what we've lost sight of!

The king stopped in his place and turned on himself with fear that this terrifying roar that comes from far after he heard the sound of a big fuss near the door of his room and doubled the loud sound outside coming from the sides of the palace.

When the door opened quickly and the wall slammed hard until the king hugged himself in dismay. The chief minister, along with the Commander of the Royal Guard, the first responsible for protecting the king and his family they were the first to enter the terrified king's room. In a glimpse, the king's eyes expanded after he saw the soldier lifting their swords and carrying their shields for the first time inside his room, along with the senior leaders and the chief minister holding the small poison box and the other hand holding the antidote, until the king makes sure with sadness before someone pronounces that this is the beginning of the nightmare explanation.

Then the chief minister jogged to king with pale face and said with fear, trying to use the kindness of what could be in this catastrophic situation: "My king, that is..."

The king interrupted the minister's talk and told him to shut up quickly without looking at his face, to see for himself if the rest of the nightmare that took place in his palace abroad and when he arrived at the balconies in quick steps to see the tragedy of the kingdom's deferral.

Suddenly, at a moment when he did not imagine it in his life, he saw the face of the nightmare right in front of him flying into the sky of the kingdom and spreading terror to everyone, as he had just done with the king, but in a more painful and gruesome way, A reflection of the flames of fire appeared in the eyes of the king, who did not stop bleeding tears of fear and grief together as he saw the kingdom's cities transformed into a pile of rocks on top of some of them, and crushed everything that was moving underneath her.

The king shouted heartbreak after putting his hands on the edge of the balconies: "Oh, God, what do I see? We have been cursed! We have been cursed, what is this creature?" Then the king gazed high and said shocked: "Tell me it's not Radenback?"

The minister said with scared eyes: "It's him, sir, and we don't know how to get like this!" He watched a black lion the size of a dragon fly over the kingdom as if he had come out of the crypt of a legend of a thousand years, it has six wings falling out of its feathers. It has sparks if it falls on anything that makes it like ash.

The sounds of death were mixed with the sound of stone-throwing and walls falling on innocent heads. Neither the cries of a child nor the elderly was no mercy, and spirits filled the sky from the widespread spread of death.

The lion fired a loud roar like a frightening thunder and said angrily: "I am Radenback. Neither the king after today nor the kingdom anymore. I am the king of this world and I am the kingdom of all you miserable creatures!"

Then the angry lion fired the most flaming and burning fire into its flame up to the balcony of the king's palace who stood incapacitated and lost everything in moments until he fell to the ground before being stung by the heat of Radenback Fire's anger from the depths of his raging hollow.

The soldier was rushed to be like a shield over the king and behind them the ministers and the senior commanders horrified until the chief minister said: We thought he was dead, my king, and he came back suspiciously, and he was already a demon out of hell. "Now, Your Majesty, we don't have time to realise our souls and you are the first, Your Majesty."

The king looked at the minister and then giving him the stink eye with a cold look amid the heat of the situation and said spitefully: "If you thought this would make me forget what you told me when I consulted your dream, I won't forget your hatred for the boy, Archie, and your deception for us and he was more honest than all of us."

One soldier shouted from outside the room: "The ogres broke into the walls of the city, and possession the rest of the cities and left only our city and the palace. If we don't run away, they will spill our blood in minutes and whoever has not been wiped out by Radenback Fire will be torn apart by the ugly ogres."

The chief guard says firmly: "Everything is over my king and only thing we have to do now is survive. The escape plan is ready to flee to the sea to the southern part of our cousins. So that we can be reunite again before the secret exits closes down or then we have to face our painful fate, which is beyond our capacity because it is something we cannot bear and I'm afraid so, my king."

The king looked at his burning kingdom for the last time from the balconies and then he bowed his head and started crying like a bereaved person.

The minister quickly pointed out to the Guard Commander and gave him an order to carry out his mission and took the king and went quickly before Radenback Fire reached them or the legions of the ogres and ate them alive.

On the way to the secret exit, the Guard Commander told the minister, wondering, "What about our imprisoned boy, he was a winning paper for us!"

The minister said with a whisper as he pulled his robe behind him: "You said it yourself." (He was) Now he has become a burnt card by burning everything around us."

On the other side of the palace, precisely the bottom of the ground in the fifth cellar, like the Deep Trench, the boy "ARCHIE" was held in the prison alone, who was held in solitary confinement, accused of pitting the kingdom's inhabitants against the king to create chaos for the benefit of unknown external parties. He was arrested and his friends were sent to another less guarded prison in the city away from the palace.

When the walls were crumbling everywhere around Archie, he thinks this is the last moment of his life.

One of the soldiers came speeding with a set of keys tangled until it fell from his hands, the man fumbled the ground looking for keys in the darkness of the prison where everything around them was shaken until he found the keys.

He called from behind the fences on Archie: "Listen, boy, your father, Mr Abraham, has a favour for me and I will not forget it, and this is the least I can do. Go now and run from this direction. It will take you north of the palace to a secret door. You will find yourself in front of the mountains of Hydra surrounding the palace from behind, make your way towards the coast six hours away and I don't think you will arrive alive, but if you reach the coast, you will find a bunch of boats and go into one of them if you find it, because I think you will not even find a boat. But if you find one, go south and inform our cousins there that the kingdom of Hameros in the north has been occupied by the ogres and Radenback. Perhaps we can find those who support our people in this ordeal."

Indeed, the boy went panicking and lonely after leaving everything behind, and everyone who found him on his way out of the palace told him that the ogres had killed everyone in the kingdom.

When Archie brokered the road in the middle of the woods behind the palace between the mountains, he came across some ogres coming to reinforce the legions that broke into the kingdom and this was the first time in Archie's life that he watched the ogres face to face after he heard them only in legends and he was never stop representing their fight in front of his beautiful sweetheart the girl of Kling Ling village, Charlotte, until he nailed in his place over the mud when he saw the enormity of the bodies of the ogres and their hideous faces.

They were four ogres, as if they had eaten a bunch of human beings escaping from the kingdom from the remains of blood on their mouths and some of the shreds in their hands that Archie saw, and this is a thing in the boy's mind. There was only a solution to confrontation, even though the forest was widening, the boy knew from his father that confrontation was better than taking a path you didn't know.

Although power varies between Archie and ogres, he has a factor of lightness, speed and flexibility.

The idea of escaping into the forest was useless because he thought that if he found himself in a swamp. It will make it an easy catch for the ogres, but the confrontation option will make you control the choices, so you decide where your feet will go where your mind and instinct will guide you.

Archie stood in front of the ogres and said in a brave voice, mocking them: "If you can arrest me, I will show you a place where many people hide and they will be delicious food for you without any trouble."

The ogres swirled in each other until one of them threw a giant truncheon he was carrying.

In his hand in a surprising way, without any introductions to kill the boy, but he easily overtakes it because of its large size.

Archie took a bunch of mud filled with a bunch of small stone and ran towards the ogre, who threw him with giant truncheon, and threw him by mud filled between his eyes, caused them temporary blindness, then turned around and the other ogres mock them laughing and said, "Come on, grab me, you dirty idiots!"

The angry ogre attacked the boy, raising his hands upwards and screaming angrily, but the boy lightly slipped between the giant ogre legs as a field rat, the ogre took the huge truncheon again and threw it at Archie because he couldn't catch it, but the ogre missed the target and he hit the other ogre foot and then he got an eloquent hit, that made the injured ogre angry and attacked the other ogre and fought as fierce wolf.

The boy fled between the legs of the ogres and after a long journey of trouble he arrived at the port. All the boats were crowded to the fugitive until he shouted and called for someone to stop and take him but it seems to be written to him this miserable fate, this day is like doomsday and everyone wants to survive themselves.

The he saw a young child crying and shaking from the cold after his parents forgot him from the intensity of fear. This provoked the ire of Archie, who took the child on his back and excitedly told him: "Hold my back well if you want your parents or you will never see them," he said with confidence, "Fear is not prevented from dying, but it also prevents life."

Then he jumped a swim to catch the boat and as soon as he realised the boat he threw the child inside, but the strong wind that disturbed the waves increased the wave slaps on his beautiful face.

Even surprised one of the boat's passengers hits his hands holding onto the end of the boat, and he said, "We will not all drown in order to save one person. I'm sorry, boy. It's your destiny today. May god have mercy on you," then the man struck a stronger blow on Archie's hand that saw him escape the intensity of the pain that had exhausted his powers and found himself like a toy being thrown by the waves in an attempt to search for the straw that would have him like found a lifeline.

In the midst of this frightening and cold feeling of the most important moment of his life, he found himself inside a vortex of bubbles trapped inside and suddenly the mouth of a giant whale came out from the bottom of those bubbles and swallowed Archie at the blink of an eye, then dived into the depths of the dark sea on this most unjust and blackest night in mankind's history.

Chapter 2

KING'S DREAM

At that time, King Archie I was the son of Solon. He inherited the legacy of the king's father (the king of blessings) until he was able to extend his influence over all the sprawling lands of the kingdom in the south of the Earth after the great deluge that divided the collection of many kingdoms. The young king even opened and expanded until he arrived a strange land in the far south isthmus named "Faloha".

It has a great well called "Berhout", so black, so mysterious as the mystery of a life beyond death, so full of water.

Even the visitor of this well does not need a bucket to scoop up from it enough to stretch one of his hands out of it without bowing his body. But the one who looks at her water imagines that he looks at a black lake and not at a well from the size of her opening and from the intensity of her blackness that sees the reflection of the moon and the clouds so that whoever sees that reflection will show that he looks at a painting of art painted by the sky in the hands of the angels that will never err from the clarity of the reflection of the beauty of the sky in its magical perfection.

While the king and the soldier sat near the well and the sky was black and empty of the moon, as if heaven, it wore the darkening dress as a sad fate that brought them to their last day, comforting an unexpected moment.

The king wanted to walk a little closer to the well to explore a need in himself to hide it from everyone after the soldier put their journey and prepared the most to sleep after the trouble of the trip, and once he approached the well, he imagined that he saw the reflection of a girl's face towards the tip of the well on the surface of the well's water washing her hair, although there was no reason to reverse objects on the water like the moon, after the sky filled with clouds, and then quickly raised his head and his hand on the sword sheath saw nothing!

So he think it might have been a fantasy and then he stood a little bit in his place without moving and turned his head towards the soldiers, but he didn't turn his body until he felt his chills which made his body hair rose from its strength and he felt it and realised that an immaterial spirit hovered around the place, that's when he threw his eye at the well again until a girl saw the facial features unclear, darkness clad everything in it except her loose white dress, she stood like a soulless body looking at him without any movement until he was assured of the sincerity of his expectation and presumption. He knew very well, what it meant to see the reflection of human's face in the water and then had no effect and knew very well the secret of this body that the girl was.

The soldiers witnessed the girl as if a ghost were sitting with the king, and she did so until packed their faces and they leapt and jogged towards their king, raising their weapons. They surrounded their king, pointing those sharp and tall swords at that strange girl.

However, King Archie I raised his north hand upwards, marking that they would do nothing no matter what, he was able to protect himself only to order otherwise. Then he told the Guard Commander quietly: "Go back to where you were! The commander replied: but sir, we won't leave you alone maybe this girl is an ambush!"

The king said with an angry tone: "I said go back to where you were and I won't repeat it again! The commander and the soldier have already returned carefully."

And their eyes didn't divide that weird girl, nor did their king, and their souls were shaking in fear. It was worth it, fear and stress.

The girl's long black hair dropping down her shoulders moved down her knees and swung in all directions without there being any wind, even if it was a passing breath of air, but the king did well to believe that she did not come from all but trusted him.

Until the king dragged and took a weighted step towards the girl, raising his head, reminding himself as a great king who owns the ends of the earth, and when he approached her, she moved her hands, revealed her hair, which covered her hidden face with her hands, and fully revealed her face, her face was like the face of the angels of the severity of his whiteness, who on one day did not think that he would see a girl with such superior beauty. The girl seemed never to be from the world of mankind, making the king's eyes protrude from it place he was smitten by her as he meditated and examined that extraordinary beauty and said passionately that he did not hide it: "If our kingdom is the wonder of the Earth, you are the second wonder of earth, then silence and he turned his eyes in the details of her beautiful radioactive face that steals hearts?"

She then spoke abruptly and said pale lips of extreme thirst, which was evident on her pale, white face despite the luscious beauty, "You are the son of king, the Marr?" It was a surprising question, like what he had surprised before with her presence, and then he said, "Yes, I am. How I serve you, strange girl?"

She smiled a loving smile with a sharp eye and said, "No one wears crowns except you and no one can come here unless (King the Marr), when I found out he had died, I said, "You must be the son we heard."

"And what did you hear about him? He likes to hear from people about him and promise you that he will."

She said longingly, "They say he is brave and he takes what he wants out of fear of anyone and I came to him myself from my world for a need that I don't think anyone will spend except him."

Despite his excessive courage to be reckless and occasional haste, especially with regard to important decision-making, he never chose between war and negotiation and always chose war for his love of fighting and battles since he was a young boy and his sadistic delight by shouting at those he crushed and seeing himself always triumphant, even at the expense of physical and moral pain, except that he was mild and graceful and not easy to involve deception or dragging him into something else he might want.

And here the king realised to the girl's destination and realised that she had the intent of being at the well, but said in himself and if so! Such beauty deserves to sacrifice so much, and then he says, a little relaxed eye down, "They hit the truth, and if you want to be a princess on any floor of the earth, it's easy for him to do that to you, but isn't he entitled to know who you are?" She said, "How can the captive girl be a princess, Your Majesty?"

The king marvelled at her word, but inherited a little cleverly and then said, "Whoever captivates like you has done your injustice, but if you were in place, you would do the same!"

And here he pre-empted her request knowing in advance what she wanted to get to, but understanding that a girl like her could not be alone, that she belonged to someone, that her presence here was isn't coincidental, of course it was planned, and that she was closer to what she wanted to salvage from that, that which she owned whoever he is.

He would not have made the girl put him in an awkward situation with anyone before he knew. He wanted to extract the word from her before he promised her something, and then he found himself embarrassed in his implement, not afraid or weak of him, of course, but he knew for sure that she would get into things that he was indispensable, especially after he was assured that she was not from the world of the humans and these people were very rare to come good.

Then he replayed the same question, "But you didn't tell me who you were, girl. It seems to me that you're not from our world, if it's hard for you to say this. I knew this, and you don't need to say it, but tell me who you are."

She nodded with sadness, expressing her disappointment at what she had heard, and then she said, and that next smile went with his eagerness on her lips, "It doesn't matter who I am! If I don't find my need here!" Then she approached him even more, including a great scare. He did not move from his place. He continued to stick like a nail in the wall.

She then put her two hands on her stomach until it became clear to the king that she was pregnant in the last months. She calmly raised her head, looked at him with her pretty face, put her right hand on his heart until he felt free in his heart. If you are strong, get me out of this captivity, I don't know the doors open, king! And if you can't, then no one can but the boy with wolf fangs will do and that's not in our lives!

And then she freakily said, looking behind her eyes, like somebody's running after her, "He's coming! He's coming!" And before she blinking with the tip of her eyes, the king collapsed, and the girl turned into a smoke thread that faded in a twinkling, in the daze of the soldiers, who rushed to their king to lift his head off the ground and ascertain his health until he assured them that he was still alive.

When he opened his eyes, he rose freaking out and asked them quickly, "Where's the girl? Where's the girl? Where did that girl go?" The king was as if he had woken up from a strange dream that was buzzing until he ran crazy toward the well until the commander of the soldiers called him, "We saw you only when you blacked out. And about the girl, your grace, the air evaporated in blink or as if the darkness had hijacked her!"

The king felt that he heard a voice of distress around him, but he didn't know how to find him.

But it seems that the sudden, most important and scariest thing is yet to happen. While the soldiers surrounded their king and the well until they heard the sound of a snarl and a roar with a breath like the wind lurking with them.

The body was horrified. That voice was no stranger to their ears and before they know its source.

The clouds revealed the full moonlight to illuminate them as the lightbulb at night to reveal the source of the sound until some shouted with fear and others crawled back, with their eyes staring hard ahead of an unexpected scary thing that made confident strides, seemingly indifferent to many of them and their sharp weapons, until the soldiers set up a narrow circle around the king.

Until a black lion appeared to them twice the size of a regular lion, they never seen before of him, moving his very long tail from above his head a sign of the beginning of a battle that would only end with the death of one side.

However, the king's courage contravened all this, as the king came out despite the rejection and warning of the commander of the Guard, but the king ordered the expansion of the road to come out and meet that monster face to face. Indeed, the king raised the blade of his sword with his hands to be separated between him and the lion.

After the king pondered the body language of the giant beast's and realised that he would attack them immediately.

He asked the soldier to give him the shield and take the fencing position.

Announcing the acceptance of the challenge, he asks them to be careful and asked them to strike the lion with one blow when chances arose, after they dispersed and trapped the lion from each side, and commanded his soldiers to prepare and when the king decided to attack, he stopped suddenly with astonishment when the lion uttered an eloquent human tongue! Moving his tail like a wrestler waving his whip in the battle, he said, "You assaulted the land of the king of the Lower Worlds and worried his sleep with your hordes. Otherwise, you tried to insult me when you were a party to whoever wanted to betray her husband the king until I swore that no one of you would return to his home only a torn body."

It was surprising for them to see a lion uttering just like them and also surprising that he was intent on killing them without any unannounced, warning or even prior threat but telling them what their destiny would be, the king said angrily trying not to show any fear, "It doesn't mean that an animal like you pronounces, it means that you've chosen the challenge without asking who's in front of you. As for the ownership of the land, there is no king on any land as long as I am on it."

The lion made a few silent steps as the custom of the cats, but his envelope with the wrecker of spirits showcasing his massiveness and prestige, declaring that he was the king of all this land and no one else in defiance of the king, the beast released a great roar that would have made the forest wake up from its sleep. The birds fled their nests until they covered the sky from their abundance.

The lion then said with his terrifying fangs, "Your ego seems to have blinded your eyesight, O son of the perished kings, and I had my revenge with your malevolent father, but he got away from me. Now the heaven brought you to cut off your lineage forever, I am King Barhout the great ruler of the kingdoms of the underworld."

The (King Archie I) surprised because he knew about King Barhout myth, but did not know that he was a lion until his consciousness came back from the crashing of ideas and remembered that the formation of any form of creatures is a quality of jinn and then realised that he was in front of a really dangerous thing, but the king is stubborn and will not renege on his decision or his prestige will go among his people.

The irritable lion completed his speech and said, "You have overstepped your limits, king boy, you will not have any presence after I finish these words?" As quickly as lightning, the lion jumped on the king, exploiting their preoccupation with the state of fear that surrounded them and dispersed their thoughts.

But the power of the king's intuition was faster than the treachery of the savage lion. The king threw himself towards the right and fell to the mud, avoiding the attack with the claws of death that came out to kidnap spirits.

Before the lion once again turned to the king, the soldier had showered him with a barrage of arrows, some of which hit him, but his grace and superior speed looked like a spark of fire. No one could predict its movement, direction and gravity. The lion jumped at a glance towards the well, diving into it and flying the water drops at them in a daze akin to his sudden appearance.

After surviving the first direct threat, he almost ended his life, the king shouted, warning, "Now prepare for Plan B. Such a beast will not leave us in our state. He believed and he lied. He will return and his return will be even more violent. Now, let's split into two parts around the well, a section aimed at the spear, and a section aimed at its arrows. Those with spears will start to have time to prepare the other batch or to pick up their spears while the snipers occupy them. And I'm going to be on the front foot like bait and that's going to make all the monsters focus on my way and here's going to be a great reliance on you to cut his back to make it easier for us to kill him later."

Indeed, the plan seemed perfect, especially as many always overcome the courage until the king heard the sound of bubbles coming out of the well breaking the silence of the sleeping well amid moments of terror.

Here everyone took their positions and got ready and the king was more careful approaching the well. They fully believe that the lion's exit is just such a matter of time as their belief in the existence of this well before their eyes.

But unexpectedly the water of the well calmed down and all the bubbles disappeared from its surface as if nothing had happened here until the king approached, and the blade of his sword was caught this time with his hands and placed down from it, even if he approached the well no more, but he carefully bent his neck to see and look at the water of the lake until he saw the strange girl face again, which caused his excitement and relieved him. This prolonged the look until he looked on his sides. The girl might have turned up again in the same way as she did and then watched the girl's face on the water slowly turn into the lion's face. He felt hard to move himself around as if the paralysis had hit him until the lion came out of the bottom of the water to push the king away after he had been hit by a powerful smash.

The king fell to an injured ground and the lion ponds above him this time, but the barrage of arrows and spears was faster than the reaction of the lion and struck him with force in all parts of his body until he became angry and savaged and decided to leave the king and avenge those who injured him moderately, some of which were eloquent, but the fire of revenge was even more intense.

But the fire of revenge was the hardest to make him feel anything until he killed the most soldiers, but the commander of the guard was clever and realised that the battle was on its way to losing, as he crawls like a snake from the middle of the fierce inflammatory battle between the unruly lion and the king's soldiers.

He arrived at the king, who appeared to have been fatally injured in the face and dragged towards the horse carriages and rushed to the kingdom, leaving soldiers and the black lion to eat each other without anyone feeling their escape.

And it was only two nights in progress that they stopped a little to heal the king's wounds and then go all the fast to the kingdom until he succeeded in reaching the kingdom with his king, but unfortunately the king returned to his deathbed and is no longer a light hero like what always belonged to his kingdom.

The (King Archie I) had three young sons, like cubs, and they inherited the beauty of their mother, the princess. Catherine, but he had a younger brother named The Chamarosh. He was a loyal friend of evil from people's fear of him and his king brother never feared more for his family than he feared for his brother. He had been reluctant to reach the thorn and had caused many greedy and powerful in the kingdom to exploit his unclean intentions to get rid of his brother.

They told him they would be his right hand, which they would convince the people that what Chamarosh did when he stole his brother's throne was for their own good and for the sake of the kingdom, not the other way around.

But evil always has to end and end all those who got involved, and they didn't hesitate to look for any plan to get rid of the king who stumbled in front of them. Everyone loved him and respected him, except these criminals until they found their purpose in his brother, whose interests intersected and his covenant in the throne with the interests of these aspirants even in the food of the poor miserable.

Until they put their hand in his hand to work against his king brother in order to turn on his beloved king brother in his people. If the six Guard commanders had not stood a barrier around their king, Prince Chamarosh would have been able to carry out his vile schemes, which were quickly frustrated.

King Archie I knew about it and wanted to get rid of his brother, but no one felt but always the things go the other way of our will. When the king woke up from his coma and realised his state of health and the seriousness of his injury, he knew that he would die soon, if he did not die, he would be wiped out by his brother and his brothers, traitors and criminals. The greatest fear was on his young sons and wife, whom no one would protect after.

And he knows that now he is in a state of weakness and he cannot do anything, he also felt that his sprawling kingdom would collapse and fall sooner or later because of the many aspirants and those who want to come out of the rule of the royal family, which has spanned more than a thousand years.

He wanted to write his guardian. He didn't know how he would protect his children after he died and how he would divide those leaves between his young sons, knowing that everyone lurks with them, first of all their uncle.

The grieving king felt great pain and sadness until he saw that dream one day before his death, which was like a message of rescue and mercy to his sons, who had no one from their father's distance. The vision was basically a heavenly and tight line of what would happen later as in each other's lives.

The king saw three lights emerge from his palace to the north of the Earth, illuminating the darkness of the north, turning its cold into warmth, melting ice and overturning the freezing and lifeless lands of the north into green meadows and plains, as if a hand from the sky had been wiped by a magical swab.

He has witnessed the Earth replete with all the beautiful creatures that running between the fields of flowers and roses interspersed with white rivers of their purity and serenity, he never saw her like it.

He thinks he saw heaven, and when he woke up from his penultimate sleep and saw the doctors around him, he said, "You can't keep death away from me if you have my recovery, you will drink from it so you don't die like me."

Then the pain of death increased until he ordered the chief priest, who is the spiritual father of the king's family and of all his confidants. He was one of the most famous interpreters of dreams at the same time and the priest did not hesitate after the king told him the dream until the chief priest said, "I can only see it is a dream of salvation, Your Majesty, from what you feared and which was accompanying you in the last period for fear of your sons and their fate after you, if this dream is real, you must send your sons immediately to the north, or if they stay here, they will be killed after your death. You know that many of those traitors wish you were dead, first of all, your brother will overturn the king and they will not hesitate to clear your sons and husband in any way, ways to have no one to demand the throne after you."

Indeed, the king carried out the priest's advice and ordered the gathering of their three children and their mother and ordered the writing of his will, which was also in the form of a new constitution of the new properties in the land of salvation the north.

The king then ordered his children to hear the guardian's presence of their mother and priest before someone later read it to them for fear of being misrepresented.

The guardian has included the following:

None of his sons received a penny of his share, but when they left for the family's resort in the northern lands, they all settled there in the resort, which was used by the royal family to spend the summer, to escape the heat of the summer of the south in the Hemyaros kingdom.

Move secretly now and immediately after completing the guardian's hearing and writing.

The eldest son (The Mar II) is the Governor when he reaches the age of 16, where the constitution stipulates that the heir shall be governed only after the age of 18 and thereafter Topa and then Amoulai.

The peaceful transfer of power between the brothers does not entitle any of them to appoint one of his sons as heir except Prince (Amoulai), who was after no one to cause any fighting between the brothers and their sons, and then their prestige goes between the nations and all their history and glory goes away.

He also wrote in the testament that his brother Chamarosh must be the king after his death and the guardian of the minor princes who was not summoned to attend because he was considered the greatest danger to the young princes and this item in the testament was merely a trick to blind the eyes temporarily so that his sons would find time to escape the kingdom before he could news of the king's death spreads!

Hence, (King Archie I) will guarantee their uncle's satisfaction and not think about getting rid of his nephews for at least a few days because of his preoccupation with celebrating this kind of news. At the same time, he will guarantee his children's lives so that they can disappear from sight until they reach the north in peace while his brother is busy arranging his funeral and announcing new appointments to the royal palace.

He also asked that no one of his sons attend his funeral in order to buy time to escape with the money they can carry and from the loyal members of his entourage who he identified as six military commanders and the father priest (Rabola).

Everything happened as quickly as the king and priest arranged. The young princes fled under the cover of darkness with strict protection from the members of the elite from the Royal Guard, whom he trusted, as he trusted with his sword, taking advantage of their high security positions in the kingdom. This facilitated them in the profession of eliminating many obstacles and silencing Chamarosh conscious spies deployed in the palace to acquire the right opportunities. In the face of darkness, they prayed for their kingdom for the last time with heartfelt sorrow, thus they slipped quietly into silence that was not without the tears of parting, leaving the land of south and the throne of the great kingdom from behind them forever or to a known time.

Ten years after the death of King Archie I, the three princes succeeded in

forming their kingdom in the lands of the north.

With the help of the priest (Rabola) and the six leaders, the oldest of them was only twenty-seven years old and Prince (The Mar), his brother (Toba) was twenty-two years old and the youngest (Amoulai) was fifteen years old.

The princes helped build their kingdom so quickly and facilitated that there were no potential competitors in the lands of the north, which were almost empty of a few simple gatherings of simple locals where the presence of the three princes in their land was a great livelihood for them until they called them the pond princes of the joy of livelihood, that they found evangelised their parents and neighbours.

In addition to the abundance of wild life and the fertility of the land that has not been in its custom, since the new arrivals fleeing from the brutality of their brothers came to the north until the bitter cold abruptly receded and baffled the knowing, and was not like before, and snowfall by more than half, which led to the continual flow of silver streams and wide glaciers.

In particular, deer herds, reindeer, wild buffalo and other rodents and various types of migratory primates from various regions of the north to these patches of good and blessed land, which were called crescent land.

In the south, where evil turned on its people and that great kingdom turned into a bloody rink of conflict, they did not stop until they shed the blood of some of them. They fell apart with blood and hunger. The poor died and the rich was killed because of the covenant to share the country's wealth.

The lack of a firm leader is obeyed by others.

The owner of the land became one of her thieves and instilled the system of banditry, betrayal and selfishness in his followers, which was a direct cause of great murder among tribes and peoples rebelling against the old kingdom slaughtered by their disabled sons. Those who appeared in the conflict among themselves were the result of the killing of King Chamarosh in one of the battles of discord that erupted from the spark of his hand. The kingdom then fell like the elephant killed on the ground and hyenas devoured him from all sides. The fall of the Hemyaros kingdom shook the land of the south and all tribes began to escape and become independent with their different entities and formed weak villages and towns unable to protect them from each other. This has increased the proportion of immigrants to the new world of the north's secure and meaningful world for safety and housing.

Some people's disasters are other's benefits. The new north kingdom was in the process of construction and expansion and in the need of the labour hands.

Of course, they will not find the best and guarantee of the people of the south with whom they have social relations, just because of whatever bad history occurred to them in the south, where the construction and construction market was in the need for skilled labour, which flourished and grew until the bones of the born kingdom, which has become the heart of the world.

Chapter 3

BEFORE 150 YEARS

More than a hundred and fifty years ago, there was a great earthquake like no other.

Until all the creatures of the Earth at the time embraced that this is the day when life ended on Earth when the waves of the Great Lock Lake separated the southern and northerly landmass plates swept across.

The waves swept through the quiet banks of the land in the worst day of history since the first deluge and swallowed all its confrontation on its way from villages, cities and even kingdoms.

The inhabitants of the southern bank of land had the largest share of ruin and destruction because it included the majority of the sophisticated human settlements.

While the bank of the great northern Lake Luke was not inhabited by simple villages made up of the nesting of some farmers and fishermen, in the end this anger of nature led the southern plate to diverge from the north by a large extent until the lake turned into a vast sea that divided the Earth in half.

As a result of these natural changes, the Earth's southern layer rose upwards, announcing the birth of a mountain chain that was like a natural barrier.

So now, standing on the bank of the north coast, he can only see before him a tremendous series of mountains, with only a few small grooves reaching you to the land of the south.

Of course, if you survive the waves and the violent water currents, in spite of the catastrophe, the inhabitants of the south were able to gather their diaspora again, and they reviewed everything they could until they rebuilt a new kingdom, but far south of the south so as not to repeat the tragedy of the past.

In many years, they have created for themselves an independent entity and a radioactive civilisation, one of the first civilisations to be formed in a short period of time, from which several human settlements have branched in a few years.

But this civilisation has not been able to continue like so many human civilisations because of the covetousness of the human being who worked under the authority of race and religious affiliation and tribal entities as a concept in which the system of government in which they administer the lives of others by various barbaric or malicious means with a good face must be based all in order to adapt nature to any form that corrupted the human soul with power and took it to the hell.

With her hands and not with other creatures, after all these years of life, all that structure collapsed and it wasn't the inhabitants of the south again flew refugees to the more fertile, fruitful and fruitful lands of the north until they were small villages scattered along the coasts of the north's lands or what they called the new world where our story would be.

But the things go the other way of our will.

Once again, it's like the curse of their fighting between them is after them wherever they are.

When there were several successive earthquakes, it contributed to a deep half-kilometre crack on the surface of the mud earth, and a leaning cave emerged that had no end as if this was one of the great transformations coming to the new world in the north lands, such as what the people of the south called the new settlers of the northern Mediterranean lands, whose lake was once the cave, as if it were the tomb to which people's souls would be drawn by force from where they were not counted, where the cave was home only to creatures that were the ugliest, most terrifying, deadliest and most dangerous on Earth, not only to humans, but to all of creatures living on land.

They don't even know the meaning of mercy between them.

Not even in the stories of the ancient but a few human beings rarely exist, such as the scarcity of this event and what came with it.

These creatures were later named by the local population as an ogre of fire for binge eating where erosion, eating, eating and not saturating until they are cheated by sleepiness. These ogres were somewhat body-shaped, but very large body-built, more than four metres long, two metres wide, as if they were moving idols of their toughness and desperation, and they had a few short legs.

Smelly never knew the use of water, small eyes thick eyelash hair as an elderly elder aged 120 years, the ogres were completely visually impaired and invisible, relying on going out into groups to track each other's smell for the strength of their sense of smell, which exceeds the sense of sniffing the dog three times. Almost naked, covering their butts with a leaf-like rag tied together with some of the two ends like spider web in its weakness. This is for females only. Men have only a set of leaves to cover their penises. But their butts were almost exposed to make it easier to spend anywhere without needing to look for a hide place.

In addition to a large belly hung over their belts with full of pimples and stinky boils.

The way they got food was to catch everything that moved, and if they didn't find, they had to kill the weakest of them by cutting them alive, whether they were young, old or even pregnant, and the victim was eaten to the ground, including bones and hair, and everything that came to your mind at the moment of imagining that disgusting scene, where they didn't have no trace on the victim because of their excessive brutality.

This continued underground for an unknown time until they went out to the surface of the earth as if the door of paradise had been opened to them wide open, when they saw all those prey and different of various kinds of animals that were abundant in their fertile and diverse Nordic nature until the ogres were saying indignantly after they saw bliss: If we knew all these blessings above our heads, we'd be underground one day in that torment.

They started hunting animals by throwing them with the huge truncheons they carried, so this was their only weapon that their little minds were able to make, but in fact it was more lethal than any other weapon made at the time because of the supernatural bowler's power.

They started hunting animals by throwing them with the huge truncheons they carried, so this was their only weapon that their little minds were able to make, but in fact it was more lethal than any other weapon made at the time because of the supernatural bowler's power.

They evolved until they got to hunting people who were more easily than the rest of the animals, especially children, women and the elderly, where the most people lived in simple tents and cottages that they made from branches of trees and their palms after they were displaced. This was one of the main reasons for the increasing number of ogres whose reproduction outweighed the breeding of rabbits in their natural life cycle.

Even the female ogres after emerging from the darkness of the Earth and its inferno into the heavens of the Earth became dead only after having more than fifty ogres in less than 20 years, doubling their number from a few tens until they exceeded 3,000 individuals. The ogres lived in a very complex social order despite their stupidity, lack of understanding and understanding of humans or even some other creatures living with us in this world.

However, the leaders of the ogres, called the Prakhia, were regarded as the elite in the world of ogres, where she had a little bit of a human mind.

The world of ogres has been under the leadership of the most famous ghouls in their history who was called the Two Heads.

It came to the masters of the land of the north and they were the remnants of the royal family fleeing the collapse of their kingdom in the south, where they gathered all the remaining human beings on the coasts and lands of the new settlement invaded by the barbaric ogre's herds to their city, which contained a palace and praised a wall that could not be broken into from anyone, where they called the second Hameros kingdom city. It was later known as the city with six towers of intensity and height to be the centre of its observer for any occupying attacks and this helped them to fortify their kingdom further and became as a precious jewel in a steel box that no one can prejudice.

The first founders believed that a strong foundation from the outset for any kingdom must be basically one of the most important pillars of the growth of any kingdom and its control over the earth is to fortify itself first before considering expansion and this is what the sons who repeated scenario what their grandfather (King of Bliss) did and found before under the slogan "My shield before my sword".

Every time the fences and towers were reinforced by another building on top of it to double its thickness so it was called the marvel of the north and even in the whole new world, anyone who saw the fences of the kingdom thought it was a pure iron cast building because of the use of the latest advanced construction techniques for the first time by pouring iron tar between the fence poles and rock building blocks until it became the fence for all who saw it as a one piece of steel, not natural and a piece.

Of course, this was not free of charge, but it cost the treasury of the kingdom a lot of money, but the doctrine and constitution of the new founding fathers was right. If one of them would have been able to pay that money in order to fortify the kingdom, the king would not have existed after the ogres of fire appeared in public.

The kingdom became the expression of a ghost kingdom on many nights and to evaporate everything in a glimpse and lost long effort years in the blink of an eye, but it seems the wisdom of king, First Grandfather, the "King of Blessings" or "The Publisher of Grace," like the so-called inhabitants, resonated and had a very great effect on the future of everyone who came after him. He believed when he said that you would not succeed in protecting yourself, exposing you and your consent if you sharpened your swords and your armour was worn out.

The kingdom was located in the crescent area, which lies in the middle of a crescent-shaped mountain formation, as if the crescent had already fallen in this place, and they had more than 60 miles from the coast. The kingdom consists of twelve complementary cities and all cities are subject to central rule under the rule of the king in the Palace of Government or what is sometimes often called the Palace of the Throne. It was considered the largest independent construction built in the history of mankind. In addition, all kings who succeeded in the kingdom were keen to bring and use the best engineers and the famous scientists around the earth to strengthen the fences in various ways and revolutionise.

Chapter 4

THE ARSH

Less than a year before the devastating attack on the kingdom by the great lion Radenback, there was a small, peaceful and reassured village whose livelihood came effortlessly.

It was located in the northwest of the kingdom and seven days away from the horseback. Next to it is a long, black mountain chain called the black barrier, which is like a natural dam between the two sides. The village, like jasmine flower, opened up below the black compost pile due to the frequent planting of roses and seasonal flowers amid its picturesque nature of open plains and ridges separated by some ice streams that are increasingly displayed every day and the small collapse of sunshine reflected on its torturous waters from time to time.

Introducing Archie Abraham In the quaint village nestled between rolling hills and verdant plains, there lived a 17-year-old boy named Archie Abraham, affectionately known as Archie, Archer, or simply Archie. He was the kind of boy who exuded an infectious zest for life, with a curiosity that knew no bounds and a heart that beat with the rhythm of adventure.

Archie was strikingly handsome in a way that seemed almost ethereal. His medium-length, lithe frame moved with the grace of a musk deer, a creature common to the vast plains that bordered their village. His dark hair, always slightly tousled, framed his face in a way that was both roguish and endearing. The locks were long enough to nearly cover his ears and reached the line of his jawbone, giving him an appearance that was perpetually windswept, as if he had just returned from some grand escapade.

His eyes, a deep shade of brown, sparkled with an undying curiosity and a hint of mischief. They were the eyes of a dreamer, someone who saw the world not just as it was, but as it could be. His gaze could light up with the tales of far-off lands and mythical creatures, capturing the imagination of anyone lucky enough to listen. His skin, tanned by the sun, bore the marks of many adventures—scratches and bruises earned from climbing trees, exploring caves, and racing through the fields.

Archie's personality was as captivating as his appearance. He was moral and kind-hearted, always ready to lend a helping hand or offer a word of encouragement. His brothers looked up to him, seeing in him a figure of boundless energy and unwavering courage. And Charlotte, the girl he adored, often called him by his affectionate nickname, 'Archie.' To her, he was more than just a boy from the village; he was a hero in the making.

Since he was four years old, Archie had been enthralled by the stories his grandfather would tell him. These were no ordinary bedtime tales but epic legends of ogres and Kyopteryx—wild, bird-like creatures that were as fearsome as they were majestic. His grandfather, a hero warrior in the kingdom's army, spun these tales with a vividness that brought them to life. According to the legends, angels themselves had descended to fight alongside the kingdom's army against the ogres. These stories, filled with bravery and the clash of titanic forces, fueled Archie's imagination and kindled in him a burning desire to become a knight.

Archie's dream was to don the armor of the kingdom's knights, to wield a sword with the same valor his grandfather had shown, and to protect the realm from the legendary monsters he had heard of in those enthralling narratives. He longed to encounter these creatures himself, to feel the thrill of battle and the honor of defending his people. His heart yearned for the day when he would ride into battle, his name sung in songs of glory, just like the heroes of old.

Despite his youthful exuberance, Archie was not naive. He understood that the path to knighthood was fraught with challenges and dangers. But it was this very knowledge that spurred him on. He trained diligently, honing his skills in swordsmanship and archery, ever hopeful that he would one day be deemed worthy to join the ranks of the kingdom's protectors.

To his friends and family, Archie was already a hero. His determination, his kindness, and his unquenchable thirst for adventure set him apart. He had a way of making even the most mundane tasks seem like an epic quest, imbuing life with a sense of wonder and possibility. And as he stood on the brink of adulthood, the village could see in him the promise of greatness, the spark of a future knight who would one day be spoken of in the same breath as the legendary warriors of yore.

Archie Abraham was more than just a boy with a dream. He was a beacon of hope and inspiration, a reminder that courage, kindness, and a love for adventure could transform the ordinary into the extraordinary. And with each passing day, he edged closer to his destiny, ready to face whatever challenges came his way, driven by the stories of his grandfather and the belief that he too could become a legend.

They didn't see the angles on reality, but they saw his wings appearing and disappearing between the superiors of the Resistance Army, and his wings were like swords shoving necks, where the guerrillas were flying like stones thrown from catapult weapons!

Archie grew up and still lives within those legends that accompanied him at all stages of his life until he painted for himself another world that is his only knight around all these legendary tournaments and battles that he will fight and save the world so that he used to always come out every morning holding his own wooden sword waving and shouting the words of the threat blatantly at his voice, "I'm going to amputate your head, you ghoul with two heads behind him."

Little brother Arthur, who fell to the ground from over giggling, and he says, "My brother went crazy." Archie went crazy and completed the rolling on the floor from the intensity of the hysterical laughter.

Archie was completing his adventure in the virtual world and jumping on the trunks of giant oak trees with lightness of macaque monkey and faster than the leopard and from the oak tree to branches of weeping willow trees or known locally as poplar trees. In order to reduce the accumulation of snow in the winter, which causes the only main road of the village to be blocked and all the village people's carriage rid to come and leave, as well as the supply vehicles to be transported from outside and inside the simple village, where most of them were engaged in growing seasonal crops for their livelihood like Abraham's family or they have a lot of acres and they hire some workers from abroad to work to their advantage as the majority of the Kling Ling's family, more than half of the village's 80 inhabitants are human.

The enthusiasm within this boy did not stop for a day until some village monks thought that the boy might have suffered some kind of insanity from the goddess, who was a little young, but he hates visiting the temple and sitting between his parents with the villagers and watching the priest prostrate that idol and offers him sacrifices and sometimes speaks the idol and he cries his grief.

But Archie saw no reaction from that idol until he got sick and got his mouthfuls out of curiosity and got to the podium where the priest was on one of the important occasions, which got into the synagogue with the most villagers, got out of the chair and stood next to the idol that the monk was clamming underneath. And in the midst of surprise, distrust and resentment of his parents from that act, which was deemed insulting to Goddess, did not receive any example and then Archie said to the priest, "Raise your head, I am now a partner with this idol in judgment!"

This caused great embarrassment for his parents in front of the inhabitants of the village and the great priest and the surprise of the attendance, which rose among them, the grunts and glances of strangeness swirled in each other. Many of them frowned that they had already desecrated their most important spiritual and religious beliefs.

Since that incident and the hostility between Archie and the temple in its severity, his father has been reluctant to go to the synagogue from the abundance of speeches and tips given by the priest to him by his son, Archie, who angered the goddess and robbed him of morality according to the words of the monks! They often order him to send his feisty son to the kingdom so as not to affect the village boys, according to the monks.

Archie did not care about it all. He viewed the priest according to his reasoning and proper acumen as a group of quacks and beneficiaries to the detriment of the inhabitants of the village. He continued to live in his own world in search of those legends, whose mind embodies him that he sees in front of him. Sometimes he finds those monsters hiding between the trees and chasing them. He had a strong feeling inside him that there was something inside him that started to grow older than before and that he should do something in his life rather than take orders that he felt were restricting him in realising his dream of battles going on in his subconscious to his truth but where and how?

His father's voice pierced his ear calling his name from afar. "Archie... Archie...Archie..." If he mentioned his name the fourth time, he knew there was a misfortune waiting for him, but not so far, at least.

His father asked him violently, knowing the answer beforehand, "Didn't you go to blacksmith man to bring the shoeing horses, like I asked you?"

Archie was disappointed with a stupid smile knowing the stupidity of what he did and said, "I won't lie and say forget but it stole me when I was training for the duel and when I remembered a little while ago you were rushing me to find time and execute what you were asked for!"

His father looked at him sharply, and said in a rough accent, "Let's say you wanted me to do the job I gave you? Isn't it?"

Archie responded quickly with fear, defending himself and hiding the wooden sword behind his back from the prestige of his sunken-eyed father and a thick, irregular beard, "No, no, no, Dad, I didn't mean it."

His father interrupted with one sentence, "Shut up and give me your sword. Before I order something else, you might not like it!"

Archie took a deep sigh until he stood on both ends of his fingers and a painful dip in his stomach and said himself (how foolish I always repeat the same mistake and I don't repent) he knew well what his father would do, the situation ended with his wooden sword being delivered. With the sound of the sword being brought, Mr Abraham liked Archie more than his brothers, and so he was intense with him in order to refine him in his own way, which he believed would make him a man who would walk in the footsteps of his father, the former leader of the Royal Palace Guard. This is not easy under the fierce rivalry between the brave knights of the kingdom to win the confidence of the king, who has set conditions that no one cannot pass unless he is entitled to that position on his father's knee.

Archie's father seems to have learned of news from the kingdom that might determine his son's future.

Chapter 5

CHARLOTTE

On a day filled with billowy clouds hanging like fluffy pillows in the sky, teenage Charlotte walked out of their beautiful farm towards her grandmother's house. She carried a handmade basket crafted from banana leaves, filled with ripe cherries she picked every morning from her family's Kling Ling orchards. These orchards stretched across a wide swath of plains, creating a picturesque carpet of the most beautiful sights one could behold.

Charlotte's grandmother, a resilient woman battling the ravages of time, awaited her daily visit. Orphaned of her parents, Charlotte lived with her only surviving family member in their family home. The house was a small but charming abode, surrounded by the farms her parents had left her. Despite its modest size, the house was a testament to Charlotte's love for beauty. She adorned the balconies with flowers and filled every corner, inside and out, with vibrant blooms, reflecting her elegant taste and pure nature.

Charlotte herself was a vision of grace and simplicity. Her clothes, though simple, were always elegant, chosen with care. Her long, chestnut hair flowed in gentle waves down her back, and her bright blue eyes sparkled with kindness and intelligence. She had a gentle, nurturing demeanor, a trait she inherited from her beloved grandmother. Charlotte adored her grandmother, and their bond was strengthened by the daily rituals and shared stories of a time when the world was simpler and filled with magic.

As she approached the house, Charlotte spotted her handsome boyfriend, Archie, carrying his little brother's sword. He had lost his own sword as punishment from his father, and now wielded the smaller blade with a mix of defiance and pride. Charlotte's eyes widened with happiness and love at the sight of him.

"Hello there," she called out, her voice warm and cheerful.

Archie, seemingly engrossed in a daydream, turned to face her. His heart nearly leaped out of his chest with joy at the sight of her. "Charlotte!" he exclaimed, his face lighting up with a smile.

Charlotte teased him, "Is your sword shorter, or is this your brother's?"

Archie laughed, a sound that was music to her ears. "It's Arthur's feisty sword," he explained, "I took it so that no one at home gets hurt again."

"How are you, my dear?" he asked, his eyes twinkling with affection. "You look more beautiful every day."

Charlotte blushed and replied, "If I knew you loved flattery so much, I'd be happy to have you shower me with it every day."

Archie grinned. "You, my dear, are all the girls I could ever wish for in one."

She laughed shyly, her cheeks turning a delicate shade of pink. "It looks like you want to go to our secret place and see what the clouds hide for us, doesn't it?" she asked.

Archie nodded, his confidence unwavering. "Yes, my darling. No one understands me like you do. Will you come with me, or is there something that will keep you?"

Charlotte's eyes sparkled with eagerness. "Just give me a few minutes to put this basket inside, and I'll be right with you."

Archie couldn't resist reaching into the basket and grabbing a few cherries. He popped them into his mouth, grinning mischievously. "These are as delicious as the girl carrying the basket," he said, flirting shamelessly. "What's your secret, Princess Charlotte?"

Blushing deeply, Charlotte turned away shyly. "I seem to be going to miss these cherries and those who bear them," she said softly, hinting at something more.

Archie stopped walking and looked at her intently. "Why would you miss them?" he asked. "I bring them to you every day."

Charlotte's eyes widened in surprise. "What do you mean?" she asked, her heart pounding.

Archie hesitated, then took a deep breath. "My father wants to send me to the kingdom for Royal Guard candidate training. It's a big opportunity for me."

Charlotte held the basket tightly to her chest. "What's the problem with that?" she asked, her voice filled with excitement. "Isn't it your dream to become a great knight and rid the land of those wild ogres? You've told me so many times that you would be an invincible knight one day."

Archie nodded, his expression a mix of determination and uncertainty. "Yes, I still dream of that. But don't you think we won't see each other for a long time?"

Charlotte's face lit up with enthusiasm. "If you go to the kingdom, you'll fulfill your dream. I'll be the first to encourage you, and I'll even force you to go if you refuse!" She reached up and grabbed the front of his hair, drawing his head towards her. Her words were more enthusiastic than Archie expected, and he felt her hands around his waist as she expressed her joy.

Archie's eyes shone with love and passion. He gently touched her cheek and said, "But I would miss these soft cheeks and those pink lips." He brushed his finger against her lips, then leaned in closer. "I will also miss these charming eyes. You are so beautiful, Charlotte."

Charlotte's cheeks turned a deeper shade of pink, but she didn't shy away. For the first time, she felt every detail of his face up close, and she liked it. She imagined them together in a beautiful evening on the balconies of a high mansion, dancing under the moon and stars.

Archie's poetic words and gentle touch took her to the highest heavens. She felt his arms around her, holding her close. "Don't forget," she said, her voice filled with excitement, "there will be many rival knights with the same dreams as yours. I will be so proud of you if you come back as a knight. You will be like the brave hero from the legends who slayed dragons."

Archie joked, his hands still around her waist. "But there will be many beautiful girls in the kingdom, known for their beauty and elegance. Won't you be jealous of your lover?"

Charlotte laughed, a sound that echoed with joy. "I know you will excel in many aspects in the kingdom, except in love. Love is not owned by anyone but is created between two hearts chosen by the goddess."

Archie hugged her tighter, their bodies pressed together. "It is the hearts that decide, Charlotte," he said softly. "The souls that love each other live in their own world."

Overcome with emotion, Charlotte kissed him, her lips pressing against his with all the love she felt. Their moment was interrupted by the distant voice of Archie's father, echoing through the village.

Archie hesitated to respond, not wanting to reveal their location. His father didn't approve of him spending time with Charlotte, believing that love would distract a warrior from his duty.

Charlotte looked at him with a mix of love and defiance. "And now, what will you choose, handsome boy? Me or your father?"

Archie smiled smartly. "I choose you, and that's why I'm with you. But I must go to my father to see what he wants, then I'll come back to you, sweetheart." He ended their meeting with a deep kiss on her cheek.

Charlotte grinned cheerfully. "What a crafty fox," she said. "Well, I don't want to cause your father's anger any more. He looks like he's about to crack the trees around us."

As Archie walked away, Charlotte watched him with a mix of pride and longing. She knew that their love was strong enough to withstand any challenge, and she would always support him in his dreams, just as he supported her in hers.

Chapter 6

WOLF PUPPY

Lazy boy come here and help me carry these bags on the horses quickly) Archie's father knew where his son was and knew well with whom to sit, but he overlooked revealing it so as not to kill anything beautiful inside his lovely son, but not to make him feel it.

No one in this universe adores deer meat like Archie's father, especially small deer meat, which still feeds on milk. And all that bags were only prepared for a hunting trip to which he goes only with his sons.

And for them, it was more important than going to school, it teaches them to face reality and refine their skills better than to receive information and take it from their father's point of view.

And it looks like this year's hunting season will be pretty creamy.

After last year's wolf hunting campaigns by villagers that wiped out the majority of the villagers' livestock grazing in the plains, the wolves were even killing deer calves and reindeer herds that had been born, they were an easy catch, but oddly, the villagers were still baffled by those wolves that had surprisingly invaded those lands.

Early in the morning, Archie, his father and three brothers had set off on their hunting trip.

The atmosphere was beautiful and they were free from the habitual fog or clouds every morning. It was a good omen with an unusually lucrative fat catch this fall, Archie was over 17 years old, followed by twins Tommen and Escott with green eyes and light brown hair. It was clear that they had taken a lot from their mother's genes.

The boys were 15 years old and then the last cluster was Arthur Slate of the tongue and hand, who was only 10 years old and who was the most similar to his brother Archie, and Arthur was sitting on the front of the horses in front of his father.

Mr Abraham was always proud of this saddle and that he was able to walk in the footsteps of his father and just like he would never stop repeating the same sentence of his son, Archie when this horse rides (your sitting on this saddle will give you from your grandfather's soul a lot of judgment and dream in your life and true courage) and this is what his father has said to his son. Twins Tommen and Escott were sitting on a brown horse, the oldest of the horses, but the safest because it's the laziest of the rest of the horses.

Because their father always feared for them because she knew only little things and their mother loved them more than others, he was always keen to ride only this old horse, but it was a horse with a well-known breed and was also considered a source of income for the family, where he was hired as a breeding solution even though he was older.

While they are on their way to the middle of the fields and hunting grounds, Abraham told his son, Archie, "Well, Archie, you seem to have known that this will be your last trip here!" Archie didn't like that question, but he added to his concern by remembering that he was going to walk away from his girlfriend Charlotte, so he kept looking in the way, showing his disinterest or not hearing anything.

Then his father added, but to all of them said, "Make sure, my children, that whatever you want you to want, will only come to you with hard work, such as ploughing the earth with his hands, but the harvest at the end will be more a valuable treasure than food for several days. Learning any profession will make you not need to ask people, but become the king of everyone, but also remember that opportunities don't always come the same size.

"Your uncle, Mr Albert, has become a man of great affair in the court of the king and is even close to the king himself. He will give you an important job there. Of course, after proving your success in the course of jockey's candidates, do not think I will ask your uncle to fold the road and make you a knight with his help, and you are not worthy of that.

"Or to become an important man in the future who is not worthy I am a man who I do not agree to give any worker a sum of money without working for that money unless it is honest or tipped from me and I will not agree to believe in someone and I have the power to make my need I may always be hArchie with you because I know that soft will make you beg people your needs.

"We are in a world where no one will mercy you if you don't rely on your hands unless you lose them. You, Archie, head of war in this family if you succeed. Your brothers will succeed after you and if you fail, your brothers will fail after you and I know I won't live to see your future. This life has put each of us at a temporary age with a beginning and an end."

You growing up enough, not good to be a boy in your age he can only hang out with that orphan girl in village neighbourhood. Even if she is the heir to all that wealth, but the Cling Ling family won't leave you to take their daughter from them easily. They have done so much to reclaim and cultivate all these lands. It will never be easy for them to give them up.

"So, make yourself from now on to shut up and abolish the moles. Think about what you're going to do after I leave this world and how you're going to feed your mother and your brothers if you're not one of the knights in the kingdom? Will you work as a servant at Cling Ling Farms? Or work as a mourner of their horses, or you'll clean their dung, or you'll milk them cows?"

Finally, after a long silence, Archie said, "But Dad, I didn't ask anyone to look for work. I became a man and I was able to work for myself!"

Mocking him, his father said, "My son must not lie to yourself. You must be very realistic. You have become a young man enough to understand what is going on around you. You know that there is no business in our village other than farming, selling coal and milking cows. I don't think a boy of your age would like to see his girlfriend collect cow dung or work rent wood for others.

"Whoever will insult you, and whoever will treat you as a slave, and I will not lie to you, son, if I told you that I see in you my father's face and violence even at the end of his life, he was as mobile as you and had a dream and aspiration. If not for death, we would not have lived in this village after ordering the king to return him to the kingdom and all his people as a tribute to his fighting and his reception in all wars.

"But it's good that your uncle is a generous and insatiable man who loves the good of people, unless he reminds us that he has taken up these high positions after having to abandon me under the pressure of that fascist gang that wreaks havoc in the palace.

"I am so glad that he is interested in you, Archie, after the last letter we received from him, and you will be honoured to meet with him and his family when the time is right."

And then he smiled yellow smile and said, "Don't forget, too, that he has a beautiful girl who looks a lot like her mother. Her name is Isabella."

Archie said, "Now I know everything you're planning, Dad. All this is to be my marriage to the uncle's daughter?"

Before his father answered him, the sound of concussion cut off their talk and it was noisy. It was the sound of the hooves of a very large musk deer flock covered by a dust pile, as if it were a cloud heading towards them. It seemed like it was a good time.

And here the father glimpsed the members of the herd from behind the bushes, which appeared to him, and the treasure had been taken to him without making distances for it and also without exhausting the horses.

The father instructs his sons to quietly stop without causing any fuss that might shift from the herd's path. The herd was about 40 metres away from them until they stopped part of them to eat from the Earth's plants and some of the fruits falling in the autumn.

Come on, brave boy. Prove your worth.

Then he looked at Archie with admiration, and he said, "Get your horse up now and go north of the doughnut, Tommen and Scott, go to the right. When you hear my whistles, start showing some fuss and turn on the sounds of creepy animals, then the deer will have to go forward towards me and I will lie between these stumps and then I will snap them up arrows to catch more of them without seeing me."

The boys carried out the line like what their father asked them to do, while Rush turned around with his horse, trying to tread carefully from behind the woods trees that blinded the herd of vision, but the horse stopped suddenly and showed signs of dismay. What do you see? Gifting? What are you going to freak out? It hits the Earth's by his hooves trying to alert Archie to progress would be dangerous for them, I think he might have been confused by the hoof sound of the herd's feet when they got closer, but Archie seems not to have had much experience with horses, so his understanding of horse movements was as limited as his understanding of what was going on in the universe around him, of course, sitting in a remote village would not make you experienced something especially at such an age unless you ask for it yourself.

Archie tried several times to relieve the nervousness of the horse and his sudden and frightening tension at the same time but to no avail.

Calm down, horseman, do not cause the displacement of the herd and then cause me great embarrassment with my father. This is not his time now. The horse retreats this time even further until he lifts his feet in front and makes the sound of his purse out of his mouth.

The horse's strong reaction was a direct indication of the horse's anxiety.

Until Archie stepped down and took control of his horse after dragging him from his forehead with strength and attracting the bridle with force until he calmed down a little bit. Finally, Archie absorbed from the horse's gaze, which was concentrated high between the shrubs until Archie turned and his hands still held on to the horse's head and his eyes searched for what might answer his question.

And here his eyes fell from the bottom of his right out of the way on a grey dense haired wolf puppy not like the rest of the wolf puppy.

He was hiding between the giant trunks of trees that came out of the ground and formed a wooden Archie that overlapped with each other like they were made by a sculptor. The frightened puppy retreated back to dive further into the darkness of the bush. Archie slowly advanced as he crawled on his feet towards the puppy, who put his tail between his legs for fear of this curious creature.

Archie subconsciously smiled a happy smile of luck who finally hugged his luck. He was fortunate to feel the taste of happiness in his tongue. His dream was to have a wolf puppy but only found the stray village dogs on which to learn how to tame these nice beings and make friends.

But it was what left her when she grew up or sometimes sent her to his girlfriend Charlotte as a gift sometimes or as a temporary deposit at other times because of his father's dislike of dogs because of the abundance of barking her on the pedestrian so that his father took three of the puppies Archie brought home.

He put her in a wooden cage and threw her into the village river, causing her immediate death. That accident was a black day in Archie's life. After his grandfather died, the six-year-old then swore not to enter the house of any of the puppies so that it would not cause her death like what happened with those poor puppies.

He perched on his knees to meet the puppy to get him out, trying to humour him and he says in a kind voice, "Come on with me. I'm sure you'll be happier with me than you are with your parents," but he was away and the puppy was retreating back more and more until he started howling in a very weak voice.

Here Archie's feelings calmed as he reflected on the beauty of that puppy as he howled, which he imagined howling while embracing him from his extreme love of puppies until he became despondent about it.

Archie felt so beautiful to get what one wished and dreamed of.

He even swore he wouldn't leave the puppy at all costs.

Rush mimicked the sound of the wolf howling as the sound of a true wolf

howling from the intensity of his love for finding his little dream in this place. In the meantime, the wolf's feeling changed suddenly and his fear resided, he lay on his hands and put his head on them. He felt that there was a link between them after he exchanged the same voice and then moved his ears forward,

announcing acceptance of his friendship in principle.

When Archie hearing his father's whistle to start cordoning off his reindeer

herd, but his puppy preoccupation was bigger than all of that, Archie noticed that the wolf was a little limp, so he couldn't flee far from the beginning until Archie realised that one of the puppy's feet had been broken, "Oh little man, what happened to you?"

Archie's father surprised that the herd was running towards Archie, from which he was supposed to make sounds that frightened the herd, just like his brothers did on the other side. That was enough to make his father rage. He knew that there was a failure on the part of Archie, and then he appeared to shout at his voice.

"Archie, AaaaArchie, AaaaaaArchie, AaaaaArchieiiiiii," said four times until his son Arthur put his hands on his ears from the intensity of his father's voice, and saying in his loud voice, "What are you doing, Archi?"

Archie remembered when he was patting his hand on the head of the wolf that he had forgotten to frighten the deer, but it was too late that the deer herd was shaking the earth and escaped from his brothers, who scared the herd from the southern face of the bush. Even the horse was frightened and fled for fear of the herd before being stabbed by those sharp horns intertwined with each other for many of them and driven with force as spears in a garrison battle.

Because the height noise of the herd the wolf puppy also felt scared until he tried to escape from Archie's hands but Archie grabbed him before he fled so he wouldn't die under the feet of the herd...

And because of his wild instinct, the puppy inserted his tusks into Archie's hand. "Oh, come on," Archie said in pain, "You bitten me, puppy. This is my penalty, little man! Because I wanted to save you and protect you!" However, the puppy did not escape his hands until Archie ran behind the trees to try to catch up with the horse before moving further away and away from the path the fearful herd would take, but the herd was a barrier between Archie and the horse, which disappeared into the crowds of collective fear.

At this moment, his father and brother arrive at him, and they realised the fear of being hurt, until he came out of the trees and pointed at them with his hand and the puppy in his lap, calling, "I'm here, Dad."

Tommen Escott Arthur Ascot Inn Speeding. "Are you okay, brother!" They breathe a sigh of relief and their eyes go around looking at him especially their father because he loves him so much, he considers him all his life.

Despite his inordinate reluctance to deal with him permanently, Tommen says, "We worried so much about you, brother. What happened to you, and what puppy did you have?" Little Arthur fell on the horse and fell on his face, but he did an indifferent acceleration until he ran and embraced his brother like he hasn't met him in years! Don't worry about me.

"Look what I found," referring to the puppy who fondles his hands and forgets about his misfortune, he was happy with what he found more than he lost until his father said to him indignantly, "I see that you did not learn from your mistakes in the past, and now you repeat the same mistake, but the most painful that you do not seem to be touching or sorry for having done bad and failed us because of a puppy."

Archie said with resentment, "It happened so fast, Dad, and I didn't see a herd of deer coming and—"

His father interrupted him quickly, saying, "Where's the horse?"

The embarrassment on Archie's face does not know where to obscure his gaze at his father, who is catching his anger, "Everything happened quickly Dad. The horse stopped progressing after this poor puppy freaked him out. When he started to get nervous, then he retreated from fear and refused to complete. When I was trying to calm him down, the horse and put the puppy away, the deer herd had arrived. I couldn't do anything, this caused the horse to panic and escape, as well as the puppy and I fled to save ourselves before drowning in the middle of the herd."

"I was right that it was time for you to go to the kingdom, no matter how hard I was with you, but you are my son, and I can't crush you in order to learn, like what is being done to the jockeys' candidates in the kingdom. Look at yourself and see what you have done has caused us to lose one of our sources of income that we have been relying on for a long period of time not only this but also lost a precious catch because of a dog puppy!

And you know I don't like these animals, but it seems like you don't want to learn and still live teenage lives."

In order, not to provoke his father, he quietly said, "It's a wolf puppy, Dad. A wolf puppy, not a dog puppy."

Mr Abraham's silence to cool his fire after their loss of that precious catch made him feel so frustrated that he decided to cancel a remainder of his journey after feeling a broken passion and hope inside him that he could not deny in return—he knew very well that his son adored animal husbandry from a young age and had a dream of having a puppy wolf, but some lessons had to be given to the boys at times. Otherwise, he will never learn from their mistakes.

If each situation goes through an understanding and without any advice suitable for each situation or without proper punishment. Mr Abraham completed his reproach and said, with his judgment, it has a lot of lessons, "Well, we will see if this puppy is able to carry you on the back to the village!" That word caused the twins to laugh until one of them fell off the old horse.

Little Arthur became angry at his brothers' laughter and said, in a furious voice, "That isn't funny."

Then he took his tongue out, and he made a mockery of them amid their father is astonishment, who finally smiled knowing well Arthur's love for his brother Archie.

Archie seemed a little broken, knowing that he had made a mistake that had caused him to lose something important to his father, but once he looked at the puppy who was licking Archie's hand as a thank him for what he did to him, he felt the tenderness of those who comforted him until he said, trying to call his father and relieve him of punishment, "But I told you, Dad; this happened so fast and I had no reason to do all this! I also caused the rescue of this injured puppy."

His father answers, but this time with a lighter, quiet tone.

After witnessing Arthur's sympathy to his brother, "If you were really eager to do your duty, which I asked you to do whatever the reasons were. At this moment if you are a knight in the battle, it is your action that determines whether you lose, kill or survive, or you may win. You've been between two choices either completing your mission or leaving what you're asked to do and being busy enjoying the hobby of collecting dog's puppies."

Archie answer excitedly, "But Dad, he's just a little puppy and he's injured, too, I never would have left him like this."

His father told him with advice, "If you were really clever, you would realise that this catch is far more important than leaving your top job for an injured puppy that won't do you any good. Your action was a reason why we lost our catch and one of the three horses I relied on for our livelihood. You didn't imagine how much I struggled to raise these horses to secure a source of income that would protect us from begging asking people, but now you have to bear the price of your mistake, which will be nothing before you repeat the mistake someday in your life. Because when life decides to punish you, you will be punished by a fierce punishment, you will wish you were dirt."

The father and his four sons return to the village empty-handed but loaded with loss on their backs after losing their most important horses and the royal saddle, which was the pride of the family.

Everyone was on their horse except Archie, who was sniffing behind them with his feet as a prisoner of war carrying his beautiful puppy, but the fatigue had exhausted them to come down Arthur and jump off his father's horse to walk with his brother to relieve him of fatigue, play with the puppy, and when he got tired, he came back to ask his father to carry him on horseback.

Until that situation provoked Mr Abraham's laughter with all his heart until tears came shy of his hArchie eyes, which did not bear that spontaneous attitude among his sons. Until his heart was soaked after watching his son, Archie reeling from drowsiness and fatigue. He even stopped and dismount and carried Archie on the back of the horse with his younger brother after the puppy had been taken and Mr Abraham had completed the walk on his feet for more than two hours until they had all arrived at their home.

Archie saw in a sleepover that Charlotte stood in front of him in his bedding and wore a pink, pure silk, soft-shaped dress as a smoothness and her hair is unusual.

She smiles and tells him to marvel with a basket full of cherries, "Where are you, Archie, why didn't you come on the date?" Then he saw behind her a girl with a very white face who was whiter in his lifetime, wearing a long black dress in it, but not knowing the shape and features of the brightness of her face, until her face became dark, and that light disappeared from it.

Archie saw in a sleepover that Charlotte stood in front of him in his bedding and wore a pink, pure silk, soft-shaped dress as a smoothness and her hair is unusual.

She smiles and ask him with a basket full of cherries, "Where are you, Archie, why didn't you come to our date?" Then, behind her, a girl with a bright, white face, was whiter than any creature he had seen in his life, wearing a long black dress, but he did not know what shape and features of the brightness of her face, until her face became dark and that light disappeared from her.

He did not know who she was or what she was, whether she was human or demon. What he more afraid of is that she had long claws like sharp eagle claws. He approached from behind Charlotte and placed one of her claws on Charlotte's neck. He felt he had lost his ability to speak and move.

Then he watched a long tongue wrap around his face as a python snake full of saliva as she wiped his face from up to down and a faint voice came out of it saying, "Someday I will taste your delicious flesh, but once he opened his eyes awake from this nightmare," until he found his cute puppy resembling a beautiful doll, he licked Archie's face with his little tongue and kept licking Archie's face until he got out of his bed and grabbed the puppy with both hands.

And he was angry and raised him high, and he said, "Really, you'll eat me when you have opportunities?"

The wolf gazed marvelling at Archie, marvelling at his friend's reaction, and then let out a light bark as if he says, "No, I do not betray who feed me and save me."

Until Archie noticed that the injured puppy's foot was completely repelled and drew a medical gauze as if a professional doctor treated him until he realised that it was his father who did this when he was overcome with extreme drowsiness, due to the fatigue he received while applying his father's punishment for his missed hunting trip. But strangely, Archie noticed that the wolf looks like human looks, not animal looks, where he felt like a wolf whispered to him the same sound, he heard in a dream! Until he decided to go back to sleep again after feeling very sleepy.

Chapter 7

SHADOW AND NECKLACE

Archie woke up from a deep and indulgent sleep like a bear who woke up from his winter slumber and his stomach knocked on the food doors until his steps take him towards his room window overlooking the infinite plains directly to see what time it is from this day until he saw the golden sun threads have started to fade from the west.

Then he realised that the sun was back in the trick and it was night, but it was still too early for Archie and what he intended to do. He looked down at him and found the puppy of the grey wolf trimming his tiny claws in his trousers.

Oh, no, this is the most beautiful pants I have, and I don't want it looking like the one I threw at the old box, so stop it, ya... umm, Archie remembered that he didn't call the puppy any name, but that he didn't even think, but an idea occurred to him, after he was all thinking about his date with his girl Charlotte, knowing that his days in the village were few.

So, he decided to go out and go down the village where the estuary of the waterfall meets the river and they hug without anyone feeling like when he meets his beautiful girlfriend Charlotte almost every night, he knows it's hard to have Charlotte waiting for him at this time she wouldn't have expected him back from the hunting trip or at least she must be asleep.

The truth is, Archie and Charlotte were dating at the same time at the beginning of the night, and they were sneaking of their homes, and sometimes the encounter lasts until the end of the night when the moon is complete in the middle of the month and their souls are lost in a world of love in which no one else lives in it except them. And the enthusiasm was ignited inside him knowing that he would surprise her with the beautiful gift he dreamed of, so he insisted on going to the meeting place despite knowing that she could only come here if he had great luck.

Indeed, he came out speeding, carrying his puppy in a small burlap bag, in order to avoid the rain if it happened, and sped off towards to estuary of the waterfall, but like what was expected, no one found except the sound of the roar of the waterfall and the frogs croaking until wind came from the north. Consoling himself and frustrated, said, "It seems that this wind is a harbinger of me to go away instead of waiting pointlessly, at least no matter now, I can deflect my head on my pillow and I am comfortable with the conscience."

Then set his head down. Looks like everything these days is going against me. I don't know why, but maybe good. Then he went back where he came from. While he's coming home on the way, the wolf barked angrily and grossly. "What happened, wolf? What worried you?" Archie raised his head quickly after someone gestured between the separating spaces and the walls of the houses as if to watch him?

Archie felt anxious and scared and continued to anticipate the situation. He might have been a passing person. But that shadow continued to look out of the narrow road openings between houses from time to time, "Who seems to be watching me? Is it Charlotte?"

It was not even Charlotte, then he decided to break the suspicion with certainty and go to it himself that when he arrived, no one, even found the wolf back with his ears as if it felt like there was a danger close to him, but Archie completed the road, saying maybe what I had today was enough to make me imagine things around me, and with a glimpse of lightning passing from the front someone remained and disappeared in a glimmer!

Archie thought it might be a giant bird shadow, but no one knows and surprised it again. The same scene repeated again out of the pews of houses, but this time it started to become clear that it was already a person, not a fantasy like what he thought.

He was stepping out of the alley and entering it again, and he was a person who had been sent to specially observe it, so he thought maybe an intruder thief wanted to steal from the village and found no one but spray at this time of the night's stillness and the quiet of the village.

So, he decided to act. He tried not to observe that unknown invisible and when that head was absenting between the walls, he sneaked into him as a rock snake with speed and tranquillity between the wall of the house preceding the wall of the house behind which that disguised unknown was hiding, also taking advantage of the sound of the wind, which became an auxiliary element to hide the sound of his feet and movement... The wind was running too fast against Archie's direction, but it brought with it a very dark cloud.

It hid what's left of the moonlight... Then he sneaked through the narrow alley until he almost walked on the tip of his toes to ensure his movement was secret, and then he watched one of them from behind at the end of the alley here.

Archie confirmed that he was the person he wanted and then put the puppy.

He pointed out to him that no noise or sound was made and closed to him the cover and in unaccounted seconds, Archie had reached that anonymous invisible in silent steps, as he walked on the sand to grab him with his hands from his shoulders and made him turn around quickly, and then asked him an angry question, "Who are you and what are you doing here?"

The unknown person turned and was grieving like the one who stabbed a dagger in the back and had a very white, with dark-haired girl who had her eyes sprinkled into her eyes, Archie's gaze lies on her wide eyes, to penetrate her glamour into Archie's eyes to know the meaning of the sedition of angelic beauty for the first time wondering with deep silence in meditation for this beautiful face of any planet coming... He was only an inch apart, between him and the girl.

Archie relaxed from his grip and asked her after his veins quietly froze and he was confused by the girl, "Who are you?"

Without permission and before he said a word, she turned her face an attempt to flee like a caged bird and he tried to realise her with his hand, but his hand held something in her chest like a necklace and in a glimpse, the girl disappeared from his hands!

Archie comes out of the narrow walls of houses, quick behind her, calling for her. "Wait, I swear I will never hurt you," but in seconds she became a smoke thread that faded in the dark of the night? Where did she go so quickly and how did she disappear in a glimpse? He looks in his hand. It was a very small emerald necklace with a very glare and glow, and he sees it as weird shapes and close to human shapes, and then it moves like gel from a non-specific and unclear shape.

He caught his hand holding the necklace and raised his head a last time, he might find it around. He stands perplexed. He wonders who this strange girl is, this late in the night and in our little village? He looked around everywhere, but it was dark, the master of the situation then he felt itchy in his leg, and when he looked, it was the little wolf was fondling his trousers again, laughing quietly, taking him and completing his way home, still hoping to come again at least to order her necklace.

And when he got home, he brought milk for his new friend and took it to the roof, and he made a bed there.

He embraces his little puppy after extending on his bedding on the floor of the house to sleep under the bright moon light, which only displaces those clouds so that the remaining Cling Ling people enjoy this most wonderful lunar look.

There is no doubt that the moon is a friend of those who don't have a friend at night. It comforts the sadness of lovers and restores the hope of those who have lost hope in life.

When Archie put his head on his pillow, they began flying for his world, which transcends stars and galaxies, and he felt a grounded air breath that caressed his tresses with cold smoothness.

Until he closed his eyes a little more delicious with that moment and the little puppy in his lap until the sound of the peaceful wind symphony blowing from the far north from the highs of the mountains guarding the peaceful village as if the musician was the same dreamy full moon who had overlooked them from behind those clouds that had come to continue into the morning.

Archie would not have slept but the face of this strange girl, whose necklace is still in his hand, was forgotten by the decoy of the empty date and then opened his eyes and lay on his back, to meditate on the sky and the unstable dragging movement as he extended on his back. Even imagine him for his sake that he actually sees that face in the liver of heaven until his meditation punctuates the sound of snoring the little puppy... Sleepiness was stronger than a moment of love and admiration... Even he is also in a happy and comfortable sleep with the smile of his contradictory share of this day.

Chapter 8

BEE'S WAY

In the early morning, there was a group of carts that had arrived from the kingdom loaded as usual with goods coming from the kingdom that were not available here in the village. The carts belonged to some traders who received some benefit for providing such services to the villagers and saving trouble and money to go to the kingdom. In addition to the mailing vehicle from the kingdom to the villages and vice versa, the latest news of the kingdom from various sources comes to all villages.

His makes the arrival of these vehicles in the village an extraordinary day. This convoy came only once a month and sometimes in the winter only came more than three months later due to poor weather conditions at the most time. The residents of the village came out of their community to ensure that they had the goods they needed before they were executed.

Mr Abraham was the first to arrive in the Bees Road area, the main corridor in the village to the mail carriage. He was like a longing lover to arrive in the letters of his absentee sweetheart and did not know that she had been in the arms of another until he found a post from Mr Albert, his brother-in-law and his children's uncle.

He tells him that he must expedite the dispatch of his son, Archie. It has been decided to submit a payment of the boy candidates for special security and strategic reasons that are difficult to explain in the letter and that if he can send his son tomorrow or even today, he must not hesitate according to the letter written carefully by Mr Albert indicating the importance of the matter.

The news was good for Mr Abraham, who did not focus on the rest of the exact words in Mr Albert's letter. He wished him happily the moment he would see his son, Archie, who had become a knight of the king and who would be bragged by the people of the village.

They went rushing home to ask Archie's mother to tell her son and ask him to prepare himself to travel while he went to the market and buy some travel supplies for his son, who will not delight in this news. He enjoys with his dear puppy on his heart, as well as his sense that the mysterious night girl will probably come at any moment as long as he hangs out in the roads at night and day to ask for a gathering. And then he enjoys meeting her and looking at that beauty to enjoy the rest of his souls as well.

Once the news came to Archie, which was expected, he realised that there were things he had to accomplish quickly, first, the wolf he didn't choose a name for. And he doesn't know who take care of him after his travels!

Knowing that the puppy had no place in this house after travelling, Archie said, "I have to spend two needs in one order this time I have lazed so much from getting the simplest things done so that it is now like a knot I have to solve before the count ends to the number ten or it could be a game loss."

He ran as a rush after feeling that in fact his expectation that he would sit in the village another week was a delusion of laziness and procrastination, but the winds blow counter to what ships desire, don't postpone today's work for tomorrow so you don't have to meet your simple needs. Then you find yourself like Archie running through village roads exhausted to the core looking for Charlotte to say goodbye and deliver the puppy as a covenant, as a farewell gift at the same time and probably she will forgive him for his sudden unexpected travel, he promised her many times with promises he would do when he met, but here he tried to realise the sword of time before it cuts him.

Until he felt the warmth of someone's hand on his shoulder, followed by a soft voice near his earlobe, "Where is the handsome boy going to?" He turned until he found whoever was looking for her. Charlotte was on her way to the farm a little late for the good of the coincidence, until he said with a breath snapped of running, "You've shortened us the time, it looks like it's going to be too short!"

Charlotte said by mockery, "Let's prolong it if it's short, and I'll order the goddess to do it if we can't, but first of all tell me why you were anxious, it seems like you were running to escape the two-headed ogre."

And then she made innocent laughs and calm as her face quiet, Charlotte didn't notice the wolf puppy in Archie's lap, which was covered in cloth until moving and issuing a faint bark, she was a little curious until she said with her eyes on the puppy, "Did she go back to the hobby of collecting dogs?"

Archie said, "I liked your sense of humour coming out of your lips, Charlotte," and then he dropped his head and put his hand on the cloth. He told her before he revealed what he was hiding from her, "That's what I told you one day and that I would get it," and then removed the whole cloth from the puppy until Charlotte saw the puppy that opened his eyes and started.

It was like a baby indicating to his parents that they would talk to him to start daily life lessons with them and then he stopped moving when his eyes fell on Charlotte until his eyes went between Charlotte's face and Archie's face until a long velvet smile smiled with her happy silent cry on Charlotte's face, "Oh, a wolf puppy! I can't believe what my eyes see."

He handed the puppy to her and tells her with a smile, "I don't hide you, Charlotte, it's my gift to you, even though I love him, but I will give you nothing but the most precious thing I have. And this puppy is the most precious I've ever had, my darling Charlotte."

Charlotte's face blushed until she became a mature red berry. As soon as Charlotte caught the wolf puppy, the puppy stared to Archie and then to Charlotte, and he didn't know if he was sold or handed over to his true mother, then she joined him to her lap with great tenderness until the puppy delighted in that act and dipped his head between her two little breasts, dwelt on the move and covered his face with his ears, as if he had already returned to his mother's lap.

Until Archie joked, "Come on, little man, this is not your mother, and I don't think she has milk in her little breasts."

Charlotte gave him a sweet smile and said, "Are you jealous of the little puppy, Archie?"

With a broad smile, he replied without uttering one word, agreeing to her question until she said to him, "Right, but you didn't tell me what his name was?" Archie says, "Actually I was worried about named him what I came to you for hearing, my dear Charlotte. There was an update on my travel subject. I didn't know it. I only knew a little earlier from my mother that I might be travelling tomorrow or after tomorrow!"

Charlotte was wistfully silent after the fact that he had gone so far and then

he added, "There was a rush mail from the kingdom asking my father to send me as soon as possible, because of a sudden change in the date of the Royal Guard session. Otherwise, I will miss my chance."

He didn't complete his speech, then Charlotte's eyes were drowned with tears that seemed to race between them in her fluffy cheek until she seemed to be sobbing at her intensity and sense that it was farewell.

Until he approached her after meeting their eyes and after he saw the effect of the news on her, just like he expected, and then he said to his lovely girlfriend, "Don't grieve, dear Charlotte. This is a must, but I promise to get back to you and I am one of the jockeys that everyone in the village will be proud of and the first of them is you, Charlotte."

She interrupted him and said, "Nothing matters to me but that you will not be late for me. No one here but you are, Archie. I used to see you every morning and evening. So how will it be my next day? I don't know when I will come back and when I will meet you again." She wore more tears until she collapsed like rain and got wet the puppy head that lifted her head and seemed to lick her clothes.

Archie took advantage of the puppy's awakening to lighten the mood, saying, "But you didn't propose to me a name for this beautiful gift! I have I promised myself that I wouldn't name him until you made a choice."

The girl says when she wiping away tears with her other hand, "I will call him HArchieey!"

"And what did its mean?"

"It means I remind you at the moment I call his name so I can feel you in front of me and still next to me until you come next to me again."

Archie already said, "It was a beautiful name," and then he uttered it a few times until the wolf turned to him and Archie asked him, "Do you like it?"

The puppy answered him with a staggering howl, announcing the approval, Archie said, "Then you are HArchieey from now on," and then hugged her with a force he has never done before and he says, "That I will miss you so much, darling."

"And I'll miss the smell of you, but I think it's our short parting that will excite me the most and that will comfort me in my estrangement too."

And then Charlotte says in Archie's lap, "Honey, don't forget that little HArchieey is between us and is afraid of choking on him."

"Oh, sorry, I forgot because I liked your smell."

Then, without prejudice, his little brother Arthur appeared to tell him with interest, "Finally, I found you, Archie, that my father was looking for you and saying that he had agreed from one of the owners of the carriages to get you outside the village tomorrow to the main carriage station and he brought you several travels, including a new item."

Charlotte says, "How are you, Arthur? It's been a long time since I last saw you and you must have grown up, handsome boy."

Arthur did not answer her, but rather gave her a look of hate, unjustified hatred from Charlotte's point of view, because his actually was the only one in this village that hates Charlotte and that he always said that she was the reason why his brother had disappeared from them when they were at the time of play and did not return until the play was finished, which caused a kind of jealousy in little Arthur's chest that was built between him and Charlotte.

On the morning of the travel, Archie's mother came and carried with her hand her son's carpet, after processing all the necessary luggage for his trip.

Within it is a great bitterness that no one can experience but how hard it is for either parent to separate their eldest child in particular if it is the first time that they will experience a bitter experience of thinking and fear that they never used to.

When his mother stood in front of him, she said, holding him in a long-sleeved dark navy shirt, "How beautiful you will be. Your father made sure to buy the best shirts in the colours that you love."

Archie couldn't bear the idea that he would say goodbye to his affectionate mother after all this age he spent near her and didn't even disparate her one night until he jumped and he hug her forcefully.

"I know you won't disappoint your father in you and you'll soon be back to us with heartfelt badges."

"You have that, Mom. I'm not the one to disappoint, even if I travel the longest distances. But you promised me before you would tell me a secret, and I always insisted on you, and I think now is the time."

She said, "No, my son, don't say this. You will definitely come back and cook you the dish of the goat's shoulder that you love."

He laughed, but he said, "But you have to tell me what my father should have told me."

She answered shrewdly in order not to open his mind to matters older than his age. This could distract his mind and bring him into doubt leading to the damage. "It's a long story, son. But I'll cut you short. If you get there to the kingdom and succeed in your knight role, your uncle, Mr Albert, will tell you everything you want to hear, even if it's heavy on you, but you have to believe it. He's the only one who knows the secret of your grandfather and your father and the secret of your father's entire family. Either I tell you know anything I can't explain to you and the time is too tight and your father and brothers are waiting down to say goodbye now, my darling."

Rush down for breakfast until he was seen by his brother Arthur, who ran up to him and snuggled him with force, telling him, "My brother, how are you going to differentiate us like this? And who will lead us to fight the invading ogres in the woods and draw the plans of smart battles and run away before they can get you ugly ogres, especially their big biceps."

He laughed high from the bottom of his heart and then Tommen confidently said, "No, Arthur, I will be the right alternative for Archie and it will be an opportunity for you to see our skills, which I have never seen before."

Arthur said mockingly at Tommen, "If the ogres saw you, believe me you would have done it in your pants, and that made Tommen frown his eyebrows with anger, then he came down from his chair and rushed to Arthur to slap him, but Arthur hid behind his brother Archie until Archie told Tommen, smiling after silently look him, "That's how you would do your little brother if I left, Tommen?"

It was a polite question, and in his time, it was a pre-travel message, and then he added his fingers to his brother's thick hair, "You and Scott were responsible for Arthur, no matter what he said, he would stay our little brother."

Then he grabbed Arthur's hair and drew him to him and said, "I know Arthur has a long tongue, but he stays the nicest and best in this house. You should go beyond him." Until Escott came with a glass of hot milk, and this was the most important thing for Archie, breakfast.

Archie said, "I always tell my brother, Tommen, that Arthur is a lot of chatter and his tongue is disowned. But he's our little brother and I have to take him for granted."

And then he hugged the twins until he entered Arthur after he crammed his slender body between them and said Archie with a pronouncement locked in his eye, heart, chest and throat complaining about his situation and examining his patience after.

Until their father entered the door and witnessed the sight before him, he said, commenting on Archie's words with optimistic wisdom, "Go back to us quickly if you succeed in your mission and we will all be happy with that and you will not wait for us to leave again, unless we rarely—"

"I promise you will not be bored. There are things that will not make you sleep the night from drinking, eating and all your eyes and your heart liked, but not at the expense of your main mission, your heart and your reputation."

Archie rides in the horse carriage parked outside which will bring him to the nearest point to gather travellers' carriages from the village to ride from there and then go to the kingdom. Archie's heart squeezed in grief as he saw the features of grief on his parents' face and his brothers and waved their hands so that he could not open the whole fingers of their gloom and bad moment, like he's holding the whole horse cart on his back from the weight of pain of separation.

Archie glimpses his poor mother as she wipes away tears so that she can't hide her grief and she speeds him inside the house to complete the wailing on her lovely son and the essence of her life, Arthur caught up with the horse carriage while saying goodbye to his brothers with all his enthusiasm, as if he were going to no longer return him until he fell to the ground. Archie could not bear those scenes to try to gather his strength and possess himself a little bit. He overcame the feeling of tears silently until the carriage arrived near the end of the road leading to the village junction when they dropped the carriage commander to turn quietly.

Then he watched Charlotte, who was going to his house, realise that she had been too late to run towards the carriage until she had taken too much action and the wolf puppy followed until her fingers had touched Archie's fingers for the last time, but the carriage was too quick to hold her hand and she cried loudly, "Remember that bees always return to the path of the bees that came out of it, and you will return to us like the bees do I love you, Archie, and I will love you until the earth buries everyone on it, until she give up running and he stand."

Archie could not respond with his word and could merely stare at her beautiful green eyes, until she had her hands on her heart and everything in it froze.

The carriage disappeared between the trees of the road outside the village and he sat at the end of the car alone, broken and put his hand on his cheek, contemplating the sky completely empty of everything in it, as if it was a sign of the beginning of a new page in his life that started from this moment.

Suddenly, the horse stopped violently and issued a neighing loud, the front of the carriage hit the back of the horse, which arose with fear until Archie almost fell off the carriage after rolling inside it and crashed into the front of the elevated carriage, Archie's face comes to back side of the carriage.

The driver of the carriage quickly came down to guide the scared horse as he said, "What an idiot girl?"

Archie rose confused by the features and said with fear, "What happened?"

the driver said, "That a girl appeared surprisingly in front of the horse carrying a puppy with her, which was like a ghost I don't know, but she disappeared in a glimpse like she did and I don't know how she disappeared? As if she were a gin or a witch, she almost caused us catastrophe if not for God's kindness!"

He asks the driver, "A girl holding a puppy? Are you sure?"

The boy's eyes circled around him in all directions with great interest, but Charlotte couldn't get to this place before us. This is impossible, but could it be the girl I saw yesterday. "Would you describe it to me, please?"

The man did not hear Archie's question, shouted at the horse more quickly until Archie felt that the carriage might disintegrate its parts as it travelled so fast because of the high sound of the dysfunction and screeching of the wheels and the shaking of its rusty spikes.

Archie fearfully calls for a peaceful arrival at his destination, after more than half an hour of concussion and a stomach waving over that old carriage, they had arrived at the gathering point of the carriages carrying travellers from and to the kingdom.

The driver snicker and said in quick words, "Come down, boy, we have arrived and you should have tried to rush to find you the carriage that will take you to the kingdom, so it seems that the atmosphere is changing fast and it will rain in a little while, and the majority of the carriage may come back if the rain is heavy, the road becomes more and more, and this hinders their arrival. Some fear that they will find themselves alone in a place where they will be vulnerable to bandits or lone ogres, so it's faster before it's too late."

The poor boy came down speeding from the carriage. He believed in the words of the driver of the carriage. He assured that the drivers of the carriages may leave early because of weather. The place is isolated and far from any residential gathering. The village is at least three hours away from walking. Because of his rush down, almost one hundred pounds fell out of his pocket, which was what had father given him, he did not feel it until he arrived at the gathering of the horse carriages and then stopped a little and thought that the money in his pocket would come out to make sure that everything he had to negotiate based on his budget. His father told him to show his firmness and toughness with the owners of the vehicles because they were men famous about greed and exploited the conditions of the travellers because there was no other competitor who took the residents of the village to the kingdom other than them, but when he entered his hand.

Archie looked anxiously at his hand as it pulled out all his pocket with everything he had until he found it was just eight pounds! Oh, God, that's just eight pounds! No, it looks like I put the rest in the other pocket! But unfortunately, his hand came out of his other pocket empty handed! Archie said in himself, and he felt so much inside him that he felt like he needed to shout his voice out to get out of that illusion that he thought had a monster clutch that sucked into his body every hour more and more.

But with equanimity, he took control of his anger and progressed towards the first carriage and stood next to it. The grief and inspiration covered his face until that beautiful face withered and became like a rotting pear until he found the commander of the carriage and he lit a big pipe, not without digging, it's like a woodpecker made. Then Archie asked the man who was careless to having a customer at a time when the customers rarely came here, "You're the owner of this carriage, sir? How much is a trip to the kingdom so I'm in a hurry?"

The owner of the carriage looked at Archie in disgust and checked it from the bottom to the top as if looking at the wheel of his carriage and then turn of his face and completing the sip of the pipe and then saying after blowing the smoke like a black cloud in the voice of careless at all, "Fifteen pounds, boy!"

"What!" Archie said in shocked tone.

"What? Fifteen pounds to the kingdom. You seem crazy because I didn't ask to fly me to the kingdom."

The man came back to sip the smoke and said coolly, "Well how much will you pay?"

Archie strictly said, "Three pounds, and I think it's a lot!"

At that the man threw in contempt and said, "Do you see that I am a donkey in front of you to carry you on my back and run you for seven days with three pounds? I've wasted a lot of my time go now before I get up and hang you from your feet."

Archie's silence and anger were on his face, and he preferred to go away quietly instead of responding to this indifferent and impolite man. Even if he agrees, the journey is long and he travels with a man with such an ugly psyche, he will have a lot of danger.

Indeed, Archie carried his bag and drove away after saying to the man thanks quietly and humbly, although he did not deserve to be thanked for his scandal and mismanagement, but Archie realised from the first, that he was already in an unenviable situation, so it seems that the value of the trip will be more than he has.

Archie continued to ask the seated carriers but found only the cheapest price and was twelve pounds with begging and was also more than he had, he didn't tell them what money he had so that he wouldn't repeat what happened with the first carriage owner until he got to another carriage and said to himself, I have to be honest this time. And he went on with his steady steps and with optimism over the unusual while in this miserable psychological and material situation until he stood before the man and said, "If I may, sir, I want to go to the kingdom, but I don't have enough money. I'm ashamed of you, but I like to tell you the truth so, I don't waste your time and my time."

The man threw him a sharp look and checked him thoroughly and was putting the saddles on the horses to prepare to move with potential customers and then turned his face away from Archie, to complete his work of equipping the horses, until he said from behind his horse, "Well, how many do you have, boy?"

Archie said embarrassingly, "That I only have five pounds, but I want to give you three pounds, because the whole amount I have is barely eight pounds enough for me to buy me some food and help me on my journey to stop me begging people, and then I will manage there in the kingdom, because someone will be waiting for me."

The man interrupts him and says firmly, "I did not ask you to tell me the story of your life, boy, but of course this money is not enough for a long journey like the kingdom's journey, but I will do you a service not to your pretty face, but to me you are an unhappy and miserable boy, okay?" He pointed his hand at a carriage that was standing alone from the gathering of horse's carriages. The man completes his advice, "He's going anyway to the kingdom a little later. Tell him you came from Mr Jamangan and tell him to look at me and he'll get it."

Archie felt he would fly from the intensity of joy. His frowning face changed since the morning and his playful spirit, which escaped her imprisonment, returned to him. Archie ran, accelerating and it showed in his face until he reached that man, who climbed into the chair and grabbed the barricade.

"Hey, sir, hey, hey, hey, sir, are you going to the kingdom?"

He shook his head and said, "You seem to be a customer of anonymity, boy. Yes, I'm heading to the kingdom. You should rush to ride and rush to put 13 pounds in my hand before you go up!"

Archie said with a smile, "I came to you by your friend, Mr Jamangan, sitting there," looking at him, Archie pointing his hand, and when he turned to Mr Jamangan, he was disappeared, as a puck! Marvel! Oh, my God. Where did Mr Jamangan go to?

The owner of the carriage looked at the place that Archie referred to. He didn't see anyone there and said, "Listen, kid, I don't have time to waste with you, these games are exposed and old, although your facial features don't show that you're a con boy." Archie felt tight in his chest and disappointed so much that he felt like a bird flew happily for the first time in the sky until an arrow hit him and dropped him into a deep valley for no end.

Archie did not care for the man's speech and insult what he was most interested in finding Mr Jamangan searching with his eyes worried about Mr Jamangan several times, but unfortunately, he was not the kind of person who would like much to ask for something from one and himself to beg no one no matter what, until he decided to walk away from this man so that he would not hear more humiliating words than he heard.

Until he got a little away from where the carriages were gathering and then put his bag on the ground and sat on it and came back again to comfort himself with his misfortune on this miserable day, then he put his hand on his cheek until he felt like he was empty from inside and didn't know what work anymore.

This is the first time he finds himself in a strange place and people are unfriendly and a very tight time before the night comes. But one must always know that there is no lasting sadness and it seems that what happened is like an arrow of joy that broke through the barrier of grief that surrounded him enough time to break it!

"Are you looking for a carriage to take you to the kingdom?" Someone's voice was next to him! Archie raised his head a little.

That's when he saw a short black-haired girl in a tight dark dress from the top and wide from the bottom covering her feet, wearing a black hat with a turquoise thread attached from the back in a very complicated way until she looked like a jasmine rose in it, most beautiful look... He kept staring at her until she cleaved her lips at a wide, quiet smile with eyes waiting for an answer until she noticed the intensity of his focus in her beautiful hat. Then she looked up

from behind her eyebrows to keep it up in his lengthy looks in her hat until she leaned slightly forward and said in a whispered voice, "Did you like my hat?"

It seems that Archie was thinking really too far with that hat, but in fact he had the right to marvelling like this. She was the girl most like Charlotte with the different colour and shape of the hair and the length of the curtain, and even the hat as if she wore Charlotte's distinctive hat and had the same colour as turquoise tape as her! Archie has in his eyes, a question, a set of questions.

After he wiped on his face, "No, I'm sorry, but your beautiful hat reminded me of someone. It's like a Charlotte hat." She put her back to moderate.

"Um," then yelled for a bit and bite her lip, and she said, "Well that's nice, but you didn't answer me handsome boy, were you looking for a ride to the kingdom?"

Archie said, claiming stupidity, "Yes," but then he yelled for little bit, not knowing what he was saying and what he was talking about and how she knew that! And then he quickly replied after he realised that it might be his life saver before dark, "Yes, yes, but how did you know that I wanted to go to the kingdom and who are you?"

The girl said, "I watched you ask those idiots. And I knew you didn't have enough money to go there in addition to the rudeness of those guys with you. It was easy. I heard what they said and everything between you and them because I was by your side, but you didn't notice my presence. I'll make it short for you, handsome, because you seem tired and frustrated, and neither am I in a hurry, but look at that carriage." Pointing her finger at a place behind his back and then seeing a carriage that had never been seen before. It was the most beautiful shape and magnitude of those horse's carriages.

The fancy carriage dragged two of the horses so black they had thick hair in their feet. The hair of the head of that horse was of many beautiful black hair paddles and they were characterised by the harmonious shape of their bodies and the beauty of the shape of the head and they seemed of rare breeds.

And whoever owns this luxury carriages and this rare and these horses is not a normal person, until the boy preaches well and breathes joyfully again.

"Don't be too late. Take your bag and follow me." Then she turns her back on him and walk in front of him towards the carriage. He quickly rises behind her to make sure that what he actually sees is real or fantasy? He even watched her ride the carriage and told him loudly, "The chances are not successive and take all what comes to you and do not waste your opportunity with so many questions."

Now Archie made sure it was real, not fiction, and he ran up to the vehicle with his bag, even if he got to the carriage door and said, "But how much is the fare to go to the kingdom in this carriage? I think it's too expensive."

The girl laughed and put her hand on her mouth in shyly and said, "This time, leave it on me, I'll take care of it." And then she added, "Oh, I didn't ask you for your name?"

"Archie is my name, Archie, but does this carriage belong to you?"

She ignored his question and repeated his name in her lips. "Archie... Archie... Archie. Hmmm it's a really nice name and light on the tongue!" Archie was a little preoccupied with arranging the placement of his bag inside the carriage safe and while the girl's elbow had planted in her own and put her index finger on her chin as she looked at him admiration, then he notice that there were eyes watching and checking on him and then he slowly turned to not embarrass her and she quickly turned her face about him, he told her to express his great thanks:

"I can't express my gratitude and great thanks. You saved me from trouble. I don't know how I would have been."

She never answered him again and she said, "Go on, horses." After she put both hands on her knees, which were on top of each other like a queen on her throne. She stays silent, not saying a word since she ordered the horses to move and moved so abruptly that Archie did not notice the presence of a driver of the carriage, but he realised that he was relatively safe as long as he was with a girl of such kindness and generosity, despite being afraid that this girl was hiding behind her silence and that mysterious personality, and then he decided to exchange with her the same silence.

There was a long silence punctuated by the sounds of horse hooves as they made the distant way but which drew Archie's attention and added to the uncomfortable suspicion that he had not heard the sound of the wheels of the carriage or even felt any vibrations in the speeding cart as a flying carpet with imaginary wheels.

Chapter 9

THE STRANGERS

Archie put his head on the carriage window. The sky was cloudy waiting for any word from the generous girl, but it did not happen until he drops off into a deep sleep. And was helped by the quiet movement of the fast-paced carriage so that he thought of the comfort and tranquillity that he was still in his warm bed embracing his little puppy with love.

While he took up sleep that made him feel like shutting down all those windows that opened him the doors of fear and misunderstanding and lost hope for him in a moment to hear a sound that penetrated the glass of the carriage window on a revival but not any sound... It was an angelic voice that snatched his soul from the horizon and from behind those enormous black clouds that slowly faded to be replaced by a glowing polar twilight with the beauty of the glamorous spectrum that dazzles the viewers in the middle of the sky as if they were dancing poplar clothes that were decorated and wore the most beautiful so as to dazzle the attendees.

Until that most beautiful moment came in the unconscious sleep where he heard the voice calling out his name and a long tune.

"AAARCHIE, AAARRRCHII I'M HERE, HANDSOME BOY, WAITING FOR YOU..."

Then he saw that the fingers of a very white hand and it was a hand coming out through the twilight spectrum of the sloped dance, to fall on his cheek gently and it was a silk chop and not a creature's hand until it turned into dewdrops on his cheeks that made him feel cooler in his heart before he felt it on his cheek, he opened his eyes a little bit to see the windowsill and the thick raindrops racing from it against their direction and then closed his eyes from the pleasure of sleep to complete his sleep, embrace him and shrink himself more indulgently, but suddenly he opened his eyes again quickly and scared and lifted his head from the carriage to realise that h was dreaming and that the sky was still black.

He opened his eyes a little bit to see the windowsill and the thick raindrops racing from it against their direction and then closed his eyes from the pleasure of sleep to complete his sleep, embrace him and shrink himself more indulgently, but suddenly he opened his eyes again quickly and scared and lifted his head off the carpet to realise that he was dreaming and that the sky was still black with clouds.

The fingers that turned into drops on his cheeks were just a spray of rain that went in from the top of the window glass that didn't close it completely and the cart still accelerated to feel that he needed to spend his need after this long walk (he just wanted to pee).

He turns right to ask the girl to ask the basically non-existent carriage driver to stop and spend his need in the open, but once he turns on his right to see that there is no one else in the carriage! Archie rose rapidly and freaked out until his head violently hit the high ceiling and then he floored down the seats holding his head and howling from the pain and then a little silence after the pain eased until he burst into laughter and fell on the floor of the carriage and still in a fit of laughter, saying indignantly and sarcastically from himself, "What was happening to me, it seemed like I was going to be crazy."

Until Archie preached well and ensured that he would find a helpful reply from the driver about the girl must have come down in a place and then asked him to complete the to the kingdom, so he wanted to know at least anything about her to remember her.

That's how poor boy was thinking, but he didn't know what to hide for him. Otherwise, it would be preferable to sit in his village if he had the misfortune he would face.

He got out of the carriage after it stopped and accelerated the steps towards the front to talk to the driver, but he was surprised that no one was in the cart driver's seat! What is this? It's like jumping too fast to spend his needs too? No, I can't be delirious. I can't stand this nasty thing that plagues me on this day anymore, but I have to pee first to catch my breath and satisfy my stomach, which is like an alarm bell, and then I'll try to comprehend what's really going on with me in this weird carriage.

It was raining so heavily like a waterfall from the sky without introduction that Archie tried to hide well on the side of the road among the trees to urinate comfortably, and as soon as he shaded himself under the thick leaves. It was like an umbrella rain until he felt that he was born again after he relieved his need and felt a good feeling and the activity of a bear in him again. He leaned on one of the tree trunks to sigh deeply and gather his thoughts under the rain showers until he was surprised by the cart moving quickly and heard a man's voice saying "Come on, horses" followed by the sound of a whip He hits the air to scatter the heavy raindrops.

Here the boy went crazy, "No, no, this is unreasonable," he ran and screamed loudly, "Wait for me, wait for me, please, I will die here, if you leave me alone in this place," and release his feet into the wind to run at full speed, and to keep screaming loudly, but the sound of raindrops falling on the ground hid his voice from the ears of the driver, who thought that he might have been a demon until he fell to the ground and stuck his face in the thick mud. But he did not stop his miserable call, as he repeated desperately, clutching the ground with his hands, "Please stop, my bag is still inside and it's all I have. Please stop. Please don't leave me here," until he gets choke up.

His eyes still did not leave the carriage as it sped through the darkness of the pitch night until the carriage vanished in front of his eyes, which was covered with shards of mud flying in the air from behind the wheels of the carriage.

While the place was very dark and he could no longer see anything but the darkness of the night that had fallen on him in the middle of an unknown land, he tried to hide his sadness and shock, so he could no longer see anything in front of him except that he must search for a shelter quickly to take shelter in it before he got sick or was intercepted by a predator or a real ogre, so there is no trick for him. Now he has been thrown into a lonely road and a wilderness whose address he does not know.

It was a strange feeling for the first time he felt the feeling of true loneliness, and that this was only the beginning of his life of exile, which he must get used to the surprises of, and that the journey was not like what he imagined and expected, but was worse, and that the surprises seemed to have taken too long, for the boy did not even reach the kingdom until he put his face away while sitting under one of the tree trunks to protect himself from the rain and began to say to himself and comfort her, "Do not be sad, Archie. It seems that these are all precursors to your preparations for what will meet you in the kingdom of candidates' training, as my father said they will mash us up from the hardness and violence of the exercises."

Until he mocked himself and said, "It seems like a very happy start, Archie," he started thinking about what he should do. He left everything he had in that bag and he stayed with only eight pounds, which would not feed him from hunger or securities from fear until his heart filled with a hArchie sense of helplessness.

What can I do now that I am stranded in this darkness and at this time where I go, sitting on his ass, leaning on an old trunk covered in dense leaves, did not stop the rain from coming down on his head to wash him and wash his sorrows with it, embracing his knees with force to his chest to fold himself and shrink, looking for warmth until I enter his head between his knees also to live a moment of silent meditation that might help him to extricate his soul from his body to lose the sense of the cold for moments until he said in an audible voice, addressing himself, "It's not easy for me to live the sense of helplessness like this."

He raised his head a few minutes after putting it between his chest until he hinted at what appeared to be a dim light intermittently illuminated between the trees, but when he progressed towards it, he was away to make him walk more than a kilo in the black forest, which was no longer affected by the feeling of fear while walking inside it.

He raised his head a few minutes after putting it between his chest until he hinted at what appeared to be a dim light intermittently illuminated between the trees, but when he progressed towards it, he was away to make him walk more than a kilo in the black forest, which was no longer affected by the feeling of fear while walking inside it.

He continued to progress without any hesitation, and his eyes did not disperse that light, despite the sounds of the tree rustling that you felt that there were eyes lurking after every step you took in the sea of darkness, which had many lows and was not ready to walk, but it was not difficult for another in his ordeal to pass any obstacle to finding a place to see him except for a few spectacles and missteps.

Because of some stems like bumps or some pointed rock that cut his fingers when he was falling on them.

And when the place was set up from the lows and the medium heights, he saw the glimmer of light in front of him, and it was only an old lantern light hanging on the door of the old house in front of him and on its side a little bit back, there were wooden houses in what seemed like an old neighbourhood or ghost village that had been abandoned for some time.

It seems that the walls of the houses are destined to collapse at any moment due to the erosion of their wood, but the presence of a lantern hanging outside the house foretells the presence of a person here at the very least, until he felt trembling from the hair of his body, as if the place was teeming with hidden spirits, he did not hear that there are houses outside their village, except some of the neighbouring villages, then he kept walking forcibly until he reached the door where only a lamp was stuck until he heard the creaking of some doors from inside the house.

He carefully stuck his ear to the door to listen, but it really seems that the houses have not been opened for decades because of the large amount of dirt on those doors and windows, as if it were a place for a garbage dump and not a liveable area at all, and he said to himself, but all this does not matter, the important thing is that I find a place to protect me from this rain and cold. Until things calm down, then I will go back to sit in the middle of the road, maybe I will find some car on their way to the kingdom, or they will take me back to the village, anyway.

He tried to open the door of the house he reached, but it was locked, and the windows were tightly closed. He didn't try to knock on the door. He just knew that no one could live here unless they were real ghosts, and that the flame of the lantern must have been the work of a jinn, but suddenly before he sat down. Under the canopy of the door of the house to warm himself a little, he heard the sound of a woman's screaming until the hair of his body stopped from the intensity of fear, and his whole body trembled, and his heart jumped between his ribs from the severity of the panic that occurred in himself.

This actually made him jump standing like a locust jump. Until the screaming rose more and more, and it came from among the narrow roads in this deserted village, which consist of more than ten houses, a broken well, and the fence of a farm that seems, in fact, to be closer to a cemetery than a farm.

Until a woman appeared in front of him, and behind her was a man trying to hit her with a thick baton, and she was screaming loudly.

Then the woman slipped her foot on the muddy ground until the man grabbed her. It almost confirms that they were indeed ghosts and not humans. The man pulled out a long kitchen knife from behind his back and surprised the woman with several stab wounds until the woman's voice was muffled and her body stopped moving in front of Archie's eyes, who paralysed his tongue as he pointed with his hand without moving from his place. His place was as if he was completely helpless from the horror of the scene he saw.

He talks to himself, "Oh my God, what are you doing, please, stop," the man runs away and lets that woman drown in her blood, which is flooded, and it forms a red river of blood exploding in his way and to make things worse came out on those screams a handful of people.

They were four men dressed strange clothes in weird shaggy and ratty faces, and they looked like if they had come out of a cave after a long period of time. Somebody came up to the body with a lamp. After a preview, they assured him that the woman had lost her life. She was killed in earnest. Then he moved the lamp towards Archie. They all looked at Archie and the man said in doubt, "What did you do to her, strange boy!" Then another approached the murdered woman and shined the lantern on her until he saw her bloodied and shouted, "Oh, my God, how did you kill an innocent woman? You look like a thief or a rapist!"

Archie said defending himself, "No, sir, she was caught up by a man and we hit her with the knife. I saw him with my own eyes. I was looking for a place here to sleep underneath and I was on my way."

The man threw him sharp and cut him loud and told those around him, "This boy is the killer of this woman. He must take his penalty. Hold him immediately."

Then everyone raised their lanterns towards Archie, who felt so angry that he filled an unknown fear and then said in angry voice, "How dare you accuse me and I'm the only witness who saw the killer. I'm not a killer. I watched a man fight with the murderer, take a knife out of his pocket and stab her in front of me."

Then Archie went silent to think very well and said inside himself with a whisper, "Oh, my God, it seems that I am in real trouble this time and it is very catastrophic, what should I do? And these people seem determined to arrest me and I am innocent. They might will judge me in one of these houses, and it might be this crime was a setup between all of them to get rid of this poor woman for some reason, and I don't have any proof of my innocence."

At a crucial moment led by survival instinct, and prove beyond a shadow of a doubt with certainty then he releases his legs to the wind and flees from among these criminals and stranger people such as the deer fleeing from the lion's claws, seeing only the effect of the mud in their faces, which left him behind from the intensity of his speed, his jumps until someone blatantly said, "Release the

savage dogs to kill him, he runs away from us. Catch the killer alive or dead." Once he hears the sounds of the dogs behind him, he realises that surviving alive in this day will determine the fate of his life.

The men and their dogs set off behind him as a herd of hyenas who had not eaten food for a long time, but Archie was the fastest running and jumped. Running between trees and jumping was his favourite game with his brothers in their village.

So, he knew how to use tree trunks and branches to his advantage, where he relied on jumping between branches and logs of trees intertwined with so many stumps and surpassing them accurately, which gave him great progress on bloody dogs and also ensured that he did not stumble on clayey land until he reached the main street with his hand on his heart, for fear that he would stop from tiredness.

He saw nothing but complete darkness in front of him until he saw that the road was surrounded by the walls of the eternal prison in which he would be imprisoned inside it for the rest of his life when he was accused of killing that woman if he surrendered to fatigue.

Until an ear drum sounded the wheels of a carriage speeding from behind it and as soon as it turned around, it might seem like a fantasy. The rain, fear and fatigue had made him hallucinate, not until he saw the flash of a faint lamp penetrating the heavy rain fog then he decides sit down next to an empty tree trunk and snaked at himself to be caught by those men and their dogs, he didn't know if he'd catch up the carriage or that those men would catch him first! His exhausted body could not complete the run after optimism in the moment of loss, that the carriage must have been a rope of survival, and when it approached it was a real traveller's carriage dragged by six horses and not just a teenage fantasy that sees his dreams squandered by steps, to escape an unknown destiny.

So, he said and breathed out fatigue dust (Now, Archie, either jump on the back of the carriage, or throw in the fate of the humiliating doom)

The carriage had a little bit of speed. Luckily, Archie, the road had clay soil and a lot of rain, which forced the cart to calm down a little before speeding up after it went over the muddy road.

In the meantime, Archie had implemented his only plan to survive those demons and attached to the carriage from the back, and he ruled to sit on the pedal of the cart and hold his trembling hands on the handle of the rear carriage door.

Until he felt a severe headache that caused him to lose control of himself and almost fell to the ground until he raised his head by force and said, "No, no, no time for fatigue now." Then he watched the dogs and behind them the men had mediated looking at him with their eyes in which sparks were not extinguished by heavy rain as he moved away from them as quickly as he got away from his travel path.

Finally, he felt as if he was breathing as much life as he liked the fragrance and wind of the plains overlooking his small bedroom on a beautiful morning.

His miserable soul finally calmed down from the torment of fear and running into the unknown.

And then he turned his face on the stranger men and their ugly dogs until he noticed that one of his shoes had been cut off from the whole bottom and said to himself, "This is an opportunity to make fun of these idiots," and then he took off his grooves and raised his head to tell them of these shoes.

To remember, the Knight Archie passed through here. But he soon realised that they had suddenly faded from the front of his eyes, as if nobody was there! The terror of those people still lingers inside it until he thinks they've disappeared to get ahead of the car and stand in front of it!

So, he thought, what he saw in that village was that these stranger people would never look like natural human beings, but he said in himself to reassure and not burden, thinking:

If this wasn't going to happen, even if I believed my intuition, but they couldn't get to the front of the car so quickly, if they really had the power to do it, they would have preceded me and grabbed me before I ran away, and then he went nervous wondering and said, "But now I don't know where this cart is going, and I don't know if it's going to bring me closer to the kingdom or anywhere I can find who's helping me with this (then take a deep breath) at least better than meeting these demonic faces."

He was curious to see from inside the cart until he tried to keep looking out of the back window. But he saw nothing. It's made the rain and its coolness like a mirror where you saw your face. More than you can see from inside until he wipes his hand on the glass and sees a women's hat blocking half the window.

They seem to have the real luxury of the features of the hats and luxurious clothes, as well as the size of the cart and the number of horses that drag them until the girl's eye falls on his eye and quickly lowers his head, and he complains, "Shit, shit, she saw me!"

Chapter 10

LOVE FAIRY

Archie woke up from his nap in the back of the carriage on the sounds of the neighing horses, accompanied by the echo of the place.

He had entered his hands in the bracketed doorknobs in order not to fall asleep, the carriage had calmed down a little as if they had reached their destination after the rain had stopped and clouds had erupted and the stars had blasted the wild forest road as if it were angel lanterns to guide from the shadow of the road until the carriage had already stopped.

Archie said, confused, "Oh, my God, how long have I fallen asleep? I have to jump before somebody comes and see no wonder I will once again be unjustly accused of being a thief or a bandit."

The carriage is full of suitcases and it is not surprising that those in it are highly influential and have those who guard them inside, and then he came up with his idea and said, "I found it, yes, and indeed, it was a beautiful thought that would not make him leave the cart that saved him. At the same time, he would disappear from the eyes, like the puck, where he decided to hide down the cart until they decided to move."

What are the seconds until he heard the squeak of the car door opening from the inside and then the sound of a walk until he jumped out of his place, speeding down the car, and then he saw a number of legs coming down from the cart, and it seemed like a boy, a girl and a man expected and saw him until he heard the voice of the woman saying with great satisfaction, "Finally, our bones moved from sitting long. How long do we have until we reach the palace?"

The man who seems to be her husband says, "At about 6 o'clock in the morning, darling. We'll be home. We'll have to get to the junction that will lead to the monarchy and then take it north and complete it to the palace. Within two hours of that junction, we'll have arrived and rest from the disturbance of that city and the emergencies that don't end."

The woman said, "But it's enough that you don't feel bored at all."

To which the man replied to her, "It's enough that you're with me and you're not in the wretched village of Kling Ling."

Archie was shocked by their words and knew that one of the spouses belonged to their village or that he was a Kling Ling but who were they? He also understood that the cart would not go to the kingdom, it would take a completely different route through the kingdom when they arrived at a place called the junction of the kingdom, then Archie said, "Thank you so much, couple. You showed me the course of my journey. This is better than being away from the kingdom. I will go down there in the junction and wait until one of the travelling carriages has come to me, so I am on the right path to the kingdom."

Then he heard the woman say to the girl, "Elizabeth, where are you going?"

The girl says, "Nothing, Mom, I just want to take a tour around the carriage to move my legs, shoulders and back from sitting as much as you do." The girl wanted to make sure that what she saw was real or fictional without showing it to anyone so that no one would question her speech, and that was to be careful to safeguard the soul from the age of people. Then Archie noticed that the girl as if to carefully examine the back of the boat as an investigator in the land of the crime and this work is done only by an affectionate and highly sensitive human being.

Archie was claiming goddess so that the girl would not look down the carriage to reveal that it was impossible for him to fight four people while he was at the top of his weakness until the mother joked, "Well, come on, Elizabeth, come back now, before you're kidnapped. We won't find enough time after that to look for you."

Strangely, the girl whispered while standing like she was talking to Archie, "I opened one of the bags inside which contained sweet biscuits and honey cakes baked in the king's palace and then made sure to close the bag well. I made sure to buy what I wanted myself from the kinds of luxurious desserts." And then she called on her mom, okay, mom, and actually she rode the whole family, and then Archie moved back before the giant wheels ran him over and he went up in the back of the carriage to get ready to go with them, and he just became a passenger from the passengers even if he was an illegal passenger.

Archie remained busy with the idea of how he would know that he had arrived at this junction called the junction of the kingdom and he had not seen it in his life. He would also not know how he would see him if they passed by him and the time at night more than he was concerned with what the girl did with him! And will they stop at this junction? But I didn't see her facial features, but her voice still rings in my ears like a bell. What a truly generous and compassionate girl.

The suitcase installed behind the cart had already opened to less than half until he saw small boxes the size of the palm of the hand of cardboard with drawings that would make you think about eating the box before you saw the inside of the beauty of the cakes painted in a way that would make your saliva flow even if you had eaten a whole sheep and more exciting that its wrote on those cookies the name of Elizabeth, until he assured her love for these bakes.

But he took a box with more than ten pieces and he took his inside and threw the paper cocktails.

And he put all that in his pocket until the necklace he had kidnapped from the strange girl in his village, hanging from his neck then he said, "It looks like this necklace will be my gift to you, lady Elizabeth. I can't think of you other than this beautiful necklace who I don't know how much it is. She may one day bring me together, Since I don't know what's inside that beautiful witch with the necklace, but not all shine is gold." It might just be a thief or a house-trickle looking for a catch at the end of the night.

A few hours later, he opened his eyes to a feeling as bad as leaving the village. He even worsened and unexpected. He felt so bad in the cheek and the rest of his body that he opened his eyes and saw that he was lying on the road and that he was not on the carriage! What happened!

The carriage appeared to have crossed an uneven path, leading to the fall of Archie. He had not tied himself to a rope in anticipation of such a situation to associate himself with the carriage, or perhaps the satiety of sleep caused him to fall painfully, which is why he fell. It was time at dawn and the sun was still ashamed behind the clouds of the red morning.

Archie sat on the floor and started meditating on the place. And see where he is now from the junction of the kingdom? Is he still far away or is he over it? The darkness seemed to crack a little, and Archie preferred to rise to make sure that he did not suffer an adverse injury that could hinder his plan, but he seemed to have only a few scratches until he sat rubbing some bruises in his shoulder, face and ribs and stretched on his back to feel the coolness of the soil and the smell of clay mixing with water to collect the spirit of nature and its coolness as a natural medicine for his psychological and physical condition.

A few minutes later, he got up to explore the land he was sitting on.

When he stood and raised his head, he saw a wooden sign in the middle of a crossroads with more than one direction.

The kingdom has an arrow underneath it pointing towards the kingdom.

Another arrow wrote above it 'Long Bridge' and now knows that this family is from that patch of land that has never been heard of.

But he was very pleased that he feels he had fulfilled all his dreams when he realised that he was already still on the right track and that he had found the junction of the kingdom and that this would be reduced to a lot of thought and insight that had no place in Archie's mind after all. But what he noticed; he drew his attention to the fact that the place was completely different from the forest that was penetrated by the only street from which he had come.

Archie said in his own mind, "If I sit down waiting for someone to arrive and nobody comes, see how I'm going to spend my other night? Where am I going to sleep in these plains that seem to separate me from the nearest human congregation?

"I have to strive myself and myself to find what works for me behind me. These hills are so pervasive that no one in this life will benefit you if you don't benefit yourself. The place was full of small lakes and dark green hills like a looming black cloud where there was no sign of even a glimmer of hope that a creature would come to this place like a green desert. I'm the only creature to walk here," but that did not hinder him from walking and feeling that he was the only one in this world.

If quite the opposite was no evidence of anyone but the sun that began to shine on the flowers and greeted the place with the sounds of some little birds, then Archie went on walking alone, gazing all around like a rat lost in the fields after losing its lair until he said optimistically, "I escaped the darkness of the woods, criminals, and savage dogs. How could I not live in these vast, beautiful and shining fields in the warmth of the sun? It's only a matter of time, Archie. Happiness will come to you."

Then he said, "This is the only high hill to which it seems that the road to it is not wet, perhaps I will find fruitful plants behind it or something that has benefited from it." He ascends the hill until the road straightened when he reached its top and seemed a little smoothed downwards, then he descended with him down and there at the bottom of the hill, and after many thoughts swirled in his head, he found himself in front of a small hole as if it was for a fox or a wild boar.

It has a hole open that can enter a skinny person the size of Archie as if a carpenter had separated the entrance to the terrier on its size... The opening was like a crater on the side of the mountain, and then he took some small stones, and he lost throwing them violently inside the terrier, so he could be sure if one of the animals in the area could not open a door of battle with a predator who did not have a weapon to confront him, and he continued to stick his ear every time.

To make sure the terrier is completely free so as to ensure that the place is free and that it is temporarily a place where it is better than walking in the ground. Until he gets himself some food, something must fall out of his hand to eat other than some pieces of Elizabeth's biscuit or until the traveller's carriage he expects to arrive and may not come forever.

As is the habit of the weather, it quickly becomes cloudy black clouds, like

heavenly waves, foreshadowing of a storm of heavy rain, until Archie says, "May this help me too fast for a while until the Goddess has mercy on me and release my food from anywhere."

The earth of the terrier, which they were surprised was wide from the inside as if it were man-made and not an animal terrier, was blocked until I thought it was the home of the kingdom's first inhabitants before the great flood. Take out the whole pieces of biscuits and devour it all at once and then complete the rubbing of his feet with continued heavy rain to occupy himself from the length of the vacuum until the drowsiness takes him back and deflates around himself and presses into good sleep safely.

When he woke up, he found himself at the dawn of a new day, and he didn't expect to sleep that long until he repeated the same conversation with himself. He said that this biscuit must contain something. Like there's a secret in this biscuit.

He was pleased when he heard the sounds of movement outside the terrier, as if it were a good day's insignia, and when he came out, the smell of dust mould mixed with rainwater was in place until he stood on both ends of his toes to inhale that natural recovery, as if he were supplying new energy and vitality; until he saw a rabbit eating with his greedily and said happily, "I'm not going to die and this rabbit is next to me. But umm, hey, how am I going to cook it, and I don't even have a tinder box, and I don't even have a fire, listen, Archie, don't put the cart in front of the horses, always remember that, catch this rabbit first, and then you will find at least a lot of solutions that will ensure that you have food, even if it's a raw meat?"

During one moment, Archie jumped like a cheetah with all the swooping force on the rabbit, which jumped lightly. He fled quickly towards the other hill and ran behind him again until he threw himself with both hands to hold the rabbit, but grabbed the air after the rabbit jumped off the top of the hill in a wonder.

Until he found himself lying on the edge of the hill's abyss with his eyes looking down and witnessing what he wasn't expecting find in this place, even not in dreams, until he said surprised, "Could I believe what I saw?" Then he rubbed his eyes again and sat on his knees, focusing more on the bottom of the hill, saying, "Is this a dining table or I'm I dreaming? Oh, God, the smell is so strong, it's like I'm in my mother's kitchen. Yeah, it's a food table," and then he sneaks down the hill.

Even pinching himself once, twice and three, oh that's enough, but does this make sense? It was a two-metre food table full of life, joy and the joy of the hungry with various types and varieties of food that was put into the moulds of the rare mammoth ivory and scattered the most food outside the table of its abundance.

Archie nailed about the luxurious journey with all this food, and he said enthusiastically, "I knew that Goddess would release my share of food, they would never be satisfied if a good boy like me suffers and starves."

Until he paused, he said, "What if the food table of one of the kings who went out on a hunting trip? Because there is no logical explanation for the existence of this food table in such a place without any trace to humans?"

Then he approached with caution the table and reached out to the grilled chickens and the BBQ smoke escalated from it as if it had just come out of the oven until he cut it leg out until the suspicion was removed. Yes, it's a real chicken, and he start eat and he turned to reassuring him, and then he sat on the table, but he still looking around him for fear, like a hyena that stole leftovers of the lions and sat corroded with fear, especially when he saw the hot chicken until he released the monster inside him to devour everything eaten in front of him. He almost choked when he wanted to swallow a persimmon before completing the first bite that was still in his throat from the intensity of his greed and gluttony for food without completing his chewing for fear that the trip will fly away in front of him.

When he finished eating and tucked his stomach, he threw himself back to the ground, and he says, "Thank you for this blessing that I would have been dead from the starving and thirsty."

He began to contemplate the sky and those birds that play between the white clouds as they obscure the blue of the sky so that the view grows more beautiful and in which the hope resurrects and remembers his play with his brothers as he smiles with the intensity of satiety and the more wonderful feeling of survival from doom. It seems that I will soon fly with these birds saying it with immersive happiness. He closed his eyes and began to lay in the realm of fantasy until he got up quickly and wrapped his head to the right and north to check for the thousand times. And said to himself, "It seems that I have entered another world or that I have already reached wonderland and weirdness that we have only heard of, in stories!"

"This time I won't tire myself of walking or running again until someone finds me or I find someone. This food will make me not need to foraging for days. If this place becomes my home, now I have to take a tour to explore the back of the little hills. I may find a cave or a terrier where someone lives."

Archie went on like this for seven days when he came to the dining table in the morning and in the evening, he found different food until it was the morning of the seventh day and once the clouds cleared, the sunshine revealed a jungle behind the hill that was blocking Archie's vision. Thick snubber trees teeming with tapered pine trees and other bifurcated trees, many flourishes from various plants, penetrating a schedule of several shale grades that lands water from a spring that suddenly emerges as a greenish and flowering oasis in the middle of an endless desert.

In the meantime, the morning had come to an end and the place had glowed after the sun had mediated in the sky, as if it were a flashing flame that reflected its glamour on the ground, and the place had grown more joyful than after he had brought out his blessings to the little guest until Archie was surprised, "Hey, that looks like a jungle!" He realised now that he should expect everything to happen after all these strange things that happened with him like a strange food table that seem like it came down from heaven, and then he said, "Now I'm going to feel the excitement and I'm exploring that forest, it's a more interesting place to look for one of these plains like carpets."

He raised both sides of his trousers to the knee and decided to walk inside the small river until the forest mediated. He thought that walking inside the river, which seems to emerge from the inside, would be the easiest way to enter with all pleasure to the depths of that place and would avoid him losing time. And once he found himself in the middle of the place to find it dark and even intensifying all the more and somewhat cold, despite the brightness of the sun and the warmth of the place outside and completely devoid of sounds, only the sound of the creek and the sound of hitting his feet on the water of the river.

The place was full of long-leafed ferns till it stopped with attention and moved the tip of his nose with a sharp focus like the one on which had changed the smell of the place. It smells fragrant? Yeah, it smells like human fragrance! A fragrance here? And in this human-free place? It increases even more the attention of a confused feeling and mixed between tension or optimism and this is self-evident.

Man's enemy is always ignorant. Doubt is part of his instinct. Then he decided to stop. He didn't go deep and he came off the river.

He said, "Now I must call on this person to come out right away." Does anyone hear me? I'm Archie!" And then he raised his voice more and said, "I'm really sorry. I ate your food and I kept you very little. I was very hungry and I didn't catch myself, but I'm ready to make up for it."

At this moment, the fragrance grew even more like someone opened a box of it and sprayed it all over Archie's head; from the strength of the fragrance to the feeling of shortness of breath and started to cough extremely.

He felt his burning chills while still struggling and circling himself to dig himself out of the onslaught of that unknown until he attracted his attention.

The tree branches moved with force, as if the wind of a storm had suddenly blown, there was no wind, until his eyes had risen and he moderated and two steps back when he saw a spectrum of twilight coming down like a whirlwind of a tornado from the top of the trees, Archie says in awe, "What else is this?" The spectrum increases in glow and glow until the roof of the forest is filled with the fallen spectrum in the form of palm-sized light balls that resemble rare pearl beads blinded by the intensity of their shine and gleefully pearl as if a massive cosmic explosion had just occurred.

Then it started as if the spectrum had a body with no features that dragged behind it all that beauty and swirled around Archie from the top of the tree until it withheld trees from its eye and became only spectra of exquisite made in various heavenly and transparent colours that danced around it in all directions. Oh, the magnificence of what my eyes see? Until whispering in his ear a quiet voice resonates and says, "Archie, I've been waiting for you for a while!"

All his feelings stopped after he heard that female voice... What? Archie talks to himself without speaking!

So, he thinks the scent of that fragrance went right into his ear and his soul was restored until the place calmed down suddenly and all the movements were inhabited so that he could be sure that somebody was standing right behind him and then calmly turned back with a feeling of fearful tension and curiosity to see what happened until he turned all over his body and pulled back his shoulders to see a girl surrounded by an aura of cold bright light on his eyes.

Wearing a scattered white dress, the limbs fluttered like clear chiffon wings covering the inside with the same colour and long black hair that almost touched the ground. The feet were never touching the ground. The tail of the long dress tumbled on the floor and her hair, which barely stopped moving, like the sea waves that were not don't calm down except in rarely.

Archie realised that this is an important and crucial turning point in his life and he got everything as well as arranged for him without knowing it until he said with fondness and amazed, "Welcome to the spectrum of imagination visitor with a face akin to the morning that lights up the night of the lover, keep watching the beauty of her glamorous eyes with great blackness."

Unlike the eyes of many human beings, until he reached out. He wanted to feel her face until he quickly returned his hand! But she said boldly, "Don't fear something, touch me!"

It took him a while to understand what he heard. He remembered that voice— yeah, I've heard it before a few times.

"How did you know my name and what do you mean you were waiting for this moment? Who are you and what are you?"

She continued to stare at him with great admiration and said, "I am the fairy of love that brought you here, Archie."

His face stuttered before his tongue until the sweat poured off his nose, then Archie said nervously, "The fairy of love? Bring me here? What does it amount to?" Then he lowers his voice, saying, "In fact, I thought you was an angel from heaven, and I didn't hear that fairies were that beautiful, but on the contrary, I heard about you only fear and evil wherever you were."

The fairy laughed without opening her mouth and then the beauty babe interrupted him and said that she had put her finger on his cheek and pressed him until she dived her finger into his oval cheek, "I know there's a lot of questions going on in your mind and you'll find an answer to everything, but all I want you don't ask more and hear my word, I brought you here for a good reason, and I'll tell you everything in the middle of the night when the moon mediates in the sky after the hill you went up, you'll see a light there." Then lifted her finger off his cheek after leaving a red trace and completing, "Now go and complete the rest of the dining table that you ate, and don't forget to change clothes, and I brought you new clothes to get ready to meet."

When I turned next to him, there were three pieces of clothing in white pants, a sky shirt with a long sleeve and red pads.

He swiftly turned around and thanked her. At the same time the girl had disappeared from front of his eyes just like nothing was.

"Archie... Wait for you this evening. Where we agreed," the girl's voice resonated with one of the highest trees, reminding Archie of the first date.

The forest returns to where it was and is cheated by the cold darkness as it was until he sat on his ass flipping new clothes that he seemed to be washed with the same fragrance as the girl, saying with the same reassurance, "All that has happened to me is proof that I am fine and there is nothing to date that invites me to worry and fear. All those ominous introductions have taken place to bring me to the hoop of a life that I did not dream of and that all I am in now is good, although it is also strange."

Once Archie arrived at the place of terrier and food table, for whom he was preparing his homeland, his lands and his kingdom, he turned the clothes and inhaled their smell to make you embrace all their smells from the gravitational intensity of their powerful fragrance, and then said, "If I wear these clothes now, they will be overwhelmed by sweat smell and rain mould, but so far, I don't have to let my face get bad in front of she from the first date, and that's what I'm afraid of."

He stood next to a river on the other side of the hill, where he did not stop walking from a lot of thinking about what had happened to him until he sat on the bank of the river and put his feet in his flowing water with force because of the intensification of the wind and the volatility of the atmosphere that foreshadowed a storm on the horizon.

He takes a deep breath and contemplate the scenery on the sight of the running river and is attracted by the beauty of the sound of the purple water flowing by force into the river and imagines that it floats and dives into that river and enjoys the serenity of its tortured waters.

He said very enthusiastically, "Yeah, that's what I need now, a refreshing bathroom to remove me from the fatigue. I also will clean myself from the sweat smell that started to reel, and as long as I had a pad to dry myself. Otherwise, this fairy gave me these pads, but it seemed embarrassed to tell me that it was my nasty smell that it's guided on, hahahah."

Indeed, he took off his clothes happily and climbed to the edge of the hill as he ran and threw himself overjoyed in the river as happy as the bird was flying for the first time, seeming to dive against the stream of water to avoid the strong stream of water such as the salmon returning to its homeland and once jumping towards the run of water to run with it at great speed to forget about each walker and throw all those attached to it throughout that period. I have a great feeling that I have already arrived in the kingdom, and I have found all my faithful and even more so, I have found that unless anyone in all the world finds him in the most isolated places and floats on his back relaxing sitting in his eyes and repeating in a faint voice.

Thank you, God. I don't know. Thank you, all of you. Be right, Archie, and prove it. You will suffer a lot. If there is only one God, not many goddesses be with him, then he opens his eyes strangely and say, "That's the same voice that sometimes comes to me, but the first time he talks to me about God?"

He stopped swimming and got out of the river and was naked to wear his clothes, but... surprised that his clothes are gone? May I put it somewhere else? No, I put it here. Yeah, I put it here. He searches and circles himself insanely naked and finds no trace of his clothes... Who took my clothes? He felt so bad. God help me what I do now that I have nothing but these clothes, not even a small rag, to cover myself, then surprisingly he hears the sound of the laughter, the beautiful female voice tormented, and he tries to covering his body from front and back, and not knowing where the source of the sound came from until he called by the same laughing voice, "It's behind you, handsome Archie."

It's the voice of the fairy of love. "Are you here? Answer me?" He said angry and then he heard her laugh again, but the source of the sound had gone too far. "See you in the evening, Archie." He turns to see his clothes behind him and

is covered up in his own speed as he swirls around and he may see her, but it's too late. She sees everything, and then remembering his father's words as he tells him never to believe in anyone. How much I hate my father's speeches and tips that don't end, but here I am and I will live them from this moment until I die.

Blush his face like a virgin girl and feel embarrassed by himself. I have to pay attention to every step of the day. This fairy is watching me wherever I go.

The sky clouded and the sunny, steady atmosphere turned to what was like a grinding air battle in which the thunder roars and the sky shone a bright flash that might take away the sight if you looked at it and said, "Shouldn't the weather continue like this until night, I won't be able to the moon that will be our time guide?"

Archie went to take a short nap to prepare for that unique date. He never entrusted his life to go to his terrier, thinking about how his first date would be with a creature from another world. He never heard of Jenn dating a man, not even in the bedtime stories he was widening from his mother before bedtime when he was a single child of his parents.

While he was on his way to the terrier, the table found the same tables he had eaten as he had not eaten anything.

Before?

How did that happen? I ate it until satiety. It's a great charm. It seems that this pound is not a reckless pound looking for a lost lover in the wilderness who has only eight pounds in his pocket or just a teenage girl who fell into a passion of admiration, I have to rain her with a torrent of asking him everything to tell her every news so that I have to ask one of the world's gin worlds on a day to be aware of her.

So, a shadow on his eye and disappeared and as soon as he raised his head, he saw the piles of clouds that did not end their battles, and then he completed his direction.

The terrier till I feel what is like a piercing arrow coming down from the sky with a force that wants to hit the middle of its head even when he raised his head, surprised by the flying beast of a long beak that included his wings and became the head of the sharp javelin next to him after he sounded a loud, loud squeak, then Archie went crazy and fled the ground, so that he forgot to enter the hole of the terrier that was right in front of him until they mistook the raptor bird and hit his feet on the ground.

And he hit the ground with his wings by force, and Archie fled around the hill and he screamed where the terrier was where the terrier was, the bird was the monstrous raptor from the last undiminished dinosaur and apparently was combing the place in search of its prey. The bird flew upwards to explore the location of its fugitive prey. But the wind was manipulating it until Archie realised it.

Until Archie realised that he had become like the rabbit he was after, hours earlier and he turned to prey after he was the hunter and quickly, lightly he jumped the death jump to the hole of the terrier and hugged himself, shivering with fear. Archie did not get angry at the predator's behaviour because he remembered that a while ago, he was behaving the same normal way when he was persistently chasing the rabbit to eat it.

After a time, the boy was assured that the creature had left the place until he put his heads on his hands after overwhelming drowsiness amid the noise of the gusty wind squeak and the roar of the sky's thunder.

It was a quick time for poor Archie and he became like an outcast in nowhere and when he opened his eyes from that unwilling cold nap, he saw two little red dots staring near him, Archie jumped in fear and said, "I hope no other creature will surprise me again?" But fortunately, the strange guest was the same rabbit who had been chasing him before, standing in front of him biting a lettuce leaf in the darkness of the terrier, until he got up, he freaked out that he thinks was elsewhere.

The rabbit jumped and stood at the entrance to the high terrier looking at it like the apostle who came to remind him of the important and most important date of his life is approaching, when he came out, he found that time had become the night and the fine dining table had completely disappeared and no trace remained even of leftovers. Everything had calmed down in the place where it had been so unjust black clouds were still clogging the sky, which was nothing less dark than the land underneath and felt nothing but the cruelty of the land on which he walked.

And when Archie crossed the hill, he beholds a faint light that tends to be red, like the light you see from behind the window, and once it comes so close, he finds a luminous dislike of red, which tends to be white, so that he knows that work of the fairy, and no one else.

This is the place that the fairy assigned me to.

Archie makes a hypothetical speech with the fairy and says apologetically, "Well I know you're here and I also know that I'm late for the date, but I think you know why I'm late if I actually was late!" Until she actually answered him behind him.

He turned around with longing on his face and she came in a simplistic way this time from no spectrum and no dazzling introductions. He said to her, "What is the most beautiful face?" And then he shut up, and he said, "But where are all these spectacles I saw the first time?"

She gives him the answer by her charming eyes, "I would not have wanted to distract your mind any more so that everything that happened to you is enough and I was keen to meet you and you're in better shape and be in a view that makes you accept me and that the different worlds we came from are not a barrier between us to make it easier for you to accept my talk with you."

Suddenly, Archie heard the sound of angry dogs from behind him, and when he turned in terror, the dogs of that terrifying village were there and behind them are those men who were chasing him for the murder of that poor woman until he jumped out of his place in panic and when he turned to Maya, that masked girl who kidnapped her necklace in their village. He fell on his back from fear and started crawling back and then collided with one of them and when he turned it was that unknown girl who took him with her in that luxury car and then disappeared and she says to him happily, "How sad I was that I could not talk to you on that beautiful trip, but I care that you have arrived!"

Then he jumped out of his place again while he was spinning in his place from fear and said anxiously and hysterically, "What is happening?" Until he heard laughter from behind him, and when he turned, he only saw Maya, the love fairy.

She said with a smile, "All these characters were a figment of the imagination just to bring you here and to see how strong and enduring you are. In fact, I liked you and you were as trustworthy as I expected you, Archie! And now I want to introduce you to myself, Archie, I am the daughter of great King Barhout, King of the Seven Kingdoms who has ruled the lower worlds for the last thousand years if not more. Don't ask me about this, because he's going to need special, long sessions to explain their details, and that's not important."

She grabbed the tip of his hand and attracted it to her while he was in his place. She then walked with her fingers holding the tip of his fingers and circling around him.

Her eyes were glued to his eyes and her lips did not disperse that mind-numbing smile then she told him to sit down now.

After she made the luminous ball between them and they sat around it and Maya said, "I know that some words may be difficult for you to understand, but I will answer you for everything you want to know."

Archie said cheerfully, "This is the most important thing that will make me reassured, but honestly, I am not afraid of you being with me, now that all I have done with me, but let my heart some kind of relief."

Fairy Maya laughed, "Don't be afraid, Archie. We don't eat humans. We don't eat creatures like you."

Archie interrupted her, "Didn't say that."

But she interrupted him and said, "Also going to answer you, Archie, for everything you want to know, but don't interrupt me."

Archie said with a smile, "Well, you won, Maya, King Barhout's daughter."

Maya begins by recounting her story and life in her hidden world about human eyes and the rest of the creatures.

Then, after she told him some of her autobiography, it was like listening to children's stories at least for Archie. Because it was like stories about a world that existed only in fiction and anecdotes.

And then she started talking about why they were here, and she said, "When humans fall asleep, your souls go up and fall asleep in the top seven skies, where no one realises them, and some of them continue to play in the skies until they are back in your bodies. While you were asleep one day, I met your soul, and it was sitting alone away from others in the first sky, which caused me to be curious. Until I saw you one day reaching out to the sky to eat something—then a branch of an apple tree dangles in your hand, and there is only one apple in it until it reaches the palm of your hand, as if you were complementing it and suddenly two huge black lions came out from the midst of the darkness of the sky, wanted to attack you, and when you wanted to run from them, until you lost control yourself and I saw you fall into a scary and big vortex of water and mysterious, you called my name to help you, and when I wanted to do, you was gone inside it.

"Until I saw you in the village and so I kept watching you, until I couldn't see anything that pleased me in my life like seeing your beautiful face and hearing your name. I've changed all my life since I met your soul. I can't find my comfort anymore until I get out of my world to watch you until I decided to make what I made when I learned about your travel so that it would be a good opportunity to meet you alone in a place free of any creature but us two. You can't feel what I feel right now, and you're in front of me, not just the spirit I see, and I can't touch it."

As Maya elaborated on the talk, exposing her love and passion for Archie, Archie was laid off so much in a moment of deep silence that he was surprised and wondering, really, what does this pound say? If she is not lying, I'm like the one who signed a great treasure.

It's a magical ring. I can control a lot of things, so long as it's about me.

Maya says with a whisper, "You seem to be running a lot in your imagination?"

Archie answers, "Oh, no. I listened well to you, Maya. But in fact, I am still surprised! If you're actually watching me all that time and you're like what you said, you're happy to see me why you've never come to me before and tell me! What prevented you?"

Her facial features changed for the first time since he met her and inflamed feelings wilted off her face as a rose, and she dropped her head, "Because I didn't want to risk my life so easy?"

Then she was silent for a while, Archie asks her, "Ha! Risk your life! What do you mean?"

"Well Archie, unless you know it about our world, it allows a girl to love only once, and if she loses that love, she lives in isolation forever until she dies."

"Ooh, wow." Archie showed his mockery of her sad world in a joking way. "What a cruel world is your world?"

She didn't answer him and she didn't blink her eyes with one blink of his word until he felt it was serious and he felt as if he had hurt her feelings without intending to and swallowed one's saliva to arrange other, more judgmental words.

Then Archie expressed his opinion with logic and said, "I apologise for this, but does it not seem to embody the role of cruelty in its hArchieest sense, Maya? What is the wisdom of forcing a person to have a romantic relationship for once in his life, or else he must live the rest of his life alone?"

Maya looked at him with admiration, then laughed from her heart and said, "This is what I love about you, Archie, that you are different from others and you know who you are."

Then he cunningly said to her, "Then I am the one with whom you intend to live all your life, is not it?"

She said, "Ha! No, not necessarily, I may have a relationship with someone else, but we'll be friends."

Archie said sharply, "But this is considered treason, and if you do this to me, I will consider it treason, and I will never accept this matter. Either you are my only friend, wife, lover, and everything, or you go on your way."

Maya burst out laughing until she revealed the beauty of her teeth as if it were a pearl necklace paved, She said, "You passed your first test, and this is what I told you before. What I like about you is that you are a firm person who knows who he is and what he wants."

Archie felt that he had done the role and then said with a yellow smile, "I was joking, don't take me seriously, I like to joke a lot."

Maya said, "It does not matter what is important that you do not show what others want, but show them what you want to offer them and not what they want to see in you, and this is an advantage that only one of great luck has, and you are one of those who have been given this great luck and you have given it, Archie."

Archie felt the time was right to get her biggest sleeve out. Her mood seemed to change at any moment for reasons not known. He barely knew anything about her personality until he decided to crawl a little bit on his ass towards her until his thigh sticked.

He felt like electricity that hit him and shouted shit. She said this is a natural warning that we are from two totally different worlds but to you I will do what you want to do, and then she did the same thing and glued her thigh to his thigh without something happening and she said, "That's what makes our heels higher than you humans," and before she completes her speech, he surprisingly puts his nose on the tip of her pointy nose after grabbing her by the chin.

She blushed and glowed her cheeks by freeing that soul that was being watched all that time and that was now embodied before her in a physical body in front of her eyes, his head goes back a little bit and they are only a few centimetres apart, and he said with my beau's eyes, "I have now made sure you are real! Now you've found me, Maya, and here I am. What do you think you did to me?"

A good question from Archie must tell the other what he wants when it comes to this importance of sudden attention!

She puts her two hands above his ears to penetrate the fingers of her long head hair falling over his neck, which was covered on his ears and placed behind his ears. She said with fond eyes, "If I had the love of all creatures, I would have made you drink from that love.

"Most importantly, what I have left of my life is all with you, and I just wanted to find you to tell you this, to live with you these moments for the rest of my life and to steal you from your people, but because there is an important thing that you must learn, you have created a great thing, and the news of heaven says this is a prophecy that everyone is looking for.

"But before everything you need to know from this moment that you are not the Kling Ling village boy who sits with that orphan girl and idiot short, and then bites on her lips and bare her teeth like a wolf who tries to protect her young puppies, and then complements with an angry tone as if she's talking about the evilest people on Earth, which has nothing but to hang out and collect damaged cherry beans."

That action prompted Archie to laugh high until he fell on his back holding his stomach so as not to get out of Maya's cynicism. When she describes Charlotte, and means her with all irrespective of her pretty face!

After Archie stops laughing, he realised that she knew the details of his life thoroughly and that he could not lie to her, and that the time was not right to go into details that might be disturbed by this anticipated date and this historic moment of his life and that no matter how important he tried to explain Charlotte's existence in his life.

Because the walls of jealousy were too high for any sound to cross.

So, he decided to get out of this uncomfortable conversation for both sides and he said, "Let me know, Maya! What does the news of heaven say, I've never heard anything about this, and the answer is indifferent for the first time since they met and said, You must know for yourself! But all I know is that my departure from the village was meant to go to the kingdom in order to attend the Royal Guard course. This is the dream of every boy to be one of the knights of the kingdom and I am not less than them, but I found myself with you. I don't know what to do here and, in this place,; and I didn't understand much of what you were hinting at, but I know that nothing will come to me from you, Maya, everything that makes me happy."

Maya said, "Do not worry, I will take you to the kingdom myself, and this is my responsibility, but before you reach the kingdom, I will take you to places you never imagined and you will never imagine to see in your life.

"To realise that the universe is bigger than just the village you live in or the kingdom you are going to, this will help you a lot in your next life in the kingdom so that no one makes fun of you and be your mind. Being aware of your surroundings and this will help you make decisions with a purpose far higher and more important than being a human being trapped in your own little shell and believing the world is conspiring to pull out your shell and you are actually just an abomination to the world.

"But you will be used to reach what is greater than your shell. I hope that the idea has reached you." And then she got up and said, "Give me your hand."

Archie gives her his hand like he wanted to before, she said, "And now close your eyes and don't open them until I ask you."

"Um, okay, but why?"

"I told you before that do not ask too much."

And in a moment of silence and tranquillity he had never felt before, he

thinks, like someone had deafened his ears. "Open your eyes and don't look down and remember that as long as you hold my hand, there's no fear for you." Archie felt like a pupil taking orders from his affectionate teacher, who could

not disobey her until he opened his eyes in a little half, feeling that he was not in his normal situation, and I was against the laws of nature, getting him after feeling that his stomach had reached the throat, and seeing only Maya with her hair flying everywhere, and some hugging her neck behind her darkness.

As a black painting inscribed in which the stars twinkle, like it's a saddle hanging in the roof of a heavenly house punctuated by star lights.

"Open your eyes, don't be afraid. You said that if you were with me, you'd never be afraid."

Until he felt brave and opened his eyes once again, looking with grieving eyes, he looked around with anxiety and shivered with his hair flying forward and bowed with his head down to see that he had risen too far from the ground as the bird rose in the sky, and the hills and those lands from above became like pieces cut from large carpets and he was swimming in the air and no one caught him from the fall.

Only Maya's slender fingers.

A strange feeling came over him with fear, and the hair of his head stood like the one who saw death in front of him, and he could not look down, his features gloomy.

After his suffering, he said, "Damn, you are really a witch and also malicious. Put me down, if you please." His first concern was not to fall to the ground, and for his feet to touch the ground as soon as possible before he fell, as if he was about to vomit until Maya let out a sarcastic laugh and said, "Give me your other hand." He quickly extended his hand to her waist. Instead of her hand, he pulled her to him tightly and stuck together after feeling that his body had stiffened until he began to inhale the air again after he hugged her tightly.

Maya tried to minimise his logical fear to adapt to the new situation and said, "Look in my eyes, Archie, and listen to my words. If you keep watching the ground beneath you, the fear will persist, and this will lead to your immediate downfall."

Archie remembers when he was sitting with Charlotte at the waterfall and telling her that he could challenge her to fly like an eagle that swooped down on fish at the bottom of the lake.

Then he tells her later with sarcasm while they are in the lake that she is a big fish that he cannot fly out of the lake in order to make her forget the challenge.

Meanwhile, he shrugs his shoulders, gathered his courage, raised his hand from her waist and grabbed her other hand, trying to show as much courage as possible until he unleashed the hobby of dancing inside him and said, "Let's dance now."

Suddenly and without introduction, he overcame all the obstacles of shock and fear after he asserted that there is no obstacle to the fulfilment of wishes except fear of the unknown.

And he danced it like a famous dancer on the world's most famous theatres, dragging her to him and running her again with strong enthusiasm to empty himself completely of despair, amid the fascination and happiness of Maya and her feeling that she had actually found what she was looking for, but it was more beautiful than she wished.

And she said with great happiness, "Ah! What a strange madness, how I loved this dance with you, Archie, go on, Archie, and don't stop. I didn't know that you are a good dancer and how much I was happy that you danced with all courage," and the two of them felt that they were living in a paradise that was only created for them.

Chapter 11

THE HORSE BARBORA

The two new lovers continued to dance long and did not feel the time until the morning sunshine began to emerge to penetrate the scattered clouds of heaven announcing the beginning of the first night of love between a rural boy and a princess from the world of jinn.

They sprinted further between the clouds mountains until they reached a land that no one had ever set foot before. As if it were an island in the middle of the Earth surrounded by a great river with very white water, as if it were a patch dipped in the mixture of spectrum colours filled with flowers, roses and streams mediated by rocks with white heads, such as scattered pearls.

As the most beautiful jewellery necklaces that decorate the most beautiful women, Archie says dazzling, "For God's mercy, what is this beauty? Maya, are we still on Earth or on another planet?"

Maya says, "I'm going to show you what's more beautiful than this. Let's go down first to see what doesn't happen to your mind or human mind."

While Archie was enjoying his eyes and himself the beauty of those pieces of paradise until the place buzzed with unexpected noise. A large herd of highly white horses, like snow whites, middle of their heads with a long ivory horn running towards them as if they were a luxurious reception delegation.

Until they stopped in front of them by a distance not far away, and one of them was blessed neighing with a sharp tilt raising his front feet with pleasure, and he was the largest of them, he approached as he looks like an arrogant horse that he said, "Welcome, Princess Maya, we haven't seen you for a long time. It's a surprise visit." Then he threw to Archie with suspicion, "It seems like a guest doesn't seem to be from your world."

From his throat, Archie almost gasped and took his soul out of his throat.

Who was so surprised that what his eyes saw and heard his ears? He continued his shock until he presented a little bit to the horse and sat silently meditating on it until he saw his face in the eyes of the horse, which looked like a black mirror, hiding a strange event behind her.

Then he said silently, "Horse talk like us?" This is a wonderful thing! Maya went to calm down from Archie's shock and said, "I told you would see something wonderful.

"Yes, Barbora, we haven't seen each other for a long time, but here we are again, and here you have grown a lot from the last time I saw you," and then she remembered that with her Archie and she remembered him with a yellow smile, "Oh, I forgot to introduce you to our new friend. This is Archie a nice Kling Ling boy. I don't think you've ever met a human before. I think Archie would be a good example of ease of relationship with humans!"

Then she turned to Archie and said, "I introduce you to my friend, Didifer, the master of this island. You will not find a non-human friend more honest and braver in heart."

The horse, Barbora, was young and had a great streak of pride, as no one in his kingdom was accustomed to competing with him, and it seemed that he felt a kind of jealousy when he smelled the scent of Maya's perfume on Archie's clothes. Jealousy and arrogance, if they came together in a creature, was bad for him and those around him.

Barbora stared at him with a very faint look, then continued examining him and sniffing his body until the effects of that disgusted a sprinkle of his hot breath coming out of his nostrils like the smoke of an old pipe, which causes suffocation for everyone who inhales it, but Archie controls himself as he stares at Maya that what should I do? He knew that he was an animal and this was one of their instincts, hoping that the matter would end there, after the horse finished sniffing Archie and continued to circle around it to examine it well as if it were a heap of barley.

Until he came back again to sniff at Archie's face and lowered his wide nostrils from his face and began to exhale forcefully at Archie's face, but this time he meant this to a meanness in himself, led by jealousy that ignites inside him like sparks in a provocative attempt to show in front of Maya that he is the strongest and most trustworthy friend, but Archie understands the intent quickly.

And he wanted to bridle this arrogant from the first time before he got used to it and decided to put an end to him after he put a cunning plan in his imagination and said to him, "Well, it is true that you speak like humans, but it seems that the animal, no matter how much he spoke, he will remain an animal because he believes that everything that is bigger than his body was the strongest."

It seems our friend Archie and the horse Barbora didn't get along with each other from the first time, The horse moved his jaws opposite each other in grumble and said, "It is also true that man remains the weakest, no matter how he thinks and thinks that he is intelligent, he has nothing but a lean body and barely two hands and two feet that help him to receive help from other creatures, otherwise he will die of starvation."

Maya realised that there was a battle going on between the two and that she had to intervene to curb the escalation of violence, but she was aware that she had the ability to control Archie through her ability to pull him back through her supernatural abilities, but she decided not to rush.

Archie said sharply, "Well, get away from me and go back to the herd. It seems that they are waiting for you to bring them some alfalfa, and not a sniff of the smell of his shoes is cleaner than your whole life, this will remind them that there are those who will ride them whether they like it or not unless you want me to ride you first to be an example for them. Is this your business?"

The horse said angrily, "I knew what you were from beginning, you deceptively trivial guest." Then raised its head high above Archie to show its superiority. Archie no longer sees only those long neck and her shadow from below him.

Then the horse violently completed, "It looks like I'm going to teach you literature, now that no one has taught you that."

Maya decided to intervene now before the situation exploded and tried to use her energy to pull Archie back, but she can't? She tried her magic several times without success until she thought that she saw around Archie a circle of light in the form of a halo surrounding him, but she was unable to break it in a strange and surprising way or even penetrate it... Maya realised that something was happening to Archie.

She did not understand what?

Archie was not afraid of the Barbora violence and his muscles, but stood firm and courageous and showed his fangs of dignity and said in a strong voice before the horse continued his words, "It is I, who will make everyone around you laugh at you, you talking animal."

The courage of the boy was like an arrow in the dignity of a horse, who felt his stomach shrink in fear, but he did not show it, but he showed the opposite, as he was not accustomed of anyone to standing in his way one day.

Barbora said with false courage, "Okay little boy. Try if you can and I'll make my foot hoof pierces your belly before you catch your breath! And then he made a naive laugh out of his prestige."

But Archie dominated his anger and exploited the naivety of the horse, his overconfidence, and smartly said, "But with my hooves, I will ride you against your will, in front of your people, O wise one."

The horse's face was colouring and asking himself with his hooves? How to have a hoof! Until he came down his head to see Archie's alleged hooves... But it was actually a smart, unexpected Archie trap.

The boy shrewdly succeeded in luring the cocky horse to the ambush and when the horse dropped his head to check Archie's hooves he grabbed the horse's neck hair, attached to it and jumped on his back as a hungry lion when he swooped on the neck of a huge and raging bull, Archie said sarcastically, "Now try to take me down if you can?"

The horse Barbora didn't expect this dare and this cunning trick from this skinny boy, for whom he was just a weaker creature than he expected, until the horse went crazy and was so loud as to confuse the rest of the herd as if someone was cut his neck.

In fact, it was easier to slit his neck than to ride his dignity in this humiliating way. He ran and jumped with all his strength and blood boiling with anger and indignation until his eyes were reddened as he uttered the ugliness of the word against Archie, "Now you will fall, son of a dirty human, now you will fall and I will smash you under my hooves."

He was biting his teeth violently and blindly before him, closing his mind and becoming thoughtless and thinking only with revenge and dropping the boy to kill him with all his ferocity.

The rampaging horse then went to the horse herd to pass itself in them but fled as Zebra fled the predators, until he stopped with his force to drop Archie off his back, then stood on his feet, then flew and kicked in the air violently, but the boy glued himself well, as the saddle glued to the back with strong hands resembling steel pliers despite his weak body.

Barbora shouted, "Damn it, you bastard human scum. I will teach you a lesson you will never forget."

Suddenly two horses decided not to stand by as they watched their leader come under attack by a human boy in their home estate until they set off, made Barbora in their middle, and tried to snap and bite Archie with their teeth, but that unfair intervention provoked Maya's anger and she rolled her eyes and took out the real genie inside her until she pointed with her hands at the low stallions and they quickly fell on their faces.

Maya said with resentment, "How you dare to attack Archie in my presence!"

The rest of the herd, which was about 50 horses, decided for a moment to remain neutral. Archie was a revolt in the middle of the silence they were accustomed to, and they did not dare anyone to reply to himself any insult that their younger leader, the son of the master of this place that left him after him, and Archie had cooled their boils, even for one day, as they did not see him being subjected to this humiliation.

The epic lasts between Archie and Barbora for more than an hour. The horse exhausted all its energy and anger. He did not come up with any result that preserved his face in front of Archie's hands, who threw his body over the giant horse's neck and clung to it like a wolf spider and grabbed the largest number from strands of Barbora hairs.

He gathers them in both hands and jumps next to his head in order to twist his neck down and succeeds in that until the Barbora falls to the ground to shake the ground underneath and shakes his prestige in the eyes of the herd, which will change the scene in this place forever.

That scene provoked Maya's great joy until she helps herself to show no one that she was leaning into Archie and losing her relationship with her old friend and very helpful to her. The herd was so confused that whispers seemed to rise inside the herd someone said, "Oh, my God, how did he beat our leader from this lean creature!"

That's unbelievable! Barbora seems to have taken a lesson he should have taken a long time ago. One of them is wondering, "Is our leader dead?"

One of them says, "This boy seems to be one of the sons of the jinn. He came with that fairy that always came here. This was a question that the herd asked each other to find an answer to what happened and what they saw in front of their eyes."

When Archie stood at the head of the defeated Barbora horse and said the pride of the victor, "Now you know me, horse, you will step into your heads again when you see me in front of you to know that if I fought you with the same your mind and logic, you would beat me, but I fought you with your stupidity and ego and made it a spear inside you, and it was a reason to fall to see the creation of your pride among the members of your clique, I'm afraid they won't accept you as their leader anymore, Maya felt a great embarrassment after her guest boyfriend did to her host friend, Archie wouldn't have done that, of course, because it's immoral to attack someone who hosted you at his house, but what Archie did would have done to everyone with dignity.

"Until she rushes to reassure Barbora and tell him to comfort, "To you, losing is not the end of the life, you are the leader of this land and the son of her master. Let's get up and make no one make fun of you and what happened is nothing but an even homer sometimes nods. Look at it as a lesson, not losing it, to win your other battles, or you will never succeed in your life.

"And I don't hide from you how much I was saddened by the misunderstanding that happened between you and Archie that I was so embarrassed."

The broken horse threw her into a melting eye.

No, Maya, you had no guilt that I deserved what happened to me. I got what I deserved when I misjudged and disparaged others. I deserved everything that happened to me. I must accept it and admit my humiliating defeat to overcome it. Otherwise, I will be unjust and I don't know which way I will meet others.

Archie said wisely, "Let him express his intercourse. The regret is one of the reasons for righteousness and not going back to guilt and recognition is the true advancement of every liver. I have mistaken my life so many times that I would not have prevailed over you without learning from my past mistakes and knowing my abilities and what I have. You did not create and stand out from others to defeat and cry over the spilled milk from the first test."

These words had a great impact on the resolve of the horse, who looked at Archie this time with respect and even grew in his eye after he mined him for no reason, so that he reduced the herd order this time in a very bold step to break the fear of other words and what others would think about you.

Archie went to the confused herd until whispers and whispers increased among them and somebody says with dismay, "The son of jinn is coming to us, my God, what will he do!" And another said with confusion, "He seems to want us all to struggle like our leader's defeating," until Archie gets to them, he tells them alone, "Listen, Barbora didn't lose one fight, and that's what's in our lives. But this was a test of your loyalty. Will you hold out and maintain your loyalty to your leader, or will you leave your leader at the first battle? If your leader goes, your wind will go, and your whole will be torn apart."

He remembered his father's words.

When he told him to remember, "That you must come out of your interior of the good to soak up the evil you face." His father raised him to love good and not hate others no matter what happens to them. Every creature has mistaken and lapses. This is a sense of creation. Do not try to make all others like you just try to advise and go quietly.

Archie felt that the wind attracted his clothes as they blown peacefully so that he thought it was Maya until he saw her standing three metres away with lips distributing the kinds of sexy smiles to the place and said to her, "Don't you think we're too late to arrive in the kingdom, I'm afraid it might be a reason for someone to worry about me!" Maya said, "I don't know what makes you rush to go there and leave me alone unless one of girls is waiting for you!" And then throwing him at her usual sarcasm, full of jealous smile.

Archie approached her and grabbed one of her hands with his two hands and his eyes swirled in her eyes and then joined her hand to his heart and said, "I am not the one who leaves love. And I'm not the one who leaves who left the world for him... Who says I'll leave you? If a princess is waiting for me there, I don't think after I know you, any girl, if she's his princess, will turn my attention," and then Maya quickly says, embarrassingly, before he finishes his speech, "Even if it's Charlotte!"

Archie one's breath and smiled yellow and looked at the side because he knew that the discussion with Maya about Charlotte was the unwanted and useless opening of the door of the junk.

And then he said cleverly, "Things I would have to do in the kingdom and he forced it to come closer and put the tip of his nose on the tip of her nose as the first time, but she put the question back, but more seriously."

Even if it's Charlotte?

Archie said in his own awkward I wish I had the strength and answer you, and I wish I could find a way out of this jealousy that stuck to me, until the Barbora issued a "Purr" that broke their dialogue, which was to become a knot that might not leave you later, "Ooh, what a touching view I seem to be in front of two lovers who fit each other. You didn't tell me what a sweetheart you would have been well received instead of what happened, dear!"

She blushed and said a professional way to escape this embarrassment.

"It looks like we're already late. Let's go now, Archie."

The horse joked, "Before you go, can I accompany them to be your third on your entertaining trip or will you ask me only for your secret tasks like the last one of the kingdom to Isabella the writer, Archie surprised what? Isabella and the kingdom?"

This name is no stranger. Is she a daughter? Maya interrupted him with a diving voice and responded quickly for fear that she would be exposed, she said with confusion, "of course, no, but I promise you will be the focus of our next adventures. It seems that Barbora wanted to embarrass her to draw the eyes of Archie that he has many secrets about Maya to hide from him and if you want to get your mistress's secrets, I'm your key."

Suddenly, a great black horse with two wings flies in the sky, it seems that the news of the Battle of Barbora and Archie and what happened to him has reached him. Till Barbora was deeply confused and shouted in a rumbling voice and sporadic breath, "Oh, heaven it's "Cantosa," my father!"

Chapter 12

OGRE TWO-HEADED

Maya Archie takes his hand and flies after they witness the" Cantosa" master of the real place and Maya assumes that his presence may return them to the starting point and may cause Archie to be later than his current delay, but Archie has a vertigo in his head due to overlapping questions in his head every time.

He can hardly understand until opens the door to a new mystery, trying to solve that knots in his head before it grows up and becomes an obsession that may turn into an illness about to turn his life and wishes upside down.

Even put his other hand on his head to collect the spread of headache.

She unaware of his condition, she said, "Since no one cares more about you than I do, don't worry too much, I promise that no one will be waiting for you, I know the way of life in the kingdom more than you, even though I didn't live in it."

So, she felt his hand shaking, you really feel cold darling!

Archie said in a muffled voice, "Thank you for asking me because I feel like I'm turning into a snowman soon."

Maya looked at him and pointed her index finger with a circular motion until a quick flash of light flashed around Archie and suddenly, he wore a thick robe like a very red monarch coat with white fur on its limbs and a neck that resembled the hairs of a thick polar fox tail, which was characterised by superior softness.

Because of that he thinks he enjoys drinking delicious milk in front of their warm house fireplace.

Archie was like he was bigger under the layers of that luxury robe and said hilariously, "I'm witnessing you to a witch lady, a pretty fairy."

In an unexpected moment, he put his other hand on her cheek and turned it towards her and kissed her in the lips so hard to thank her for what she had done with him, without feeling it until the Maya froze in her place and became like a cherry in her red from the intensity of her shyness and said with his passion, "How much I love you, the magician Maya."

After spending the day playing between streams and flowering fields using their magic and wonder abilities to visualise things in front of Archie for his reality as the fabrication of species of small animals such as rabbits and squirrels to play with them and run behind them.

Until she said to Archie, "Now it's the evening and it's time to deliver up that I have, which is to get you to your desires, and I'm late to see no one from the watchtowers or the walls of the kingdom," and they actually flew quickly over the dark forest that was separating the kingdom from the rest of the world from the south, about five hours away on the horses, but at the top of the joy.

They had arrived above the trees of the forest five hours after the horses appeared in the kingdom, and here Archie wanted to use her deepest love for him to ask her for answers to Barbora's words, especially about the girl Isabella!

Suddenly, Maya glimpsed a light from afar, and it increased more and more as she travelled a greater distance over the forest, until Maya realised that this light was nothing but a light of fire in the kingdom, and this is not normal.

"It seems that something is going on in the kingdom," she said, puzzled.

Archie said, "I only see thick smoke rising to the sky like smoke from the crater of an erupting volcano."

Maya answered, "But these are deliberate fires within the villages of the kingdom on the side of the wall separating the kingdom from a cave. Ogres?"

Archie said with his eyes rolling, "Do you mean that ghouls stormed the walls of the kingdom?"

Maya said forcefully, "What's much worse than that?"

Archie's face frowned and was invaded by a very frightening feeling for the first time and he feels that he is already about to live a reality that he had not imagined since he was young, but it seems that many things are going to change anymore.

They descend in a place in the middle of the forest above a high rock as if it were the foetus of a newly born mountain that had a barren and flat surface and from below it a very dense vegetation cover as if it were a sea of hanging leaves, until Archie said, "Don't you think we're still a bit far from the kingdom, or are we going to take an alternate route through sky?"

"No, Archie. I have to make sure myself so that I don't throw you to death. You have to stay here a little for a while until I can make sure of how dangerous the situation is there and the degree of danger. There is something wrong with what is happening and I must investigate this myself. You must stay here now so that I may come back as soon as possible to give you the sure news."

"Well, girl, since you are the witch and you know what's going on, I'm waiting for you, be careful and don't meddle in what doesn't concern you."

This time she flew without disappearing, as usual, and at such a high speed, that he did not know it before, until it almost fell off the edge of the cliff of the boulder that came down, as if a gale-force wind had struck it.

When she approached the city walls, the night of which turned like the morning of a very tormented day, the cries of women and children were intertwined, men were spooked, the wheels of fleeing carriages were squeezed and dust was mingled, buildings were torn down with fire smoke and the smell of destruction and ruin everywhere.

Maya enters the city from over the fences while overlooking everyone who was in it until she sees the legions of ogres that use huge batons with all the violence to kill everything that moves in front of her and even the frogs are not spared.

And not only did it, but it was carrying large, swollen trunks of trees, like one of you holding matchmakers in his hand, which beat people and burnt them down in a brutal way, laughing and continuing to hit the walls of the houses and another holding a number of people, sitting on them and crushing them to death.

Another is the erosion of the heads of all children, men and women in its grip.

Even dogs and horses were not extradited from them. The savagery was in front of Maya's eyes in the form of these stinking creatures that created a chilling blood massacre.

In all her life, had never seen anything like this, but in those tales that she could hear about the battles that her father, the king, had fought with the kings of the gin, or imagined that she had already heard them.

Maya lands between the flanks of the houses in disguise and shows his passage in light from a wall to a wall that spies to listen and investigate more about the inhabitants of the city, where the others went, what happened to the king and the residents of the palace, and where the guard went so much that was guarding the walls and the city?

Her eyes fell on one of the single ogres, and he was wandering among the alleys looking for pubescent prey. The ogres' sense of smell was never wrong.

He was very large compared to the rest of the ogres, and he had two heads, one smaller than the other and uglier, and he stuck his head on the wall of the house above the window until his instinct told him that there was a hunting. Inside, when Maya saw him, his hand enters the window of the broken house to pick up a five-year-old girl screaming terrified as if she wished her soul would come out before looking at that frightening monster for another second.

And then the little head says to the bigger head in a raven-like voice, "Well, it seems that it is a small meal that will not satisfy one of us, what are we going to do with it now, should we divide it in half?" Maya did not endure the child's screaming, afraid of that hideous creature.

It's awful what she'll see if she doesn't move and do something right away before it's too late, until Maya shouts his call in a strong voice, "You ugly ogres! What do you think of a meal larger than the one in your hand that satiates you until morning?"

The ogre turns its head back and watches Maya hanging between the earth and the sky with her shiny dress flying everywhere. The ogre approaches her a little to watch what seems to him that dinner has come down from the sky—the ghouls have a congenital problem with their eyes—and they are not smart enough to distinguish or perceive the difference between the creatures around them, but all that matters to them is to kill and eat everything they hold in their hands, wherever they are.

Maya unleashed her trick and the magical method of fairies in seduction and sent sweet words as if they were poplar flutes to become like a narcotic drink for the mind and the arrows of her eyes shot with a strong and intense focus in the eyes of the two-headed ogre to pierce his eyes with her magic until he was numbing and completely paralysed, his eyes whitened and his mouth opened.

And she said to him, "I'm your lady now, and let you leave the baby right away!"

He relaxes his huge hand.

No feeling and the baby falls and Maya picks it up before it falls on the floor. "And now your ugly ghoul goes where you came and ordered your army to

come back immediately and no one remains here," the two-headed ghoul said as if he were a slave carrying out his master's orders, Your Majesty's command, until he turned back and they were back, but he couldn't walk on his feet, which were hardened by the power of magic.

Even sat on his knees like a camel and he looked crawling and completed his way out of the walls of the kingdom they had breached, and he was flopping his heads between the walls of the houses like the one who have epilepsy.

Maya glimpsed the shadows behind her from over the walls until she ran to the child's house and quickly hid. An ogre was astonished when he saw their leader crawling strangely and thought he might have fallen into a winery and over drinking. What are you doing, boss? The rest of the ogres gathered to see their leader in a humiliating and strange situation, and he did not say a word as if he had completely lost his speech, and this increased their fear for their leader and they all became nervous!

The leader ogre did not even look at them (since ogres are small-minded creatures that cannot quickly understand or infer what is happening around them or what happens to one of them, but rather the method of error and repetition that most animals use in search of food) and as soon as they saw him heading out from where they entered, and one of them got up By blowing the trumpet two annoying blasts, which is the sign of the exit and heralds the end of the invasion, and all of this is because they saw their leader leaving the cities of the kingdom from where he came.

Other ogres hear the sound of the trumpet, and the rest blow the trumpets, and the sound of trumpets is loud throughout the city, thinking that their leader has ordered that.

The hordes of invaders appear to retreat outside the kingdom before they reach the kingdom's palace, one of them calls out in a voice, "Come on, let's leave."

The youngest of them called him and he had a man leg in his hand who did not finish eating it... "Hey but I only ate two men and I didn't like their taste, they were old and stinky!"

Another hit him from behind him. "Didn't you hear the sound of horns, you clumsy? They said that the two-headed chief left. Do you want the chief to be angry with you and cook you in the pot, like your brother cooked before?" It was the habit of ghouls that if they did not find food for their leader, they would slaughter the weakest or the youngest and present it to him to eat. They were merciless creatures and never knew fear.

Maya was following and hearing everything that happened. She realised that she had inadvertently saved everyone who remained in the kingdom alive from these ogres. "I can't believe what happened. That two-headed ogre was their

leader? And I was the reason for their exit!" Out of joy, Maya hugs the innocent child whose parents fled and it seems that they forgot her from the horror of the disaster and fled with their lives, and in the meantime, Maya hears one of them open the outside door of the house forcefully and impulsively Maya says to the child, "Do not be afraid, my little girl, you are now safe, no one will harm you and I am with you, listen to everything I tell you and do it. And I'll be around watching you."

The little girl shook her head in the affirmative and said spontaneously, "OK, Mama!"

My mom! Maya repeated Mama word in astonishment with her lips without uttering it, as it opened in her heart what had not healed since she was born, how much she wished herself to utter it even once when she saw the boys playing with her in the palace when they finished playing and they called their mothers with longing and joy (it was the word 'Mama', a great impact on Maya, who was deprived of seeing her mother) But those feelings are spoiled by the sound of footsteps running hastily with fast steps on the ground and suddenly she becomes silent the voices after they reached the door of the room, to move the door handle down slowly, here Maya put the child under the bed and then Maya disappeared.

"Laura, Laura, my daughter where are you?" A man and a woman were calling in a sad and crying voice.

"My daughter, Laura," was calling for the woman and crying very hard. "The ogres seemed to have eaten her!"

The mother knelt in her grief, thinking what she thought happened, and suddenly the baby came out after hearing her parents' voices, "I'm here, mom, I'm here." Maya sees them without seeing her. She's overwhelmed with feelings of joy she can't hide. Tears pour down her cheeks and turn to the sky and start flying. Her tears flew through the air like raindrops, motivated by her joy at saving that child's life, and she was at least one of them happy.

Maya could not complete the flight. She softens her heart. She mixed celebrations of joy with their celebrity and grief. She remembered that moment as she embraced that girl, Laura, and remembered this word, Mama.

And she remembered, watching the parents hug her with great love and that she had been deprived of that beautiful moment and that she was the only one who was excluded by fate among all those whom I knew who had no mother until she stood in the middle of the sky like a withered rose trying to suppress what was inside her but she could not, the concern is great and her breath hardly

came out of her body like a bird captive in a cage. Then she returned to sit under the courtyard of one of the walls of the destroyed houses, after the rain fell as if it was a mercy to extinguish the fires of evil and malice caused by the ogres.

She sat and hugged her knees and cried, but elegantly, without moaning or wailing, and covered her face with her hands, ashamed of everything in her life, not knowing why she felt this way.

She said consoling herself, perhaps helping her to get out what was bothering her chest and holding her breath, "Why am I not having a mother?"

My father neglected me and I became like the only one despite everything he had, but this does not suffice me about having my mother with me.

She raises her face to the sky and says, "I wish someone would hear me and bring my mother back... I wish someone would hear me and bring me back my mother..." she said, bitterly crying.

Yes, the fairy of love, nothing ever sings about the mother, so whoever has a mother should praise the God of the heavens, who made him a mother among the many who have been deprived of this blessing. Enjoy the presence of your mother in your life and make her a princess because she will leave one day and you will cry more than Maya cried in this influential moment.

Archie is still waiting Maya's return, sitting with the feeling of loneliness, the jungle and its darkness, and he is curious most of the time about what is happening in the kingdom and about the cause of the burning fires. Did the ghouls really invade the kingdom and that he will see it with his naked eyes for the first-time face to face? I wonder what Maya found, and when she will return, and when he will reach the kingdom that he has long awaited to reach. He already felt that it was too late, as the moon had disappeared, the darkness increased, the sounds of croaking frogs, and the silence prevailed throughout the forest, except from the sound of raindrops hitting the surface of the leaves and branches of the trees.

The boy became frightened in himself after having an undoubted feeling that there were eyes watching him from behind the dense trees after he heard the sound of branches breaking, suddenly as if someone had thrown a small stone from his right, turning Archie with his speed and anxiety.

After being aware that the sound could not be of a passing creature, it was the sound of a stone thrown from a man's hand who wanted to divert his attention from the face where he was, this trick would not have worked with Archie until he gathered composure and said, "I know you're hiding between trees for a need in yourself, and I understand them, but I'll give you safety to be afraid. I won't hurt you. I also don't know where I am." It was a brave initiative from Archie to feel the other's strength and confidence.

So much as the moments of the beginning decide how to deal with the other with you.

And then there was a long silence in which some birds came out of their dens freaking out, and Archie grew more anxious and tried to prepare for any surprise and decided to return to the high rock so that he might be safe between the dense leaves that he would not rule out that the stab would come from anywhere.

He sees nothing but the fear he seized, throwing the stone around him from was repeats all directions and he no longer knows where it will come from!

Maya blunted her tears and tried to take her grief and remembered that she was here for a purpose and no time to waste it on what it would no bring back tears. Oh, I really delayed on the poor Archie, forgive me, darling.

When Maya reached the forest where she left Archie and came down from the white rocky hill, wondering, "Is this the place or am I wrong, or not, really, it is the same place and this white rock, no one is here?" Where do you think Archie went? She called to him in a low voice, but no echo reached her, and then she rose into the sky? Perhaps seeing it from above will give her some hope, but it is of no use. Her physical and psychological state is unable to use all of her magical properties. She had exhausted all her strength to stand against the two-headed ogre, and now she was experiencing a breakdown in her body energy, but she had another solution which was to soar into the sky for a longer distance to try it out. Invisibility.

The atmosphere of the sky helps her to reveal the locations of any soul she wants to reach her and she closed her eyes as she climbed more and more in the sky until she found herself trapped in the sky by four (flying jinn) the private guards of the king entrusted with them all the tasks of research, protection and implementation of the dangerous tasks of King Barhout, the father of Maya.

"Madam, His Majesty the king is looking for you and asking for your presence at once!"

Maya stared at him in shock until she furrowed her eyebrows in anger and said, "Or might he remember now that he has a daughter to ask about? Tell him I'm not lost and I know when I can go back to the kingdom. Tell my dad I'll be back tomorrow and I'm enjoying my day here."

Their leader, who was called Chraklis after he caught her, replied, "No, madam, we will not return unless you are with us. These are the orders of my lord the king. I am very sorry." Maya realised that she had to use some trick, as she would not leave Archie in a dangerous place and in a wild night alone, because she would bear the full responsibility. If anything, bad happened to him, in addition, she is obliged to take him to the kingdom, because she was the one who caused the deviation of his path until he reached this dangerous place without even having any weapon to protect himself with.

She said with cunning, "Come on, go ahead and I will follow you, but the commander of the Guard was intense and very intransigent and Maya knew it very well. Come on, follow me. There's no time for the gamers." Maya's angry as she tries to free her hand, "What are you doing, Chraklis? Leave my hand right away. I can't understand that."

Chraklis said, "I'll leave you only at the palace." Then said, "Come on guard hold her."

Her heart and mind squeeze and worry for what will be solved with Archie without her!

In a desperate last step, she deliberately dropped her shoes and said that "My shoes fell, you idiots, let me pick him up." The guard bowed their heads to watch the shoes fall into the woods and on his omission from the guard, Maya pulls her hands out of his speed as a professional lightness player and flies fleeing them towards the kingdom.

They might clash with the ogres to find time for herself to escape and hide. Certainly, it is not enough for her to keep pace with the strength of the guards and their speed (the jinn) which is like a burning meteor.

From house to house, among the destructive meridians and the piles of scattered, burnt trees and guards behind her, they were like her shadow, but the small size of Maya compared to them helped her get into narrower places, so that it appeared that she had lost them because of the many smokes of the fires sparked by the ogres heading to the fence from which the ogres came.

The ogres behind him were like a long corridor in the middle of the forest towards the south of the kingdom through the hole they dug in the wall of the wall and surrounded by a long rocky corridor that leads to the mountains that surround the kingdom and does not know the end of it, where the ogres cave that backfilled on them... while she was in one the houses peeked from the windows of the house and watched him from the side of the door, waiting for the right moment when she felt that the guards had completely missed her, to set out on that road and said to herself nervously.

Now I must hasten to get out and take off quickly, for my intuition tells me that they are very close to me, and when she came out of the house in which she hid, she took silent steps against the wall, quietly, as if a bird was on its head, and she saw the shadow of a giant wing, and one of them had descended to the top of the house, and that shadow did not show any movement. It was as if he was standing on top of the wall next to which she walked, reflected by the moonlight, which suddenly came out like a light in the darkness, until the moonlight faded as quickly as it appeared and did not return and that shadow disappeared with it.

And when she had the opportunity and saw that the road had opened its doors for her to go to the path of the ogres, and when her feet crossed the corner of the house, she turned with fear and she felt something and did not see anything until she collided with the body of Commander Chraklis and looked at him with the looks of the one who lost his life in an instant! Who surprised her with a blow from his wing that made her unconscious.

Meanwhile, unfortunately Archie was kidnapped while he was trying to find out who was occupying him behind the trees of the forest, and he was covered with a large burlap by three unknown individuals and taken to an unknown destination.

Chapter 13

HIDDEN WORLD

There is only one way that leads to this world and enters through it, which was like the neck of a bottle whose head ends with sharp fragments that are inescapable for the rest of the creatures if they wanted to enter this hidden universe and filled with strangeness that human science cannot explain or reveal its secrets, it was a dark and frightening path with something that makes smiling a path on your lips, and kills every belief that you may see what makes you happy at the end of the darkness and lack of air that makes you feel that your neck is in the hands of the hands of a ghoul, preparing to extract your soul from it, unless you are one of the creatures of the people of this world and this is the secret of the inability of any creature other than the jinn to enter This world, no matter what his ability or whatever knowledge he has attained, entry into this world will remain forbidden except for the jinn and their companions.

The road leading to the world is not strange to you that it is an ancient and deep well to infinity, and as for whoever approaches this place, his fate is either perdition or disappearance, it is (the great well of Barhout).

In which the battle of (king Archie I) took place.

With that scary black lion and strange unknown girl whose secret no one knows, and perhaps there is something we will know in the coming chapters.

The well was filled with water to the end, and it seemed to the onlookers that it was, but in fact it was just a barrier and a gel screen covering the water's surface from the top just to make everyone who approached the illusion that it was a full water surface.

But the one inside it is lost, like the one buried in the grave. Will never returns. It has a fetid smell, unlike well water, which is known to people.

When you go down to the well and break through the gel barrier, you can hardly see anything at all. It's like on a dark night in a deaf room with blind eyes.

Even if you approach the edge of depth, you will see your eyes in the room and light them with their lanterns to see underneath a cave hole, as if the dawn light had emerged from it towards the right from the bottom of the place. When you enter it, and see that at its end it looks like the outer space of the universe, even if you get to the edge of this tunnel, you feel like you've reached a crater looking for the edges of that crater.

See only if you stand on it from the magnitude of the vacuum and this great vacuum has a mixture of colours mixed between the colour of the morning twilight and the dusk of the first night until you feel that you can breathe like you breathe in the upper world, where seeing the sky and its colour feels the breadth of life and freedom as opposed to the beginning of the descent into this world.

Who feels like you're going to a dark grave inside an abandoned mine.

And when you throw yourself from the tip of this great vacuum that makes you believe that you are standing on the edge of the universe until you see down from you a dome of light in a dim colour the same size as this great vacuum has covered the sky of that vacuum and can't go down this vacuum unless you breach this a great tomb.

Whoever enters the tomb will see wonder you will see what is more like from the world of mankind, but in a different beauty, palaces, houses, streams here and there and pierce those strange cities built in a way that resembles human settlements but strangely.

It's a big world where you can only see the light in the longest mountain under this tomb. It has the palace of one of their kings or, rather, the only king of these worlds. When you pass the dome from the top downward and then look at it, and it's above you imagine that you're touching the red twilight.

There is no day here but almost a night long. Some of their homes are carved in mountains and others are cities created from melted bricks with several dark colours that distinguish them from only some of the different colours of light that are inside it.

Meanwhile, the date of the day of ornamental was to hold the annual ceremony, which was an annual day. The mountain that embraces the palace of the kingdom was lit up in its entirety. It served as the palace of the universe in their entirety until most creatures from all the poles of the underworld flocked to celebrate. The sounds of trumpets rise from the top and centre of the balconies of the beautiful palace, which is well built in a dazzling way for everyone who saw it, calling for a sound from one of the middle balconies of the eight-layered palace.

O people, O great people, O people of the great Barhout, our great king will come out upon you now, and it is an honour for eyes to see, and voices to be heard, then the heralds and trumpets stopped and murmurs rose among the crowds.

To watch and hear their king, who only sees him once every fifty years, for some of them will see them for the first time since they were born, and once all royal protocols and artistic reviews are over.

Until King Barhout came to them with stature and majesty and with all the adornment, and around him were the fairies who carried the end of his long robe of blue colour and embroidered on both sides with a golden ribbon devoid of lustre that he had drawn. A long white beard, bright white, and its tip almost touched the ground despite its height. Of course, this is what distinguishes the jinn kings. They were descendants of the giant jinn, unlike most jinn, they were somewhat short in stature, with the exception of the flying jinn with wings, and most of them worked as guards. The king and the kingdom, and they did not eat what the other jinn ate, but they offered them tree bark and honey to feed, and this was their food only.

The look of the king was dazzling for everyone who saw him holding a stick of pine trees in his hand, which was polished with a golden line that rotates on it from the bottom to the top in a unique geometric shape.

At the head of the stick was a dragon's head with an open mouth, and wings behind its ears, flapping as long as the king's hand was holding the stick.

This stick is a simple example of one of the delicate crafts that distinguish the jinn in the field of industry, its extreme precision, and the ability to make strange things that humans are unable to do except with a supernatural effort, and it may not happen.

And he made us different so that life could continue and serve one another, and not underestimate the value of your family or yourself because you were born differently, or less in size, or did not like your appearance, but look at those who are less than you, then turned their heads to a direction outside the crowd on the right of the palace and said:

"You see those jinn who are on the other side next to the place of the palace lighting source from below! He was a short worker, green in stature, ugly in character, and had wide ears with many openings, like a doomed beehive, and he had long hands. A long corridor that has a stone shelf filled with oil along the outskirts of the palace in the form of a spiral that surrounds the palace wall from bottom to top."

"That is why they are enslaved and their weakness is exploited for this deadly task that no one wants. These creatures, my sons, are called palace servants. From the moment one of them begins puberty, he is used in this task until he dies. They have no work but to burn wood and keep the fire like this until everyone leaves and then He turns it off in the morning and they leave) He almost sees nothing on their faces except extreme misery and looks of sorrow, especially their father with a broken heart, and he watches his sons looking at the other boys as they have fun and run with his feet and eat from here and there in this big party while his sons have been deprived of all that and even more so hard work and hard work! They are only happy with the presence of Maya, the daughter of the king, who is the only creature who cares about them and tries to make them happy, and I haven't seen her for a while."

The two children looked at each other with some regret and disappointment, then one of them said, "We are really sorry, Dad, we promise not to repeat this." They looked back shyly at that grieving man and his two children. That weeping scene really affected them, and they thanked their father for that precious advice.

The king speaks from the balcony with enthusiasm and confidence, "O people, I promised you centuries ago, and I fulfilled my promise to you to make this kingdom relax and live in safety until the wrath of heaven clears from us and we possess the top and bottom of the earth and dominate the creatures of the earth and those on it, then the voice of loud applause and exalted voices and chants praising me their king (long live the king, long live the king, long live our King Barhout, the Great)." (As is the custom of defeated peoples) completes his speech and adds, "The dome is close to breaking out of our kingdom, and then we will conquer the earth and dominate everything, and you will enjoy the moonlight, which is our energy, and the sun of the earth, which is the source of the continuity of the basket Our food will be the beginning of the eternal life that you promised them."

The legend says that the jinn in the past were seven kingdoms and they were fighting among themselves and they owned the whole land before people came until they decided to stop the shedding of warmth among themselves so that what remained of them would not become extinct due to the death of most of them in wars in which no one was victorious until they agreed to share the land among themselves with justice and equality.

But they transgressed and broke their vows and fought among themselves again until the curse of heaven came upon them and condemned them all to live in the narrow lower world and surrounded them with that dome, and that they would not come out of that world until after three thousand years. A female fairy who will be queen over them, then a throne will descend from heaven in a land that has no description, and whoever sits on him is ruled by the sky to rule all the earth and those on it as long as the throne is immortal. Although it was just a myth, it may not come true.

So, it was difficult for seven kingdoms to live in one world, and his great murder occurred among the seven kingdoms in which King Barhout allied with three kings and they held the covenant of safety and peace every time with one of the four kingdoms and then attacked it at night and exterminated it from the hatred of her father and so until they exterminated the four kingdoms.

What was king Berhout to sow sedition between the two kingdoms, he pledged to them and then make them fight between them?

He claimed neutrality and his failure to intervene in favour of one of them on the pretext of respecting the covenants between them until they weakened each other and eliminated them by striking one man, enslaved the remaining inhabitants of those deceased kingdoms and made them servants and slaves in his kingdom.

This is in short what happened in the underworld and between the kingdoms of jinn in the previous centuries and why they stayed underground so long.

Complement his promising words in the ears of happy crowds. Now I invite you my dear people to enjoy, dance and celebrate this great day and forget all your feelings and worries and leave what is in your mood.

Spread out and rejoice, then hit a side with his stick on the floor to shake the balconies with a signal of the end of the speech and turn back, standing from the honour.

The shouts of the presence and the cheers of the king's life (and the immortal achievements), which were real and dusted with it, but unfortunately are built on the bodies and skulls of their sons. The simplest did not get the crumbs. All the wealth of the kingdom was shared by the nobles in the kingdom.

Since the king went until the king's guests from the nobility of the kingdom and the king's entourage went to dance in haste, it was their need to entertain themselves from the righteous red tape they had forged since they were created.

The community's untouchable class of the present, the most suffering and the most impoverished, sped off like hungry hyenas on its prey to the binge tables of food and feasting. In a chaotic and unpleasant scene, the sounds of the guard came with the noise and shouts of those poor hungry and seemed to clash between them to organise the place that turned out to be a real war square, which drew the king's attention to that heart breaking situation until he stopped walking and looked at all those people with a kind of sorrow and mourning what was going on in the kingdom. Contrary to what he had said and bragged about in his prepared speech as if he had seen the starvation of the people, his kingdom would soon come to an end.

The rotten lining around the king had eaten up all the rights of the people, leaving no one to eat after them from the treasures of the earth of the underworld full of some good.

And they were a reason for the king to forget that class of the people of the kingdom, or perhaps it is the deliberate forgetfulness by the king to make him rule and authority and make them in this state to be in their need always and they find no way but to wait for his mercy and generosity for them from their rights and wealth that should have been in their pockets and not in the pocket of the one who does not own it. (The king and his entourage)

The king looks around him and does not find his daughter Maya, and he asks his minister who is accompanying him as a shadow and says, "Why do I not see my daughter, Maya, here today, or was she one of the absent?"

The minister replied hesitantly, "You know, Your Majesty, that Maya did not like to attend these celebrations ever since she attended him for the first time in her life, so she has not attended the rest of the celebrations yet. Perhaps you know more about her than I do, but I have commanded the private guards to go and find her at once for Your Majesty's sake, to see her as you asked."

The king took a deep breath and then took it out of the depths with great frustration and quietly said, "Right, but every time I watched her go around with those miserable creatures around the palace with her nan. But I didn't want to flip her joy into her unhappiness. How stubborn she is. I rarely see her smiling as if grief had worn her since she was born on that disastrous night. She often likes to isolate herself from others and not to confuse anyone and feel happy only when she meets with her friends. I don't know what made my daughter adore their councils, and all the boys and girls in the mansion who want to sit with her and accompany her?"

With a yellow smile, the minister said, "Do not worry, my lord Maya, a young girl. Perhaps she has found tenderness with these creatures, and you know that she watches both boys and girls of the palace with their families, and that the field jinn are small creatures that have no family, and perhaps she felt something of the similarity between her and them."

The king turned to the minister and gave him an angry look until his eyes turned into yellow eyes, as if they were the eyes of a lion, not strange to you. He said sharply, "What do you mean, Minister?" Those words were like a slap to the king, who never cared about his daughter and was only concerned with satisfying his desires with the maidservants, and the minister knew that very well.

The minister stammered and tried to correct the misunderstanding in a voice like a rattlesnake, frightened, "No, no, my king, cut my tongue if I meant something wrong, but I was hinting that the reason for her love to babysit the servants and the madness of the fields, maybe she feels that she is higher than them and that she gives them and wishes them out of her grace and the generosity of her father and this is a feeling, good for a girl like Maya to enhance her sense of herself that of real princesses and will sharpen her skill to deal with others in the future since she doesn't babysit you much and this seems to me that the instinct of leadership runs in her veins, my lord.

"And this is very reassuring. They are very simple, and Maya is a very gentle and kind-hearted girl. Of course, this matter will make them very happy while she is sitting with them, and this will spread a generous picture to others about the beloved king raising his daughter."

It was a wise and convincing response from the minister to escape his slip.

Maya did not actually lie. When she said that her father, the king, did not feel her presence, the king was not at all giving priority to his family life, which Maya was all he owned after the death of his wife immediately after her birth in Maya.

It was forbidden to marry another woman in the law of the kings of the jinn if his wife died if she was of the same lineage, but it was permissible for him to marry every day a woman from the maidservants, and the next day brings another woman, and so it was for King Barhout as if he was a womaniser more than he is a king who will not be inherited by anyone after him, except for this girl who will one day become the queen and the rightful heir to all this world.

Chapter 14

Jungle Boys

The kidnappers open the gut that they put a burlap inside as if it were a dead catch caught after a long effort.

Indifferent to the fact that there is a human being that they carry inside this burlap and that he has been hurt so much.

Archie took out his head and blindfolded eyes to breathe life after almost choking from self-distress inside the burlap, which was designed primarily to place the dead cruiser and not to mankind a living distance to the place where they settled.

After they have spent walking for more than an hour in the dark and heavy trees are known, descending, including those inside it, striking in the sharp rocks and the stumps of hardened trees with common limbs, leaving those who touch them to bloody remembrance. And the poor boy had the biggest share of all that, but his patience for pain made him bear all that pain until he bitten his hand so that he wouldn't make a voice of pain in order not to weaken against those who showed him courage and fear from the beginning that didn't benefit him.

So quickly, they unshackled his hands and left his eyes covered until there was a suspicious silence until Archie begged after he became weak and painful, "Don't you have food? Tell us who you are and what you're doing here in this jungle?" One of them is asking Archie in a threatening tone. His voice was as sharp and disturbing as the raven is when he fights with the other crows. Then another came forward and lifted the cover on his eyes. Then Archie raised his head with dismay to see three masked people around him, as if they were ghosts in the darkness of the forest.

Tell us who you are and what you're doing here in this jungle? Someone wonders Archie in a threatening tone. His voice was as sharp and disturbing as the raven's veil when he struggled with the other crows. Then another came forward and lifted the cover over his eyes. Then Archie raised his head with dismay to see three masked people around him as if they were ghosts in the darkness of the forest.

The he knew they were boys from their voices and body sizes.

Until he saw behind him a slick rock only one metre away, he crawled back and turned forward so that he wouldn't say that he wanted to run away. He wanted to take a stone from the ground to throw at them. He thought they were bandits and no one would hesitate to rush him by stabbing him with a dagger or throwing a spear for whatever reason, he told them in a twisted voice of pain, "I don't know who you are and why you kidnapped me, but I need treatment right away. I can't talk about the severity of the pain." The same boy with an ugly voice responds to it. His name was Adrian.

"Accusing you, Haha. Hear what he says! A little while ago, he asked about food, and now he wanted treatment. He didn't seem to be out of his mother's mansion."

The other colleague replied to him, and his name was Luca with a sharp tone, "And why you realised he was lying and he came from his mother's mansion like you claimed he might be a poor boy and he actually seemed to suffer. He saw the burlap crashing into his force in those sharp rocks when we were carrying him, why not take him to the camp and then get the doctor Sebastian to examine and treat him.

"We give him food so he can answer our question and then tell everyone what we found!"

Adrian replied angrily to him, as he did not like Luca's response to Archie and he felt that he was arrogant, "Well why not breastfeed him from your goat's breasts?"

Luca violently answered, "Well for what I look like. But he has to ride on the back of the donkey like yours in order to get him to the camp. A donkey like you can only disturb people with its ugly voice."

It raged between them until they almost fought until their third, Charlie, said, "Enough, you savvy. You insulted each other in front of this weird boy. You showed him how young you are. Now it is decided by all of us that you support Luca's idea and that we take him to the camp to confirm his safety first before he gets any hated. It seems from his coat, that he is the son of one of the princes, but we will look for his story leisurely. Now there's no blame if he doesn't answer. Enough of what happened to him."

At these moments, Archie's imagination was clear about the nature of these boys, how they fit into each other, and whether they are not all the same minds and thinking. This is what delighted him a little bit and made him hope that he would miss meeting the rest of the gangsters so that they might not be thieves of the beginning and that Adrian's cruel and imperious behaviour would not reflect what others might be like.

The boys Charlie and Luca took the injured Archie on their shoulders until they arrived at the camp headquarters at a distance of less than half a kilo. The dawn began to hang slowly after the darkness had eased and the thickness of the trees was reduced until they arrived at a place resembling a green square with no trees but from the remains of an earlier tree block.

The boys Charlie and Luca took the injured Archie to their shoulders until they arrived at the camp headquarters at a distance of less than half a kilo. The dawn slowly began to hang after the darkness had eased and the thickness of the trees was reduced until they arrived at a place resembling a green courtyard free of trees other than the remnants of an earlier tree block.

Archie as several camps and a young boy fire, on what it looks like to warm up and make breakfast.

The remainder of the four were clogged and covered themselves with black- dyed cotton sheets to absorb the most of the sun's rays.

That visits them to resurrect these days of the year. Until the scene of Archie from behind the two exhausted eyes looked like a bunch of bodies preparing to burn and then scary obsessions in himself and that was the fate of those who had been abducted before.

Until he was placed on the floor on an empty bed beside the fire, until he stretched on his back from the intensity of fatigue, twisting his luxury robe, which Maya gifted, put his head on the headrest, closed his eyes, forgotten everything around him, and entered into a blessing of physical and spiritual satisfaction after his suffering.

And then he opened his eyes to the sounds of a swish around him.

And someone who he thinks is sleeping like mummy is moving and removing the blanket from over him and then asking someone about breakfast! And here Archie wipes his heart out a little bit and knew they were the rest of the gang, not like what he thought.

And while he is, he doesn't know what they're going to do now.

Until the boy sitting on the fire stove rushed to them for breakfast, and he seemed to be the youngest of them, and he was gentle among them from the features of his innocent face, his blonde, brown, thick curly hair, which seemed to have not completed the thirteen-year-old, his name was Clementine, and then he asked impressed, confused, and his cooking spoon was still with his hand, "Who is this boy? And what happened to him?"

Adrian said in his unpleasant voice and his usual rude style, "Nothing for children with these things. Go and complete your task. I am starving harder than ever. I don't smell anything delicious than what you cook for us, your frivolous cook!"

Clementine threw him in half an eye and another eye looking at the strange boy with a luxurious red robe. It seemed to Archie that everyone used Adrian's rude style until he was confounded by Clementine with the same rude style and sarcastically when he said to Adrian, "Since when has the crows distinguished between human food and decomposed corpses?"

It was like a painful slap to Adrian. Everyone laughed until Archie, despite the intensity of the pain and fear. Luca raised the sound of his laughs to piss off the hateful Adrian even more.

One of those who was sleeping under the sheets was covered in a lot of laughter so that Adrian would not be angrier, Archie turned to Clementine in a name to open a door of good relationship with one of these kidnappers and told him with a whisper after Adrian went disappointed.

Archie said, "How cute are you, boy, and then he reached out to him to shake hands and said I am also one of your brothers, but I am new to you." Clementine extended his hand to Archie, shaking hands until they were interrupted by a gloomy voice close to them among the shrubs, saying indignantly, "I seem to have missed a lot of things during my absence and no one told me."

He was a boy different from the rest of the boy in size and length. He was prestigious in the body and personality.

Presents them with four rabbits with his hands.

Arrows were still in their necks dripping.

Abominable Adrian runs into that boy and says to him, "No, sir, we wanted

to surprise you with our precious catch for the day, without bothering you, Mr Leader."

A strong boy looks at Archie with a small eye as the rich arrogant looks of the poor beggar who seemed to be the master of the place, not just one of the bandits or someone fleeing his country and wanted for justice. His name is Nathan, he whispered Clementine Archie from afar in a faint voice and his head to the ground so that no one could see his lips moving and said if this boy asked you anything, tell him I don't know until our leader Alexander(the ghost) comes, Archie didn't understand Clementine speech, but all he concluded from Clementine was that this boy was not good, and so did Archie from the very beginning he saw him throw Nathan rabbits to the ground and advance towards Archie as a nervous lion, who implied that another lion came to take his place.

With strong strides on the muddy ground, Archie would not seem comfortable at all. His heartbeat accelerated further. Nathan knocked a dagger out from behind his back and waved it towards Archie, who was still sliding on the ground and had no food or treatment until he approached Archie.

To insult him in front of others, this is a habit of insulting every new guest who enters the camp, where he never showed any sympathy for the boy's pathetic view, some of whose limbs still bleed and did not bandage.

He said, "Who are you, boy, and how did you come here?" Adrian fired his tongue as long as usual to be the master of the news until Nathan, and told him to shut up, raven, or I cut you off your tongue, didn't I tell you a few times not to respond on behalf of someone, idiot, unless I asked you to? Forgot or remind you of this dagger!

The red-bladed dagger looked more like a pickaxe, but the smaller size was a strange-shaped dagger, and it seemed that it was never even used to cut a leaf from its cleanliness, and the glamour of Adrian's silence until he listened to his swallow sound of fear.

Nathan was a cheeky, savvy, insidious person who inevitably possessed such mysterious eyes and his prominent forehead must have been so, rarely until he sat on his knees beside Archie's shoulder and then entered the tip of his dagger in the middle of the robe and dragged it quietly.

Archie was looking at Nathan's eyes more than he was looking at the dagger just knowing that this person in his heart was what his uncomfortable eyes showed to them at all.

Then he seemed to feel the robe, the limbs and the scalp of the beautiful collar, and he said with wonder, "I never smelled such a spectacular fragrance in my life and did I not see in my life a robe so luxurious that it had no stitching and no indication that it was animal skin, not fabric?"

Until he saw Archie's dirty clothes that you want, he realised that a robe couldn't be for one like Archie.

Then he says, "He turns his dagger in front of Archie's face and moves it in a provocative way."

Until his face came up with a sly smile to show no good and he said, "Where did you steal this precious robe from, professional thief?"

And Archie told him quick, in his usual intuition, "If I were a thief, I would be like you now!"

Nathan blocked his face and stopped waving his strange-shaped dagger and looked back to make sure that someone heard him from the boy to determine the size of the insult he was subjected to until he saw everyone looking at him and then lowered their heads for fear.

Wow, thief and tongue bully! His breath was coming out of him as a teapot steam and then he added, "Do you see this dagger, boy?" Archie still exercises silence but keeps staring at Nathan's angry face, and Nathan laughs maliciously.

Ooh, he scared me so much, and then he turns his whole body behind him back to the others to say, "Did you watch this prick fox threaten me, it scared me and made me shake from these looks," said Adrian and Fat Martine, who did not wash his face from sleep.

"We are, sir." Our feet shook in fear of those very anxious looks! They completed the feigned laughter to the satisfaction of their master while others shut their mouths like sad prison doors for the innocent inside and didn't comment on anything because of Nathan's misbehaviour with this wounded captive.

Which was not the covenant they had made since the foundation of this camp, and with a sudden and unexpected step, Nathan applied with one of his huge hands, like the palm of a brown bear, on Archie's neck, like the neck of a deer, and strangled him tightly, as if between them an ancient vengeance to heal what was inside.

Archie's eyes widened and he tried to utter a stifled voice until he stopped begging when Nathan's malevolent face.

He put the pointed tip of his dagger into one of Archie's eyes and said to him, as he ate his grey lips from his excessive use of tobacco, "I will pop those girls' eyes, you petty thief. If you don't tell me who you are, why you are here, who sent you to us, and where did you get this robe?"

Archie shrugged his shoulders and then his head to understand that he could not speak, but Nathan was like a monster that caught his prey and had not tasted the taste of meat for days. He was blinded by his pride and narcissism and then added.

"Try to be smart and you will find one of your eyes rolling on your stomach," Clementine shouted at the top of his voice.

Nathan stopped. "Stop now. This is contrary to the laws of the camp that we swore by. Look at him that he is injured and you have prevented him from the air and you want him to admit all that and he is in dire need of treating his wounds that ooze blood. This is not your right to deal with a prisoner as if you want to get rid of a sterile dog."

Nathan turned to Clementine with sparkling eyes and said angrily, "Look who finally said it. I didn't know you could speak. I thought you were speechless, Clementine."

Meanwhile, Archie was gathering his strength without being aware of Nathan, where he was silent for a long time until he took a deep breath after devising a tight plan to get rid of the grip of this monster, even if the difference between them was vast in strength and preparation.

Archie joined his right fist with force as Nathan was on top of it and dealt him a blow between his thighs, injuring him in his testicles.

It falls to the ground and wriggles over the mud as a snake that grapples with its end.

Archie forgot about the pain and his weakness. The moments of danger make the weak cat a wild lion so that he could get out of his trick and beat Nathan's hand, which held him to the dagger, and then grabbed Nathan's hands and put them behind his back, and he threw his other hand on Nathan's neck, and then threw his whole weight on the floor to tighten his fist as well as a professional wrestler in combat.

It was like what happened between Archie and Horse Barbora, so sure enough, Nathan fell into the evil of his work until he started screaming, let me go, thief, save me, idiots, what do you look at! Until Adrian and Martin were both chubby with Nathan's help.

But Luca put one of his feet in front of Adrian, who stumbled immediately and fell over the fat Martine, got the slim Adrian into his coma.

In the blink of an eye, the situation turned in favour of Archie, and amid this astonishment, the others woke up to the impact of the battle and the loudness of

the voices. One of those boys said with blatant fear, his name was Pablo, and he was one of Nathan's followers, "Damn who wants to kill our brother Nathan, what audacity and what cowards how do you stand and watch on. Our brother was like this while he was being attacked and ran looking for his dagger."

As for Archie, he tightened his fist and twisted Nathan's wrist more forcefully until it almost broke amid the moaning of Nathan, who seems to have lost his strength completely after those two painful blows. He increased his enthusiasm if he wanted to take his right in front of others. This is a chance that will not be compensated to break his prestige who believed that their leader until he jumped on his chest and pointed the dagger into Nathan's eye and said to him with the sweat on his nose, "An eye for an eye", then he stuck the pointed tip of the dagger under Nathan's eye, who did not move. He was silent to push the blade of the dagger from under his eye.

The eyes of the two were piercing each other's eyes like two wolves, swearing that one of them would die this day, then said Archie, warning, "It seems that you misjudged, your clumsy bull."

"And if you had dared to do more than that, I would have stuck your dagger in your eye and cut off your head and made you a memory and laughter at the same time for the group of fools you lead."

But Nathan was not to give up so easily after he smiled in the face of Archie a false smile that was dyed with the makeup of reconciliation and forgiveness and said to himself, "There is nothing more despicable than to smile in the face of a dog that you wish to spit in his face."

Until Nathan was surprised, Archie, who was sitting on top of him, kicked him from behind with his knee to throw him to the ground behind him, and finally jumped on him to pin Archie from under him.

But Archie's hand still grabbed his wrist, trying to push Archie's hand away, but he didn't succeed until he used his teeth to bite Archie in his hand hard, but Archie turned on him again and started strangling him with both hands after he put the dagger between his teeth. All this was in front of everyone who did not move because the custom stipulates that if two people clash, no one should interfere between them until the battle ends with the victory of one of them, because it is considered a man-to-man battle.

Fighting intensified in the mud, punching each other and squabbling like rabid dogs, but Archie's small size and light weight enabled him once again to overcome Nathan's powerful punches and grab Nathan's neck so tightly that Nathan tried to get rid of Archie by stretching his hair with both hands, but Archie had wrapped his entire body on Nathan looks like a giant python because of the devotion to the prey that caught it, except by surrendering to the inevitable fate.

Archie tightened his fists on his neck and began waving his hands at his loyal followers who woke up and who did not hesitate to pounce on Archie with sticks and hit him and drive away their friend Nathan from him quickly before it was too late, Archie was beaten so badly that he passed out.

Nathan sighed with his hands on the floor, then raised his head to look at Clementine, Luca and Sebastian, who didn't interfere.

He said with great anger, "You have revealed to me your intentions, you tramp, but you will regret it, I promise you. Well, what's going on here? Why all this crowd? Are you holding a contest this morning?" Another voice from behind the camp came from among the trees, it was the voice of the leader or the true leader of this camp or the founding father of this gang until Clementine, Luca and Sebastian rejoiced and Clementine rushed to tell him about the matter But Sebastian caught them and said he's in his mood now let him wake up from his drunkenness, but Nathan and his faithful followers of him in evil, whose faces have shrunk and become like rotten gourds, it was Alexander nicknamed the ghost.

"Come on, tell me who won to share the wine with me until tomorrow morning, and as I progressed further, I realise through the tracks that there was a fight that had taken place, it seemed that I had missed a lot here, what a loss I wished to be present to enjoy watching what I missed from a fight I haven't seen a fight for a long time and haven't found anyone He also fights me because all the boys in these days have become like girls, so we no longer know who the man is and who the woman is, what a ugliness this miserable life is."

He was walking and swaying left and right, as if he had completed his night drinking all the liquor of the forest.

He carries in his hand soft river pebbles, throws them up a little and picks them up again before they fall to the ground until he approaches Archie while he is lying on the ground, and his mind was not fully conscious to notice accurately, so he left half of his mind drinking and left enough to carry him to the camp in order for him to sleep peacefully. Then he asked quietly, "Who is this who sleeps in the royal robe? Is he dead? Or is he sleeping?" Then he kicked Archie in the back, you tell me are you sleeping or dead, boy? He was already drunk until Clementine told him that he was injured and that he was in a critical condition, and he fainted due to the heavy blood flow.

Pablo jumps in addressing Alexander to cover up the poor boy's misdeeds and says with a false smile, "He was drunk and couldn't sleep in his place from too much drinking, so he fell here and because we would take him to bed to rest until he woke up to tell us."

Nathan said, "It's not your habit, Alexander, to come this time. Maybe there's something wrong with you early, or is the drink done? But don't worry, my friend. Lucky for you, today we have two kinds of fine royal wines. The Kling Ling wine that was a gift for my father and has not been used yet. I still keep it as a gift and I don't think I will find better than you for giving this precious gift that suits your hobbies and unbridled internal desires."

"Yes, yes," Alexander said he burps and flops on his feet over Archie and does not disparage him, as he still contemplates that boy lying on the floor and his strange clothes.

And then he says, "Yes, I want some drink that you said to me, but I want this sleeping boy to give me. He must know that he sleeps only at bedtime. We are in a state of war. We came here to be a liberation front for our kingdom." And then he shouted at Archie, "Come on, Sleeping Boy, wake up, or I'll give you a relative of the ogres and the wild birds that are endemic to this forest, and then make stupid laughs and keep laughing until he falls on the floor."

Nathan pointed out that they would take him to his tent to sleep until the effect of the wine went.

The next morning with the light of cold dawn brightening. Empty of warmth badges, Archie wakes up after two full days spent in his coma. He found himself lying on a comfortable sponge bed inside his tent. No one shares it. He seemed to feel the pain in his forehead and the rest of his body he no longer felt a few tingles of pain.

And his condition has become better before until he ascertains in his own decision that these are not a wicked gang and that Nathan and his followers seem to represent a different thought than the rest and he will discover this for his own sake.

Archie came out of the tent to see ten metres from the fireplace and had a teapot.

No one was around the stove this time, but the whole camp was completely free of any human being.

He felt a strange quiet and knew that these boys had a routine to walk on, like they were in a real camp, and as soon as his instinct got him to the stove to see what was there, and then with a covered plate, he smelled of delicious food, until he lifted the lid, if a loaf of hot bread, mArchiemallow candy and a number of eggs knew that the boys was not far from the place, and he said, guessing, "They seem to have eaten their breakfast and left this to me. This is what I understand. If otherwise, they have not entered the food Jovi, since I left Maya's dining table. I don't know how long this has been! Until Archie ate all of what was in front of him, if with a quiet laugh, come from behind him, freak out, if the kindly boy," Clementine says, "Don't be afraid, would you like more? Your name is Archie, right?"

Archie said, "yes and you?"

"I'm glad to know you, Archie, and I'm really sorry for the bad hospitality you got, but to you, Captain Alexander has learned everything and will punish whoever abused you, especially that bull, Nathan. I'll be honest with you, but I don't know you that we were so happy.

"When you walked all over him, he is an unethical arrogant, but don't worry anymore. Friends are busy working out like a day, either swimming, hunting or performing some routine tasks. We also have more food, so don't worry how much you want and don't fear anyone."

Archie smiles, laughing at the boy and having the opportunity to know who they are and their story here in this remote spot, but preceded by Clementine by asking, "Tell me from what country you are, Archie, and what were you doing alone in such a wild forest?"

Archie said, "Does that differentiate if I tell you that I am from this kingdom or from that village?"

Clementine, in turn, reacted against Archie's expectation and said honestly, "Yes, it will make a difference. It will make a difference to me. Your name was heard only because anecdotes and historical narratives. The truth I has felt that since I saw you for the first time that you are not a son of the kingdom and that your presence here must have a strange story."

And you were wearing a fancy royal coat that had never seen him before.

He threw the bread crusher, which he had in his hand when he remembered the precious coat and rushed towards Clementine by force, dragging him from his robe and nervously knotting his eyebrows, "Where is the coat who took it?"

Frightened by his reaction, the little boy, who retreated back a little and said a scared smile.

"Hey, don't eat me. Don't be afraid that your coat is saved. We took it to clean it. And as to why you're kidnapped, if you're asking, I don't know anything about this, and I can't guess either. This is the first time I see someone being brought here and he's tied up. Maybe they thought you were a thief or one of the kingdom's spies. And that's what you should know, either why we're here, like I said before, space and time don't allow me to tell you all the details.

"But what I can tell you is that we are a resistance group with noble goals and we have a noble leader as well, and at the same time we have another leader who owns the dreams of his sapper and believes that he will become a king one day and that is why we are divided here in many things and what happened to you was one of them You know, you look a lot like my younger brother, Arthur?"

Clementine replied, "Oh, really, and where is this your brother Arthur to see if he looks like me or are you lying to me to get a lot out of me? But what I can tell you is that we are a resistance group with noble goals and we have a noble leader as well. At the same time, we have another leader who owns the dreams of his chef and believes that he will become king one day. That is why we are divided here in many things and what happened to you was one of them."

Archie says after the anger went, "You know, Clementine, you look a lot like my younger brother, Arthur?"

Clementine replied, "Oh, really, and where is this your brother, Arthur, to see if they look like me or are you lying to me to get a lot out of me?"

Archie realised that Clementine is a boy who is not easy to manipulate. After this reply, he realised that the boy would not have spoken so openly because of his naivety or his young age, as he thought he would not have made it out to a stranger.

But he knew what he wanted to reach, and those words suggested that Clementine wanted to know what kind of people Archie might have.

And it has a lot inside it that he wants to impose, but he seems to have found no one to listen to, so Archie noticed the lad's attraction to him quickly.

But Archie preferred to slow down more so that maybe this is a trick or a representation to get his entries out of secrets, so both sides in this situation are in anticipation and wary of the other.

Pablo calls on Clementine loud, "What are you doing with this idiot? Didn't I tell you to prepare us for food?"

"Clementine," Archie said, "You gave me your word that nothing comes out of our conversation."

Archie still registers all these faces and their actions in his imagination. He would not have forgotten what they had done to him from the outset, although he saw that he did not deserve to be treated like this because they kidnapped him without leaving him enough room to justify his presence in their forest, they said. Archie picks up a piece of bread from the floor and clean it until Alexander's voice called him, "Let it and we will make others for you. We will only satisfy the guest. You have the right to us, guest. Then he approached and everyone was behind him, including Nathan and Adrian, and Martín, and Pablo on his side, and Clementine, Charlie, Luca and Sebastian on the other."

So Archie smiled at himself and said, "It seems like the time for truth is now and it's the date of the account in front of everyone." The truth is that Archie has no fear of anyone anymore after he has read the titles of the book This gang well and understands it properly in his way.

In his customary way and now he has to take advantage of what has happened to him and he has to protect himself and we will not say that it is time for revenge because this was not an Archie impression. He is a nice boy, even with the one who misrepresented him wrongly, as happened with him since he arrived here, and because he wanted nothing more than to return to the kingdom road in order to get to safety and send the good news of his arrival to his parents.

Alexander said to Shush after they all gathered in front of Archie around the fire stove, "I got what happened to you and I'm going to give you what he did and to be fair, I listened to them all and it's time to listen to you and tell me what happened, and I'm going to tell you who has done you right now and everyone else to be an example for the rest."

Archie did not respond, but he really wanted a provocative need in himself and started wrapping his head right and right like the one that stopped his horse and didn't know where he left it until he stood on both ends of his toes trying to look behind Alexander and Nathan, the question marks painted on all of them and took their eyes into each other and also turned back to see the attention of Archie, but only saw the long pine trees manipulating the birds with tenderness.

Archie's action prompted the curiosity of those present. He even wanted to outrage them and provoke them to come out misguided so that they would become more divided after realising that they had been divided since the beginning, especially Nathan, who was irritable and flaming and could not hide anything inside him. He came out with intense anger and shouted until his size doubled. I studied this tramp from the first time I watched it, it deliberately ignored the leaders of this place in order to pit others on us, so I did what I had to do as a leader when I gave it a lesson that he would never forget.

Alexander said quietly, "You have to calm down and I think you've acted enough with this boy. Now it's my turn. I hope you shut up a little bit and leave your nerve inside you before it exploded." Nathan Alexander threw his hatred and then he mumbled and cursed inside it.

Alexander raised his eyebrows with delight, expressing a hidden admiration in Archie's heart after looking at him at length from the bottom up and realising that he was not an ordinary person and not a thief, as he was told, "Well, Archie, it seems to me that the nature here is your admiration and it really is. You will like it more when you go into it to see the wild raptor chick that we're looking for our next scheme."

Until Archie sarcastically said, "It's so beautiful and exciting, but what I'm so confused about is that I didn't see your mothers here."

A group of boys as old as those around you should have been at home, eating, drinking hot milk in the arms of their mothers, not gathering in a wild forest in this cold.

Nathan went crazy and my nose widened until it had a rampaging bull's nose and he said, "Didn't I tell you he wanted only to insult us in our house to get the rest out of here."

This is for a knowledgeable spy and I can only see that he succeeded in penetrating us if you let him proceed further, you will find ourselves prisoners of the leader Glister who leads the task of returning us to the kingdom, Alexander replied to him, in turn, "I told you not to utter his word, Nathan!"

Then Archie continued my speech with a provocation, "It has sparked my curiosity that his morning in the same ages says that they are soldiers and they call you the titles like the ghost and the leader on this mule that is next to you (meaning Nathan)! Until most of the boy laughed, which made Nathan explode angry until he took out his dagger and shouted like the monster and he set out, he wanted to attack Archie, who did not show any mark to fear, as if they had a sea between them."

When Alexander cried out loud and sharp on Nathan and said, "If you dared to do so or touched his hair from the head of the boy, I swear that I will make your head in your hands."

Nathan turned to Alexander, after impatient, and said, "Are you insulting me in front of everyone for that idiot? It seems you didn't realise what you did wrong, Alexander."

Alexander answered, "I commanded you, and you did not listen. I told you to leave it to me, but you let your anger control you, and you received your share of the humiliation which you wanted for yourself and which I did not want for you."

Then Alexander turned to Archie and said with a smile, "Well, Archie, you said yourself that they should be by their mother's side, eat food, drink hot milk in their mother's arms, and what you say is true, but what you didn't know was that these boys lost their mothers and some of them lost their mothers and fathers and even their homes, no. They are the walls left for them to drink hot milk under, and no mothers have to lie in their arms, because there is no one for them except me and Nathan. We are the oldest and most familiar with what is happening in the kingdom from which we come and in this forest in which we camp.

"In general, Archie, I forgive you. Of course, you are a stranger and you have no knowledge, but this is a summary of what you witnessed and why we are here. Now tell me, Archie, which country are you from and why are you here in particular and at this difficult time that the kingdom is going through?"

Archie shrugged his shoulders and let out a loud sigh, expressing regret inwardly, embarrassed by what he heard, "Thank you for my apology for my ignorance of what is going on here and about the condition of the boys. I am from a small village in the far south at the foot of the Black Mountain called Kling Ling. My father sent me here to meet my uncle who works in the palace with the king."

Alexander's eyes widened as if he approached an answer that might be from the most beautiful thing he will hear, he said to him in a politer way, "Your uncle works in the palace for the king? What is your uncle's name, Archie? I may know him. My father has also been working there for a long time. I was one of the residents of the palace, and I am familiar with the names of most of those who work in the king's court."

Archie said happily, "How wonderful, I am more assured now that my uncle is called Chancellor Albert, I am not lying to you if I tell you that I do not know what he looks like, I have not seen him even once in my life, but I have a book that I carry from my father that he sent with me to my uncle Albert in order to join the course of cavalry candidate's royalist."

Alexander's face discoloured and he was silent for a long moment and said to himself, "No, it is not possible."

Archie's face shrunk and said, expressing his astonishment at Alexander's surprise and his silent reaction.

"Is there something in my words?" Alexander muttered calmly and said, "There is no one named Albert in the palace but one person and I know him and he is the advisor to whom you said your father sent you. What puzzles me more is that your eyes are the same as those of my sister, Isabella! Archie felt as if a bell was ringing in his ear when he heard the name Isabella, he had heard this name from his father and from the horse Barbora before, but what does it have to do with it?"

Archie's astonishment grows more and his longing to know the matter boils over, as if he is close to solving a puzzle that he has been wanting to solve for a long time. Then Alexander asked him, thinking, "Is your father's name Abraham?"

Archie said, confused, "How did you know that?"

Alexander interrupted Archie's astonishment and hugged him with great force and eagerness until he heard the crack of Archie's ribs, and Alexander repeated with great eagerness, "You are my cousin Abraham, you are Archie Abraham, whom I had heard about and never seen in my life. What an unexpected coincidence."

Fat Martin said with frowning lips, "It seems that a love story has begun in this forest!"

Luca hurriedly replied, "You'd better be silent, barrel, and not talk about your master like that."

Then Adrien said, "They talked a lot and now they started embracing each other. We don't know what else we'll see after this sudden love that came down on us and how long it will take like this, I can't stand this hunger since morning?"

Sebastian says to him, "Are we in the evening to say since the morning that we are still in the morning, and it has only been an hour since you ate breakfast, and I watched you eat half a plate of eggs, how did you become hungry so quickly?"

Clementine said, laughing from behind him, and this was his opportunity to mock one of his worst opponents in the camp, "It seems that he forgot the bathroom door was open and did not close it well, which preferred the eggs to get out quickly. Ha-ha-ha."

Adrian said, "I will teach you a lesson you will not forget when I am alone with you one day, you idiot cook."

Archie is still rolling his eyes and hands drooping while he is in the arms of his cousin Alexander, amidst everyone's surprise. Fantasy, "But tell me what's going on here and what you're doing here aren't you supposed to be in town?"

Alexander said, patting Archie on the shoulder, "I will tell you everything and you will know everything that happens here, you are now one of us, but we must prepare the situation in the camp for this happened, but the question that preoccupied me is how did you come to this haunted forest and cut off roads, which no one enters alone but perishes?"

Archie said, "I will try to explain it to you in a simple way, but before that give me back my coat."

Nathan claps his hands up and turns around and says sarcastically, "What a touching story I see before my eyes or this. Is he the one who was waiting for you, great Commander Alexander? Isn't this thief supposed to be tried and investigated to find out that he is here? It seems that this Archie thief has charmed you and controlled you, or does the master commander have another explanation, Alexander?"

Alexander said sharply, "No one is a thief here except the one who accuses others of thieving as long as you do not have the proof. But now we know that Archie is my cousin, and it was a surprise to all of us, and it is natural for the situation to change and everything change, unless you are determined to accuse him unjustly without evidence, then you must say that so that we will give you a response that suits you and suits you for your accusation."

Nathan said, looking at Archie with maliciousness, "I don't care about all this, and I don't care who he is, but it seems that you have forgotten the covenant between us that no one enters this camp and does not become a member of it until after my consent and you and not only you decide, but it seems that your joy in this cousin of the one who entered between us, as a spiteful devil to separate us, he has forgotten you about all those commitments that we have."

Alexander realised that Nathan's hatred and malice were so ingrained that it was very difficult to convince him, though he would continue to seek him in order to get revenge on Archie in any way. So, Alexander decided to put the boat rope in Nathan's hand and make him make a quick and decisive decision. "I don't think your words matter," he said. After what I said, then let it be my decision. I made it and I know what is in the interest of this group, and I was the one who had this idea. It is foolish to think that I will abandon my cousin Archie, in order to extinguish the fire of hatred that seems to eat you as fire eats wood, so it seems that the son of Uncle Archie is a real brave man and we need this kind of man.

Nathan smiled mischievously and said, "So that's what you say?" Well then let us see if this cousin of yours will spare you from me and the rest of my followers in the camp. I will now put an end to this nonsense and announce that I and my companions withdrew from the children's camp, then turned around and waved his hand to his followers, the religion, who made up half the camp with him, but he was surprised that no one moved except Adrian and Pablo.

As for Fat Martin, he lowered his head in embarrassment and fear when Nathan gave him a glaring look, until Clementine said bravely for the first time after ensuring that everything had changed and Nathan had no word on them anymore, "Sorry Nathan, we all want to stay here and no one wants to leave Commander Alexander, no matter what."

Hatred appeared on Nathan's face, like that of the crocodile that had robbed his prey, and he replied sarcastically, laughing, "Look, even this dishonoured cook has become an affair, insulting his master. It seems that it is a scheming that you have devised at night among you to get rid of me, and you will soon pay for it."

Alexander replied with disdain, downplaying Nathan's threat and impact, "Don't need to look at us. We have a lot to do. Take with you who you want. Leave unpleasant friends of you who want to stay with us and continue with this group and who you want to catch up with this maverick rogue."

Nathan mumbled and said, "His heart is flaring. Goddess alone knows that this tramp has charmed you, but I will promise you. You, Alexander, will be the most remorseful about this!"

And then leave, disappointed, and no one knows what to hide in his sleeve from plans for revenge that he might not imagine until the demons.

Chapter 15

WONDERS JOURNEY

After more than two months in the camp, Alexander explained to Archie why they were there and that they could not move towards the kingdom during that time period because of the proliferation of military scout fantasy to search for them and release their spies and dogs around the kingdom as lawless and create a wayward difference against the kingdom.

It was difficult for the young men to find an entrance to penetrate all those military crowds with capabilities and an extremely dangerous and capable number that could easily capture them if they approached. And Archie was convinced because he thought Maya didn't have to find him at any moment, but he was disappointed, and his wishes went in vain, and she didn't come even in a dream, forcing Archie to park his bitter reality, which would be a reason for his parents' unhappiness, grief and worry about him.

Waiting for a miracle, he had changed the equation of a closed position on each side.

In the afternoon of a chilly day punctuated by the warmth of the golden sun's face from behind the dispersed winter clouds and on the omission of everyone who was at the tip of the forest among the trees on a fishing trip.

He abducted a shadow from heaven and quickly disappeared. Only Archie, who was dressed in his clothes after washing it and drying it to catch the rest. When he raised his head to the sky, he saw nothing and turned around to see the boy. Maybe someone saw what he imagined was something in the sky.

But they were talking to each other and didn't seem to pay attention even through the shadows again in reverse.

He said, "I hope this is one of Maya's surprises, and I will drink happiness if it is, but as soon as I enter his hand in how much of his robe until he snatches the same shadow, he hijacks it faster, so that Archie tries to walk faster backwards as he looks at the sky between the scattered clouds, but he stumbles upon his rock and falls on his back and face to the sky."

It's like fate tells him that I made you see what others saw to be a vow and what really happened unless he expected and witnessed what his eyes did not see in his life and felt that his body was not stronger than a heavy surprise. It was that shadow of what is but the shadow of the giant raptor.

In the sweeping attack on his prey, until Archie realised that the boys were the target of that flying beast, and Archie screamed loudly and forcefully, flee, run away until his voice was packed, and Alexander heard a voice.

Alexander heard the sound of shouting and others turned anxiously to glimpse the wild bird as it swooped on them and shouted at them all, run your skins into the woods.

They all dispersed in a number of different directions and had been trained to do so before, distracting the raptor, but there was a target with the same sights as this predator and on his itinerary. Clementine was running to get into the woods, but the hungry raptor was faster than the Clementine reaching the dense forest trees until his claws were inserted into the backpack.

Hanging by Clementine back to put the little catch in it, and he found himself rising upwards, but unfortunately the raptor couldn't rise too high, because his speed was forcing him into the woods first between their dense trees and then going upwards, and that hindered the predatory bird to escape with its prey quickly and to move away until Alexander realised them and hung Clementine's foot, trying to pull him down before they rose upwards.

Upward and the fall would be painful or perhaps killer and would end their lives in an instant, but it was unfortunate that he noticed that the Clementine shirt had turned like a noose on the boy's neck, who had blown his face because of his inability to breathe.

The bird shouted frightening shouts and raised his wings with all the strength, and then the bird screamed frightening screams.

It's like a giant screaming in your ear drum.

Until the blood flow from Alexander's ears, he feels quite the opposite feeling like they're all falling to the ground.

With great speed, he saw the branches of trees climbing upwards. It was a quick landing that led to them hitting several branches until they snorted on the ground like they had seized and kicked the raptor on top of them, and his huge body was crouched over the bodies of Clementine and Alexander!

Everyone came to the jungle to catch up with their leader and little brother to save them before it was too late. Lucky for them, the bird did not roost them all over his body, but only one of his wings. His body was attached to the body of Clementina, who was the most affected of this accident.

He received a sudden and very extraordinary spear blow that ensured that his skull was penetrated from behind until the tip of the spear settled between his eyes.

Sebastian speeds up to examine Alexander and Clementine, who is called the camp doctor. His father is also one of the palace doctors who is accredited with his expertise. He inherited little skill in this area from his frequent contact with his father. He said with confidence, "I assure you there are no serious injuries, but Clementine will need some urgent treatment, and it doesn't mean he's in a critical state, but let's take them to the camp now and see what we do."

Archie told Luca, out of the camp, "Is this the first time you see such a creature?"

Luca's response is smiling, "We are in her area and in her nest, but in our experience, she comes out only spring and summer and her skin does not protect her from the bitter cold like the rest of the feathered birds. You have seen for yourself that her body is completely featherless. This is the secret to our confidence in setting up the camp in this area. These giant predators spend the autumn and winter. In a deep hibernation until spring arrives but the exit of one in this cold timing was a surprise to us unexpected."

Archie continued to paint his conception of the strange world he has lived and lived in since he emerged from his village and of the kind of place and nature of his inhabitants. This jungle, which Maya left him alone, was not just a forest like any other, but a forest of death for him. And it is now understood that his abduction by gangsters was more good for him than he thought, but if he stayed waiting for Maya, who would no longer suffer the darkness of the haunted forest in fear and anticipation, he would not know the end of it.

Alexander rose as if he had been out of memory for several years, with his face looking like something was in his mind, and then he said, "what happened? How did we fall from the top and we were about that monster's feet? What happened? Did anyone see something from that moment to tell me what happened?"

Archie talked and said smiling, "Yes, while you were in the battle of life and death with that bird, I saw a spear with a shiny head on the ground and its grip made of piano wood and as I ran towards the woods to follow you until I realised that it was useless to run and that the only solution would be only to use the spear, which by the way was heavy on me, but I was skilled at throwing away, until I hit this dumb creature."

Alexander sighed after feeling cold chills running through his veins and released a deep blossom of satisfaction and said, "We're lucky, boy, to have you, or we're in the raptor's stomach. You have shown our courage and proven the authenticity of your noble metal, Archie. That spear was a gift from the king to my father and it was more a souvenir than a real weapon. Even his headers were made of real diamond metal and his name is pride, so I give it to you as a symbol and a humble gift on your great deed."

Archie smiled as the spring response smiled with great joy and said, "No, no, I don't deserve this."

Alexander interrupted, "It's an order. Take it and make it your third hand with which every forehead we will face on our way, you are the gift of heaven to us and we need to like you."

Archie tried to grab the javelin from the raptor's pyrotechnic head, but he was surprised by the strength of his skull and its cruelty, as if it were a marble head, until he decided to cut her head off after taking out his throat until he noticed the bloating of the bird's belly and thought it was due to body rotting and then said with suspicion and human curiosity, "He must have eaten something big. I must open his belly to see and cut the doubt with certainty. He may have swallowed a human being."

And indeed, I splintered the bird's belly into it. It was puffy belly because of human eating, but it was surprising that a thin, pink leather bag came out. It was a bleach placenta that rushed out and grew rapidly.

He drove out of the bird's belly and pulled out his mouth like he was waiting for this moment to perform honesty.

To her people before it's too late.

Until 20 eggs like ostrich eggs came out and had varying spots of size and colour that smelt unpleasant Archie fleeing away with his hands on his nose from the stink hole of his scars, which combined the odour of decomposing the body and coming out with severe sickness. He then stood a thinker and said astonished after absorbing it late, "Oh, my God, she was pregnant with all those eggs and we killed her? That was her ovary, not her stomach, like madman was ignorant."

"Alas, so forgive me, my God, for we were defending ourselves and were not to spoil the earth and kill your creatures for the sake of pleasure. It is a sad thing for me to be the cause of this."

And he did not complete his words until he saw some eggs moving in half a circle around themselves and colliding with each other and soon pleasure entered his heart quickly When I realise that the eggs are still alive.

He did not know what to do in this case, until he cut the leaves of the trees to remove the sticky remnants of the placenta and collected them all, leaving the spear and heading towards the camp, informing everyone of what he had found.

And what the forest gave him, Luca said, "It seems that she is pregnant, what we were looking for?"

Charlie replied, shaking his head in denial, "And how could he find what we didn't find together? He meant hunting, and they didn't catch anything big, since the winter covered the place unusually early."

Luca said quarrelsomely, "After he killed the raptor with such a blow from such a distance, I am not surprised by anything from this boy, and it seems to me that he will become the joker of this camp."

Archie, jogging approached, cracking a wide smile that they had never seen before, and said with great eagerness, "What a wonder, my friends. Look what I found. Look, it's the eggs of a raptor that I snatched from its guts before it died and it's still alive."

Luca's eyes widened and he moved away from the trunk on which he was leaning, but Charlie did not spit his lips and walked silently towards Archie as if the bird was on his head until they were shocked when they saw the eggshell cracking and their bodies shivered after Archie had laid the eggs on the ground and began as if she wanted to speak from her excessive movement.

"Didn't I tell you, Charlie," said Luca, dumbfounded. "We've turned the woods over six months ago, looking for them, until we almost perished if it weren't for the kindness of heaven when an angry raptor attacked us to protect their nest."

And they were still around it until they all hatched with the help of Archie, who was breaking every crust out of it. The beak of one of the raptor chicks came out of it to run and fall with its emaciated legs between the feet of Archie, who was their mother, until Archie said tenderly, "Sadly, I killed your mother and it seems that this is a divine punishment to bear the consequences of my actions and to be the one responsible for keeping you alive," and so it was.

Until a voice said from behind his ear, "Your Eminence, your heart, Archie, you are a noble person, but you should know that exaggerated kindness will not benefit you anything. These are predatory creatures that do not feel what you feel, and when they become strong, they will not differentiate between those who fed them and raised them until they become strong, and the food is their nature, my brother. If you try to change it, you will find yourself among the losers."

Archie wisely said, "I will not try to change anything, but I will give her of love and mercy. The one inside me until it runs out When she says that I'm not you. In the eyes of nature, I robbed these chicks of their mother's tenderness."

Alexander grabbed one of the chicks, and he was aggressive, and he tapped Alexander's hand so hard that he laughed, and he looked at him and said, "It seems that this will be their leader, and I will name him from now on X if he has a life," then he took out his dagger from behind his back and put his pointed tip under the eye of the chick and then pulled it down quickly until the chick's face made a long wound the chick shrieked in great pain, and Archie jumped up quickly to snatch him from Alexander's hand and said angrily, "How crazy are you doing this?"

Alexander said quietly, "You will grow up quickly so that he will remember me and remember him that I love to be in contact with leaders everywhere."

Charlie said, "But they are twenty chicks, so they will need abundant food, and this is what we lack with the approach of winter and the scarcity of hunting." Archie Woo said, pressing on the chick's wound to stop the bleeding, "I did

not ask you to feed them, this is for me alone."

After a whole week passed, as if they had only been in the evening, the raptor

chicks had grown up and started running on the ground, but they still stumbled and staggered, their legs were still soft, and waiting for their wings to strengthen, they were not created to run on the ground. Then to see what his reaction would be until he was about to flee between the feet of Archie, and he was his mother who breastfed him, and he did not forget what he had done to him, as if reminding him that he would take his right, one day.

Meanwhile, Archie wanted to tell Alexander about the fires he had seen in the kingdom, which might have been invaded by barbarian ghouls, and he said knowingly ignorant, "I knew before I got here that there were huge fires that took place in the outskirts of the kingdom, and he could see the brightness of their light from a distance. Far away, and I think it is a dangerous thing."

Alexander said, reassuringly, "Yes, it happened and we expected it, but do not worry, we received news from the kingdom that the ogres had withdrawn after they launched a surprise attack on the walls of the kingdom and caused great harm and terrorised everyone who was there, but they failed to reach the palace and that all those fleeing that brutal attack started to return to their homes, and the king ordered urgent aid to those affected, and the most beautiful of this is that the strategic food stores were not attacked by ghouls, as they were in a far and safe place that ogres did not reach. Reindeer and deer to the far south. Towards the coast, due to the intense cold here and the abundance of snow, and one of these herds must pass from here, but we do not know when specifically."

Archie was surprised to learn that Alexander had attacked the ogres, but he did not show it and continued to give a surprised look.

As if he did not know anything and did not tell anyone for an unknown reason.

Archie took advantage of this moment and wanted to know what Alexander had told him during the last period.

"Would you please tell me, Alexander, what is happening here, and the story of these ogres, because I did not understand much of what you said, at least to understand what is going on around me. I do not understand exactly what made you think about such a matter despite your young age and despite the danger of the matter and the danger of the place in which you reside and the impossibility of what you seek from a kind of view from my point of view, at the very least, do you not see that you are exaggerating more than it should."

Alexander adjusted his session, leaning against a rock covered with rabbit fur, and said preferably, "Overall, everyone says the same thing, but in the details, there are good intentions and lofty goals for this matter. He who possesses these two qualities will never be disappointed.

"As for the story of ogres, it is an old story that has been renewed in our time. To summarise the situation for you, these are creatures of little understanding, driven by the instinct of survival in an unbridled manner, but despite their lack of understanding.

"However, they were able to make a large incision in the wall each time, and this is a matter that puzzled the kingdom's scientists, engineering experts and military leaders, as it penetrated the kingdom's walls, which are like a steel shield.

"Modern regular armies cannot penetrate it, so how can ghouls without understanding do not have any scientific or technical level? Until the Committee for the Protection of the Palaces, which was headed by my father unanimously, was convinced that there must be a human factor between the ogres and the secret of their penetration of the walls of the kingdom, and that this human factor is the evidence of the ghouls and their secret to penetrate the walls of the kingdom in some way.

"And here a bigger problem occurred. Opened a wound in the palace that has not yet healed, when my father and your father, who was then one of the guardians of the castles of the wall, told him that he was later transferred to the leadership of the king's guard.

"They asked the king to conduct an internal investigation, but what drew attention and raised question marks was the opposition of the priests and some ministers to this matter on the pretext that it was an insult to senior court officials, which would lead to the spread of internal confusion among the general public and doubts about the capabilities of the palace to protect the population, they said, which made the king He tends to believe them in order to avoid spreading any chaos after what they said to avoid spreading any chaos among the public who were in a pent-up and charged situation, like sheep waiting for the moment they entered the slaughterhouse. Hence the division occurred in the king's court, and your father was one of the victims of that insidious battle that took place in the corridors of the palace.

"As for our presence here, Nathan and I decided to do something, which is to lead a long-term rebellion with which we support our people in the kingdom to prove the correctness of my father's view and that there are traitors around the king they must be exposed, but we must catch one of the ends of the thread that they wove around and outside the palace, and it was my choice for Nathan, because I knew he was a serious person and believed what I believed in.

"As for the boys, their families were victims of the invasions of the ghouls, and the rest were suffering from the oppression and indifference of their families for family reasons, and this helped us to convince them to join us while ensuring that they would get food, housing and freedom instead of working in restaurants or shoe-shoes. They did not earn more than the insults they were exposed to throughout their work."

Then, Archie asked him, inquiring with his eyes on Clementine, and this was also another opportunity to find out about this boy, who he finds confusing, and he could not understand his personality despite his simplicity and kindness. Alexander answered with a sad face, "Clementine did not live his childhood like the rest of the boys, he suffered greatly in his childhood, so his father was a cook in the palace until he was unjustly accused of being behind the attempt to poison the king, he knew my father very well that he was innocent. But on that day the king was in a day of decoration and family celebration until he drank excessively and was told of the intention and stalking by some of the stalkers of my father.

"The matter prompted him to immediately execute the innocent cook without a trial, and no one knew about this sad and heinous event until the early morning after the execution of the sentence, and this was a great shock to my father. And to all fans of Mr Polo.

"Behind that incident was one of the priests who saw that my father had respect and love for everyone in the palace, including the palace cooks. This was one of the obstacles in front of the priests' plans to control all the palace staff to enforce their plan and to deliver a fatal stab to the king as my father realised, but he lacked evidence, so they wanted to get rid of all the circle surrounding my father, which they saw as a barrier between them and the king, and my father still suffers from this filthy fragmentation to this is your day this incident had a profound and painful effect on Clementine's mother until she died of that tragedy. Then Clementine was sent to one of his uncles, who owned a blacksmith's workshop, and Clementine was nine years old.

"But he did not treat him like a child, but rather he treated him like owned slave like a ploughing ox, which made him hard on him in many cases, up to depriving him of food, and sometimes he was punished and prevented from entering the house, as he slept outside the door of the house in miserable conditions, as if the world had been overwhelmed by this boy. The poor thing until I received his story from one of the blacksmiths and told my father his story.

"My father did not hesitate to sponsor him in his other house with his second wife, who did not have children, as he hoped that Clementine would be a gift for his wife to compensate her with the tenderness of motherhood. She was not happy with his presence as a son, but she was trying to use him for another purpose, and when she saw me, she tried to make Clementine look like a servant, but soon he would embarrass her when he told her, "Mom, present, making her face become embarrassed in front of me." I consulted, and after four years, he became one of the founding followers in this camp, and I will not hide from you that he is a skilled cook by nature. It seems that he inherited the genes of the art of cooking from his father.

"Since that day, I have seen in him the face of my brother, whom my mother did not give birth to, but I did not show him that so that he would not be deceived and depended, so that I could see him live in his truth and become a man capable of protecting himself, and so that no one would look at any help I give him as favouritism because of our brothers and this is what made me treat him like any other person. But from me, he is my younger brother, beloved to the heart."

Archie said, "This is a noble act of yours and your father, and I am not lying to you that I reciprocate your feelings from the beginning. He even reminds me of my little brother, Arthur, every time I see him."

Alexander stared for a long time at Archie and asked, "Your brother, Arthur? Your brother Arthur? I did not know that you had a brother with this name, because I knew that you had two twin brothers, not one of them had the name Arthur."

Archie said, "It seems that our news was cut off from you before the birth of Arthur, yes Arthur. The last cluster in the family, and now tell me about you, so I did not understand that you have a sister with eyes that look like me, and her name is Isabella, and is she your age?"

Alexander smiled, laughing. "Yes, I am not joking, and so is her face, so that it looks more like your sister than my sister. If that happens, and we can enter the kingdom, you will see her and see the similarity between you two. She is a girl who loves reading, especially reading stories and novels, and she has a very great knowledge of many stories and legends.

"She was even warning me about the haunted forest and the black goblin and the mysterious character called the (healer) and the dragons, and about a catastrophe that will happen one day because of it, a narration of darkness that no one can escape from, and things I would not have believed had I not been aware of some of them recently, such as the haunted forest and the black goblin after I confirmed the story. As for the other stories, I still believe that they are just nonsense, but considering that my sister may not care about you much, as she is a reclusive girl who only cares about seclusion and delving into those strange stories.

"Right, you didn't tell me, Archie, how you got to the heart of this forest on your own from the village of Kling Ling," then he said jokingly, "Don't you tell me that you arrived in the forest while flying on the back of a winged horse or

on the back of a dragon. Ha-ha-ha-ha, these are the stories of Isabella that she can't stop telling me every time I sit with her."

In fact, Archie was surprised to hear this about Isabella and said to himself that it seems that Isabella has supernatural abilities to bring imagination into reality, but is it possible that Isabella knows Maya? "Ummm, well, Alexander."

Alexander said, "Call me Alex, so you can shorten yourself this long name."

Archie said, "It remains a beautiful name. Well, before I was kidnapped when I was in the woods, I had someone with me and he brought me to the woods because he wanted to help me get to the kingdom in order to get to your father after a long-lost story longer than the nights of the cold winter that almost caused me to be lost forever.

"But while we were on our way at night, we saw the outbreak of fires in the walls of the kingdom and its houses, then he told me to wait a little while to explore the matter and then I was kidnapped and I no longer know anything about him."

Alexander put his hand on his cheek and listened carefully until he asked, "How did you let him go alone to cut that far away from the middle of the desolate forest to the kingdom?" Then Alex said, recalling, "Oh, but how could you see the fires in the walls and houses of the kingdom, when I know that it is impossible to see the kingdom, or even its very high towers?

"And you are in the middle of the forest because the trees of the forest cover the sky, in addition to the lower level of the forest than the great hill on which the kingdom was built."

Archie confidently said, "That's right, Alex, but we saw everything clearly when we were in the sky, me and Maya!"

Alex frowned, his eyebrows stuck together, and said in astonishment, "What? When you and Maya were in heaven? Who is this Maya and what do you mean when you were in heaven?" Suddenly, the sound of a loud call interrupted them. Luca was screaming. The messenger arrived. The messenger arrived. He was a jockey on the back of a saddled horse, raising his front legs until he stopped near them, and the boys behind him looked at him like a farmer's longing for the clouds of rain in the dry time.

Until the knight jumped off his horse and almost stumbled, until Alex said pessimistically, "This is a bad omen. He is hoping for a big promotion and he will hit three birds with one stone when you, Alex, break your father's thorn, and prove that your father is your supporter in this rebellion, and here the evil wing of the kingdom will be victorious.

"He prepared a squad of three cavalry squads, about twenty horsemen, to besiege you from several directions. Therefore, you must hurry to escape towards the coast, even if the road there is fraught with dangers. But it is easier for you than to twist your father's hand to subdue him, and you are the reason for that, and I have brought you food for your horses, and I may help you to stay as long as possible until you reach the coast."

Alexander said in his misery, "Losing is easier for me than being the cause of my father's humiliation and breaking his thorn from those criminals. Thank you, Leon, I appreciate that."

Then Alex looked at the forest with great sadness, knowing the bad and dangerous of what he will face in it, "And I do not hide from you that the hope before you have vanished by sitting here, if you head forward towards the village of Kling Ling, they will realise you quickly. Spies are everywhere, the lands are flat, and it is difficult to escape or hide. If the choice is towards the north, the chain of black mountains does not end, and you will not be able to climb them except by the rise of your souls."

Then the knight Leon added, with his eyes revolving between the boys, as if he had noticed a big change. "Who is this boy? And where is Nathan?"

Sebastian said, "He is the son of Abraham, Alex's cousin, and he is the best kind of man he takes as a supporter."

The knight said, "Or is he the son of Abraham, the former commander of the king's private guard?"

Alex said, "Yes, it is him and I think he will surpass his father."

The knight rejoiced and said, happily overwhelmed with happiness, "How glad I am to know you, Archie. Oh, I forgot this book. From your sister, Isabella, Alex, I asked to give it to you, so that it might benefit you or instil in you a love of adventure and patience until you win, as she said, How lucky you are to have your sister who asks about you every morning."

Alex laughed and he said looking at Archie, "How much I told you that she was a girl from another world, if you gave me a dagger, it would be better than these papers. Keep the book, Archie, and enjoy reading it."

As soon as Archie grabbed the hardcover book, as if it was a thousand years old book, as the girl seemed to be writing deeply and immersed, and revisited it many times, as it seemed that it had been used up a lot, and it was titled Another

World, until Archie felt a cold shiver in his heart, colder than the cold north wind when it suddenly blew and when he randomly opened it, his eyes widened greatly as he saw a drawing of a white winged horse riding on his back a man in black clothes from his head to the soles of his feet, no trace of any features of any part of his body until curiosity became more and his hands sweating and he turned the pages quickly until he was shocked by what he saw and turned his head back, shocked to himself, he said, "Damn this Maya!"

Chapter 16

REBELLIOUS PRINCESS

Maya looks from the balcony of her lofty room from her father's palace at the sky of the underworld, surrounded by a huge red dome from the top, limited in scope.

She missed the real sky, which flew in its pure, calm space, which had no limits to its beauty and subtleties, which always dazzled it from scattered clouds and sometimes harmonious as a rug, like a luxurious bed on which only those with great luck and shining stars and a full moon light as a shining lamp, or in the form of a full moon, like a knight of girls' dreams and nights. Half luminous as the succession of night and day, and the dreams that robbed hearts and souls, and nights in the shape of a crescent moon, like a dream that she wanted to cling to and embrace forever.

All this made her feel that her days were not the same, and that her life was part of the lives of others whom she knew in the upper world, unlike her life in her own world, which she felt was living inside a book whose pages were full of spider webs that she could not.

To live with complete freedom in whatever she wishes and wants, and that her days are repeated and that it is forbidden to mix with only a certain class of creatures, and of course, Maya should have also not taken a step in this world except with the knowledge of her father and the guards around him. And her character that refuses to live shackled by these restrictions, for her exit to the upper world was like exiting from the sandy fire to the Gardens of Eden, but to return to the fire again, no, and none of us should do and think about what Maya thinks, unless the obstacles are great and beyond one's ability.

And while she was in this state and inner peace with herself despite the tightness in her chest, she placed her beautiful chin on her hands and rested on them on the shelf of the high balcony wall, while she saw the highest red sky of the kingdom, and beneath it the city seemed like a sea in a wild night interspersed with the lights of luminous and radiant lanterns to illuminate the paths of those who walk in it. At the height of her enjoyment, she closed her eyes and the cool breeze hit her cheeks.

Until she heard laughter like the laughter of young children, as if passing by in front of her, it did not disturb her peace, but rather made her heart happy. That was how happy she was in the company of the young boys of the palace, from the sons of servants, workers and others, until she saw those two little fairies playing in the air in front of her balcony, each one with four transparent wings in bright phosphorescent colours that did not stop moving. As if honey was poured on those wings, they were more like the wings of a royal bed, the royals, and they wore a beautiful green dress, the length of which ends at the bottom of the knee, and only a little of their beautiful and radiant skin colour is visible.

It was common in the sky of the jinn world to see fairies at night in abundance.

They are stars that adorn the sky, but they are more dynamic, more beautiful, and more dazzling, despite their different beautiful colours, as if they were the gift of the Creator to the people of this world, who only sees light a little.

"It's you two beauties, will you come close to me so I can enjoy watching this beautiful dance!" (Maya's call was to the two fairies)

They look at each other and look at her again. "It's Princess Maya. She's calling us." They come right away. One of them says in her beautiful voice known about the little fairies, nodding her head, greeting her queen, "You are our pride, my lady, to ask us to approach you, and to you it is a nice feeling that we will be in your hospitality tonight."

Maya's face was filled with joy and happiness as she spoke to those two fairies, "Your beauty, you two witches, how I wish I was as beautiful as you two," they came closer, "But it is not hospitality befitting two beauties like you."

The two genies say, "A favour does not need anyone to tell others about it. Everything in it answers everything that others want or what it is. You are beauty and you are all magic and attraction, my lady."

Maya welcomes them, but the intention seems to be something else, "Is there anything you wish I could fulfil for you?"

The two fairies say, "Being here with you, my ladies, was in itself a wish."

Maya says, "So, what do you think of you being as my bridesmaid in the palace?"

The two fairies are astonished, "What are you really saying, my ladies? Maya, yes, I will not find anyone to relieve my sadness but you." (Maya shows a kind of sadness on her face to affect the two fairies for a need in herself.)

The two fairies say, "Your Majesty cannot be sad anymore while we are here. Just unless you point us to it and we will implement it immediately, even if you want us to dance for you all night, we will never stop until you get bored or sleep."

And the other said, "Stirring feelings at the wrong time may harm, so you should not provoke any feelings inside you, my dear, except for your feelings for us now, for it is what you need. And as for what's inside you, leave it temporarily so that you can be happy in this moment."

Maya was very pleased with these positive words and felt that she was in front of two clever fairies and that she had been able to guarantee their loyalty in principle from others who did not feel, but there was one thing left, Maya turned her body from them and greeted the door of her room, then said in the tone of a little girl, pleading with her mother, "There is something in myself, but it is difficult for me, but it is very important, but I find it easy for you, and if you do it, this will be the beginning of the covenant between us, you two beauties."

The two fairies said, "My dear ladies, we are under your hands. Tell us what you ask for, and it will be in your hands."

"I want you to bring the keys to this room that the guards have outside, and to know when they are there and when they are not. That's all. Do you find any difficulty or adventure in the matter? Is that or is it dangerous for you both?"

The two fairies said, with confidence and enthusiasm, "Your Majesty, Is that all that matters to you and grieves you?"

Maya said, sympathising with her more, "Have you seen that, you two beauties, that my concern is easy, but it bears a heavy burden on my chest, so your mistress is no longer as happy as she was because of that key!" Then she pretended to wipe her false tears.

Until the two fairies said, "Don't worry, Your Majesty. Give us a little time, and we'll give you what pleases you." The two fairies spared no effort to make the little princess happy.

Until they broke through the door without the need to open it. This was one of the characteristics of the little fairies that they did not need a gate or a window in order to enter anywhere they wanted. The fairies come out and cross the corridor in the absence of the guard who was sleeping in a deep sleep, and they take the key from him and quickly return to Maya's room who as soon as she saw the key in their hands, her heart fluttered with joy and happiness before Maya uttered her lips.

One of the two fairies say to her, and her name was Affray. We have accomplished the task. This is the key to the room. But the timing does not matter. We can make the guard sleep a deep sleep.

He does not wake up until after a whole day of sleep, the looks of joy and happiness on Maya's face are enough to remove her sadness and bring her out of the depression of the loneliness that she returned to again after leaving Archie in the forest alone, in the meantime, Maya realised that in her hands there are threads of hope, but she must be good. Otherwise, any mistake may turn those threads into noose ropes.

Maya opens a golden jar that was on one of the shelves and takes from it three pieces of sweets, which are not found anywhere, or rather it only made for her, and say to the two fairies this is the contract of friendship between us, come on, each of you take a piece and I am a piece.

Then Maya continues, "So, listen to the plan now and prepare well, you will be my companions in my path forever from this moment, and we will then go to another world that you have never missed before" (with a joy that was never seen on Maya's face before) The enthusiasm within Maya was equivalent to the joy of the mother of her finding her son the only one that was lost and I found it after I lost hope in it.

The two little fairies came out of the room's door to pave the way for Maya's exit, where the guard was falling into a deep sleep.

One of them opens the door for Maya and the fairy Affray precedes them to make sure the road is clear. Maya hurries to get out and is preceded by the fairy Zara and the fairy Affray waves to them at the end of the corridor to advance and that the road is empty.

The corridors in the palace were long and teeming with many bends and many rooms and windows decorated with gilded copper lanterns to increase the power of the lighting, from which the fire was never extinguished.

Maya hurries, but suddenly one of the doors opens in front of her and one of the guards comes out, and his pale green and foul eyes fall into Maya's innocent eyes that were filled with fear, as well as the expressions of astonishment on the guard's face.

Because he knows that she is locked up in her room by order of the king and her father. Then the guard asked her with a hint of doubt, "How did you get out of your room and who brought you out? Unless you're on the run?"

Maya says to herself, and she is still silent, I must show him the truth.

And before Maya began to speak, a very beautiful singing voice, like his melody, came from behind the guard, who began to sway in place from the intensity of drowsiness until he closed his eyes from that sweet melody that came close to his earlobe and drowned it in singing. It was the fairy (Ezra) who was working like a shadow around Maya was expecting such surprises to happen, so she tried to precede Maya with steps forward, the guard falls to his feet, as if the angel of death had taken his soul.

This amazes Maya, who shook her head and smiled from her heart at the supernatural work of the fairy and the greatness of her act. And if it were not for the lack of time and the difficulty of the situation they were in, Maya would not have hesitated to bestow the fairy with the most beautiful thing she owned. Her hands were lighter than a feather in spending everything she owned for the sake of making others happy.

So how about someone who helped her and gave her so beautifully while she is in dire need of that help!

The fairy Affray arrived and she says curtly and she has missed some action, "What is the last of you and why are you standing here?"

The fairy Ezra says, "Nothing, the poor guard wanted to sleep, and we helped him do that with love." Then she turns to Maya and says jokingly, "Isn't that so, my lady Maya?"

"With the cunning smile of friends, of course, beautiful, and he had that, and I hope he will have a good sleep."

The fairy Ezra says excitedly, "So, let's offer our beautiful services to everyone we encounter and finish this matter before it requires services beyond our ability." The three laugh as if they were on a walk on a river of the rainbow from the intensity of what affected them that enthusiasm that strengthened and eased their relationship with each other What a dangerous task that they started in such a short time.

Maya's father had ordered a magic bracelet to be placed in her hand, his job to strip her of all the characteristics of the jinn, and thus she had lost all her abilities.

Of course, if she had not been stripped of all her magical abilities, she would have been able to escape from the palace and escape with ease, although she would be chased by the flying jinn, who had very miraculous properties and more impact.

They had to find a way out of the palace. They couldn't get past all those floors full of guards. Of course, the multitude overpowered the courage and the angelic voice of those two little fairies, who were considered the most important of their fairy weapons to Maya, "Now we have passed the first hurdle, the most important one, and now we have a way. Get out of the palace, Maya."

"And what do you suggest?" The fairy Affray shyly asks Maya.

"Aren't you supposed to have a preconceived plan before?" Maya says, embarrassed.

"Oh, excuse me, it happened suddenly and it crossed my mind for the first time since I saw you, and I never thought of this idea of escape, but listen, since we are here in this place, we are safe for a while, but the only way out of the palace is the main balcony, now at this time of the night, no one can pass in front of it, not even the guards. My father always goes out at the end of the night and begins to contemplate this sky, but this rarely happens because of his constant preoccupation with his infinite wives."

The fairy Affray says with joy, "So, beautiful, then we will hurry to reach the balcony, and then we will fly together!"

Maya says worriedly, "Oh my God, I forgot that these walls in my hands prevent me from using my abilities and therefore I will not be able to fly with you."

They looked at each other in astonishment and said, "Ezra, what, my lady?"

Maya says, embarrassed for the second time, "This matter left my mind and I got excited that I apologise for what I caused you and I got you into my own problems."

"You don't mind, my lady, but tell us, how can we get rid of this bracelet that is in your hand? There must be a way to open it like there was a way to wear it!"

Maya says, "Actually, I don't know, since I woke up with it in my hand, I started feeling very lazy and my body became heavy."

Affray said, "Wait here, I'll be right back!" "Where will you go?"

Ezra says to Maya, "Don't worry, my lady, Affray doesn't say she will do anything unless she is sure of it and his success at the same time."

"Come on, go quickly and don't be late before the news of Maya's escape spreads," Ezra says to Affray.

Affray goes like lightning and disappears from sight. Maya tries to untie the bracelet from her hand and hits her on the walls and on the floor at other times, but to no avail, but the bracelet was shining more and more every time Maya hit her more.

Here, with cleverness and wit, Ezra realises that the radiation from the necklace is only a warning that the holder of the bracelet wants to get rid of it.

"Your Majesty, stop quickly! Hold your position without moving, so that the light really dims." Ezra's prediction came true. The light that radiated and dimmed from the bracelet was only a warning to the commander of the guard who put the bracelet in Maya's hand that Maya wanted to get rid of the bracelet, and a few seconds did not pass until the alarm bells sounded in the corridors. It has the servants' and guards' rooms and Maya's room at the end of the long corridor, and the voices of the guards' feet and their voices begin to rise here and there, while they are still hiding at the door of one of the deserted rooms.

The footsteps of the guards are getting closer and closer, and the Adrian hormone in Maya and Ezra has reached its limit.

But with the cleverness of the fairy, Ezra realises herself and remembers what abilities she has. The fear and the horror of the situation had forgotten her before.

Until she found herself breaking through the door of the deserted room they were leaning on, and if the shadow of the guard looked down on Maya, her eyes staring at that shadow, suddenly she finds herself being pulled back inside the door and suddenly disappearing.

And when the guards arrived, they looked at the place and searched here and there and found nothing. Then they continued the way in search of the fleeing princess. It was Ezra who opened the door and pulled Maya with all her strength in time.

And in a quick reaction, Maya hugs Ezra tightly. "Oh Goddess, how I feel that you are a gift that has come to me from heaven among all creation." Maya cries hard and continues to hold Ezra, who seemed to suffocate due to her small size compared to Maya.

Ezra tries to cough loud to understand that Maya is in tears that she cannot breathe, Maya releases her in order to allow her tears unconscious of what she did to this poor little girl inadvertently. Finally, Ezra breathes a sigh of relief. She walks away, fearing that Maya will come back to notice her again.

Little Fairy tries to search the dark room with curiosity that pushes her inside. Rather, she unleashed herself eager to know exactly where they were. It was a very dark room.

Maya says in a broken voice, crying to the fairy Ezra, "Go directly in front of you and then up from the right to the end of the place and you will find a rope. Try to pull it down."

Indeed, Ezra did what Maya asked her and found a golden rope that she would not have seen had it not been for the intensity of its shine, but it was rather heavy. What?

As for Ezra, the rope was pulled smoothly, as if it were a thread of needle being pulled from the tailor's poison. His curtain rope consisted of two pieces that moved away from each other to the right and the left to let out a shy light that increased as the distance between the two pieces of curtain widened, and the rope continued to withdraw despite Ezra stopping that.

Ezra turned her head back, so it was Maya who was pulling the rope with her, and slowly, a beautiful dim light appeared, illuminating the darkness of the room until the corners of the dark room were illuminated with a light as if it were the full moonlight in the dark night, as if it had revealed the beauty of that room and the luxury of the furniture that was surprising and comfortable to the eye. Maya came forward and opened the balcony door that was covered by the curtain.

The fairy was stunned by what she saw and said to Maya, "What is this place, Your Majesty, Maya?"

Maya answered in a sad voice, "It is my mother's room, Ezra, my mother, who I have never seen in my life and I have never touched except through this picture." (It was the picture of the charming mother of Maya).

Hanging on the wall with the stature of Maya, holding it with a golden frame in the form of four fairies that stick to each corner of the picture frame.

Maya stood on the balcony wall and placed her hand on a statue of a small fairy that was decorating the balcony wall. Maya's mother loved those little fairies. An aesthetic painting, even in the smallest details. Maya's mother was not just a wife and mother (she only realised pregnancy and childbirth from motherhood), but she was a creature like him that was not created in this universe throughout the ages, except for very few, and she was of dazzling beauty.

Long, shiny, bluish black hair, dragged behind her, and this was one of the beauty traits that Maya inherited from her mother.

Until the day came when Maya's father ordered that the fairies not enter the palace again, so that they would not remind him of his wife, whom he considered the light of this universe, and whose death was the reason for his neglect of many things, one of which was his daughter Maya because of his excessive drinking and the large number of maidservants around him that he wanted to forget about. It goes through, but to no avail.

The fairy stands next to Maya's shoulder and puts her head on Maya's in sympathy for her in this sad moment that does not pass for a moment but that she remembers her mother from time to time, but that kind princess could not control herself until she collapsed in a new wave of crying and mourned her luck that did not unite her with her mother even once.

While they were comforting each other, a very white cloud approached them and evaporated quickly as if it were a bubble and exploded revealing what was inside it.

She is the fairy Affray, and with her a group of fairies carrying a rug of corrugated carpet that resembles layers of red waves, large in size, which may be seven meters long and three meters wide. Come on, Your Majesty, quickly, says Affray, and Ezra looks at her in full happiness, and says to Maya, "Didn't I tell you that Affray does nothing without knowing what to do she does! But now, come on quickly, my lady, let's move." A lot of time has been lost. Indeed, the rug is approaching the balcony until it becomes attached to it, and Maya jumps on the rug and begins to move away from the high balcony of the palace, then he sets off by himself without anyone touching him, to the highest sky of the underworld.

Affray says to Maya, "This rug is commanded to get you out of here, so if it rises, it will go off like lightning and will never stop until it brings you out of the underworld. Rest assured, Your Majesty, we know what we are going to do." Affray turns to the fairies and thanks them, and they all say goodbye, and the rug comes out and speeds up more and more to the top of the kingdom to penetrate the red dome.

Maya is surprised to see her father while he is on the balcony looking at her as if asking her (Why my daughter), but with more strange looks, as if this matter was expected to happen one day, Maya did not stop looking at her father's eyes while he looked at her as if it was a look of farewell mixed with several asking him where and what is this matter that it makes a girl who lives a life of luxury and her father is the king of this world to think of escaping while the rug before it reached its speed and approached the sky of the underworld.

So, the flying jinn, numbering five, surrounded the rug from all directions, screaming the fairy in the rug (O flying carpet, I command you to reach the height of your speed and to break through the clouds and to lose the soldiers behind us)

The rug responds with a firm voice, as if it were the echo of a cave, "Well, my lady."

Affray says to her sister Ezra and Maya, "Hold on tight, we are facing a very difficult matter." The rug disappears from the eyes of the flying jinn among the clouds, and suddenly they appear from the side of the rug again.

One of them stretches out his hand to hold Maya, the pound jumps up, and she bites him in his hand, and Maya holds her before the strong current of passion takes her, due to the speed of the rug, the rug exceeds the flying jinn again and they appear again.

They are behind the flying carpet but this time each of the flying jinn was holding the edge of the rug in order not to escape from them.

Affray looks at Maya and says to her in a loud voice, "Cut the bracelet, I will cut it quickly in any way."

Maya begins to bite the bracelet, as it was made of emerald bracelets, which had two iron bars of copper, and they were tied with a rope.

Maya tries to use all her strength and bites and bites in the hope that she will cut the bracelet, but the situation started to get worse, as the jinn slowed down the speed of the flying carpet until it remained between them and the sky of the underworld, a very large black cloud.

The speed of the rug slowed down so much that they almost thought that it would stop until the rug entered at the beginning of the dark cloud. Here, the jinn took out ropes and tied the rug on each side in order to establish their control over it. Maya glimpsed a button in front of her, as if a revelation inspired her to something, as she rubbed a rope. The stubborn bracelet with all its strength was at the tip of the wing of the fairy, which was like a sharp moose until she cut the bracelet and got rid of it, and she felt as if a thorn had been removed from her chest, and she felt a force inside her, like electric charges flowing through all her veins. Her face resulted from such a rapid transformation in her Soul Physique.

But she resisted that because of the embarrassment of the situation, which was for them the last chance, and she says in a low voice between herself and herself (we will not leave hope, I will not leave hope).

Meanwhile, the flying carpet had reached the midst of the depths of the terrifying cloud, which rained down on them with continuous thunder and lightning until the place became darker, like the darkness of the dark dawn before it cleared.

Maya throws the bracelet away to get rid of the flying jinn tracking them. In the darkness of the cloud, the jinn had put their hands on Maya and her two friends, but what happened was not considered, a shout came over the place that made the flying jinn scattered in the air as if they were leaves scattered in the air from the strength of a storm wind.

It was Maya, she regained her supernatural abilities, and she caught the two fairies, Ezra and Affray, and put her hands on their ears and hugged them. In this case, Maya no longer needs the flying carpet, because she can now run faster than the flying carpet, driven by the enthusiasm of what she did, which was the last hope. Then it goes as quickly as possible out of the sky of the underworld and heads to the only exit that separates the upper and lower worlds.

Maya breaks through all sound barriers because of its high speed as if it were a lightning strike, even if it came close to reaching the dark path of bats, which was the exit gate from the underworlds, or specifically the historical well of Barhout.

Affray and Azar say to Maya, "Now it is our turn, Your Majesty, to show you the way."

Maya says to them and fatigue has destroyed her, "It is for you."

The two fairies leave Maya's lap and set out in the pitch darkness to illuminate the path in front of Maya with their radiant wings.

But in the meantime, Maya senses that something is in their tracks and thinks that it is only the captain of the guard, so she hastened a little.

But she knew that the one who followed them was closer than she thought and that he was around the corner to surprise them and catch her, but this time she showed a different feeling for what was inside her, and Maya did not find anything but to confront him with her fears instead of continuing to escape.

Until I made a sudden and dangerous decision this time and stopped in the middle of the pitch-black darkness of the cave and suddenly turned back.

To face fate this time face to face, it was really a brave decision that stopped the impulses of fear that were in her from the first moment of escaping, but the surprise was that what was in their tracks was nothing but the flying carpet, which was one of the most important factors for the success of escaping from the palace and the underworld. Without it, the plan would not have been completed and would have been executed at that moment.

Maya lit her eyes to reveal this hidden stalker until she said in astonishment, relax the tension of her tight nerves, that you are the flying carpet?

He replied, "Yes, I am the flying carpet, Your Majesty, I would not leave an order that I commanded until I completed it! Even the two fairies didn't expect that, oh my god, it's the flying carpet!"

The two fairies rush and start jumping on him and playing with him joyfully and merry when they meet again in the midst of this darkness in which there is no light but the light of their wings, despite the worrying situation in which they are, but that did not prevent them from expressing their joy and happiness, even for a moment, did I not tell you, my majesties, that it is something.

Maya says, "I didn't know that I would be so happy with you. It seems that he has come at the right time. I can't stand it any longer. I can't hide from you that I have tried a lot and that I can't go on any more than this until she threw herself on the magic carpet from the intensity of fatigue."

Ezra said in a sad tone, "Poor Maya, how much she suffered today and how much she cried as well, but now it's time for you to rest and it's our turn to finish the rest. Come on, you magic carpet, take us to where you are commanded, and go to the world of light and lights, a world beyond the earth."

"Ok madam," magic carpet said.

And the it set off carrying the three girls on top of it, but quietly and with peace of mind they had not found for a whole night.

Accidents happen suddenly in our lives and it is not necessary that you wait for a happy event to find happiness, but sometimes it is behind the biggest tragedies that you encounter and you think that it may be the reason for your end from the earth and your destruction.

However, your belief in your dream and holding fast to it becomes like the rays of the dim morning sun, which only turns the darkness of the night like death into a light like the birth of the hope of life again for all creatures that cling to the hope of sunrise to seek life anew.

Maya wakes up and finds herself in a small hole surrounded by two fairies and a magic carpet covering the hole of the hole as a protective curtain for them Where are we! Maya says in a wailing voice the two fairies eagerly answer, "We chose to rest here a bit. We found this place and felt it was safe and we didn't want to wake you up Your Majesty, you were in dire need of rest after what you went through."

Maya came out of the hole and saw that everything around them was covered with snow white that had fallen heavily while they were falling into a deep sleep and warmth like sleeping by the fireplace of his hearth.

Even the lake, which was a little close to the hole, had already frozen, Maya rolled her head and sometimes her eyes in amazement. Here and there, as if something caught her attention, she came out of the cave crawling on her knees amid the astonishment of the two Gentiles who thought that Maya might have lost the ability to walk, which raised their fears for her. Maya approaches the small lake from which a small stream was branching, then turns her head behind her into the hole. Then it seemed to her as if the place began to change colour in front of her with the colours of spring until she wiped her eyes to make sure that it was a pure fantasy.

The two fairies say to Maya, while they are in a state of doubt and terror, "As if the place had liked you, Your Majesty?"

Maya to the two fairies, "Did I tell you to stop here?" The two fairies looked at each other, wondering, "You have been in a deep sleep since you fell on the magic carpet, while we were in the dark cave! Yes, I like it and how I don't!"

The two fairies look at each other and wonder on their faces! Maya continues and her mind was farther than it actually was, or she was delirious in herself! Then she added, as she spoke to herself, "It was the first place he brought me here!"

Then she looked at a place close to the hole and behind until she got up and walked a little, and there was a piece protruding on the ground, rectangular in shape, three meters long, and there were small pieces here and there that had been covered by snow. It was nothing but a beautifully shaped dining table covered with pieces of heavy silk cloth. The snow melted easily and the food was ready to eat since Maya put her hand on it.

The two fairies were still watching in amazement and silence what their eyes saw. The effect of that moment on that gentle fairy, Maya, became apparent when she learned that chance had led her to the same place of their first meeting, Archie, as if the clock had turned back a little.

But this time without the beloved Archie.

Ezra said in amazement, "How is this, my lady! Where did this food come from, here, in this frozen place, in these pots?"

Then Affray also says, her eyes focused firmly on the pots, "But hey, aren't these pots like the pots for the palace kitchen, or am I imagining that!"

Maya gives them a sad smile and says, "This is what brought you here with me, and this is what got me out of the kingdom, my dear. I no longer think about what my priorities are now, do I follow my mind or my heart? And if I did this or that, what would the consequences be? The pound of afar is approaching it. We have been with you from the beginning. We will support you, help you, my dear. We will guide you to reach what you believe in without turning around to the consequences.

"If each of us thought about the consequences before he thought about reaching his goal, no one would move on this earth, we must move forward, Your Majesty. All we ask of you now is to gather your strength, and we will take you on this journey to the end, and remember, Your Majesty, the end will not be worse than what we are in. So be it, as long as we are on the path of hope, we will not lose anything."

The words of Affray, that little fairy with a wise mind, had a high morale boost and a very strong impact on the soul of the already collapsed Maya, psychologically, emotionally, as well as physically.

Maya looks at the magic carpet and says, "How can I call him?"

Affray says, "What do you need him for?"

Maya says, "Every time I look at him, I feel very sleepy, it was indeed one

of the most beautiful things I put my head on."

Maya says like she heard from the fairy, "O carpet of the wind, come to me?

And quickly the magic carpet came to the bottom of Maya's feet and slipped lightly from under her until he dropped her on top of him."

Maya laughs hard and says, "I didn't want this, the wind carpet." Then he suddenly threw it from his back onto the snow, amid the silent and embarrassed laughter of the fairies, until the fairy said, feeling a laugh inside her, "That he executes every word said to him with one letter and with all accuracy."

Maya, lying on the ice and mocking what happened, "Oh, well, I understand now, so I must choose my words very carefully, or else I will find myself in a situation that is not to be envied, like this situation that made me laugh in your eyes."

Lying on the snow, she takes a handful of snow in her hands and says firmly, jokingly, "Now you will pay the price for your laughter at me."

Until she took in her hands as much snow as she could and made it into two balls with her hands, then threw the first snowball at Ezra, who lowered her head, and the snow was in Affray face.

Who was behind her sister, Ezra turned and burst out laughing at her sister, who did not hesitate to take a handful of snow and throw it in her sister's mouth, who made Maya enter into a fit of laughter until she also received snowballs from Affray and even the magic carpet was not spared from those snowballs, which he, in turn, took some snowballs with the tip of his robe and started stoning everyone without exception and started to have fun and run in the snowy plains between the four of them once while they were on the ground and times while they were flying in the air. Happiness and joy on the faces of the three girls who went on an adventure that they did not expect. Beautiful laughter rises across the quiet white plains that witnessed the most beautiful meeting between two beautiful people belonging to two different worlds that do not meet.

Until the sky played the sounds of the violin and the scene of the warm morning sun rays penetrating the cold heavy clouds of snow as if there is a glimmer of hope coming to catch your heart and change your sadness into a joy that you did not expect to happen at such a time and place.

Perhaps this is what the three fugitives were lacking to remove the shipments of fear and heavy worries that accompanied them throughout that difficult night and so is life if you do not have time to enjoy it, laughter and fun do not expect someone to give you part of his time to be happy in it. Only you can create and create happiness for himself, even in the most difficult circumstances, because your sadness will not bring you joy and will not fulfil your dreams.

Only you can do it and you can do miracles with your mind, hands, feet and tongue. Just unleash your imagination and work with it.

Chapter 17

BLACK GOBLIN

Heavy snow has been falling since the beginning of the morning on the camp, to inspire peace and tranquillity in the soul, to ease the fear of the unknown that they were forced to.

Therefore, they have no choice but to go through this forest inhabited by evil to reach the coast, and then leave their hometown behind them beyond the sea in the far south, and they do not know when they will return, or they may never return to their kingdom and villages.

They had prepared breakfast before the morning hope dawned again, and they were in the abundance of freedom that might be taken away from them at any moment if they misjudged time and situations.

It was agreed that they would move while they were divided so that they would not be arrested if they fell into the ambush of Commander Glister, who would not stop until Alex was arrested, as if he were on a werewolf hunting trip that terrified the world.

He realises what will bring him great benefit if he succeeds in hunting him, thus the adventure ends and every dream collapses before it sees the light.

Alex chose the style of the wolf pack in leadership, where he is the alpha in the foreground because he knows the way more than others, and Archie is the betta leading those in front of him from behind to protect their backs with a proud spear.

Alexander approached Archie, who was busy feeding the raptor chicks, who were very attached to them and had signs of ferocity early on from the way they were eating.

They fight with each other in fierce battles that do not stop until after the intervention of Archie.

And he said to him in a whisper, "Let's hurry to move so that we realise the longest possible period of this day, and the day of this day will not be long," but Clementine, who used to spy on speakers and intrude most of the time, had another opinion with a sudden spontaneous question behind Alex's ear, "But how will we ride our horses in the midst of these snows that may make us deceive us while crossing the lakes and rivers that you told us are in the middle of the forest?"

Alex said, "A smart boy, so we had to move. Now the water does not freeze in an hour, not even in ten hours. We will need five hours at least to pass the most difficult part of the forest, so walking along the river will help us to shorten half the time and more than half the trouble of walking instead of crossing the forest, but caution remains the master of the situation, and we will need half a day for the forest to freeze. If the snow continues to fall like this.

"Then we will turn on the river to continue the path and avoid the biggest surprises that may hinder us, which I do not think we will face extraordinary things, but here the metal of strong men appears.

"Boy, if we thought everything would go well, we'd be in our mothers' homes now, Archie. But hey, since you said lakes and rivers would freeze! Why not wait for a day or at least half a day to walk over the lakes and rivers than to walk beside them since you told me that the road is full of intertwined trees and thorns and some natural obstacles such as hills and cliffs!"

Alex replied in turn, "If I had time, I wouldn't have said anything other than what you said, Archie, but you yourself have heard the warning of the Knight Leon from the Glister campaign, which I do not guarantee that they have already reached the outskirts of the camp, they will not hesitate to hunt us as we were hunting birds. But there is only one outlet that we can go through, and it will bring us back to the kingdom from under the earth."

Archie said with great eagerness, "What happiness, but how?

Alex said in frustration, "I am afraid that I will disappoint you, because it is in a place that is several leagues away from us. It is located inside a deep cave. It is better that we first focus on escaping and surviving, and then we will have other future plans to return, but now our presence here and our return to the kingdom is literally over."

Snow is falling twice as fast as if a giant has opened snow bags on their heads and advanced towards the forest. The thickness of the horses' ankles, which seems to be going to need more effort than planned. As for Archie, he was on Clementine's horse flanked by him, and on his back, was the large bag and inside it were all the raptor chicks, which were strong boned, until I learned to fly leisurely.

The place seemed to become more and more narrow for them, with the tightly intertwined trees crowding around it, and the slopes chasing the very white heights, and the place seemed to be lost for the first time.

But the insistence within them to triumph over themselves more than anything is what made them not fear a path Alex knows as well as he knows now that with his friends there is danger lurking in the way that only time separates them from.

After more than five hours of walking, they reached the end of the road besieged between the trees and rocks of the forest, as if a door had been opened for them to enter a spacious place, where in front of them was an area empty of all trees in a circular shape, like a frozen lake, of equal length and width, approximately four kilometres.

Archie was more than tired of the heaviness of the raptors that were gaining weight day by day and said murmuring, "I think it is the right place to take our breath and rest for a while I feel like I carry a mountain on my back Oh heaven, have mercy on us."

Alex replied angrily, "But if you drown, then don't blame me."

Archie said, wondering, "How do we drown while we are on dry land?"

Alex answered confidently, "This place is nothing but a fragile frozen lake, and if you ask me, I will choose to rest among the trees, even if the place is narrow, but at least I will ensure that there is no surprise like sitting on the surface of a frozen lake."

Archie indignantly said, "Damn is this a lake? How is that and no effect or any features of its existence!"

Clementine said that the severity of the heavy snowfall hastened its freezing and hid the features of the lake and its shores.

As for Sebastian, when he realised that they were going to stop here, he got off his horse and put his things and took out the portable bed and threw it over the snow and wrapped it on his body and fell asleep quickly without anyone asking permission. His strength did not help him to listen to the endless arguments and discussions.

Likewise, Luca, who was yawning all the time, as well as the others who got down on his knees and dipped his head in the piles of snow, and some of them fell on his back with great relief, like the one who entered heaven at that time Alex realised that everyone's fatigue had reached a great amount.

And he said, "Then, let this be our temporary resting place, and whoever wants to eat, let him eat what he has of fruits without cooking, so that we can make it easier for us to move later, before it gets dark."

Until he looked at the tops of the trees and noticed as if a wind was moving its upper branches against the direction of the wind, which he sensed its wind as it struck his face, which made him feel a deep fear in himself, which he thought would happen and hide it from others so that it would not lead to an early break in their resolve while they rest.

And as soon as there was peace and tranquillity, they calmed themselves, the snow stopped and the wind blew even more. They heard the sound of a woman's cry, as if demons had violently snatched her soul.

Everyone noticed, and Clementine said with horror, "Did you hear what I heard, or am I imagining?"

Fat Martin said in panic, "I swear I heard a woman's scream!"

The source of the sound suggested that it was from afar, but the fear made them feel as if they were among them until they realised that there was no safety here and they had no longer drowsiness.

The sound was repeated again, and the horses shrieked with fear and turned around in confusion, until all the boys gathered in one place, eyes trembling with fear, and they looked at the other, perhaps hearing what would reassure him and tell him that this was nothing but the sound of a passing winter wind, even if it was a lie.

Alex looked at Archie with pale eyes and said, "I told you I'm telling you that I'm lying some of Isabella's stories and believing some of them, and here's one of hers that seems to come true now."

"I don't see that you mean the black goblin! Right?" Archie said slowly.

Alex said, "But she only goes out at night, and when the moon is full in the middle of the month, according to the novel, and I believe her now."

Archie said, "And did she describe her to you and how to escape from her or how dangerous she is or have you seen she before?"

Alex felt that he was weaker than ever as he looked at the boys and how the time would pass on them while they were in anticipation. Archie wanted to go to get the novel and see it, perhaps he would find something useful. He realised that Alex had entered a spiral of intense psychological fear until Alex told him,

"Don't go, she's read everything, and nothing will stop her except to rob the souls of what you find in front of her. As for the solution, I have prepared a station for this expected moment, which is to hurry away, and when evening comes, we put the horses behind us and in front of them and we are in the middle of them. If she come from any direction, she will pounce on any creature that has a soul in front of she, regardless of its size and type. Otherwise, there is no other solution, so let's hurry as fast as we can to set off over the frozen lake."

As soon as they set out over the lake, it suddenly became dark and quietly as the room was after the candles had gone out.

When the time of fate comes, everything changes and miracles and miracles occur.

This was enough to stop the horses from walking suddenly and stood on their hind feet and floundered with their front feet high in the air in fright, then circled around themselves several times without stopping, as he felt the angel of death but did not see him, then Alex shouted, "Now it's time to get off the horses and make two horses run in front of us and the rest of the horses drag them by their bridles and put them behind you."

Indeed, they set out over the frozen lake, running from fate to destiny. There is no escape from your destiny except by embracing another beautiful destiny that may be waiting for you or may not.

Alex led the front horses so as not to get far from them and behind him the boys, then Archie held a rope with several ends tied to the bridle of each horse in order not to advance and trample them or not flee in another direction and the horses were their shield and their last fortress with his other hand held the proud spear, ready for the battle of survival, until he knows for a moment that it's time for the raptor chicks to part.

It is not possible to take their souls without any guilt, but it is enough. He was seeking the guilt of killing their mother until he stopped and opened the big bag carrying the chicks and shouted at them in a savage voice until they flew in fright without understanding, but they did not move away, but instead became hovering above them and Archie screamed hard at her and started throwing pebbles at them.

Go away, go back to the top of the branches, but she still thinks that he might change his mind suddenly, and they were the ones who saw in him their tender mother in this world, but the effect of Archie to harden them even once in order to give them life for a long life and when he saw that she did not move away, he took the arrows from his back and aimed towards them to frighten them until the chicks shouted at him while they were in the air in anger, then fled to the forest quickly while shouting pain and sorrow for what happened from Archie. I don't know why he did that, but he was undoubtedly in order to save their lives without them realising.

Alex and the rest reached the other end of the forest, which was full of tall, empty tree stalks. From the branches, it looked like a maze made of wood, and when Archie arrived after them, he dragged the horses.

He found everyone as if they had turned into stony bodies as they looked up in panic, and their eyes almost popped out of their sockets as they looked at the top of the hill on the right.

The black goblin that Archie was afraid to confront or even imagine her appearance had appeared He felt an electric shock that paralysed his movement. He did not expect that the black goblin would be so ugly, leading to death for fear, but his sense of great responsibility and focus on saving everyone, no matter the cost, made him bring out the true leader who was inside him and called Alex, and he said, "Go now and I will occupy it and I will try to offer her the horses as an offering to her. Maybe we can buy some time and I'll catch up with you quickly."

Alex said, "I don't think it's a feasible idea unless you want to kill yourself, Archie."

Archie said with shaky confidence, "It is better to die trying to survive than to die like a sheep that surrendered itself to a shepherd's knife."

Go and don't think about Archie, I know how to save myself.

He thought it was a good trick, and without realising it, he found himself calling out to the fairy in a brave and confident voice, hiding the fear of evil within him.

And he said to himself, "Death, death." Then he shouted loudly, "We thought that you are the queen of this forest, and that the queens honour their guests, and that we are waiting for your generosity."

After she was watching the escape of others, she saw him from under the darkness of her face, where he could see nothing but two eyes of burning blue fire, and her thick and long braids in the form of red cobra snakes with prominent teeth playing everywhere in the air.

As for her body, it was like a bird's nest stick covered in a black loose rag. Archie's heart trembled in fear, unable to control the nervous horses as he hid behind them and felt the shaking of his eyes and blurred vision as she approached him after she came down quietly from the top and has a rustling sound that makes you want to scratch your eardrum so hard, he felt that he must and it has a strong effect on his eyes. Perhaps she was taking his sight from him until he looked at the tip of the spear, which was made of thick diamond, and saw the fairy coming to him in the reflection of the diamond surface of the spear tip, so he avoided looking at it until she said in a voice like a creaking and whistling of the wind, "You will have what you asked, boy!"

Until I stared at one of the horses and fixed a place and even the horse was approaching it without feeling its head!

Archie looked in astonishment at the horse, whose body was twitching vigorously, without moving a finger, and it came out of its anus with a lot of dung and huge urine, until he saw the horse's skin sticking to the bones of its rib cage, like the one who died of starvation.

This demon has done all this with this strong horse, so how can I when I am a weak creature?

In a moment, he felt, as if an ember was burning in his chest, he wanted to remove it from its intense heat, until he was surprised that it was the necklace that Maya had given him, and he could not bear to leave it in his grip due to its intense heat, and he said, thinking, "I don't have any weapon now. Perhaps this necklace that came from the world of the jinn is my only hope."

Then he threw the necklace as a last solution into the body of the black goblins, which quickly sank into her body until she suddenly stopped, and the horse fell down like a mummy of bones covered with skin.

The goblin looked at herself in a frightening silence until her body started to ignite from the inside as smoke seemed to come out of her body after she froze in place as she looked at what Archie did not comprehend what he had thrown inside her!

Until the evil goblin felt that what the boy had done was not normal, he paralysed her without realising it, but it happened in the blink of an eye, but it seems that the effect of the necklace was stronger than just a burn, which made her open her mouth very slowly as if she wanted to get something out.

Until a loud scream came out of her in the form of a wind with a strong fire that threw Archie and the horses away from it and rolled hard on the ground until they fell among the surrounding bushes, which were like a nest of very intertwined branches, it is like a pile of fishing nets stacked on top of each other, and the forest caught fire from the intensity of the scorching sound of everything that reaches it.

Only Archie who looks the necklace had a role in his fortification.

The forest is burning and the snow is falling again, the fire is lighting up the darkness of the forest, and the fire has mixed with snow and light with darkness, as a mixture of Archie's current situation and his rosy dreams, which he believed that this life had given him the path to reach happiness furnished with roses the moment he met Maya.

Archie takes advantage of his distance from the eyes of the black goblins and tries so hard to crawl through the thicket of bushes that has become a veil between him and the angry goblin seeing him on the hill until he is shocked when he hears Clementine's voice calling, "Where are you, Archie!"

Archie grumbled, "What the hell did that idiot come up with now and at this time?"

Archie had no escape from advancing, crawling under the canopy of the bushes, and succumbing to the thorns and sharp edges of some razor-like rocks hidden under the snow, trying to get close to Clementine's voice, until he came out of the heap of bushes and pointed with his hands to Clementine whispering, "Look here, Clementine, look here, you idiot!"

Archie did not find it necessary to accomplish the task himself, after realising that there was something he was looking after and guarding, and he did not see it or realise it with his eyes, but at least that feeling grew inside him, and this made him sharpen his resolve with determination and courage despite the ordeal they were in.

He got up and rushed towards Clementine and turned his head back to make sure that the place was clear and realised that the time had come and that the goblins, no matter how much harm they had suffered, she must return to them until he jumped on Clementine and put his hand on his mouth for fear of screaming or showing an unexpected reaction.

He had caused them to draw the attention of the goblins hidden behind the burning flames behind them, but Clementine could not control himself until he started crying and his body twitched violently as he pointed his finger up a little, then Archie understood that before turning his head and then slowly turning his head and raising his eyes a little and if the goblin was standing in front of them few steps away, her entire body was ignited and turned into a mass of black fire with sparks of snakes that writhed above her and released their poison in the air.

To spread all the drops of evil that come out of it to all parts of the forest and infect every living body, and with a voice that does not resemble her voice for the first time and is sharper on the ear, the goblin said, "Have you heard that snake poison harms a snake? More than one tyrant and their demons perished at my hands until they fled and left this land to me alone, so what do you care about a human being who has no trick or benefit for himself!"

Then the goblin laughed in a very malicious voice, a laugh full of smoke like an old smoke that made Archie put his hands to his ears to avoid harming the sound of her murderous laugh.

Then she added, "Now you will see how I tear your limbs that tremble with my claws, and I will enjoy your screams with you, and with my little children I will enjoy drinking your blood, which does not seem to be sweeter than the taste of those who preceded you."

She looked behind her eyebrows at her evil thirsty snakes that launched an attack on Archie, who was able to turn his fear into a flame of anger from the fire of anger and survival instinct until a white aura formed around him with a strong flash a thread of rays like lightning came out from between his fingers towards the goblins, and their raging snakes made the heads of the snakes fly in the sky of the forest until all those flaming heads fell on the snow as if they were meteors from the sky that hit the earth!

Archie did not believe what happened and what he saw?

The snakes were killed with all this ease, which caused the goblins to be savage and expelled all their anger until their size tripled. Against everything that is his enemy, no matter how great his stature.

Archie grabbed the spear to deal her a decisive blow, but it seems that Archie miscalculated the back force of the pound, which was not intimidated by that spear, which to her was like a piece of worn wood, and did not give him enough time to pounce on him as a claw at the prey with all its strength and weight until it fell on Archie. His back and crouched completely on him until Archie felt his face crushing in the snow as she said in a voice like a crackling roar and grabbed his face with her terrifying bronze hands and directed him towards her eyes.

He knew that she was not doing this in order to give him some parenting advice, but rather in order to take his soul from his body, which for her is considered a meal, as he saw the tape of his life in the eyes of the goblins!

She opened her mouth and only saw a dark black hole in front of his eyes, expanding more and more as she sucked the sparkle of his eyes, and he felt numbness in his limbs and severe dizziness in his head, as if he had surrendered to his end and his destiny this time.

But suddenly something strange happened, as the goblin began to stiffen and lowered her hands from Archie's face and lifted her head back with staggering steps, distributing her screams, unable to move, as if someone had dragged her by the hair, unable to control herself, and as the goblin turned to look behind her.

Even the beautiful fairy, Maya had used all her power to stop the goblin's magic and weaken her power and she says to the goblin, arching her eyebrows, "You won't get him as long as I'm alive!"

At the same time, the two little fairies, Affray and Ezra, were trying to raise Archie's head and get him out of the snow pile to breathe again.

As Maya continues to use her power to drive away the malicious goblin until Maya rises to the top to release all her power and absorb the potential energy of the goblin demon to burn it completely, causing the goblin to shrink in size and her body begins to wilt like a cut rose.

Meanwhile, the goblin spoke after feeling that she had lost the battle after she tasted humiliation and brokenness. She said, begging Maya, "I will give you something that no one in the world will give you. If you promise to leave me, I will give you the secret of the healer, Masa, and you will not find in this universe anyone who gives you that secret. Only if you leave me, I promise to leave you and leave this forest forever, and you will not see me forever."

Maya says with suspicion, "It is one of your schemes that is not hidden from one of us. You felt that your death was approaching, demon."

The goblins said, "I am too weak to turn against you, as you can see, I have no power and no help, I have completely lost my strength. There is a tree called the Adam tree that grows only one apple in a lifetime, and this plant does not grow until once every thousand years. Whoever eats the apple lives and never dies, and that one person should eat it and no one should share it with him, otherwise it will not do him any good if he shares the apple with someone else. And that this tree is not only found at the top of Mount Clementador, the highest mountains surrounding the kingdom, the goblin demon had magical energy for those who listened to it, attracting him to it without realising, and this is what happened to Maya, who listened completely, the offer is generous and tempting."

Until she finds herself subconsciously approaching the black goblin and the goblin continues to transmit its magical energy towards Maya without her feeling it as she listens to that strange secret, Maya felt numbness in her body and was unable to control her movement. When she approached the savage goblin, she was surprised by calling her with her tongue, which was like a chameleon's tongue, five meters long until it wrapped around Maya's body and began squeezing it after she dropped her to the ground, and indeed what happened, Maya suspected him of the malice and treachery of the goblins, and the battle equation changed here, as the old goblins became the one who controlled Maya who was overthrown by the goblin's tongue like a thunderbolt that stunned Maya and paralysed her abilities completely and she was unable to do anything. The goblin pulled Maya towards her and did to her as you did with Archie, to take her soul from her eyes, and she put her eyes in Maya's eyes to steal her life from her.

As for the two fairies, she collapsed with weeping and weeping, until Affray started throwing snowballs at the black goblins, and Affray said to her, "You filthy devil, leave my mistress at once, filthy tongue chameleon, come on, leave my mistress, at once, take this and this and this."

And she keeps throwing snowballs that were for the black goblins as if they were the buzzing of flies.

She couldn't do more than that and in a fleeting moment, like the angel of death kidnapping the souls, a bright, sharp sword cuts the tongue of the black goblin and the tongue knot untied from Maya's body, and she heard a voice from behind her approaching and talking to her to check on her, is she still alive?

But it seems that the goblins do not want to end the matter at this point. Rather, it seems that they are determined to have a very bad conclusion for everyone, after she rose again, and she is rising like the eruption of a dormant volcano and roared with a savage sound until frightening bats came out of her body and flew to the sky and returned to attack everyone. The goblins raised their hands higher and muttered strange words, like a magician casting his magic spell. Until the trees began to move and rub against each other with great violence, and the branches smashed, and the winds blew from all directions, until the two little fairies almost flew away with the wind.

If only they were caught by that saviour who was none other than Alex, but it seems that the goblins have regained their energy until they swell up again.

Which forced Alex to cover Maya and the two fairies with his body from the blowing of the evil winds that turned the broken tree branches into stray arrows in every direction until they thought that they were impossible to do.

But the goblin did not complete that terrifying muttering, until the spear of pride in Archie's hand had pierced her skull and completely destroyed her and her evil forever, after she had fallen on her face and her black blood had stained snow-white with her uncleanness.

For the first time in a very long time, as our time is far from the time of the creation of the universe, this forest will rest and find calm, and the worst creature in the world will be absent from it forever.

The legend of the black goblins ends and all the creatures of the jungle will rejoice on that day.

Alex turns to the back and only sees Maya's traces engraved in the snow that was thrown over him, she rushed to Archie and put his head on her thigh until she lifted him on the magic carpet, the warmest on the ground. Amidst Alex's scrutinising gaze, he forgot about Archie, to the surprise of what this girl and the two fairies around her were, and where they came from this giant rug.

It was amazing until Alex told her how he was now and his eyes did not stop checking every part of her!

Maya felt a remorse and that she was the reason for everything that happened to Archie, otherwise he would be in the kingdom now enjoying prosperity and security. She did not even hear Alex's voice until the fat Martin said, "It seems she didn't love you from the first time, Alex, but it doesn't prevent you from trying again."

Until Maya turned to Alex with her long hair that scattered snowflakes around him, and Alex was mesmerised for the first time, as if someone had put the moon in his hands, contemplating her comforting beauty for the eye.

Then she said in a sad voice, "The poor man seems to have suffered a lot, but I am sure that he will rise quickly if Archie will never stop him. As for this fatigue, it is a simple symptom like a king's rest after a fishing trip."

Even in her analogy, she was trying to make Archie significant, and Maya turned and asked Alex, "Who are you?"

Archie interrupted them, muttering words like the one crying for help in a pale and weak voice until he said, "I can smell Maya or am I preparing for that!"

Maya said happily, and that suffocated her, "Rather, he is preparing for you, Archie."

He replied with a heavy tongue, after opening his eyes in half, "But the voice is Maya's voice, or does I also imagine?"

Maya was silent as she meditated on him until her eyes filled with tears after hearing him and she said, "Yes, this is I, Maya. I would not have left you, and you were not in need of me. How can I leave you when you need me, Archie, here I have found you now, and I will not leave you this time, because I am ashamed of what I caused you? I was the cause of everything that happened to you, Archie." Maya's words were the right antidote at the right time until he put his hand on her thigh to lean on his torso and then sat cross-legged after regaining consciousness until he saw Maya in front of his eyes for the first time since. To separate in the forest until he kept feeling her with his hands as if he was seeing her for the first time and said, "Yes, you are the love fairy who brought me out of the real world to the world of fantasy that I still live in until now and I do not

want to leave him as long as you are the one who tells the story."

Until he asked her in astonishment as he looked at the two fairies and said, "For the first time, I see two butterflies of this size and have pure human features,

or am I still delirious?"

Ezra got angry and said, "Hey, you, we are two fairies, not insects. It seems

that you have a squint in your eyes that must be fixed."

Maya laughed and said, "Let me introduce you to my two most adorable

friends, who are very credited with being here and finding you."

Archie said, "I see," and then he turned to see Alex standing, without saying

anything.

The laughter was on Archie's face with joy and happiness at seeing Alex,

"Thank God you are fine, I am really happy to see you and you are in good health."

Then he turned to Maya and said, "I want to introduce you to my cousin Alex, he is another copy of me."

Maya said, "I saw that the truth is—he was a reason to save me and I forgot to thank him for that, but I will return the favour to him one day until she turned her face to Alex and looked at him and sent for him brilliant smile, it was the reason I rescued and saved you from the black goblins and he fought so bravely and I can't hide from you, Archie, that I felt it was you because I couldn't see well when the black goblins tried to strangle me with her tongue but I knew that no one had that courage but you."

At this moment, the rest of the boys arrived, including Clementine, and as they approached, after they were assured of Archie and Alex, their eyes turned to Maya and the two fairies were in unprecedented astonishment, and they saw two fairies flying and having the same features as humans, a royal red carpet, black goblins lying on the ground and another white one standing in front of them!

This led to a temporary silence filled with contemplation, so they did not know what had happened here and who these strange looking girls were?

Until Archie stood and asked the boys a question to pave the way for them to introduce the strange guests, "Do you now see these creatures in front of you?" Mouths kept shut and eyes chasing every movement of the fairy Maya and the two fairies around her.

Until Luca stammered, "Who are these, Archie?"

Archie, in turn, replied, "This Princess Maya and these two beauties are her friends. We owe them so much they saved our lives from the greatest danger we faced here. If they didn't matter, our souls would now be heading towards the sky, and your bodies would have been buried under mounds of snow."

Everyone murmured between them in a whisper.

Until Clementine said in fear when he saw the proud spear standing on the head of the black goblins, "You killed her, Archie? You really are a knight from another world, Sebastian said it seems we have entered the world of the jinn and not the forest that we know!"

Alex said coldly, "Calm down, my dear Clementine, I share the same belief with you, but what happened has happened, nothing will change the matter. I am like you and everyone here except for Archie. I never expected to see such creatures in my life."

Then he looked sideways at Clementine and winked at him and said with a smile, "But they are really beautiful. You have to give them a gift, maybe you will fall in love with one of them."

Clementine's cheeks turned red in shame as he stared at the fairy Affray with shy looks until Affray noticed him and said sarcastically to her sister, "Why is this child looking at me as if I were his mistress!"

Ezra said, "It seems that he is waiting for you to give him some sweets that his mother denied him when he was late to return home."

Maya warned, "I don't know what brought you here and where you wanted to go, the place is in the wrong direction to the kingdom, but if you are the one who created the camp next to the carcass of a raptor at the lake, I do not advise you to return to it again!"

"Why?" Archie asked.

Maya said, "We saw his cavalry squad, I think they were knights from the kingdom, those horses armed with armour with iron thorns could only be experienced knights or a military squad that was on a mission, but the summary of the story is that the camp that was at the lake has been completely liquidated." Alexander jumped with his voice, "I knew that our adventure in this forest would be easier for us than to fall into the hands of Commander Glister, and they

will not leave us until we are liquidated or captured!"

Archie meditating-ly said, while looking at the sky as if he was talking to

someone behind the clouds, "This matter would not have happened in this way except that there were those who arranged the fates for us so that all of them would be good for us."

Then he looked at Maya and added, "And he brought you here himself, not by your will, Maya." Then he turned to Alex, addressing him, "And now it is your turn, Commander, to take us to the cave that will shorten the distance. Maya came as if she was an angel from heaven to shorten our journey."

No one understood very well what he meant or what he meant. Everyone thought that maybe it was because of the effect of what happened to him from his battle with the black goblins. He started saying words they didn't quite understand.

However, he was throwing something that he hid in himself, and he was afraid that he would reveal it to them except at a known time so that their thoughts would not be distracted.

Alex said, "It looks like they'll get here when the snow stops falling, and they might realise if we don't hurry before they head into the cave, and I don't think they realise we're going there."

But the experience of Commander Glister and with him in the search for antiquities is second to none, so that the king sometimes calls him the title (the loyal dog of the kingdom).

Even dogs are incapable of chasing fugitives, but Glister does not hesitate to use the worst and most despicable methods to catch up with whoever he wants. Either he catches us or we kill him if we can.

Before he killed us, Archie said in agreement with his words, "You are right, we have nothing to lose, either we die the death of the brave or we live the life of cowards. This is our chance and you will not abandon each other." Then he addressed Maya, "Is it possible that you will take us all to the kingdom now?"

I approached him and whispered in his ear, "You alone, yes, but all your friends yes, too, but not with me, but on this magic carpet. He is under your command. Just ask him to take you anywhere and you will see?"

Archie said, "Is this true or fiction from one of the novels?"

She said with confidence, "Try and ask and you will see."

He told her, "What should I do?"

"Say, O magic carpet, I command you to fly with us, and to remember the

name of the place only!"

Archie came to the front of the magic carpet and did not understand that what

he had to do was really like magic if it happened.

And in the blink of an eye, the rug rose from the ground, and its limbs

fluttered like the wings of a bird, punctuated by the sounds of clapping its limbs, like a dreaming bird that sings and unfurls its wings across the vast sky amid unexpected surprise and bewilderment for everyone who was in the place.

"Oh heavens, it's true?" Archie said while laughing at the surprise, then he turned to Alex, who was in turn turning his hands in astonishment.

"Now we don't need to go to the cave, and all our suffering will be over and we will reach the kingdom in a few hours or much less," said Archie exaggeratedly. Fat Martin took Luca and Sebastian's hand and began to drag them to dance on the ice until Clementine clasped his hand with them and they all danced for joy without feeling it. It was like joy, even in the most frightening of situations.

And they sang the sound of singing until their feet, which were not used to dancing on the snow, almost betrayed them.

After Alex listened to Archie's idea and saw the new reality, he thought more realistically and said:

"I am afraid that I will disappoint you, my friends, but I will not disappoint your joy with the presence of this rug and the great burden that will remove it from us, but you should know that our arrival in the kingdom these days is a real disaster without any exaggeration. The walls have ears that have been planted, and no one will sacrifice his life in order to hide rogue boys in his house. This is if the reward that was placed on our heads did not spill the saliva of some, and that we would have entered the lion's den with our feet. As for crossing the road through the cave, it will lead us directly to the bottom of the kingdom, and from there we can set up a secret and secure camp that will be a strategic centre and no one will ever expect it. Then we launch communication campaigns to reach my father, so that we may find internal support or important information that may lead us to something useful.

"In addition to the presence of these super friends, unless you want to go alone, Archie, I won't stop you, because you are an unknown person there, knowing that the time for joining the Knights Candidates course has expired a long time ago, so you must choose your path now carefully."

Luca said, "Summarise, Alex, what are you suggesting to us now?"

Alex said after taking a breath, "My suggestion to you is that we fly this miraculous carpet to the highest peak in this forest."

Maya said, "It is true, Archie, this is a wise idea, but it remains up to you. If you want to go alone, you know it's easy for me."

Archie said, "If I had wanted to leave you, I wouldn't have come here in the first place."

Fat Martin yelled a frightful scream. They rushed at him looking at him as he pointed his finger at the black goblins!

"Damn it," Alex said after seeing what shocked them, the black goblin had turned into a girl lying on her face until Archie approached after he pulled the spear stick from her skull and flipped it on her back.

She was indeed a blonde girl in a village dress, with a belt wrapped around her waist, and holding his necklace in her hand.

Archie turned to Maya and asked her, after he carefully pulled the necklace from the corpse's hand, "Do you have any knowledge of this?"

Maya said while looking at her in panic, "I think, but I can't be sure that I missed a lot to know!"

Archie said in a louder voice, "Do you think or expect? There is a difference."

She said worriedly, "No, both, and because what I heard about had no sound logic or famous support, except for some legends that say that the black fairy was a beautiful orphaned girl of unknown parentage until one of the jinn kings raped her and cast a spell on her so that she would not tell anyone. And then he banished her in the distant forests, but after what I saw, I will adopt all the tales I had heard."

Archie said in a loud voice, with a face worse than what he saw himself in after he had killed a pregnant raptor. "For the second time, I will be the killer of an innocent creature! I wonder what sin I have committed to cause all of this to happen to me, is it heaven's revenge on me because I wronged someone? Or was God angry with me because of an act I committed and for which I did not hold myself accountable?"

Then he raised his head and said to Maya sharply and suddenly, "Tell Isabella to improve the plot next time!"

Alex tapped his face with his hand.

Maya said, confused, "What?"

Then Alex said, "There is no time for argument, let's dig a grave for her and bury her instead of crying over those who will not return." Indeed, they dug a grave for her and put her in it without shrouding her.

But what they didn't see in the girl's body was that the black blood turned into real red blood and was returning to her body instead of bleeding out, unlike usual. Is she still alive or is this the work of the devil?

Chapter 18

GLISTER

When all the boys reached the high cliff at the top of the forest on the back of the miraculous rug, they forgot something important Which is that they tied the only horse that was left to them after the rest of the horses fled down the cliff in a lonely tree at an orphan rock.

And an element that attracts the pursuers, just as a piece of cheese attracts the mouse into the trap, and this is one of the threads that Commander Glister will grab to reach them while they are unaware.

As for Maya, she brought them a trip of food like the one that Archie brought but less variety, less food, and less important than the one she brought to Archie in the great plain, and then she left with the two fairies for a need in herself.

After all that long rest after an unexpected trip, Archie woke up a few minutes before the dawning of the morning.

Fortunately, it may be enough to spare them a catastrophe, on which the sun will rise, if it is delayed more than that in a few minutes.

If it is a few minutes longer than that, that is, if it is not already late. Until his attention was caught by a light of fire at the end of the cliff that dispelled the darkness of the height of the place and eased its coldness until he felt an apprehension within him that made the tension pulsate with every sweat within him.

Archie came a little closer and saw the fat Martin sitting around her, throwing the remaining wood to breathe the warm fire in the frigid dawn.

And before he reached him, he heard the sound of the neighing of a frightened horse purring a lot, and these were warning signs from the horse in order to release him before the danger approached, and the sounds of footsteps surrounded him, many far away, but it was as if they were revolving near him from the intensity of the calm and silence of the place. He could hear the sounds of chicks of birds in their nests.

His eyes bulged after realising that they had realised from the cavalry of Commander Glister, even if he was not sure of it, but he had to be more careful than necessary until he jumped on the fat Martin from behind and closed his mouth and said to him in a whisper violently, "What did you do, you idiot!"

The boy's face turned pale, and he said, after seeing the frailty of Archie's face and his uncharacteristic words, after he loosened his hand to let him breathe.

Martin said with fear, "As you see, the cold deprived me of the pleasure of sleep, and I wanted to help myself by myself without waking anyone."

Archie jumps up and pours water on her to turn her off and says to Martin, "Go fast and wake Alex without even raising your voice. Run out without asking, your fat idiot."

Then he said to him, pointing his finger at his lip, "Shut up!"

Archie opened his eyes on the end of them and glued his ears in the air to listen carefully and make sure of the sound coming from below and said to Martin, "Go now quickly." Then he turned and crawled on his knees with his palms toward the edge of the cliff from where the source of the sound came.

Then he stood on the ends of his feet and walked crawling like a snake until he heard again a voice louder than what he had felt before, and it was the sound of rocks falling and breaking.

And it seemed to him that the sound was getting closer to the edge of the cliff where they reside.

And he himself believed that the sound would be a natural sound of rolling rocks from above, and when he made his head, the first thing he saw was the helmet of one of the cavalrymen covering his head and four others under it.

I was sad from what I saw when there was not enough time to warn others.

The climbing knights were hidden around the corner from reaching the top of the cliff and here Archie must act forced to make himself some advantage over them temporarily and give enough time to warn the others to rise in a capacity better than to rise while captive and the enemy's weapons over their heads if they had not penetrated their skulls.

Suddenly there was a terrible silence in the place, as if the knights sensed that someone had exposed them, but that did not prevent them from advancing, but Archie was better prepared to receive the first unwanted guest in a more appropriate way than his honour.

When the first knight put his fingertips on his hands on the edge of the cliff, expressing his happiness to his friends who are directly under his feet, he says to them with joy and good tidings with malice, "The plan has succeeded, we have arrived successfully, and we will win what the commander promised us!"

But he did not finish his words when he heard a voice from above his head mockingly saying, "Yes, gallant knight, you have reached your end, and as soon as the knight raised his head to see the source of the sound, he found the ends of his hands had parted from the cliff and found himself falling very quickly to the bottom of the abyss, sweeping with him all those who were under him let out the loudest cries of bad ending, which awoke from their intensity everyone in the forest terrified of those cries that precede the moment of the exit of the criminal spirits from the bodies, and it was a cry that no one can escape from before the sunrise of the day, which will reveal a painful massacre."

Archie roared loudly as thunder, "Wake up, we've been revealed! They have revealed our location, the cavalry, that we are under attack, pick up your weapons."

Alex gets up after Martin wakes him up but quickly jumps up when he hears Archie's distress and warning him and asks out loud, panting and his eyes are ahead of him, damn them how did that happen?

Everyone panicked until they ran towards their weapons lying here and there but the shadows of dawn in that leap moment were like fog, causing them to collide with each other.

Until Alex called out loudly, "Quickly take the turtle position, the truth."

Alexander did not understand the situation clearly, so he thinks the knights have reached the surface of the cliff and that the fog was a barrier between them until Archie said to him, "Alex, take four of the boys and stand on the right of the cliff, and I and the rest will stand on the left of it. It seems that they have found a way to us, and we will be a thorn in their way up here until they despair of going up."

The plan was prepared on this assumption, as each team stood in a position of readiness, sharpening their daggers and aiming their arrows to repel any possible attack, but contrary to what they thought, there was no counterattack, but rather calmness prevailed in the place, contrary to what they expected.

On the other hand, it seems that the knights and their leader below realised that they had found those who were following them, regardless of how they climbed to this high and confusing place, as much as they could not be reached and besieged.

Archie said nervously to himself, "Where are you, Maya, it's your time now."

Until Clementine shouted, recalling, "Where is the magic carpet, that this time is more time than the time that has passed, it will save us from this predicament!"

However, Alex had another opinion and said in a low voice, "No, even if the rug is here, we will not ride it to reveal our secret that the Glister squad has bows and arrows with automatic adjustment, long range and accurate shooting, in addition to the fact that the Archers are among the most skilled Archers in the kingdom are roving cavalry Archers, in addition to that we lost dark element and do not forget that if they see the rug, we will have revealed to them our most important weapons and our most important winning cards, and suppose the worst case is that we have all been arrested or one of us is arrested, we will be tortured unbearably in order to reveal the secret of the magic rug.

"And I don't know anyone who can bear to keep any secret while he is under the hands of Glister, they will not hesitate to do the impossible until they find the magic carpet! Which Glister will consider as an invaluable treasure to be proud of in front of others, and will be promoted to a rank he would not have dreamed of, and this is what he seeks I will not allow him to occupy the largest positions in the country at our expense. Rather, I am the one who will seek to rid the kingdom and my father of his tyranny and wickedness to relieve pressure on my father from one of the directions. They have surrounded my father and it seems that they are close to closing in on him."

Then he asked Archie, "Where is your fairy girlfriend?"

Archie said without hesitation, "If I knew where she was, I would go to her right away, even if she flew, but she told me that she would be close to us and that she would come back, and I still trust that she knows what is happening and will return at any moment. And I hope that that moment is now so that what we do not expect to happen does not happen."

Alex saw the fear in Archie's eye and said to him reassuringly, "Do not worry in both cases, we have the advantage now. Their number, according to Maya's words, was about twenty knights, and after the fall of those who infiltrated here, I do not think they are more than three or four, so the number will be in the range of fourteen to fifteen knights who are besieging us with the deadliest weapons."

Charlie said, "Oh really? Thank you for this disappointing reassurance, Alex!"

Luca said excitedly, but how long will we be trembling and waiting for them like prey, afraid of predators while waiting for them to attack.

Sebastian said, "I don't think they will attack us after what happened to them, at least not after an hour or two."

But the response came quickly, and while they were chatting, five pointed hooks fell on the surface of the cliff and plunged forcefully into the cliff's rough floor like spears!

It was tied tightly with iron chains of small size, but very interconnected.

Clementine said angrily to Luca, "I wish you hadn't spoken, you pessimist!" He whispered spray inside him as if fate was listening to us.

Sebastian shouted, "Are you waiting for them to come up to ask them to let us go back to the kingdom or what? Let's cut the ropes of those hooks before they go up."

Archie wisely said, "No, do not cut the hooks now until we are sure that the knights have climbed and reached the half way of the basement, and because it may be a plan from them to draw our attention with these hooks and then turn around and climb from other places!

"Therefore, we must remain in our places for a period not exceeding five minutes at least, until we ensure that they reach the middle of the foothills, and then we surprise them all in a quick attack and cut the ropes of the hooks to ensure the fall of the cavalry from the highest distance and then make sure of their death and the loss of the largest number of cavalries.

"In doing so, Archie, Alex, and Luca broke the chains of the cavalry, which they thought were ropes, causing them to be late. Until one of the knights climbed to the roof and ran quickly to stab Archie, but Alex was faster than him and rushed him with a flying dagger from behind in the back of his head. As for the rest, they fell dead from the top of the cliff in front of their leader, Glister, whose eyes shone with blue fire from the intensity of anger and the hidden hatred that leads him to all these evils.

"For Glister, it was like a warning not to get any closer, and that your fate would be no less than the corpses of your soldiers. It was a more severe loss than me, Commander Glister, but what struck him with oppression is that his loss was not in front of an experienced army, or in front of a legendary crushing beast, or in front of a king of mighty kings.

"What made him fall into a fit of hysteria is that his humiliating loss happened to him at the hands of rebel boys who do not possess even the simplest weapons of his knights, armed with various types of weapons and skilled in fighting the difficulties and guerrilla fighters who bear the highest royal decorations and who have repelled the invincible barbarian ghouls many times and times!

"It was a humiliating disaster. He does not know how he will manage his face, which is stained with the shame of humiliation that did not happen to any of the leaders."

"Except he who was promised by his supporters that he would become Minister of Defence. This position will guarantee him and those around him a striking power to achieve what they desire with all their comfort.

"But a fearless leader with a stubborn, rock-hard head like Commander Glister cannot let this matter out of the context of this moment, even if it costs him to transcend moral norms, the nobility of knights, or even the decadence of thieves. If the description is correct, the bad intention of this tyrant, who seems to have been infected by ghouls, has been infected.

"Glister settled on his impostor plan in himself as he put his two hands on his kidneys, which he felt were bleeding sharply forcibly from the humiliation wound he had suffered in front of his knights, and that this would leak to the ears of the people of the kingdom, so the matter would reach the king, then his ball would be completely burnt before he burns the king's fire.

"This fire of anger will be nothing but a prick of a needle in front of what will be a great disaster for him if he does not immediately curb his anger. So, he turned to the style of prostitution, because it is the only way to win over the boys at the top, perhaps to gain some time."

He saw that the cliff was now fortified, after the boys above alerted the presence of the knights and thwarted all their attempts to climb, in addition to the disappearance of the element of darkness, which was a natural cover to carry out their infiltration.

He called out in a voice faintly menacing that is not covered by anything, "I know that you are the one who leads these poor and deceived boys, and I know that you are accompanied by a boy named Archie, and that you know, Alexander, who I am, and how much I know your father, and that you know how terrible you have done to the king's knights.

"Who sent us personally to bring those with you back to the arms of their mothers, whom you hurt, Alexander, by stealing their children from them, to send them to the hell of delusion and darkness that you drew for yourself, you renegade of the law and disobedient to his father.

"And you, called Archie, I knew that you were the son of the deposed leader Abraham, who was plotting to overthrow the king, who had the credit of making your father a seasoned leader. But this is how dogs always bite those pure hands that extend to them when they find no one to sympathise with them, there is no doubt that you are like your father. But after all this, the king has given me an order to treat you as young men who have kept the way, and they must be returned to their families, not as criminals.

"If this indicates anything, it indicates the piety and wisdom of His Majesty, who knows very well that your presence outside the kingdom with these thoughts will make you criminals. Now let's go down so we can end the matter and get back together and announce your repentance."

Everyone was surprised by this amount of information about them, especially Archie, who was very upset by what he heard from Commander Glister about his father until he clenched his fingers and joined them and everyone heard the cracking of his knuckles.

Alex said to him coldly, "Leave him, this is a dog of wretchedness."

Archie remembered the hadith of his father when he told him while advising him to avoid the evil of anger, as it would destroy him. Meanwhile, the commander was walking in implementing his plan without anyone knowing what was going on in his mind, which is filled with the heads of demons.

Then he winked at one of the sniper knights to get ready and take a special position a little away from the bottom of the mountain so that the vision would be clear in an attempt by Commander Glister to drag any of Archie or Alexander to the edge of the cliff above in order for the sniper knight to grab him immediately from a distance and between the huge tree trunks and then it will be A painful blow, in the event that one of them is injured or managed to kill him, will cause them to shake, and will hasten their surrender.

Commander Glister continued his series of threats, but did not choose his words well, so his words were without effect, contrary to what he had hoped.

Then, after he caught his breath, he said, "I simply ask you to go down and surrender yourselves without shedding any other blood. Otherwise, if we can

climb up to you, I will not be able to secure myself from carrying out the execution directly and throwing you from above.

"But I left you another chance to survive due to your young age and you know that there is no way to escape, so do not think for a moment that the killing of a number of knights will make us retreat, but there are many reinforcements that will arrive and I do not advise you to wait until they arrive because they will have specialised weapons only to torture the prisoners. We don't own it now, so hurry up, time is running out, so blame only yourselves."

After he fell silent and did not find any response from them, he decided to raise the level of his threats to a more uglier and bold level. He said to Archie, "I see that you, Archie, are a good boy, but you have fallen into the nets of the black widow's brother, and they will suck your blood and throw you a lifeless corpse. Did no one tell you that, or did they tell you that they were angels shine a light in the kingdom?"

Archie stared at Alex, furrowing his eyebrows, then added Glister recounting his offensive and provocative speech, "I advise you if you don't mind yourself, you should fear for your father, mother and brothers too, because we will reach them in no time. I hope you have understood my words well, subjugated mufti."

Alex said to Archie, "Don't answer him that he wants to provoke you, leave him to me this time!"

Then Alex answered sarcastically, "Have you, you coward, finished telling you that story that your mother, who was killed by thieves, told you while you were looking at them until you wet your pants with fear when you were a teenager?

"If you could do anything, you would have done it before you spoke, but you cannot and never will. I advise you to leave now before you lose the rest of your men, and then everyone and those in the kingdom will know that the gallant commander has exterminated his proverbial bloody squad in the face of all the dangers have been completely exterminated at the hands of boys who have nothing but daggers and worn-out swords like children's toys Do you expect the king to welcome you?

"This is if he does not take pleasure in executing you and orders you to be cut alive while you know that His Majesty the king is lenient in everything except to see a military leader insulting the kingdom's army, so how if the loss is the same as your loss now? Think quickly, Glister. You miscalculated this time and fell into the evil of your deeds. You are faced with two things, two of which are both worse than each other.

"You will die at the hands of the king, or you will run away now, but we will find you, and we will find you, and we will cut off your head and send it as a message to the king to let him know what strength and valour the rebels have reached, and this is the closest it seems."

Archie had thought about his plan, and did not tell anyone about it, in order not to be disappointed, for not everything was said until he came to the edge of the foothills to locate the commander and rush him with a spear.

But suddenly the bottom of the slope covered thick black smoke rising towards them, but it was not like any smoke coming out of the fire, it was smoke with the smell of burnt meat and the others smelled the smell then Archie decided to look up his head to check the matter.

He looked so focused that he saw a pile of twigs and timber that the knights had gathered and placed the bodies of the dead soldiers on top.

Until Archie's eyes fell for the first time into the sunken eyes of Commander Glister, his beard is untidy, thick moustaches' full of grey and tall, whose length is known from afar.

Then Glister shrieked loudly, and his voice reverberated, and the forest was swift as the sound of the screeching wind of a storm.

"Do you think you will be able to terrorise and blackmail me, kid? Ha-ha- ha." Then he pointed his finger at the sniper knight who was hiding among the bushes until he fired a lightning arrow from his automatic bow to hit the desired target, making him look like Alexander.

In a blink of an eye, Archie realises that there is something deadly among the dunes of smoke heading towards his face, and with his wit he tilted his head a little to the right, but the traitorous arrow did not prevent the traitor from hitting Archie's cheek and causing him an injury that would have been fatal if he had not moved his head at the last moment a few centimetres until he threw himself and rolled with his hand on his face from the speed of the arrow, everyone was so shocked that they thought that he had been hit directly after they saw the arrow passing Archie to complete his way in the sky far away on the horizon.

Everyone rushed out, thinking that Archie had been killed until Alex grabbed Archie's hand and removed it from his face to see where the injury was.

I know that this unclean criminal will not rest until he kills one of us. Then Sebastian was asked to investigate the severity of the wound until Archie got up after seeing blood dripping from his hand and said with regret, "You don't have to, I will be with you as long as the soul is in this body until the last beat. But I did not imagine that there is a leader so despicable and mean to burn the corpses of his knights who were with him instead of handing over the corpses to their families!"

Alex smiled a false smile and said, "You are good, Archie, and you will see and see many things in the coming days that will change your view of this miserable cruel world."

At the same time, Glister had rejected the idea of besieging the place for several days until they surrendered of starvation, as he intended to do something else until he ordered his knights to leave.

After they killed the only horse that belonged to the boys, and burnt it with the rest of the corpses of the knights so that the boys had nothing left to eat.

Unexpectedly, Maya appears in front of them like the one who came out of nowhere, with the two fairies and the magic carpet. It is the appearance of the real jinn as well when they are exposed to humans without any introduction until the other boys almost fall to the ground from the shock of the surprise.

And the first time her eyes saw the place of the wound on Archie's cheek until she came close and saw the blood on his clothes and his hand and said, arching her eyebrows, "It seems we have missed a lot."

Clementine said with great joy that he was to fly. In the air to embrace her, "Oh, my goodness, your fairy friend, Archie, has come at the right time with the rug."

Those eyes stared at Maya and especially at the two little fairies that look like dolls but fly like birds until they frowned upon their faces when they saw those admiring looks from all those eyes like the eyes of monsters staring at their prey waiting for the opportunity to pounce until Luca approached and extended his hand to touch the wing of the fairy Affray after being dazzled by beauty The colour of their wings and the charm of their appearance make you feel that you want to eat them more than you look at them for a long time.

After throwing him hateful, she said, "What are you trying to do, you ugly?"

Archie said on his face the happiness of meeting again, "You missed the excitement, Princess."

She responded in turn with two painful eyes, as she put her palm on his wound and moved her palm on the wound in its place, then something strange happened, as Maya's hand lit up from inside to the outside of Archie's cheek and

a faint light shined from it that made Archie laugh and shake his head and then his shoulders and take a laugh and he says, "This matter tickles me, what did you do, even if she raised her hand, as if the light of his cheek was shining from white, and he did not see any trace of any wound."

"So," Alex said in amazement, "You really are a witch!"

Maya replied with a frowning face, "If it wasn't for Archie, I'd show you what you didn't like, I don't like being called a witch."

Archie said to her calmly, "Calm down, my dear, Maya, and make excuses for them, as you did with me, for man is an enemy of what he does not know."

Then he said to the others, "Why are you besieging me as if I were the enemy? Go back to your positions!"

Alex said, "Glister and his gang have left where they came from, and I can't say for sure. However, he either wants to give us a chance to get down, or he has a backup plan, but in both cases his going only means that their danger is still hovering around us like bird's hovers around carrion. You won't leave it until you leave it until you eat it."

Maya interrupted him and said in a firm tone, "I told you that I would not allow anyone to harm you as long as you were alive."

Alex looked at the others and pursed his lips and said with admiration, "This is the love that I have not heard of since I was born."

But Maya stood away and said we will be back in a little while, "I promise we will not. We're too late this time, and then she flew into the air, fading between the clouds and the two fairies. Is Alex true when Archie discovers the truth, or is Maya's love true when she confesses what she's hiding?"

Maya saw in Archie her whole life, and there was no one equal in her eyes or who could match his place in her heart, and she would not abandon him, and no one would be able to wipe her tears or stop her from pouring out if she sheds light on his loss or loss.

There is no doubt that she will not go for a walk in her hidden world this time, but rather to avenge the wound of her lover.

Maya does not see what others see, perhaps she was under the influence of blind love or to carry out a plan that she had prepared.

She and the two fairies saw from behind the mounds of clouds above the forest, Glister, and the remaining cavalrymen with him, taking a different path to the path of the kingdom, amid the trees of the forest, which ascended to the sky non-stop from its highness until they settled at one of the forest's springs.

Which was an ideal place to stop in order to launch another campaign whose type and time is unknown until they got off their horses after tying them to tree trunks and the feeling of humiliation accompanies them more than their shadows until Glister became like a wounded wolf in a very dangerous situation.

When he realises that his end is near and that he has nothing to lose.

While they were busy preparing the place for the temporary residence, the horses moved in fear and were neighing violently. One of them fled and dragged with him the knight who was holding the bridle and his lizard in front of everyone and they looked until he left him after his face fell into the mud of the forest, but the rest of the horses continued to purr and steam out as thick as if they were saying we don't want to die here. And she was trembling with terror and panic after she saw what the human eyes had not seen, until one of the knights said, "I only see that there is a predator waiting for us!"

Then the tangled trees behind shook, shrouded in a darkening darkness under the thick branches, with the sound of breaking, as if someone was making a way towards them, until Glister said with all courage, "Get ready, we are facing an unavoidable animal attack."

Then he sharpened his sword and said thinking, "I only see that it is a herd of grey wolves or a giant brown bear. Prepare the automatic arrows and put the horses behind you. We are the ones who protect it, not it. Otherwise, we will be stuck in this forest and we may have to eat each other in order to survive."

This was the closest explanation to Glister and the most powerful stimulus at the same time, but the shaking of giant trees full of leaves and huge fruits was baffling and no animal could do this until those huge fruits fell on the heads of the knights and their horses until fear reached their throats and they gathered around each other and they made Commander Glister in their midst for fear of him And after he lowered his sword, he said, "This is not the work of an animal, until that suspicious expectation was broken when a huge, dark-black wolf appeared in front of them, gaping its mouth open for a row of fangs that they had never seen and did not look like familiar wolves until some of the knights dropped Archieers from their hands and retreated in fright, but Glister had an opinion."

Another, he showed great courage, contrary to what was in the minds of all knights, Glister surprised everyone when he attacked the wolf instead of the wolf attacking him, wielding his sword and waving it with his hands.

He said to the wolf with courage as if he was fighting a knight, "If you are my destiny, then show me your courage, you beast, but in a way, contrary to what was expected of the wolf, he retreated back and disappeared without turning his back on them until he suddenly disappeared among the pile of fern trees, and this behaviour caused strangeness and high tension until they heard a loud howl coming from behind them, in contrast to the place of the wolf that appeared in front of them, and they turned quickly, their legs trembling in place."

Until one of the knights behind them shouted, "help, help me, help me," and as soon as they turned until his voice was cut off and there was no trace of him and disappeared just as his voice had disappeared, then Glister rushed with two knights who fired arrows into the pile of trees to ensure that there was no danger in case their leader entered to save the kidnapped knight until they heard another knight screaming behind them (rescue me, oh, save me, save me) and he was dragged and dragged from his feet among the trees in the darkness of the forest, and they found no trace of him except that his fingers with which he ploughed the ground left him, seeking help without finding them.

Glister went crazy, and he had a vertigo in his head, as if he was alone in a forest revolving with everything around him, and he almost fell until a third knight screamed frighteningly.

Glister looks at him as he is dragged into the woods, without moving this time. He realises that it is not the work of a wolf.

Even a group of wolves is an act of supernatural abilities that they do not have the strength to confront, and he knew that he must escape, but to where?

Until he decided to surrender to his destiny and chose confrontation after feeling the pain of his heinous act and what he did to the bodies of his dead knights, and he said miserably, "I have always expected death, but not in this way, and it seems that God has taken his wrath on me and I only see that I have received my punishment!"

Until he thought that there were many black wolves surrounding him among the trees and running quickly in a circular motion without seeing them, and he kept spinning around himself quickly, waiting for where death would come to him. It caused him to cut accidentally to the end of his face, it made him pour out a lot of blood, he drowned his beard, which was dyed red, made him fall on his back, and I think he was spinning in the belly of a hurricane, he didn't know, and he was about to pass out and he didn't know whether he was conscious or unconscious, and he couldn't speak anymore until he collapsed.

He has that someone is standing in front of him, but he does not see him until a girl's voice comes from behind his ear saying to him, "This time we let you escape from us, but the other time if you try to hurt Archie, we will take you part by part." The words ended, and everything in front of him vanished, and he closed his eyes, and he could no longer hear anything, and he lost consciousness.

Chapter 19

PARTING LOVE

Archie rushed toward the rug, like a happy wave above the sea, on a summer's day, seeking the warmth of the sands of the beach to rest on and he said, "Now, now, brothers, it is time to set out on the magic carpet. Come on, gather all your things, and don't forget your shoes and weapons, because we will never come back here."

Clementine asked, "Who else is your fairy friend and her companions?"

"Of course not, because she's right behind you, Clementine," said Archie, smiling, pointing his finger over Clementine's head. "Which will not hesitate even for a moment to do everything to help us escape from these predicaments

in which we almost drowned if Maya did not come. Isn't that so, Maya?" Everyone looked at Maya while she was wearing a black cloak, unusually and she said to Archie, in a voice closer to a whisper, "Aren't you supposed to

have taken the rug out to gain time? Or have you forgotten what I taught you?" Archie said hesitantly, after taking a deep sigh, thinking he might be reprimanded in front of everyone, "Umm, no, I did not forget, but after listening to the advice of Commander Alex, we decided to wait until you return to discuss the matter together, and there is nothing better than the matter being a consultation between friends."

Maya gave Alex a fleeting look and then turned her face away from him and said arrogantly on purpose, "I thought you were the leader, Archie, but it doesn't matter, I understand this to others at this moment, but well what did you suggest, Commander? I may share the idea with him, or revise it if there is a bug, if we suppose so. Then, she shrugged her shoulders and said to the two fairies, after she winked at them with the edge of her charming eye, wasn't she, my dear?"

The fairy Affray said reluctantly and hurriedly, "Yes, yes, my lady."

Her sister Ezra said sarcastically, "Without discussion, my lady, and they knew that their mistress's words were directed at Alex in an indirect way, and so did Archie and before him Alex and after them the others."

No one was hidden from Maya's facial expressions, nor her flattering manner in dealing with Alex from the first time until Alex approached her and said in an admiring tone and with a smiling face, in keeping with Maya in her childish style.

"The truth is Archie is our leader here, but due to my humble experience, I advised them that we should not fly to the kingdom directly because the guards have become stricter since the kingdom was exposed, and I think that you—"

Maya interrupted him in a provocative and rude manner and said, ignoring his look at his face, "I know everything that happened there in more detail than you when you were hiding in the woods and cutting off the road, O noble leader!"

Then she turned to him for the first time and continued her attack, "It does not seem to me that you do not have a solid plan except for some wishes that you have in yourself and that you seek to fulfil through me!"

Archie quickly responded to Maya and was angered by her sloppy talk that she was used to!

And he said, "But you did not let him continue, there is something that Alexander referred to, and I would have liked you to wait a little longer instead of this torrent of accusations."

Ezra went towards Archie, with an angry face, and said in her gentle voice, as strong as she could possibly have, "You don't raise your voice to my lady, so you don't know what you did a while ago in order to avenge the wound in your face that no matter what you do, not even a simple thing of her love for you."

Archie said a surprised, "What?"

Alex interrupted them, saying in a cold tone of much tenderness, "I don't know why you were angry with me, but did you know what happened after the kingdom was subjected to that barbaric attack? Of course not. As for me, I knew very well what exactly happened, so my plan was built on the smallest details of the architectural construction of the kingdom, its cities and its security system, in order to avoid any mistake that might cost us a lot."

Alexander did not exaggerate with these actions, but on the contrary, he was very happy to break the barrier of disregard that Maya placed between them. He longed for this moment from the first time he saw her until he imagined that there was no one around them, only they were alone looking at each other and

exchanging looks of admiration, if not more than that in the boy's wild imagination.

Maya did not act in this way because of her bad manners, but rather to block the way in front of Alexander, who Maya felt that he was infatuated with her in a suspicious and exaggerated way, which made her deliberately insult him or belittle him in front of others to alienate him from her, but it seems that there is no benefit in all of that.

Alexander continued his speech in exasperation and said, "The plan was to fly to an unknown cave that only a few know. It is fortunate for us that I am one of those few who knows that cave, and the road will be somewhat long, but the percentage of danger is determined by our actions, unlike direct flight to the sky of the kingdom, which will make our fate in the hands of others. This is what almost everyone agrees on, or at least."

Maya replied while twisting her mouth after feeling that she had made a mistake in her behaviour and opened a door for discussion with him, contrary to what she wanted and said, "What about the night? What if it is raining and cloudy? What if the weather is foggy, Eloquent?"

Alex realised her ignorance of most of the details of the technical and military matters of which he knows more than anyone here and said to her with a sarcastic smile, "If I hadn't thought of that, the flying raptors would have devoured the kingdom's army and all who walk the earth, O noble girl.

"But there is an invention called a spirit-catcher that is placed on the walls of the kingdom to sense the presence of any flying object from a distance, even if it is from behind the clouds or in the darkness of the night. Therefore, the cave option remains the most appropriate and safe option."

Maya's face shrank and became like a rotting peach, and she felt as if she was completely naked in front of everyone.

Even Archie who tries to patch up some of her mistakes often did not help her like every time, but she insisted on her steadfast pride in the midst of the storm of embarrassment and put her hands on her waist and said while looking at him from the bottom up nervously, "Aren't you the son of the king's advisor?"

Archie knew that Maya might embarrass herself more because of her stubbornness after letting her fight her losing battle to have a lesson for the rest of her life, then Alexander replied with a dead smile, "How do you know that they will tell my father when I know that all or most of the commanders and guards in the king's court are in a fierce war with this father, if they do not get rid of me without anyone feeling me or make me a reason to twist my father's arm and humiliate him. If what you think of it will succeed, I would have been the first. Whoever suggested this, and when we stayed in this forest, we were forced to go through such an adventure that makes us throw ourselves to death every time."

After Maya's sterile argument with Alexander, Archie stood for a moment in front of Maya, after he let out a sigh that came out from the depths of his heart.

Then he approached her and whispered to her in her ear, indifferent to the gossip of the Fairy Affray while she was hovering around him in anger, and her voice was like the sound of the annoying buzzing of mosquitoes, and the looks of others, or even the mistrust of some:

"Will you leave me alone like the first time? You don't know how sad I really was for losing you for a few days, like the one who lives without a heart."

Maya's face turns red when she sees other people's jerks chasing her between unimpressed eyes and lurking eyes. Embarrassing thoughts attacked her from all sides, as happens to any girl in such a situation, and she could not respond or resist the magic of the distinguished perfume of Archie, which was still stuck in his clothes like what stuck in her mind on the memory of the first meeting until she ran towards the magic carpet to stop the waves of those romantic words before they fell. In the quagmire of other tongues that will haunt her forever.

Then she stood by the magic carpet, took off her cloak, and turned her face toward Archie and she said, "Then let's go and put you in the right direction to reach what you're looking for, but suddenly Luca's voice surprised them when he shouted in Maya's face with great anger for the first time."

Rolling up his arms, he said, "Listen, witch! It seems that you have taken advantage of the kindness of everyone here to ride on our backs. It seems that you come from a completely impolite environment and you should not think that helping us will make you a princess over us!"

Those words were enough to erupt a volcano that did not stop temporarily after those arguments and Maya's anger at Glister until she found this boy insulting her in front of others and he unleashed a whip of his tongue lashing her in front of everyone as the racist master flogs his disobedient slave!

Where she said, like a dragon that breathes flames, "My father, that great king, did not dare to raise his voice at me, then you, you naughty one, would come to insult me in front of the public, no and a thousand no!"

Until she gestured at him with the tip of her finger, as she muttered strange words that no one had ever heard of (Harbot Karbot Kreir Ra Shamrostar) and while she was terrifyingly muttering that spell, a strong wind blew fast, as if it had come out of the nose of a giant who was furious at the universe including it.

Everyone fell and scattered on the ground, including the two fairies while she was standing like an idol. Not a single hair of her shook until Luca rose from the ground by two meters, screaming in terror, and his soul was the one who ascended to the sky screaming in terror, "What is this that I rose, so what is happening? Help me!"

She wants to kill me Archie Alex save me, until he fell on his face like a squawking bird falls to the ground, it all happened in very quick seconds. No one had time to intervene, she knew that she must protect herself by herself, even if it was just words, if she kept silent about this. Now her silence will pave the way for others to attack her, and she must not wait for someone's pity to be her defender.

Archie hurried towards Maya, and he was afraid for himself and he said to her, "Honestly, O Maya, he's just a poor boy who doesn't realise what he's saying. He certainly doesn't know about you, so don't overreact and control yourself, because I didn't know you like this before."

Maya said while looking at the sky sadly, "I'm sorry, I can't believe what happened, and I didn't mean that, everything happened so quickly and I couldn't control myself."

Archie remembered his father's commandment to him when he told him that I would bite you son out of anger, remember this commandment, "Do not be angry, do not be angry, do not be angry."

And he said to himself, "I don't know where I saw this scene before?"

Then Archie said, directing his words to Maya in an indirect way. "Looks like your friend will do us harm if you can't convince her, Archie, that she needs to adjust herself to the way we talk and put up with each other. Otherwise, it is not better for her to suffer alone than to wait for pity from a girl who is proud of herself from top to bottom, and she is not from our race!"

Clementine said boldly, unusually, "Excuse me, Alexander, even if you don't like what happened, you must be the owner of a word of truth even if it is against your enemy!"

That talk angered Sebastian, who pulled Clementine from his sleeve and said to him, "On our side, are you on her side?"

Clementine continued his speech with logic and realism, "Because I do not distinguish in truth between a friend or an enemy, were it not for Luca's rudeness, this would not have happened. We must be fair. I see that what this beautiful fairy has done with us over the past two days is more than such a simple unintentional mistake!"

Sebastian said after tightening Clementine's sleeve stronger than before and pulling him strongly to him, "It seems that someone like you can easily sell his brothers in order to reach his sick whims! Do you think that I didn't notice your errant look at one of the two little fairies approvingly to satisfy your lust, you imperfect!"

Alex said after blowing his mouth on the ground grumbling and looking at them out of the corner of his eye and said, "Shut up now, and you, Sebastian, leave Clementine's shirt and you must learn the manners of dialogue first and not to touch anyone with your hand in order to teach him your point of view."

Then he raised his head and smiled without smiling and said Archie, "Tell the fairy that we are sorry for what Luca came from, and I apologise to her and tell her that we are now ready to move together."

Archie said cheerfully, "There is no need. She apologised and admitted her mistake and that I am seeking an excuse for everyone, as fate brought us together in unsuitable circumstances to take the time to get to know each other, but now let's finish the matter and move towards the cave, we are still early in the day."

The magic carpet flew high in the forest sky, which was suspiciously dark from above, despite the brightness of the sun on this day, as if it had become overwhelmed with sadness for an unknown reason, until its dark mountains appeared behind them that were the scene of rehearsals for real battles.

The atmosphere became clearer due to the height of the magic carpet higher than before, and the landmarks of the kingdom became clear to them as if it were a giant artistic painting that they saw in front of them from this height, as well as the six towers of the palace that embrace the competing clouds all the time high, surrounded from behind by that famous mountain of high altitude that can hardly be seen. Its peak was so high, everyone clung to each other.

After they knelt on the floor of the flying carpet from the intensity of the height and the gusts of the wind that made their hair fly in all directions until a river appeared to them from afar, cutting its way between the trees, very white from the many waves covering its surface from the intensity of its flow while they approached it more and more while the sun was in the middle of the sky after the middle of the day, and it was sending its golden rays to adorn them the unknown path they were taking, after it was difficult for them to think more about what might stand in their way again from surprises that may not come to anyone's mind.

Every distance travelled by the magic carpet increased their hearts palpitations, and it made them feel the closeness of their arrival to the kingdom, which has become like reaching the Gardens of Eden, even though they had been there for days and they are still circling around it like bees.

But fates decided that they would be banned from entering their homeland after they decided to deviate from the silence of others from what they thought were matters in the kingdom that should change for the benefit of the kingdom's residents and not that the interests of the kingdom would benefit a small group.

Until they saw that cliff they were on from afar, as if it was a small rock that was at their feet.

Archie contemplates that beautiful view from the top, as if the earth has become from below them. It is a painting of an artist who created the most accurate details. He wishes himself to be in the midst of the towering castles of the palace and how he will feel at the moment when he is in the middle and lives the moment he joins the Royal Guard.

He sends a letter to his parents, brothers, and his charming girlfriend, describing his interesting diaries and wild heroisms during the training period, and the beautiful girls call as kings flock to the king's throne because he is the most famous and bravest knight among all the knights in the kingdom, as he dreamed of being.

He took a breath and let out sighs of relief as he contemplated all those wishes in the sky, as if everything he had been waiting for during those long years had been fulfilled smoothly. He had a beautiful feeling, and it was not only Archie who enjoyed meditating and imagining, but even others share the same feeling in themselves.

Alex pointed down towards the east after he appeared in front of them from afar, the cave in the middle of a mountain ranges from the right of the river flowing with strength until Maya suddenly felt heat in her body and hugged herself quickly as if he had been stung!

She knew that something that was hers alone would happen, and he approached her, even if she looked back, she saw a strange cloud, dark in colour, like a cloud. Loaded with rain of torment, the flash of lightning does not stop shining inside it, as if it were a giant electric charge that wanted to swallow them! Even if she approached them, the sounds of lightning rumbled violently inside her, which shook the carpet with waves of lightning sound and its echo like a sea wave.

Alexander said with great fear in himself, "It is a strange thing about this cloud that left the whole sky to catch up with us."

Maya turned to the cloud and said, shouting loudly at the magic carpet, "Hurry, flying carpet, to where I commanded, hurry to the cave as fast as you can." Then Alex continued, directing the magic carpet, "It went down a little until we were in the middle of the high tree branches, so that it was difficult for this strange cloud to follow us because of its large size and the narrowness of the distance between the high branches of the pine trees, due to the convergence and smallness of the distance between the branches of the forest trees."

Until he nearly turned them over and tucked them between the thick branches hanging in the air and their little branches hitting some of their faces and scratching others until Charlie cried out in a hoarse voice and his lips fluttered like a piece of cloth from the force of the speed of the rug, "Oh, my goodness, we're doomed, Alex. You got to tell the magic carpet to slow down before it's too late."

As for the cloud, it became directly above them, which did not leave them even for a moment, as if it were their shadow adjacent to them, and perhaps if they were in the same path, it would have destroyed them.

Archie shouted, "How long is it until we reach the cave, because we can no longer see it, and I am afraid we will escape, from where we do not feel? It's right there in front of us on the river bank and all that's left for us is to get ready to do something we might not have thought of before..."

Alexander was aware that the situation would end unexpectedly and might end in pain so he started yelling at everyone, "Hold on and get ready to jump into the river when I ask you!"

The river was dividing the forest into two parts, the section in which the cave was considered one of the parts of the kingdom.

The area was considered the first line of defence for the kingdom against any invading human armies because of the density of its trees, the abundance of pointed rocky hills and steep slopes, and the difficulty of penetration by any army, in addition to about the stories and legends that make everyone who thinks of crossing this place search for another plan that this part of the earth never includes.

The fairy Affray Archie says, her eyes trembling as she hides behind her sister next to Maya clinging to the floor of the rug, "The great King Barhout, the father of Maya, appears to have been angry with an anger that he had never angered before!"

She says it while mourning her luck for this moment, then Maya said with a pale face filled with fear and sadness together, "Don't worry!" Then I held Archie's hand after suffering from the speed of the air, after her eyes shed tears of separation that stained Archie's cheek, as if she realised something very bad had happened for the first time until Archie knew that the matter was great.

She said, her hair covering her face, revealing only the features of her wide eyes, the thin pointed tip of her nose, and her blushing cheek, "Remember that no matter what happens now or at any time, nothing will separate me from you, Archie and if my end has come, you will not go except to ransom you with it, Archie. I will not leave this hand except for your own good."

The words were coming out in a stifled voice that she couldn't control herself until she broke down in tears and fell into Archie's lap as she sobbed so hard as the crying of a child who had left his mother, who will never return.

As for Archie, he felt for the first time that he was helpless, like a deaf and dumb orphan, lost in a forest and no one found him, until he felt a sharp pain in his head from the confusion of thoughts in his head, and he did not comprehend all this sudden transformation. The situation is due to a cloud!

And he did not realise what it means that this cloud within it is the king of the entire world of the jinn who is chasing them, and that this girl in his embrace is only his daughter who went out and left his entire kingdom in order to find her.

Until Alexander shouted at them and said one of his eyes on the cloud of terror and the other on the tree branches, "Leave the arms of Archie, lover fairy, and tell me what to do now?"

Maya endured her broken heart and said angrily while wiping her tears, "I'm sorry, Archie." Then turned her face towards Alexander and said, "Now you must all jump into the river before the magic carpet reaches the cave, because he can't. You must disperse for a while and then gather your scattering so that no one knows where you are going, because this cloud carries a great evil within it, and I do not want any of you to be hurt because of me. As for me, the rug and the two fairies, we have work to do."

Then she grabbed Archie's hand and said happily, "There is a lot of sadness in her."

The one who took me from you the first time is the one who will take me this time and as I promised you, I will come back to you again and this is my promise that I never betrayed, then she pointed to Alexander and shook her head that it was time to jump until Archie took her hand hard and said with trembling enthusiasm, "I will only jump with you, Maya!"

Alexander said, "I will count to three, and I will not say three until everyone has jumped into the river."

Then he said, "Magic carpet, I command you to go down as fast as you can."

The decline was more adventurous, as they would be swarmed among the overlapping branches, which might be like batons, that suddenly fell on the face, but they had nothing else.

Indeed, they all stood before Alexander said three, as if they were in a marathon with the most expensive prize. Maya says to Archie, after she was silent a little, contemplating his face for the last time, while she held his face with her hand and raised the dimple of his hair that slept on his forehead up to his nose, "This is my battle, but you go to your battle and make sure that we will we win," and before Archie even said a farewell, Maya pushed him with eyes full of tears from the top of the flying carpet to fall into the river.

And he catches up with the others, had it not been tied to her heart, she would have thrown herself with him out of her excessive love and thickening of it, and there was nothing left on the rug except Maya and the two fairies and behind them the cloud of jinn and demons that came very close to the magic carpet, which could not stand the anger and insistence of the great king of the jinn and his servants to retrieve his rebellious daughter and they all disappeared above the sky woods.

Chapter 20

SARA

In the middle of a rainy day, Archie's father rushes out to see some of his friends, most of whom were from the Royal Guard, who were dismissed from service because of the story known as treasonous of the kingdom, to tell them about the man and the news he brought from the kingdom until he entered the only bar in their village and found one of them drunk.

He hung his wet cloak and went to the table where the drink was served. The place was almost empty except for the bartender and his drunk friend.

Abraham said to the man eagerly, "I knew I would find you here, Marco, how are you, man? Are you still the way I left you before? Isn't it time to quit this habit, man?"

Marco said after burping several times, "What is there here in this village but this tavern that helps me to forget everything and make up for my mind and relieve the grief of a miserable man who has stolen everything, since you know that I am alone after they took from me my dearest wife, Sarah. I don't have children that I take candles from to light my dark life like what you have, Abraham!"

Abraham replied sadly, emphasising his words, "Do you still remember her after all these years, Marco?"

Marco clenched his fists hard and heard the sound of his teeth grinding some of them, then he hit his hands hard on the antique wooden table and the wine glass shook and almost fell if not for Abraham grabbed him before he fell.

Marco added in an outburst of anger, looking at the bartender who ran away in panic, "How can I not remember her who fought everyone to win her, and gave up my father's inheritance in the fields for the Charlotte's sake, she took my soul and my life and I look unable to do something like the miserable tree that is sawed it with a chainsaw and it groaned in pain without moving a finger I was just living for her, I mean what I say, Abraham, I was going to work for it and not from my future. I was looking for something to live for after my father died and I found it in her I didn't even wash anymore. Except by crying over her to comfort myself when I feel that she is the reason for that."

Abraham patted his hands-on Marco's shoulder, who quickly shook them away from him, Abraham said kindly, "I'm sorry, I didn't mean it, but it's been more than seventeen years and I see that you are still able to marry and have children, and you can give birth to the candles that will light your life, Marco. It is unreasonable to cry all your life for the one who left and left you, for this is one's injustice to himself, Marco, and if you do not find, I will find one for you myself." Abraham laughed.

Marco got angry and turned to Abraham and said, with spit splashing from his lips, "Would you have forgotten your eldest son, Archie if he had been away for several days? Common tell me?"

Then he was silent for a moment, in which he did not find a response from Abraham, who understood Marco's position, and continued Marco wondering by chance, not realising that this was what brought Abraham here.

By the way, he said scornfully, "What is the news of your son, Archie? I heard he was going to the kingdom to meet his uncle, the honourable chancellor, the thief Albert!"

He uttered the name of Chancellor Albert, breathing in anger, his eyes flashing in anger, and turned around to the table, slamming everything on it with one blow with his forearms, and dropping all the glasses on top of the floor with the wine that ran through the grooves of the tavern until it reached the door.

Mr Abraham replied calmly and with coherent nerves, "Take it easy, Marco."

Then Marco interrupted him violently and started shouting at Abraham, "Because he is your brother-in-law, huh! You knew what he did to me and did not move a finger!"

He robbed me of my wife. Do you know what that means? Then he clenched his fist and almost punched Abraham's calm face, who was well aware that it was foolish to go along with an excitable person.

Even worse, he is right, which means you have no reason to confront him, just wait for him to calm down.

The story of Marco's hatred of Chancellor Albert goes back to the past years, more than seventeen years ago, where Mr Marco was working as a member of the border guards in the kingdom, and in a surprising way, days before the case (traitors of the kingdom) surprising everyone.

When he was joined and promoted to the king's Royal Guard under the leadership of Abraham at the time, when he became the commander of the king's Guard in the palace, he had a very beautiful and cunning wife, Sarah, who was twenty years old, and she was also working in the palace as a teacher of etiquette and languages for one of the king's daughters.

Where she was a resident of the village (Kling Ling) also, a childhood friend of Marco, where she was desperate to close the distances between him and her until he arranged a job for her as a teacher for children in the kingdom and succeeded in that and because of her intelligence and beauty she got a job in the palace.

This was strongly opposed by Marco because he knew that some of the palace men could not bear the presence of a beautiful woman around them without unleashing their nets by trapping her and preying on her in any way they wanted.

It did not occur to poor Marco that his extreme or exaggerated jealousy from her point of view was another reason for the beautiful Sarah to give herself reasons to justify her plans that did not occur to anyone's heart.

Where the schemes of that cunning beauty, Sarah, who has great fortune in men, coincided with the changes that took place in the palace, which fate wove like a bridle of a wild horse, which makes you lead it with ease around the necks of all but Sarah.

As Mr Albert was promoted from the director of security in the palace to the rank of chief of the palace staff, and this was after Sarah got a job as a teacher for the children of the palace officials, including the king's sons. One day, Mr Albert's eyes fell on Sarah.

He thought for a moment that he had a convulsion in his eyes after she passed by him and she was directing the students to the class, so she did not finish him off with a smile radiating a light of her beauty like the light of the twinkling stars on the horizon of the sky and the smell of a fragrant perfume that is enough to tame the most cruel and violent men.

But behind all that beauty and silence, she was hiding something deadlier than the poison of the most dangerous snakes!

Mr Albert resolved at that time that this treasure, which is the treasure of the earth's treasures, should not be lost from under his hands, under him, as it is now an employee under his authority.

He did not fear for her, even from the king himself, for he knows that the king has a wife, if he thinks, just for the sake of thinking, to marry a girl he knows that the queen can remove him from the throne.

Queen Caroline, the king's wife, was a woman of tyrannical tyranny that was feared even by the king himself, although she used to offer her husband the king royal gifts in the form of stealth girls to enjoy them and satisfy his instinct so that he would not leave her bed with a legitimate wife, unless she ensured that he emptied all the waters of his lust into the body of a female who would not compete for the throne. Never.

And if this is something forbidden and contrary to their belief and may harm the king's reputation, the queen's jealousy is one of those girls, but it is easier for her than having another wife who may take over everything and share with her the most powerful women's position in the country before the king himself shared it.

Thus, she will become one of the losers and will not escape from the tongue of the slanderers.

The circumstances of the lives of both Mr Albert and the glamorous Sarah were perfectly prepared for their closeness. The first was a widowed man in the prime of his youth, with two sons (twins Isabella and Alexander), and he lived in luxury and in abundance of money and power, and he lacked from the pleasures of life except what his eyes saw of the beauty of this girl who exhausted his thought and craved his soul.

On the other hand, Sarah was an unruly girl with aspirations beyond the ordinary for a girl of her age who saw that she was lacking only a man of strength and influence who would have a ladder to climb to the wings of her ambitious dreams.

She found what she wanted when she saw the saliva of men's lust flowing from Mr Albert's eyes as he examined her from top to bottom, each one of them looking for what he lacked.

And so, fates wished, until one day Mr Albert stopped her in one of the halls of the very long palace and told her that there was a prestigious job and that he could not find anyone who was qualified and suitable for this job but her due to the sensitivity of the job.

She is to be the personal tutor for the queen's adopted daughters. The king's wife was sterile, so they decided at one moment to sponsor two girls the king had given birth to from one of the girls who came in the form of (forbidden gifts).

From the sterile queen who was stripped of mercy when she decided to get rid of the mothers of the two girls after weaning the two children to ensure that no one spoils her mood in the future.

Indeed, Mr Albert succeeded in arranging the matter without making the queen see the new teacher because he was aware of her demonic jealousy, so Satan sought refuge from her twenty times.

And because he knows that the queen, if she learns of Sarah's existence, might plan something wrong out of the ugliness of evil that runs through her veins instead of blood.

So, he decided to take the king's daughters to his private suite in the palace to be taught with his twin sons.

Of all who were in the palace, Mr Albert was adamant to Mrs Caroline for his always helpful advice to the queen and her husband, and they saw in him their true and reliable man in the palace.

Therefore, he had a word heard, free of doubt and suspicion, and this made him single out the girl Sarah in his special section and shower her with gifts and the most beautiful promises of speech, and all these unkind behaviours were taking place without her husband Marco knowing about them, and here Mr Albert realised that the girl did not need to be lured further and that she had paved the way for him of her own accord and sent him a sign of acceptance to be his wife without uttering a single word.

In order that she might not be caught by any slip, if her poor husband knew of this betrayal orchestrated by the love of his life, which was unfortunately, that love would become a dagger in his back, and when the enthusiasm of Mr Albert reached took pride in sin and was strengthened a lot by her dirty and vile support against her husband, who was the cause of what she is, and this is the nature of those who abandoned their principles and moral values for the sake of something that may not happen, and if it happens, it may be a disaster for him like the one who runs behind a mirage in the desert, the thirsty thinks that it is water in the desert of wilderness. He does not find it and lives a life similar to the life of cattle, rather he is more astray in it.

When Mr Albert resolved to carry out his plan, he ordered Mr Marco to be summoned. The plan was prepared by agreement in advance from Marco's wife, who instructed him to complete the mission to give herself to him and be his angel wife and in fact, the opposite is that he was well aware of what she wanted to do to her husband that she might do to him one day but the cravings blinded Albert's eyes.

Whoever betrays in such a way of lowliness that no one expected, nothing prevents her from repeating the same thing with you.

Mr Albert received Marco in his private office and welcomed him as if he were welcoming a king of kings and not just a soldier, to the point that he poured him tea himself and asked him how many sugar cubes he wanted to put, as if on a magical night of love with his mistress in the moonlight they were staying up late.

And he extended to him a basket of the palace baked goods stuffed with delicious cream, which Mr Marco has not and will not find like it in his life since he was born until this moment, from the pleasure of enjoying the real taste of delicious food, the most important of which is the baked goods!

Until he shouted with great admiration and the cream of the cake was flowing from his lips, "Wow, I felt like I was born again and that all my past life was a nightmare and now I wake up for the first time and it is as if I am eating from the pastries of heaven, it is not like any bakery I have tasted in my life."

And he continued his speech while eating greedily, "Imagine, Mr Albert, this matter, and that it was you who woke me up from that miserable dream to this happy reality. Which I considered a good introduction to the beginning of the conversation, which was expected from the outset that it would be moments full of tension and anger or perhaps unimaginable consequences. But you must try in anything you want to reach, otherwise the angels will not come to you with your wishes on a silver and gold plate to purify everything you want."

Mr Albert said gently and with a kind of pride, "Indeed, Mr Marco, I have brought you here to tell you a very good and last piece of news. Hmm, we may disagree, but the end will be satisfactory, by the way. Where is Mrs Sarah, why didn't you come with you?" He said it with all cunning and innocence.

Until Marco answered him easily and simply and said, "You invited me alone and did not invite my wife with me." Mr Albert laughed stupidly and said, "Ah, your wife is right, your wife, yes, I forgot." Then he stared at Marco seriously and was silent for a moment, which surprised Marco, who stopped eating after some doubts he sees Mr Albert's colour changing every moment, as if he is watching his chameleon in a state of panic, with pale eyes distracted, and then he breaks that silence and says sharply in it a kind of hidden anger, Yes my wife, and now will you tell me about the good and the bad news, and I hope you start with the bad news so that I know what awaits me because I know that always had luck against me!" Follow it with a sarcastic laugh, "huh ha-ha!"

Albert put his hands on his knees with confidence and said with a smile on Marco's face, "Your luck today is better than ever."

Then he stood and pulled his cloak from its two ends and said proudly, "I appoint you today as one of the royal cavalry knights, and you know that this is an impossible thing to reach, even if you spend your life in service, unless you get an opportunity like this that I present to you now, and remember that opportunities are precious and rare do not come twice in life, who would think that His Majesty, the king himself will ask you for himself personally without having any advantage in you!"

Marco stood dumbfounded in silence for a moment, not understanding what he was hearing. He knew that such a position would not actually find him, even if he spent his life, because these positions are given only on the recommendations of senior people and on their head the king and queen or those who represent them, most notably Mr Albert, or that you are the owner of a supernatural talent and this is not available in Marco, the simple man, knowing for sure the impossibility of reaching one of these people, and here is the opportunity, the dream had come to him asking for it on its own and without asking for it, he could not speak as if one of them had held his tongue.

Then Mr Albert said, after seeing Marco's eagerness to know the rest of the details of this prestigious offer, and of course he would not get them for free, and frowned on Marco's face, as if to make him feel the greatness of the matter, "I will shorten the matter for you, Marco, and in order to make you the happiest person on this planet, that Mrs Sarah or your wife Sarah, whatever the name is, no longer wants you, and I do not hide from you that she is..." Then he fell silent to arouse suspicion in Marco's soul.

He turned around and said, "I don't know what to say, Marco!" then deliberately silent, which made his brain erupt from the volcano of doubt and he got a little closer to Mr Albert and grabbed his robe hard and said with his eyes sparkling from them, "What is wrong with my wife, Mr Albert?"

He did not answer him until he repeated the same words, the veins of his face swollen from the intensity of his jealousy, and it seems that this is what Mr Albert

was striving for, because he knows that a person in the hour of anger is like dough.

Until Mr Albert said, pretending to be sad, and he succeeded in that, "Calm down, Marco, it didn't get as bad as you can imagine, but I don't hide from you the fact that the king has set his eyes and he is more fascinated by her, of course you will say that the solution is to get her out of the palace. No, Marco, it's too late!"

Then he shook his head and nodded at him unfortunately and interlaced his fingers and then turned around to tell him the malicious idea to control Marco's imagination and thoughts and said quietly after holding Marco's wrist, "The solution is for me to marry her!

"Why marry my wife?

"Let me continue that I am the trust of Queen Caroline, and this will be the reason for her joy and approval, and the king will not be able to do anything, because you know in advance, Marco, about the power of Queen Caroline and how the king fears her, especially with regard to women.

"If the queen had already known that the king wanted to marry Sarah, even if secretly, she would have gotten rid of her, and you would not find any trace of her, and you would lose her forever. As for my marriage to her, it is a temporary solution so that I can get her out of here to safety, and then she will return to you to your village, enhanced and honourable. Did you understood now why I brought you here?"

Marco reacted angrily after taking his dagger out of its sheath and shouting at the top of his voice at Mr Albert, who had almost fallen on his back.

"Of a violent reaction of Marco? Damn you and the king, that's why you brought me together in order to take my wife from me, you wicked fox!"

The guard rushed in and grabbed Marco's hand and took the dagger from him and pressed his hands behind his back.

Mr Albert took a deep breath and straightened his robe, which was about to fall off, and began to shake it with his hand. Then he said coldly, his eyes glimmering with malice, "You have signed a contract to destroy your life, miserable Marco. The guards have seen you attacking one of the king's most important men. You have committed a great crime, and they are punished by hanging." Then he approached Marco and whispered to him in his ear so that no one would hear him, "You have one last chance from three options. The third one means that you are the happiest person, and he is either you die, or Sarah dies, or either I marry her and you live together and come back as a happy couple as you are now with the position?

"You are now free to choose, for I am more merciful than Queen Caroline if Her Majesty knew that a savage soldier like you had tried to stab her best friend in the palace and the kingdom!"

Then he beckoned the guard to take him out amidst Marco's pale, soulless screams after he felt that he had been forcibly killed and realised that what he was working for and devoted all his love and attention to was in the hands of another man.

Mr Albert was the most fortunate person in that period, as things happened according to his desires and wishes, as if he was the one who paints his life as a skilled painter who creates in his painting and puts in it everything his eye desires and his hand adorns with it.

If Mr Marco held his anger for just a few seconds, Mr Albert would have been in an embarrassing situation. If Marco could act cunningly in return for the cunning, he was meeting, or he was silent, even for a little bit, but this is life, sometimes the world you do not win by anger, but by seeking and planning, even when you seek evil.

At the same time, Mr Albert was suffering from great pressure from the priests' gang and their clients from some ministers who sold their loyalty and dignity at a cheap price in order to abandon the protection of the cavalry leader at the time, Mr Abraham, the father of Archie, who represented a danger to their interests from their point of view, but in fact the intertwined interests were the worst thing going on in the corridors of this sprawling palace.

No one would imagine that all these despicable souls had gathered together to get rid of the commander in chief without the knowledge of the queen, who had eyes and ears in every inch of this spacious palace, which is like an entire universe made of stone.

Mr Albert shortened the inclusion of Marco in the list of new knights and put his name in the cavalry division who were under the command of Abraham as a new knight. The news reached Mr Albert that Mr Abraham would be pardoned in the case of treason to the king and queen, but it was decided to expel him and execute all those who were with him, and here was a great opportunity Albert to single out Sarah, Marco's wife, and get rid of Marco once and for all.

Where he will not find anyone standing in his way, especially that he will find a blessing from Queen Caroline, who will not like the presence of a woman of this beauty hovering around her husband's dormitory, where she will live far from the residence of the king, even if it is for a while.

For the queen to have enough time to determine the type of lady Sarah after marriage and the way to get rid of her.

Oh sorry, how to deal with her in the next few days.

Mr Albert represented the role of the innocent in front of his brother-in-law Mr Abraham when he visited him the last time in prison and that he did not know what was happening, but he swore to Abraham that he mortgaged his life and the lives of his children to the king and queen in exchange for being pardoned to return to his family alive in the village of Kling Ling instead of returning in a coffin.

Indeed, this happened, but the surprise that Mr Albert expects is that another pardon will come in which the entire squad, which was Marco among them, was pardoned, as there was a repressed defeat in the eyes of Mr Albert.

He hid her knowing that Marco would be like Juha's nail in his life with Sarah, who would become his new wife as soon as the storm of lies and betrayal that engulfed the palace was over, and that might lead to his plan being exposed one day.

Which prompted Mr Albert to resolve to complete what he had started, and he must finish it immediately, or else he must not rule out that his head will fly. Marco is still living and may use the words of Mr Albert against him,

especially since he used the name of the king to blackmail and loot the property of others unjustly, and to add to all that, many around him wish to find a slip on him to twist his hand or threaten to expose him, which will turn him into a conspiring slave and a puppet in the hands of his enemies if he is exposed the indictment of Marco.

Then he destroys the future of his children, and this is the weak point of Mr Albert. He has already completed his plan and sent a group of criminals to kill Marco on his way out of the kingdom in the prisoner carriage.

But unfortunately, the presence of his brother-in-law Mr Abraham happened in the same car that was carrying Marco outside the kingdom for deportation within the column of deportation carriage, which led the assassination squad sent to cancel the mission immediately, as they were surprised by Mr Abraham's question to them when he said with eyes filled with doubt, "Who are you? Did the king send you to give us a farewell kiss, or are there some gifts that will be in the form of poisoned daggers or arrows?"

The squad leader said maliciously, while they grabbed those automatic arrows, "No, no, sir, take it easy." Then he smiled a yellow smile that revealed the dirtiness of his teeth, which is not dirtier than the blackness of his merciless heart, "We are a special squad working to serve the king and the kingdom as well, but we are under the command of Mr Albert, we were sent just to make sure you are safe and that you arrive outside the kingdom safely."

And how even the butchers and beggars throughout the city have become among the most oppressed and have become involved with the herds that want to live under the slogans of love for the king and false patriotism, even though this matter belongs to the king himself and he has pardoned and ended and this is all there is to the matter, sir but Mr Abraham noticed that the members of the squad, whom he had never seen before, seemed closer to the hired mercenaries than to the knights.

Rather, this was evident in their sharp features and their eyes that revolved around Marco and the carriage in which he was sitting, as if they were the eyes of the wolves that did not leave the injured bull while he was among the herd.

Then said Mr Abraham, as he clenched his fist on the carriage door, fearing that it might be opened suddenly, and shook his head at Marco to do the same.

And Abraham said to him, "Well, thank you, gallant knight, for this attention, but as you can see, we are on the threshold of the gates of the kingdom, and there are no angry citizens here, and there is no danger. The carriage is sufficiently protected by its leader and his escort. We hope to meet again someday to return this favour. There was no choice for the mercenary leader but to turn away or open up, despite their superiority in strength and weapons compared to the defenceless prisoners."

Indeed, he ran away, and there was no alternative plan, only what was planned to put Commander Abraham and the senior leaders in a car alone, and the rest of the cavalry in other cars, and that Marco be shot with a killer arrow, but the situation of Mr Abraham and his friends between them and Marco and it seems that this day was not destined for Marco. Maybe, one day he will be killed, but no one knows how that will be.

As soon as they returned to Kling Ling village, Marco's old mother, who was taking care of him, died and she was the last hope for him until he shouted around the house in a hysterical voice, "Why do the goddess hate me, what did I do to her, why all this torment?"

Until he found no friend except for alcohol, he drank him from the morning and sometimes slept in the streets, and he seemed to be wandering on the face of all that period. This was the sad story of Mr Marco and the reason for his hatred of Mr Albert, who robbed him of his wife and caused the man's future to be lost.

Rather, he was also to take his life, not because he deserves it, but only because of his lust. From here, Abraham set out as if he wanted to start drawing strong relationships that were close to starvation after a long estrangement until Abraham patted Marco on the shoulder, who became for everyone who saw him as an old man in his first forty years, and all of this was from excessive drinking and growing anxiety.

Abraham said to Marco, after he put his hand on his shoulder and shook him hard, as if he was shaking his drunkenness, "The postman from the kingdom arrived today with news, then he was silent for a while."

Then Abraham continued, "Umm, but I don't know whether to believe him or not, although I tend to believe him, not for anything, but for my longing to hear anything about my son, and because it is just a verbal message similar to stories, and you know that I believe what I see, such as envelopes, for example, and not what I hear."

Marco's eyes shone with joy and he was as if he was a madman who had woken up from his illness that had accompanied him all his life until he pulled Abraham's clothes from his sleeves tightly and hugged him to him and said while whispering with eyes filled with tears, "Say that he brought a message with him from Sarah, Abraham, come on say that. Please, I know that Sarah will not forget me, and she still remembers me as I remember her, and I smell her special perfume, the fragrant Rodriguez perfume."

Abraham's face shrank from the Marco case, who weeps the rock if it uttered, but he had to use his impulse for his longing and love for his wife, he walked in a useful way instead of seeing him smash in front of him like this, and so did Abraham when he told himself this lie before Marco was surprised by it, he told him yes! Abraham said it with confidence, as if he had spoken the truth.

Yes, Marco, the courier came with a verbal message from Sarah saying that she still remembers you and that you did not leave her imagination, Marco, and that she also did not forget the smell of the Rodriguez perfume that you were using too!

Marco said in amazement, "What? It is a women's perfume and I have never used it."

Mr Abraham sarcastically realised that he had miscalculated and would have exposed his lie if not that he had captured a malicious laugh in himself in order to avoid embarrassment. He added, "I mean her perfume when she was using it. According to the courier's words, and that she is still waiting for you to free her from that tyrannical oppressor that separated you, the message ended here, Marco. But now, listen to me carefully. If this message does not change you, you will never change, and you will lose Sarah forever. Now, the vision has become clear, and the circumstances have coincided between us, Marco. As for me, I want to get my son back more than I hate those who are there.

"And as for you wanting to get your wife back," Marco said, "What do you want? I mean, it's time to go back as we were before, honourable fighters for the kingdom, and now our duty is more important than that. We will fight now for honour, land, and children. You are a strong knight. This sadness will not help Marco, nor will it bring Sarah back, nor will it bring back your youth.

"It seemed that the idea was for Abraham to form a group of comrades from the past and to investigate what was happening in the kingdom. The stories about what happened in the past nights seemed to spread as if they were the events of a mysterious novel. But now go home, take a warm bath, shave your beard, and rest, and tomorrow I will meet you, and I have gathered the men, and I will send you my son Arthur for lunch, and veal soup, which Archie's mother has prepared, and which she has opened a little stall to sell this soup, to make a fortune."

Marco said with a laugh, after his face changed colour, which became like the sun at sunrise, "You will do that, I promise when we return from the kingdom with Sarah."

Mr Abraham rejoiced well for the return of hope and enthusiasm to Marco's face, and this is what he really wanted to have the best support and a certain in their desired campaign to the kingdom.

Chapter 21

STRANGE MONSTERS

Maya's weeping face was the last Archie saw as he fell from the top of the rug until he fell on his back hard on the surface of the river.

Scattered in its wake everything that was in his mind and erased all the mirrors of his eyes to live in a silent darkness like a foetus in his mother's womb with a soul that does not see and does not feel when he disappeared under the waters of the river and settled at the bottom and disappeared from the world and everything in it for a moment as if he had been buried alive!

Until he returned again to the top and pulled his head out from under the crashing waves of the river, which had a clear effect in mitigating and absorbing the impact of falling from the top, and began to inhale the air with eagerness and his soul was panting from his mouth.

He took a deep breath and quickly screamed for help, his eyes spinning around him, his hands hitting the waves.

Trying to cling to it from the horror of tension and anxiety, perhaps he will find any hope around him to find himself like a confused bird at a pool of water. But the river swept him away from the place of the cave very quickly, and he did not know whether to search in the sky for Maya and those with her, or he had to find his companions first who fell with him until the body of one of them collided with him from behind him and hugged him quickly without knowing who was more than he realised that it would only be one who jumped before him for sure.

It was Clementine, who said happily, gargling from the water that came out of his mouth, clinging to Archie's back like a child clinging to his mother's breast. "Thank God you are here, Archie. I was sure that I was drowning because I couldn't find anything to catch, even if it was just a bird's feather floating above

the water, so I wished it if a savage raptor had pounced on me again and I don't see myself dying by drowning!"

Archie said, raising his voice, confused by the loudness of the water, the force of its rush and its waves, playing with them like dolls, "Rather, thank Goddess, I found one of you. When you jumped before me, I saw the rocks in the middle of the river and how strong the water was. I thought I would only see your corpses floating in the foam of the river. I also did not expect the river to be so cold."

Until their conversation was broken by the sound of cries around them, closer to cries for help. Until they saw Luca and Sebastian holding each other, and only their heads were visible from them, and they were holding the tip of a pointed rock that was embedded in the heart of the river like a stake, Clementine said to Archie, who was trying to swim against the strong current, "It seems that we are not far from the others."

Unfortunately for them, the sun's rays descended directly, without being obscured by any veil of clouds or a cold mist.

Like fire on the ice, which caused the melting of large amounts of snow falling at the top of the river, but fortunately for Archie, his feet touched some rocks at the bottom of the river, while the river waters lifted them up and down, as the river did not exceed two meters deep.

But the force of the rush of the water is like a gale force wind, which made Archie see a thought in his mind, as if someone had thrown it suddenly into his mind, and indeed he dived a little until he saw what seemed to be the most expensive lifeline he could find in his life and for a moment in the midst of the mixed feeling between tension and fear of death by drowning.

Where there were rocks at the bottom of the river stacked like paving stones for old horse carriage roads. He crossed the river from bank to bank under the river, then raised his head and said to Clementine, hold my back tightly.

And here is the plan, "You will hold my back well and try to lower your body down after I take a step on you, and you will put your feet on the rock that I will pass that you will reach, and so on until we reach the other bank, I know that you will do and that you can do that, boy."

Clementine said, mumbling, with signs of incomprehension on his face, "I won't prolong the discussion because I didn't understand anything, but I understood that I would be like a frog behind you, diving and showing until we reached."

Archie felt that an attempt to communicate his idea to the boy from the first time in the midst of these circumstances had failed, but he relied on Clementine's common sense and wit. "Yes, yes, well done, now you understand, frog," said Archie, joking with the boy and claiming that he understood his words.

Until Clementine's head smiled, not sure that Archie had understood him, but he continued moving behind Archie without babbling so that too much water would not enter his small hollow filled with river water.

As for Alex, he managed to get by with his experience and jumped on one of the rocks in the middle of the river and took advantage of his height and the length of his legs in particular.

And He made them like a hook, with which to catch every young boy who passed by the side of the rock, who clung one by one to his legs.

And so on until he was able to rescue Charlie and Pearl and dragged the fat Martin with his hands until Alex and the three boys were in the middle of the river on a smooth rocky hill.

As for Archie, he went to Luca and Sebastian, but before all that he must reach the shore of the bank, to bring Clementine to safety, to relieve himself of the heavy burden, and to have known the way to reach the shore instead of venturing and trying to save everyone at once.

It is better for you to arrive late than to not arrive at all, or to arrive while you are a dead body and you do not even find someone to drive it, and this is what Archie did the one who actually managed to reach the bank holding Clementine until he had that feeling full of clear victory that he had never felt before.

Despite all the great tribulations he overcame, I thought for a while that he saved all of humanity, not because they arrived safely, but because whenever he saw Clementine, he remembered his younger brother, Arthur.

Until Luca called, "Are you forgetting about us, Archie, or what? Our fingers have been cut off and we can no longer hold this rocky, jagged edge! We would rather jump in the river than endure more!"

Archie stood, tired, from the ground on the bank of the river on which he had fallen, and said with fear and confusion at the top of his voice, "No, but I am coming to you with patience, please."

He took off his shoes and then jumped into the river like a carp at a terrible speed until he reached them and felt the bottom from under him until he found a trace of the same paved rocks that spread at the bottom of the river and used them to reach the bank until he confirmed that these rocks were nothing but the remains of a human road paved over the river or a bridge that had fallen and collapsed by an agent or by the actions of the factors of nature, they all arrived at the bank safely.

Luca and Sebastian had moderate injuries in their fingers, which were cut and stabbed because of the pointed rock they were holding on to. Archie said to Sebastian, "Tell Clementine and teach him how to help you heal your wounds and he will do it, Doctor Sebastian. These are free lessons that are distributed to us for free. We must succeed. It is because later on it will be paid for and the price will be very high."

Archie saw that Alexander and the rest were in the middle of the river about forty meters ahead of them while they were trapped on the rock, and he walked by the river on the bank until he was right in front of them and shouted mockingly without seeing him throwing small and soft river pebbles at them as if they were like the eggs of a quail bird.

To draw their attention to him, their eyes did not leave the high waves of the river trying to snatch them from the rock on which they took shelter, until the fat Martin noticed him and shouted with joy, "It is our friend Archie, it is Archie, calling us from the bank—that it is Archie."

The tension and anxiety turned to hope and calmness until Martin's fat feet slipped and were almost swallowed up by the angry river waves, but Alex caught up with him at the last moment, Charlie and Pearl laughed after they saw the fat Martin rolling like a hedgehog curled on himself.

And Charlie said, with foam in his mouth, laughter at their friend, "For a moment, I thought I was watching a penguin lose its balance."

Burley replied, quarrelsomely, in an irritated manner, "I thought a fat seal rolled around while sleeping like an empty barrel. If he drowned, he should have been ridiculed in this humiliating way."

They continued to laugh until a successful pebble throw from Archie's hand hit Pearl's head, and they turned to the bank, and Archie called them at the top of his voice, "Will you sleep on the rocks or will you come to us to continue our journey?"

Alexander replied after throwing him to the side and said loudly, criticising, "He who puts his feet on the shores of safety is not like one who sits in the midst of the horrors of danger, look for ropes for us or make them from those trees behind you, for around their trunks grow climbing branches like strong ropes. If our position here does not encourage crossing, it seems that Martin has a fever."

Archie turned to the giant trees behind him to check Alexander's useful piece of information, akin to solving a puzzle at crucial moments.

And if it was indeed, as Alex said, it was a large, climbing tree that wrapped around the stumps of pine trees that were scattered in abundance, as if they were many snakes trying to squeeze the tree trunks, and as soon as he remembered to bring out the proud spear to use his sharp blade, he did not find it until he became mad as he felt his back and focused his eyes on every inch around him was terrified until Clementine saw him bandaging Sebastian's wounds and said quietly, "It seems you have lost a dear, Archie, isn't it?"

Archie with a stray mind said, "How can you not when the spear has lost pride? Oh, what sin did I do to get all of this? No, no, I don't know what happened to me. It seems that I forgot it on the magic carpet, or that I lost it in the river when I fell?"

Clementine said smiling, with signs of doubt and suspicion in Archie's eyes, "Look behind you, he is there. Archie hastily turned backwards with his eyes, and saw nothing. Then his eyes turned in all directions and every inch around him, and he did not see anything!"

Then he turned to Clementine in anger to reproach him until the spear was in his face and his blade almost touched the tip of Archie's nose. Clementine said, "The spear fell from you inadvertently, when you ran to the fairy, Maya, I took it and kept it when I knew that the atrocity of the matter was enough to make you forget it. And then these rapid events occurred, and I forgot to give it to you."

Archie sighed so hard that his cheeks were like balloons, then he grabbed the spear and sat on his little butt and said, "Now help me cut the ropes. Let's talk later about the reward."

Alexander growled and shouted, "Did you go to cut the ropes or to make a house in the tree?" What is the ugliest of this day and the ugliest surprises that we have found?

Archie gave those with him a silent look after hearing Alexander's angry shout, and a dead laugh emerged from him.

He said, "Do not respond to him, as it seems that he will unload his anger on us. Leave him for a little while, so that we can do our work without any pressure. Come on now."

Time passed quickly and they accomplished the task of making ropes from cutting the stems of those climbing trees, which were heavier than they thought.

Until Archie grabbed the end of the rope to trim it and be more precise than it is in order to make it have two ends to tie the dagger to and become like a hook to be a weight in the front of the rope when he throws it to the stranded in the middle of the river that did not welcome the presence of these unknown intruders, as if the river seems to be hiding some surprises for them while distance.

And so did Archie, and he threw the dagger at Alexander, after he tied it to the trunk of a huge pine tree, and Alex grabbed the dagger, repeating, unusually pessimistically, about which he is known to be a boy who is indifferent to everything that is coming in his life, "It was a difficult day from the beginning, and I am not optimistic about the rest of it."

Charlie replied maliciously, "I see our leader as if you are not sure that the one who sent us the ropes is our brother, Archie!"

Alexander said after pulling the rope and tying it around his waist, ignoring Charlie, "Go ahead and cross the river quickly, because the force of the water will make your body twice as heavy as it is for the rope, and this is beyond my endurance. Show me that you deserve to be knights, men that everyone fears, and now pass quickly and we'll finish it."

Charlie gave him a silent, hateful look. He was the first to cross the river while he was holding the rope that starts from Archie and ends with Alexander, then Beryl advanced, and finally the fat Martin, who approached Alexander and said to him with a complimenting look, "Thank you for saving me", then continue following the others until they all reached the bank.

Clementine was the first to be happy about the friends reuniting until his eyes glazed as he greeted them with warmth and tears in his eyes, until Martin hugged the fat man saying how much I miss your fat despite their incompatibility since they first met in the camp, but the spirit of the group ran in Clementine's blood more than anyone else.

Which buried the sound of hatred between them until that act raised the astonishment of Archie, Alexander, and the others knowing Martin's chubby hated Clementine.

But this behaviour was an introduction to everyone and a biography about the spontaneity of this member and who may be a pivotal member in the future of this gang soon, so whoever has a white heart like Clementine's will never lose.

The fat Martin stood in anger and said in a sharp tone, his hands on his stomach, which the wet shirt couldn't hold, and his navel came out from behind the buttons of the shirt, shyly, "This is the third time we find a place to rest, and every time we are preparing food something happens and we have to run away like rabbits, but now there is no excuse for you to sit and cook food and then sleep a little, for the day is in its midst, and the place looks like an oasis of safety chosen by God to compensate us for what we have been through. Look at the weather, how nice it is, even though we are at the end of autumn. The need for that is great, and not just for satiety."

Silence fell after Martin's historic sermon, punctuated by the hum of male flies fighting to win the female who seemed to be busy enjoying licking the pus of the sleeping wound of Sebastian.

Everyone had taken off their wet clothes and hung them on the branches that were lined up over their heads in both directions, in such a way that they were free from any blemish.

They stretched out semi-naked, their private parts covered only with worn- out panties that have not changed since they left the kingdom more than three months ago, as if they were on one of the islands of the Gypsy Sea in the south.

Which is characterised by its warm sun throughout the year, some of them slept on his side and put his head on one hand and the other on his ear, and others covered their eyes with tree leaves similar to the ears of elephants after they stretched under the intensely shining sun that reflected from their tired bodies.

Without any sense of her presence, like not being aware of the constant battle of memory of the flies, the fat Martin felt a deep anger within him and rolled his eyes around the place after feeling that for a moment he was talking to the dead.

Until Luca replied, laughing nervously, "Don't you see what we are in, your fat? Tell me, where are the bags with all our tools and food? Or do you want us to slaughter you like a pig? Do you not have eyes to see, or do you only see through your ugly belly button, huh? Come on, don't you see that we only have the clothes that cover us? Aren't your goddess supposed to send us food instead of this place so that the sun's rays don't want to touch us as if we were unclean creatures of the earth!"

Clementine replied, furrowing his eyebrows and shaking his head in anger, "Slowly, Luca, why all this prejudice against Martin? His question is innocent. Indeed, we are now in the best time. We hope to find ourselves and gather each other after what happened. After all, we are human beings who need food, and we are not angels."

Luca yelled at Clementine, "Huh? Are you all crazy or what? This is unreasonable! This is unreasonable! Does it seem to you, too, that we represent

fasting to your various goddess, or do we have food and we take it too much for ourselves, or what, you useless one?"

Then he continued with his teeth eating his lips, "But it seems that the waters of the river have swept your minds and you can no longer think realistically."

Clementine said angrily, looking tenser, "It's my roughness when I spoke to you as a human, I should have to talk to you like an animal because you are only good at speaking to a herd of animals..."

Luca interrupted him with sarcasm and provocation, "Well, you did if you told us that you are one of the rats of the kingdom and only understand the language of shoe slapping when you run away."

Clementine became angry and could not control himself and shouted while biting his lips. Clementine said angrily, looking tenser, "It's my roughness when I spoke to you as a human, I should have to talk to you like an animal because you are only good at speaking to a herd of animals..."

Luca interrupted him with sarcasm and provocation, "Well, you did if you told us that you are one of the rats of the kingdom and only understand the language of shoe slapping when you run away."

Clementine became angry and could not control himself and shouted while biting his lips. "Do you like me to a rat, monkey?" And Clementine pulled out his claws like an angry cat defending its only morsel after a long struggle. He jumped with his hands-on Luca's face and attacked him with his fingernails and even biting. Fat Martin entered the battle line without any hesitation and grabbed Luca's hair to give Clementine the edge. To beat Luca and heal his madness and his constant mockery of him.

Everyone woke up in annoyance to the sound of shouts, punches and insults flying in the form of spit that hit the faces of everyone around them.

Archie hurriedly approached them and got between the two quarrels and grabbed the arms of both Luca and Clementine and said in exasperation, "Damn you both because you couldn't stand each other's different points of view. How stupid are you? What would you do if you found booty and wanted to share it or disagreed with each other while you were on a night watch? And you two just couldn't stand a sterile argument between you?"

Clementine said grinning about his little fangs, "I was very patient with him and he kept raising his voice."

Luca replied, "But I was the one who was patient…"

Archie interrupted them and reprimanded them strongly, "Be silent, children. This incident will not be in vain, and you will have a different punishment, and you, Martin, will not be better off than them."

Alexander came and stopped for a while and said with a sarcastic face and a calm voice, "This is how it happens when the leader is absent, they will kill each other without any mercy!"

Alexander was hinting at something, but Archie was watching him and interrupted him angrily, "Very clear, but this is what happens when the commander is bedridden like an old woman who has rickets?"

The others would have burst out laughing, except for the three abusers, had they not captivated the laughter within them and hid it for fear that they would anger Commander Alexander and cause a crisis like that of Nathan, who left the camp angry and threatened them with woe.

Alexander felt an inner hatred for Archie that he had never felt before!

After a period of silence, then he thought quietly and decided to wait and turn the situation in his favour and ignore Archie in order to appear more intelligent and more rational in front of others.

And indeed, he did so and ignored Archie's embarrassed reply and said gently while staring at Archie, "Everyone seems to have lost their bags and this means that we have lost food and only arrows, bows and daggers are left with us, and this is not bad, as the food will sooner or later find it."

As for the weapon, I don't think the branches will give it to us, said the fat Martin, scratching his stomach, "Well, Commander, since food is an easy matter, as you said, tell us where we will eat from while we are in this place, unless you have a kitchen in that cave that you want us to head to while we are hungry."

Alexander grimaced, fed up with the dulling of Martin's thought and said, holding himself in anger, "I promise you will be the first to eat, and I will give you food with my hands."

Fat Martin opened his mouth in amazement and happiness, and said cheerfully, "Really, when, when and what will the food be? It is grilled lamb with apple pie sweetened with honey, because that is what I want now."

Clementine said impatiently, after hitting his forehead with his fist, "I am so impatient with this talk with this boy that I hate talking about food, I hope something happens to forget this talk that causes colic."

On the morning of the second day, after a night that was not reassuring, Archie and Alex did not sleep, and they became like guards awakening with great attention and concentration when they lit a huge fire to make them feel safer than warm after they heard strange sounds like howls but not howls that came from behind the cave and around the pine trees with voices tree rustle which did not cause their fear to settle on one doubt, but rather several terrifying doubts that endured all forms of terror and panic.

And when the others woke up in the morning and got dressed after a refreshing bath on the cold river shore, suddenly the forest shook up and came out of what was inside of it from the surprises and without any introduction until they heard the sounds of thick breaking of the branches from behind the trees and swaying in all directions until they all thought they were around the corner or less from facing ogres, and this is what their minds agreed upon, except Alex, who had gone away and thought that they might be the other squad of Glister had revealed their position until the bushes came out in front of them and they looked on after a terrible silence of suspicion and anticipation, until they were no longer a whisper!

Then came the surprise that cooled in their hearts the fire of doubt when they were surprised by a small spotted deer that leapt in front of them from behind the thick bush and stood meditating on their strangely shocked features!

He did not last long on his own until another jumped up beside him and began to flirt with the first, and they were more than six months old.

A few moments later, a whole herd came out walking quietly and slowly and began to eat from the green land full of fresh herbs and from the intensity of surprise, everyone jumped for joy and shouted with joy and fun and said the fat Martin, who went crazy laughing hysterically— Hahahahaha, that it's meat and he called with enthusiasm to the others next to him as if calling on him who sits on the top of the hill, "Come on, bring out your arrows, and let us hunt them all. It seems that God has answered the foolish Luca, and has surprised us with what no one had thought of."

It was a hopeful scene after moments of feeling lonely and hungry together, but something, as usual, misfortunes do not come individually until the atmosphere disturbs everyone, including the deer, when the dominant male deer issued a loud warning cry in three batches, like blowing a trumpet, and it appeared on the eyes of the herd and its bodies, traces of panic and confusion as if call to escape from death!

Yes, it is the sound of the call of danger, which means run away with your life, comrades, before they eat you alive, so is the witty Archie, who remembered the failed deer hunting expedition with his father and brothers.

The herd fled towards the river and set out along the shore without looking behind them to be sure. Then Alex and before him Archie realised that the deer ran towards the river so quickly, not to take a warm bath under the rare sunshine these days, but rather an indication of the presence of an unknown predator chasing them, and it is better to act now before it's too late.

There are moments that you have to run forward without being sure of the type of danger, at least in both cases. Running away means that you still have your whole life in your own hands, but waiting means that you own half of your life and the other half in the hands of the unknown.

Astonishment prevailed until Alexander shouted louder than the shriek of a male deer, who fled before the rest of the herd, in an unusually comical manner! And Alex said, warning in a hurry, until he wiped his mouth with a punch of saliva which he secreted from fear, "Go up quickly, the trees are beside you and the danger is ahead of you."

Alexander ran and stuck his body to the tree trunk and said, "Come on, get

on my shoulder!"

The boys did not understand. They thought that it was a joke from Alexander to ease the atmosphere of quarrels that escalated and began to repeat his screams again loudly and roaring in anger like a roaring lion. Let's run and go up as fast as possible until he grabbed Martin's chubby hair, who stood imagining him enjoying the food in his imagination, and he imagined those deer were grilled meat flies in front of him.

Alexander continued, "If you don't act now, we will be dinner for the next monsters, and this is much worse than our hunger for game. There are monsters running after this herd that will tear you to pieces." Archie runs to the tree trunk and does like Alexander.

And he clasped his chest to the trunk of the tree to save time for the others, as the pine tree on which Alex chose to climb had more and rather thick branches than the rest of the pines around them, and whose branches were rather thin and slender, and they began to climb onto the back of Archie and Alex who already had to. They carry everyone's weights above their shoulders, even though they do not carry any weapons after fear has forgotten everything.

Then everyone was sure that misfortune had come to them again, and even followed them in this far land. The fat Martin murmured, his stomach sounding warning that the food was running out, and he said as he climbed on Alex's shoulder, "Nothing new. We're going to run like rabbits again, until I accidentally blow a fart that would have made Alex go crazy with laughter, or else Fat Martin would fall on him."

Everyone climbed up to Alex, who was the tallest and did not struggle to catch the nearest branch to the ground from the first jump. Archie and Sebastian, who was late to stand on Archie's shoulder because of the injury he had in his hands from the river rock, until Archie said after he seemed uncomfortable and tired from Sebastian standing on his shoulders.

Until Sebastian turned, when he saw what made his heart jump from among his ribs from the horror of those many yellow eyes sunken in the heads of a herd of strangely shaped werewolves that were chasing the herd of deer, peeling the body from its ugliness and its very frightening form at the same time!

Sebastian, staring at her in horror, his lips trembling after the herd of strange beasts stopped running after the herd of deer when they spotted the boys on the tree stump and Archie and Sebastian were still down!

Alex shouted madly, "Damn it, it's the dopper, it saw us, and it seems that it has changed its target, and we are the prey, not the deer!"

Sebastian stopped moving and was trembling, but Archie did not know what to do except that he wanted to get rid of Sebastian, who made him move heavy and paralysed his feet in place.

And he looked up at Sebastian and whispered sharply as he tried to control Sebastian, as if he was rising from a high fever and his eyes were fixed on those ferocious beasts, "Don't look at them, you will break your neck and fall and be easy prey. Remember, Sebastian, that there are those waiting for you, and there is no doubt that the arrival of your corpse to them in the form of pieces will make them sad, but you cannot do that if you throw all your strength into your hands and climb quickly, that's all you need, and I don't think that's difficult. Come on, please, for God's sake, Sebastian, don't break yourself and us with you!"

Until Alex dangled from above and extended his leg to Sebastian and said to him, sweat pouring from his forehead, "Hug my legs with your thighs, and I'll lift you up without your hands," but all that didn't make Sebastian remove even a little bit of the tragedy that had befallen him until Alex shouted angrily, "Come on, get up and grab my leg, your stupid bastard, before you kill us!"

All that commotion caused by the increased movement on the tree and its branches caused the focus of the Dopper creatures, who instinctively realised that their prey was planning to escape to the top of the tree.

The doppers were mammals with the head of a werewolf and the body of a muscular kangaroo with claws similar to the claws of a bear, black in colour, like the colour of a gorilla, and they had long hair from the part of the head to the middle of the back, and their voice resembled the sound of African wild dogs when they communicated with each other, and they had six fangs the length of each of them more than more than four inches, evenly distributed on each side, are very sharp and jaw-dropping, they enjoy grinding the bones like a crunchy biscuit. Never stop eating even if it is full, this is the secret of its great danger.

Alex said himself and made a promise to himself that he would end the matter at once, and all he had to do was to make a quick movement to lift Sebastian, who was obstructing Archie's rise, and this would expose them to death indefinitely in a few seconds that would kill their dreams if the worst-case scenario happened until Alex threw himself in the air while holding the stems of the climbing trees and he abducted Sebastian by surprise, dragged him by his hair, lifted him to him, and then lifted him to the top when the rope returned, loosened once, to the outward direction, as if an eagle had swooped in the blink of an eye.

The ferocious doppers let out a terrifying howl to pounce on Archie before he caught up with those who had climbed up and lost their dinner until Charlie cried, crying out over the branch of the tree, "Come on, Archie, get up!" The skinny man shivered when he saw the entire herd of doppers, who numbered in the dozens with dozens, it was jumping like a deer in the air approaching Archie faster than a flying arrow, Archie turned to the tree trunk on which he was leaning and climbed the protrusions from the bottom of the tree trunk to the top and climbed until he grabbed the rope that Alexander gave him and threw his two hands on the rope to become suspended, the air away from the tree trunk until it was exposed. One of those doppers was bitten by an Archie's cloak and would have gotten him if it weren't for the difference of a few seconds, and in less than a moment one of you turned around.

Dozens of doppers gathered and their saliva filled the ground from below around the huge pine tree and howled and barked from all sides and tried to jump and catch Archie with its fearsome eyes and long tongues, they are animals it is not climbing and belongs to the canine family somewhat, which makes everyone

on the tree in a safe and secure position, and I started to smell the ground after it smelled of blood, which increased its brutality even more. Many of the herd members put their front legs on the tree trunk and some of them continued to bark while the lucky doper who grabbed Archie's cloak was still hanging in the air shaking His body fell down hard to bring down Archie, who could not climb from the weight of the doppers attached to his cloak.

In his cloak, Alex said in a loud voice, "Where are the arrows?"

Clementine replied, "We forgot about her at the river bank when we were taking a shower in the morning, and there was nothing but fear and confusion when you were yelling at us to go up to the tree."

Luca and the fat Martin went down to the pine branch Alex was sitting on and began to try to drag Archie before he gave up and was dropped by the dopper who would never give up until he got his prey.

And as soon as they lifted Archie a little with great difficulty, Alex dangled his hand to catch Archie, but the violent dopper moved his jaw with great force, right and left, with the help of his weight, who was more than three times the weight of Archie, who tried to hold on as much as possible, but it seemed that he could not stand it, and he was tired of bearing the weight of Sebastian, and the doper came and completed what was left and wasted his energy and in a sad moment of tiredness— until Archie gave up after all the miserable attempts and fell down with the stubborn dopper. It was a great shock when they saw Archie falling among those hungry monsters roaring around him as if they were dancing a victory dance and rejoiced with joy at this hunt Which will only be a simple wait before they find what satisfies them after they made a circle around it and some of them continued to run quickly around Archie with the false illusion of attacking him, and others sat down a little, and this is fortunate for Archie that the natural behaviour of the dopper and its hunting rituals require that you sing around the prey before pouncing on it, tear it alive and make mock attacks on Archie to distract him from the real attacker who will be slashing his stomach.

With his teeth like the new Barber's blades, as they seemed to have never seen or hunted a human before, Alex said tactfully, after he thought, "Hold on tight to the tree trunk and shake the branches on which you are standing violently, and we will howl and bark with all our might, and this will harden her mind a little. While I try to lower the rope to Archie, perhaps he will find a way out of it and jump into the rope."

And they did that when Alex finished saying the word (three) until the circle of siege imposed by the doppers on Archie was dispersed and they took a position of self-defence after they thought that a herd of dogs or the wolves attacked them and started shouting warnings among themselves, and some sniffed the ground to make sure.

The others went forward to ascertain if there was indeed an enemy or competitor who had suddenly stormed their lands to snatch their prey from them. As for Archie, he was staring at the dopper's eyes and legs with caution, calmness and high concentration, after he sat on his knees to warn of any attack on him, after he caught a handful of dirt in both hands to defend himself, and he

found nothing but the mud of the earth.

Archie realised that this opportunity might not be repeated in light of the

overwhelming preference of the doper herd over him until he made the strongest decision at the most decisive moment that could end his life at any moment if he made a mistake when he threw the doper's face in his eyes with the sticky mud in his hand, who was standing in front of him like a guard until the doper shouted He barked vigorously, shook his head in harm, and ran quickly everywhere, hitting his head on the ground and colliding with others like a raging bull.

He bites and snaps at him, and groans intensely in pain, but unfortunately this behaviour of Archie and not studied had a dangerous repercussion that made her let out her anger to decide to finish him off immediately.

Where they gathered around Archie very quickly and even narrowed the circle after they felt that he would escape from them indefinitely.

They were determined to start devouring him immediately when Archie realised that the matter was over after he had exhausted all options and was stranded and closed his eyes to meet his inevitable fate while hearing the cries of his friends from the top of the tree like a distant echo that was veiled by the intense disturbance caused by the evil dopper.

And he entered into a deep spiritual thought to forget the severe pain he would suffer.

Heedless of despair, comes a ray of hope in the form of a burning sun light that struck the eyes of those ferocious beasts with sudden blindness, which fled in every direction to protect themselves from those sudden rays, as if someone had set the sun beside them, and their eyes became half open and they could no longer see well.

It was a very bright reflection of the sun's rays. It was only Alexander's successful trick, who climbed to the top of the giant pine tree and took out a small dagger that was in a small pocket behind his leg muscle and raised it high to direct the bright rays into the eyes of the doper herd and made him as if he controlled the aim of his arrow towards the target with all accuracy and he succeeded and he was successful in his good idea with an effective effect until Archie felt that the evil spirits around him were far away.

And when he opened half his eyes, the situation was completely different for a moment and he realised for a moment that the world had ordered him to renew his hope for him again for a specified period, Alex called him from above with the loudest shout he had shouted in his life, "Come on, Archie, get up quickly and pick up the rope and the boys will take care of the rest, I don't think the rays may have a long effect on these monsters."

Archie tried to get up and run, but he felt complete numbness in his legs after that fall that he fell on his back, but he tried to gather his strength, which completely collapsed to get up, but he could not until he stumbled and fell to the ground.

Then he tried again hard to crawl to approach the tree trunk, but the rope was short and he needed two right feet to make a successful jump. The doppers found that moving them towards the tree's stem would rid them of these rays that blinded them temporarily and at the same time the place would be suitable for them to finish off their prey and devour it under the shade.

Until he threw with all his strength on the rope and caught him while they were the boys to raise him and in the utmost optimism, sitting on one of the branches of this tree is considered as one who enters heaven, there is no fear in it or fatigue, but the beats of joy did not last long until the same naughty dopper jumped on it.

The one who clung to his robe the first time, as if between him and Archie he retaliated hundreds of years until Archie fell again on his back and he saw nothing but complete darkness and entered into a half coma. With sadness and crying and sad looks on Alex who appeared for the first time as if he was weaker than a chicken, the dopper monsters pulled Archie from his feet away from the tree as if they were dragging the body of a dead animal, and in the midst of this scene that no one wishes for his enemies, how about their best friend?

In those moments when real men's metal appears, Clementine pulls the little dagger out of Alex's hand and jumps on the rope until it falls beside Archie.

Amidst the astonishment of everyone, even the dopper beasts gnashed their fangs for fear of causing them unexpected harm, until he attacked them with his small dagger violently as he howled and barked in an exciting and heroic scene and said sharply, raising the dagger between his blue eyes, "I will not leave him alone as long as I have a weapon, I will not accept that one of us dies because of these filthy creatures, even if it cost me my life," shouted at the top of his voice like a lion who declared war, until fear appeared on the herd of doppers in a surprising and surprising way!

Her ears were lowered and she fell back as if Clementine's voice had really scared her and in an unexpected way encouraged Clementine more and continued and raised his voice more and higher until Clementine marvelled at the loudness and strength of his voice even though he stopped shouting?

Indeed, the dopper retreated in great fright and retreated, letting out a faint moan, and kept barking among themselves with eyes sparkling with sudden fear until Clementine stopped screaming after he felt that his vocal cords might be cut off and his voice pale, but the snarling sound behind him did not stop until he raised his shoulders to his head to protect his ears from that clank and he saw a huge shadow behind him that blocked the sun from them and replaced their shadows, and as soon as Archie raised his head from the ground, he saw the doppers fleeing like rabbits and dragging the tail of disappointment between his legs! What happened?

Archie said, with panic on his face, "Do not move, Clementine, stand in your place, and do not turn behind you!"

Clementine now sensed that the dopper had not escaped from his voice until Alex came down from above and did not see what he saw until he stopped and said with light astonishment, his mouth, "May God have mercy on us! And he wished that none of those who were on the tree would follow him, as he saw a great brown bear standing on his feet, blocking the horizon in front of everyone in front of him from the horror of his size."

Archie rose with difficulty, put his hands-on Clementine's shoulders, and rolled his eyes together, then said in a whisper, "I am proud of you, Clementine, but it seems that the second part of the excitement has begun, valiant knight. Turn behind you and hold yourself and try not to make any sound or make any movement."

Then Archie took the dagger from Clementine's hand quietly without Clementine feeling doubt and suspicion of Archie's mysterious tone. He turned

slowly back until his hair stopped and his eyebrows were about to fly over his eyes as if he had been struck by lightning.

Archie said to him, "Stand firm, boy, and do not spoil that heroic deed."

The appearance of the bear was not the last moments and the flight of the wild dopper herd was a great joy that removed a mountain of worry and fear from the chests of the lost boys in this world.

The one who is ruthless, big or small, was lost in the stage of fear of death, and suddenly after the appearance of the bear they became in the stage of inevitable death.

The doppers herd was around the corner, close to killing one individual.

Whatever the importance of this individual, it remains one individual and they were spared from that at the very least. As for facing a bear of this size, it means that there is no chance of survival for all and not for one person. Even those on the tree if the bear could not climb to hunt them because of its size, it could easily bring them down by dropping the whole tree, which seemed to him like a soft cane stick, or shaken them to fall like apples from the tree...

Archie patted Clementine's trembling shoulder until his electrified body shook with fright, and he said to him, Archie consoling, so that he wouldn't be shocked, like what happened when he saw the black fairy, "As long as your body is standing, you should not be afraid of the idea of bodies falling around you, if it's your turn when you see them fall while you are still standing. Remember this. You are still standing."

In the midst of this solemn situation and the deafening silence in which only the rustling of trees can be heard, as if they were the voices of the spirits of creatures that had been taken by the forest, Archie called Alex with intermittent words, "It is safer not to move or take any step, and so is everyone above."

Fat Martin said in frustration, "It was as if happiness had sworn not to leave us forever. We didn't want to get rid of those bleak monsters, and now a giant bear comes to us, it's a great disaster?"

Archie said, "The real loss is that we all die and no one remains in us to tell our story and adventures to others, and the journey of our lives is a lie that we lied and believed and disappeared with the end of our lives. Be patient, everything has a solution, and so does this bear. We must find an escape from it, even if we have to create a hole in the air, we will create it with our own hands out of nothing.

"If the goddess wanted to destroy us, he would have done before, but this bear would not have come at this time except to save us, not to kill us, even if his features do not suggest that, but if the goddess wanted us to survive, he would send it even when you were survival on the back of the worst of creatures. In this situation, there is no longer any benefit in talking, other than a call to wait and be patient."

"I'll try to keep the bear busy," said Archie audibly to Clementine, and you try to slip quickly to the place of the arrows and spears we collected from the river, and if you ever see the bear attack us by shooting as much arrows as possible and leave the rest on us because the body language of this bear never suggests that he wants to pounce on us and his appearance and behaviour do not suggest that he saw in us the perfect meal as the dopper would see it, but the silence did not last long, until the bear broke the fragile silence and shook his huge head after having settled on the ground with his feet and hands, and speaking as humans speak, and said in a slow voice and with distant words.

"Your thought was not right, I do not kill children and I hope that you will continue your journey because I do not think that you came for accommodation or recreation here and it is in your interest to hear my words because I will not do it again, gentlemen, here I am addressing you with my human spirit, but after a little while I will destroy your tender bodies When I return to my animal nature!

"I'm afraid that doesn't happen, it will make me very sad after I finish tearing the last one of you, but I will quickly forget in a few moments, this is what keeps me alive!"

This shocked everyone but Archie was the least stunned after she looked back with this memory a little when he remembered the horse, Barbara who was stunned for the first time when he saw an animal talking, thinking and behaving just like humans!

Surprised, he said to himself, "Why do you repeat the same situations every time? Are we going around in a vicious circle, or is there something we need to see? Or are we parting of a novel that we do not know the true intentions of its writer?"

Thinking, he said, "Since the bear spoke in this way, it means that he has a complete human understanding of our minds and the nature of our thinking like what happened with the horse, Barbara, before?"

While the giant bear was about to leave after turning around with his back like a moving wall, Archie shouted at him with force and shouted, "Hey, bear!"

Alex grumbled, pointing at Archie silently, with his index finger on his lips.

But Archie was gentle and realised that behind this bear there is a great thing and that it is not an ordinary bear until he started arguing with him and said, "Since you mean what you said, do we not have the right to thank you even a little for your good work with us and saving our souls?"

The bear stopped walking and looked from behind his eyelid to the side to listen to Archie, who had come to Alex, who said with astonishment, "As if I am living in one of the pages of my sister Isabella's novel, it is a wonderful thing."

The bear continued its distance after stopping and did not respond to Archie, who bit his lip, who shouted at the bear again and slapped him with more seriousness, "Stop!" The bear stopped again and listened attentively, as if he was waiting for a signal to find out something in himself!

Until Archie said, "But tell me, how could a bear like you put a human necklace around its neck?"

The bear answered him coldly and full of anger, "I told you to leave at once!"

Luca said, his heart nearly jumping out of his ribs, "Archie, damn you, you are like the one who smashes a hornet's nest to provoke his instinct and kill us as we promised…"

Cried Martin, weeping in an ugly voice, in which all were disgusted and disgusted, "We are dead, we are dead I can't imagine who's going to start this bear first? But of course, not me!"

Then he continued crying like the crying of the child whose toy was taken, except for Archie, who remained steadfast, waiting for answers from a talking monster, then added, anticipating the response of the bear.

And calmly he said, "I saw your eyes and saw the deep sadness in them. I may be in front of you, seemingly a little resourceful creature. But my mind crosses the horizons."

Then he got closer to the bear until he was walking beside him until he touched his back gently and said tenderly, "Your eyes are the eyes of a human and not the eyes of a bear, and I see in them a lot of pain!"

Then he was silent and wanted to give the bear time to speak, but a moment passed as if it was an hour, then finally the bear spoke and said, "Don't worry about me, I have adapted a lot, but I can only give you a piece of advice. Beware, the healer masa. No one has the ability to escape from him, and everything he does will be the complete opposite later!" Then he continued walking, during

which Archie decided not to be too curious, since the situation had reached this unexpected friendly.

In order, not to weigh him down and provoke his explosion at an unexpected moment, in which he cannot control himself for any reason, and this also happens in many cases.

Then, Archie stood for a while, repeating the same sentence, beware of the healer?

After the name had been repeated to him several times before, and now it seems that he must find an explanation for the character (of a healer), which seemed to stir up mystery and confusion in Archie's soul, Archie moved away from the bear a meter away without turning his back on him.

He said thanking, "I wish I could understand what you mean or what is going on in your mind so that I can be of help to you, but thank you, bear, for this advice. Thank you once again on behalf of me and everyone and everyone who loved us in this life. We will not forget you that favour as long as I live. I promise that I will not forget you, and my friends will not forget you either, bear, and if I wanted to know what your name is, but thank you."

Archie did not stop firing expressions of praise at the bear as he turned back and turned towards the bear until he reached the bank of the river because he knew and also believed that the animal instinct could return to him at any moment.

It is not hidden from Archie through his experience in breeding dogs that it is foolish to turn your back on any predator and do not believe in betraying its instincts, but all this did not change the behaviour of the bear who continued walking away silently.

Leaving the boy between great joy and great confusion, especially Archie, who did not leave his eyesight from the bear, and he repeated in an inaudible voice, "Beware the healer," until the bear disappeared among the trees of the forest.

Chapter 22

CROWN PRINCE SURPRISE

While Maya was standing in the hands of her father and the guards around him, the two little fairies hid behind her in fear, sighing in tears:

Woe to us, woe to us, we helped Maya to escape, and we are now before the king.

Maya said confidently in an inaudible voice, "Be quiet, do not move, and stay behind my back."

Until the king said to her curiously, "How does the king's daughter behave? Is that what I taught you? And for whom? And what is the goal that you seek from behind all these behaviours that are not worthy of a girl of the same status as you? I did not spare anything for your happiness, and even if you asked for something that was not created, I will create it for you and I will make it for you, no matter what the cost is, only for your sake, it will be made and created!"

Maya raised her head indifferently and did not show any fear or confusion, as she prepared for the worst that could happen since the moment she dared and planned to escape and said with poise, "I do not want you to do anything for me or create for me things that you did not create and do not cost yourself because I lost something irreplaceable?"

The king replied, provoked by her words until his eyes widened, "What did the daughter of the Great Barhout lose that I did not know?"

She said boldly (and this is her specialty and art in which she excelled) and furrowed her eyebrows, "I lost my father!"

The guards were astonished, and they exchanged strange looks, and their features showed fear of the king's reaction until the king turned his back and said calmly as if he had caught on quickly and said, claiming ignorance, "What is the meaning of that and where did you lose him, my daughter, and how is that while he is in front of you?"

Maya says sadly, her eyes glazed and her tongue freed, "I lost my father when I lost my mother, until I spent most of my childhood crying until the soil was wet from crying a lot and no one felt me! I was hoping to see my real dad, who took refuge in his embrace after the separation of my mother!"

Maya could not stand her being affected by her words stemming from the burning pain inside her until her tears ran and continued in a louder voice, "I wanted you my real father only. I do not want more than this and not that father that I have never felt since I was created for me, you are just a person named (my father) who spends all his time with the maidservants and did not care about my presence as if I were a piece of the luxurious furniture of his palace.

"I do not want to be a box of memories in which you put everything that reminds you of my mother to cry over it for a few minutes to relieve your conscience of your responsibility for your only daughter and then return to your frivolous life!

"I have seen many creatures less than me in the kingdom, and some of them do not have a home for their children, and some of them are deprived of the blessing of hands, he and his sons, and some of them do not have money to feed his family, and some of them spend their time working in painful torment, he and his sons in order to light up that damned palace for us.

"And in order for you to enjoy your wives, and for the affluent to enjoy in that palace that was built with the torment and torment of the wretched!

"However, my father, I watched them live the happiness that I dream of, and I am the daughter of the king for whom you will create everything that does not exist, as you say. I have seen them playing and having fun with their children happily, but many of them do not leave their children wherever they go. I saw the real life on the faces of them and their children, despite their lack of the simplest things that would enable them to live a decent life.

"I felt the pain of all of them, my father. I felt as if I had no hands or feet to touch everything around me, and I also felt that I needed someone to pull me out of my moral poverty, even though I have everything. I went through all this trouble because I can't revive the dead, but I see you looking at me, but you don't see me, and that's what hurts me so much!"

She was crying so much that she needed everyone's tears from her sincere grief.

The king turned to those around him and they lowered their heads in embarrassment at what they heard. Then he rose from the throne and slowly advanced to the Maya and hugged his plant after raising it up.

Like a child who was not more than two years old, and he started shaking her after he removed her from his bosom due to his height, and said with a smile, "You are right. All right, my daughter, I promise you that everything will change, and even you will not be a child after today."

Those words made Maya and her two little fairies happy, and they thought that things had already changed from one situation to the next, and that this would change a lot.

Indeed, especially with regard to her return to her human friend and lover, and this was the first good tidings that came to Maya's mind.

Where Archie did not lose her imagination, even for a moment.

On the morning of the sixth day of Maya's forced return to her world, and in the palace in particular, who was trapped in her luxurious room until she could not see the two little fairies, and the matter worried her and the long wait, but the king promised her that he would not be patient with her all this time despite the passage of nearly a week, which passed as if a year did not. No response comes, and she only saw the maids when they brought her food, as if she was one of the prisoners and not the daughter of a king, and yet she could not convince someone to talk to her, and why did the king not ask her to him yet, after six whole days of her return to the palace?

She did not find anyone to console her but herself, for she used to sing in her sweet voice, but with melodies that no one would ever wish to hear.

The melody sounded ugly even to her ear, but she said while hugging herself from the severity of loneliness:

Go on, girl, and don't open a door for despair to kill you, perhaps my father has some important things and I don't think he forgot, because like my father he never forgets and never breaks a promise no matter how much it costs, unless he wants to send me a message or hide me a surprise!

There was unusually a lot of movement, as the female workers, servants and guards were rushing in every direction and quickly as if they were in the arena of a great party.

It was an unusual day since its inception, as if an important celebration for a great occasion was being arranged for it, but the closest party, which is the great union party that the kingdom witnesses every year, was over for a while and only happens once every year!

After nine o'clock in the morning, there were invited guests who began to flock to the gates of the palace from the various creatures of the aristocracy in the kingdom, either in luxurious carriages drawn by the finest and most beautiful types of purebred Arabian horses of exquisite beauty.

Or they walked on foot until the scene was as if they were more pilgrims to the Holy House than they were visitors to the king's palace from the crowding of delegations.

Until the royal palace hall prepared to receive delegations buzzed with the sounds of classical music, to the sound of which the king only sleeps.

But this time on the scale of the entire palace, and while Maya was captive to her room, she followed the events from her high balcony with astonishment, and she saw for the first time this huge number of guests, which imposed itself on the public taste and customary in the palace protocols and the accompanying events and occasions.

However, Maya chose to enjoy the scene better than to think about the event, for in the end the news of these guests would reach her sooner or later.

She put her hands on top of each other on the railing of her balcony and began to enjoy listening to that soft music, which she loved, because it was the most she used to do to get her out of any miserable situation she was passing by, looking at the sky and dancing in the middle with all those melodies like feelings of love lost in the crowd that complicates and contradicts things in her life.

Although they do not have a real sky like that in the other world, which made her more daring and determined to get out of her world, and in which she saw the real world that she drew in her imagination, and indeed she found it and found in it more than all of that.

Maya found in it another counterpart in existence that increased her enjoyment even more, as the one who puts honey on apple pie.

Moments later, Maya decided to ask one of the guards and even ordered him to answer her immediately as the king's daughter, and he is just her guard, nothing more.

Maya asked him sharply about the matter, and the guard said nervously after taking advantage of his young age and his lack of knowledge of the powers and procedures that are tiring in such matters, "My Lord, the king has ordered that we do not utter a word with you and that we do not tell you anything, and I cannot break the order of my Lord the king, my lady!"

This method did not work with the stubborn Maya, she stepped on the guard's feet to print her shoe trail, then threw herself back and fell to the ground on her back and the guard looked in amazement, "What are you doing, my lady?"

Maya said threateningly to the guard seriously, "Now I will scream for everyone to enter and see me fall on the ground and I will tell them that you wanted to assault the daughter of the king, and you know what the rewards of someone trying to do is to burn every part of his body on a quiet fire to die suffering the most severe torment!"

The guard's face turned pale, and his eyes almost escaped their sockets from the horror of the matter, knowing that if she was true to her threat, no one would lie to her words, and no one would repay that painful torment from him until the guard said with his eyes trembling with tears, "But, madam, you know that I did not do that and that this is unfair.".

Maya replied hArchiely and said, "You have no way of surviving but to tell me what is happening here, and not just that, but that you tell me everything that happens every day, otherwise I will not hesitate to tell my father that you raped me and violated the honour of the king!"

The poor guard felt that he heard the king's voice coming out from all the walls of the ancient palace threatening him until he cried out in a loud voice in fear, and he overcame his weakness and he pleaded, "No, no, I don't want to die." Then he got down on his knees trembling hard, "And he said, "That's yours, Your Majesty. Well, my lady, well, I heard and obeyed, but promise me that no one will tell me that I told you. Otherwise, I will be one of the dead, and I am new to marriage, and my wife is an orphan and she is pregnant now."

Maya rose with confidence, topped by a malicious smile that almost sealed it with an evil laugh. Then she grabbed her mouth and turned around and said quietly, "Come on, get out what is in your pocket and speak briefly."

The guard said, with a stuttering face, on his knees, "This day is considered an important event, according to the words of my lord the king, who recommended secrecy in the work to hold a great royal party for Mr Chraklis, the leader of the flying jinn. We did not know what the real occasion was, but we, as a guard, only knew that this day would be extraordinary and long," then raised his head and looked at Maya and said in a whisper, "I do not hide from you, my lady, that most of the rumours that we have listened to say that this great

party is the wedding of my master Chraklis rumours also circulated that my lord the king, my lady, was the one who took care of everything, but do not ask me about the bride, as we do not know more than this. And if I had something in my pocket, my lady, my tongue would have revealed it even if I refused to say it."

Suddenly their conversation was interrupted by the sound of knocking on the door of the room, an unusual sound of knocking from behind it, the voices of hums and women's clamour Maya said cautiously to the guard, "It is enough now to stand up and see who is knocking and do not remember what happened between you and me to anyone."

The guard said in fear, "Your Majesty, that is yours." Then he jogged and opened the door to see who was knocking, then came back and closed it with his hand still on the doorknob, saying, "My goodness, she is the chief maid and her maidservant."

Maya raised her eyebrows in surprise, she said, "It is strange that the maidservant comes to my room at this time! Ummm, okay, put them in and leave."

The maidservant who preceded the rest of the workers entered and was walking like a duck, behind her herd of her young in a straight line. She is the person primarily responsible for Maya and her needs.

Maya smirked at her maidservant with a half-smile and said, "What a strong presence in my wings, Mrs Alice."

She was wearing a white dress with long sleeves up to the tips of the fingers to her feet, and it had a long tail from the back, as if wiping every trace behind her from behind her head.

Those who were dressed in light green chiffon fringes, bent down to Maya and the team behind her bowed. Then she said gently and with a solemn look, "Your Majesty, we have come to prepare you for the big party?"

Maya said with a stupid smile, "Excuse me? What party is that you prepare me for without my knowledge?"

Mrs Alice tensed up a little, and intertwined her two fingers in a crooked way, she said, "Your Majesty, the king, has commissioned me to prepare you especially for this occasion, to be the princess of the party. The bridesmaid is undisputed at the same time, Your Majesty, and we do not know anything like you, but we know that there is a great party that will be held today in the evening in honour of one of those close to His Majesty, the king, and that you will be the star of the evening, so my lord wanted everyone to see you as if you were their queen and not just a princess."

Maya noticed the movement of Mrs Alice's hands holding them several times, the sudden perspiration on her forehead, as well as the movement of her toes that did not stop moving in place like a bird whose wings never stop flapping when it catches it and will only calm down when you release it. So was Mrs Alice as if she knew something but didn't want to say which. She continued to exaggerate the praise of Maya's beauty and that she would become that princess that everyone who sees her dreams of.

And that her beauty will catch the eye, and even if she is not the one who will be the one who will be the party for her because she will be the star of the surprise party?

The maidservant knew something, so she realised that she had to ease the situation and not get into a whirlpool of questions that would lead to enmity and hatred between her and the king's daughter without any guilt in her.

Maya remembered her father's promise to her and influenced her to improve her father's feelings of hope and she said in a cold voice, "Okay, miss. Doesn't it really seem like an unusual day for me? Why not come on, then let's prepare for this happy day, which looks like it's going to be a really special day."

Maya said it while feeling a constriction in her stomach, but she was certain that this day would be a special day, as long as she had been accustomed to the torment of waiting since childhood, and she is now waiting for the time of the promised promise.

In the courtyard of the great palace, which was teeming with equipment and musical bands that came from all over the kingdom to delight everyone of all colours and tastes, and the clowns of strange shapes and eccentricities and the dancers who were part human? Yes, they were some of the people who are kidnapped to work as slaves by some influential and powerful jinn in the kingdom in order to trade them and use them as tools that offer some dance arts that no creature in the worlds of the jinn can master.

In addition to some abnormal works, and they brought huge profits to their jinn owners, in addition to their different human forms from all creatures, and this is also an advantage added to slave traders in this parallel world to bring in their pockets the largest possible profit.

Among all those crowds, Maya's close friends had a strong and quarrelsome presence as well, especially her five close friends, to take advantage of this important historical event, as they do not find enough time to play with Maya, who has become a captive of her room and may even become a prisoner forever if her intuition is correct in this sudden event.

Her friends were Priyanka, who was Maya's age, the daughter of one of the leaders of the Royal Guard from the flying jinn, and her pet Foxy, who does not leave her and is closest to the red panda, but is smaller and has a long tail that wraps it around the neck constantly and has a purple colour like lavender, Priyanka loved humans. To the extent that she was often shaped by their shapes when she watched them in some annual entertainment shows and was very impressed by their intelligence and their shapes, despite their differences from humans except for the length of the ears and wide eyes, in addition to the supernatural abilities that the jinn excel over humans who were distinguished by the mental abilities that only a few classes possess. From the gin.

And Olivia the blonde with long, luscious golden braids, like horse hair, in its beauty when it waves and travels all over the world, punctuated by her lynx- like ears, unlike the rest of the jinn creatures whose ears were not like those of a lynx.

Olivia was the oldest of them and Maya was at least fifty years older, as this age in their world is considered as a difference of only five years in human life and the quarrelsome boy is always Robin with thick black hair, very white in the face as if his face was lightning and he is the youngest of Maya's friends and the shortest and he is also the only brother to Priyanka and who has several amazing talents in playing and juggling, as well as he can extend his hands to catch anything from five meters or a little more.

These super-genes he acquired from his mother, which are of a completely different rank from his father's rank in the world of jinn, as it is one of the upper ranks of the jinn classes, to which King Barhout belongs, and it is the highest rank in the entire world of jinn.

Finally, their dog Regen, a strange creature that was so black with a chest, feet and legs that were spotlessly white, and had two small wings on either side of his back, was often transformed into several creatures, all for the happiness of Maya, who was brought by Robin's father specially from one of the human lands as a special gift for him on his birthday.

Where a sorcerer would cross dogs with some creatures such as cats, horses, and hyenas, and they would die mostly except for the dog Regen, who was a Hasky dog, and a human magician had prepared him to make a savage creature with special abilities from him, at the request of one of the kings to create a special weapon for them to confront him. Opponents, especially in intelligence and espionage activities.

Where he was determined to hide temporarily, where he would disappear for a few seconds and then reappear, in addition to that, he did not have much saliva, unlike other dogs, so that it was difficult to track him, but unfortunately this did not work with Regen and they almost got rid of him had it not been for Robin's father admired his beauty and shape the unfamiliar and bought it at a high price, and the price was in fact considered cheap in this precious creature, which is a real treasure.

Boyfriends run with each other in the crowd outside the palace when the food carts gather with their low-priced offers to the party-goers, not caring except for their joy, which was like a dream story and a happy thought thrown at them after they heard news that they would see Maya soon.

Until the feisty Robin started to play irritating and he jumped to the roof of one of the small buildings to extend one of his long hands and pick up from the various foods that are in the carts, taking advantage of the busyness of the sellers, especially the strawberry cake cart that cannot pass under it without taking it and eating until full from the intensity of his love for it, but this time he miscalculated and did not hint at the presence of the owner of the cart out of his eagerness for cake, and there was a hatred between him and Robin, which is the most blinding hatred of any of you, until he grabbed Robin's long hand as it fell on one of the cakes and said, angry with an iron spoon in his hand.

"Damn you, you thief who does not tire and does not get tired of repeating what you did. Now you have fallen into the evil of your deeds, and I will cut off this long hand for you to prevent others from stealing after today."

But Robin noticed that the cart next to the cake cart contained a group of monkeys equipped for circus works, so he reached out his other hand to open the cage door and the monkeys came out with pleasure, thinking that it was time to taste that familiar delicious smell of a beautiful assortment of delicious strawberry cakes and buttered banana cakes even Robin shouted, warning the seller of the monkeys' attack, and as soon as he turned back, he saw the monkeys occupying the cake boxes, sitting on top of them, and starting to eat fiercely.

The man went crazy and exclaimed with pain, "Oh my God, what is going on here, get away, you vile monkeys! My wife and I worked hard to make these cookies to sell today and make our children happy!" Robin fled quickly, laughing indifferently, to catch up with his sister Priyanka, her friend Olivia, and their dog Regen.

Who not only stole the poor man's cake, but also contributed to the support of other thieves to steal what was left of the poor man's cakes, without caring about it, as is the custom of the immoral. Definitely this act was immoral and days will return to him what he did to this poor man. Priyanka says to Robin, "What a rowdy? Where were you? You delayed us from getting to the queens' suite to see Maya before we got lost in the crowd."

Robin said quarrelsomely, as he ate a piece of the stolen cake, "You should've just bought my favourite cake from the confectioner."

Olivia said sarcastically, "Did you really buy it? Or, as usual, you robbed that poor man's car without any regard for the losses he incurred!"

He smiled a malicious smile and said to Olivia, his face splattered with jam from the intensity of his eagerness to eat, as if someone was racing behind him to take it from him, "You can say that, but it doesn't matter that I got what I wanted and I was satisfied and that's what I care about now I can think of other things right, Regen!" He told his dog, who responded with a sharp tone and a sharp and angry bark!

As if he did not agree with what he said or what he did, Robin replied to his dog, Regen, with a mockery, "Well, what do you know, you are just a hybrid dog, you don't even know what you want to eat!"

But Regen understood human speech just as you understand each other, and with an unexpected movement, the dog Regen jumped on Robin's back, took his bag, and ran quickly among the guests' legs intertwined like sugarcane stems in the fields.

The bag had some leftover cakes that Robin had stolen and Robin screamed desperately, "Give me my bag back." He knew that Regen was only getting revenge on him, and from his constant mockery of him, the dog

Regen knew that Robin would use his ability to extend his hands as long as he could, so he was faster using his secret weapon, which is to disappear for a while. Seconds until he no longer saw any trace of him in the place.

Priyanka reproached Robin violently and yelled at him, "How long are you going to continue this daily altercation with Regen, leave him alone, Robin, and please stop doing this?"

Robin said, infuriated, "No, I will not leave this hybrid unpunished. He took the cake unlawfully, and suddenly Regen appears in front of them with his bag in his mouth."

Robin said angrily, "Now, hybrid, I will teach you manners," and when he tried to catch him, Regen had disappeared before he blinked Robin's eyelid, and so it seems always between the two, which made the others fed up with Robin's feisty behaviour.

In a few seconds, the situation changed, after there was an uproar, confusion, and great noise among the people, and the crowds stopped moving, and the voices were silent, and only a whisper was heard.

The guard advanced, raising the red palace banners, with the emblem of the fiery jewel in the middle, in the hands of each of them. They lined up like a solid structure to stand as a barrier between them and the groups of guests to prevent anyone from advancing in front of the main entrance to the palace.

Where there was a large procession coming from outside to inside the palace, similar to the procession of the king himself, except that the king is not among those inside the procession.

It was a majestic royal procession of six giant chariots drawn by black jinn horses with long necks covered with a shield of pure silver embroidered with some luxurious drawings that express the heroism of the great King Barhout. Whatever it was intended for her, and it was difficult for anyone to think of approaching her, so she was used in royal processions to frighten anyone who thought of approaching the procession from the common people, most of whom wished to meet any royal procession to stop him and ask the king what he wanted due to the difficult circumstances of life when most of the inhabitants of the kingdom under the control of the aristocracy of the jinn over all the resources of the underworld for their personal interests, not caring about the suffering of others.

Priyanka and Olivia struggle in the crowded pile to reserve a place for them to witness that majestic royal procession, especially since those savage horses that pull all those most refined and luxurious chariots are rare to see for many young people and the general public, and as soon as the moment of enjoyment begins until Priyanka tells Olivia that the real loss is to miss the moment you watched these historical moments.

Olivia said with great passion, "I was desperate not to miss any such event because I would find in it the rarest pleasure, Priyanka."

Suddenly the feisty Robin entered between the two girls and said, "I hope I didn't interrupt you two lovers!" The two girls looked at him in astonishment, then suddenly the dog, Regen, entered between Priyanka and Robin, crammed himself until he reached the front to take his place also to watch the event, but Robin did not leave him in his business as usual and slapped the dog on the head and said to him threateningly, "If you return it, your hybrid, I will lift you up to the sky with my long arms and throw you from above? What was the dog, Regen, except that he did the unthinkable, he turned around and put his head on the ground and raised his ass and let out a stinking wind as if it collected all the stink of the whole earth in this very confined place and in seconds the crowd of people turned into an arena that resembles a battlefield after the end?"

People put their hands on their noses and mouths and everyone looked at me next to him and believed that he was the perpetrator until the situation worsened and the situation became tense and chaos reigned among the crowds of those present who had lined up while watching that royal procession.

One of the women said, her face frowned and disgusted by the smell while dragging her two children, "Damn you, did any of you bring a skunk here?"

Another says, his face green from the smell, "Did any of us anger the gods? Where did this stinky smell come from?" People swarmed at each other to escape from the place covered by the mist of the wicked wind that Regen released to shame Robin here.

Priyanka couldn't control her nerves and said to her brother Robin violently as she put her hands to her nose, "What a scoundrel, enough is enough now I will tell my mother what you did today and I won't be satisfied with that I will also tell her what she did when she stole that poor confectioner, damn you, you rude one."

Likewise, Olivia felt indignation and regret for every moment she knew Regen after her little animal, Foxy, ran away, fearing the escape of people who drew the guards and they felt that something had happened and ran quickly, but they could not get any closer to the strength of the smell, as if the earth had taken all its filth to them, they grumbled well and blocked them. Their faces blew out of the stench and stink that was twice as strong as a skunk's scent. No wonder, this is one of Regen's biological weapons designed for escape.

As for the delegation that was in the procession, they continued walking inside the palace in peace and tranquillity. They were not disturbed by what was happening around them. As soon as he reached the gate, Chraklis alighted while he was enjoying a moment of enjoyment that made him pour all his thoughts on the moment of meeting his lucky girl.

To complete with her the rest of enjoying this real pleasure, which he considers a dream that was not among his dreams that he lived since he was born to this historical moment in his career.

The maidservants threw roses from the palace balconies to welcome the guest of the palace and the prince of the unexpected ceremony.

Meanwhile, while the human beautician was putting the final touches on Maya's hairstyle to be the princess of the party in the most beautiful bright look. The hair clip fell from her, and when she wanted to pick it up, it was the unexpected disaster, as she muttered words like a score or an incantation in a hidden voice that made Maya fall to the ground as if she had been killed and in amazement at the beautician and the other workers! Maya rolls around on the ground without making any sound like a stabbed snake, her eyes widened exaggeratedly and bouncing out in a terrifying way, like a floundering from epilepsy.

Her body began to tremble violently, and the workers were in fear and did

not know what they were doing, and they thought that she was fighting death, and foam came out of her mouth and mixed with lipstick, and the blackness of her eyes turned to white striped with convulsive veins of blood!

One of the workers shouted in terror until the guard entered jogging and raising their weapons after they were told that there was a breach of the privacy of the king's daughter from one of the intruders, and they saw the workers pointing to Maya lying on the ground, she breathed her last, and when they approached, they were frightened.

After they hastened to summon the palace doctors and tell her father the king of the tragedy, they gathered around her and she was still in a state of shivering and thick foam with a sound and moaning like the whining of a cat!

It seems that the events of this day will carry many more surprises than the surprise of the party itself.

Priyanka and Olivia took advantage of the chaos and confusion that had occurred and ran to the palace, followed by Robin and after him Regen to search for Maya to watch her and be her bridesmaids before she was the princess of the upcoming party, but it seems that their hope will be delayed if not disappointed, as it was noticed that there is something like a suspicious and suspicious movement in the corners of the palace. It happened and signs of astonishment dictated everyone as they looked at everyone.

No one knows what is happening and why the order of the guards is suddenly scattered like this.

Priyanka said with signs of stress and anxiety, "It seems something strange is happening!"

Robin replied quarrelsomely as usual, "It seems to me that someone is dead or on the verge of dying!"

Olivia said fiercely, "Shut up, Robin. Aren't your bad deeds enough today, I hope you won't do any more sabotage, or you will see what you haven't seen in your life?"

Heedlessly, the little red panda (Foxy) came down from Priyanka's neck to catch up with two butterflies who had entered through the main door into the midst of the palace staff crowd. Priyanka shouted, "Oh my! This is not your time, Foxy."

But Foxy was so quick to follow his instinct that he disappeared between the many legs and Priyanka sped off behind him, though she couldn't catch him with her hands, but her eyes were like a magnet that never left his movement. Olivia followed her.

On her face was disappointment.

Robin behind them, laughing, says, "What a great pleasure this morning", and behind him, Regen, gave a sarcastic laugh in support of his quarrelsome friend.

Until they became.

They were all crammed into the middle of a raging herd of bulls stuck in a very narrow gorge. Suddenly, Robin spotted the red panda Foxy and said to the two girls, "This is little Foxy, I caught him there."

Priyanka says eagerly, "If you catch him, I promise I will give up telling my mother what I did today."

Robin quickly replied, taking advantage of it, "With the black mask, you keep with you!"

Priyanka said intently, then suddenly blushed, "What?"

"What is that mask, Priyanka?" said Olivia, surprised.

Priyanka interrupted her and said to her brother Robin in a hurry, "OK, well,

you have what you want."

The red panda puppy Foxy was watching the butterfly resting on the shoulder of a servant who was holding glasses of fine wine in his hand.

He stopped for a while to find a safe footing for his feet and reach safety in the midst of the crowd. Foxy was wagging his tail in preparation to pounce on the butterfly, but Regen had another opinion when the dog jumped from behind the bartender and barked at him hard, which hastened the escape of the two butterflies, but this did not prevent Foxy and his instinct as he jumped off the ground to the shoulder of the bartender, who lost his balance and almost fell until he threw the glasses in his fear into the air and flew with the two butterflies and with Foxy, who had been betrayed by his calculations, and he also fell with the rest of the glasses and win above them, like pouring rain.

Robin went crazy and raged like a raging bull against Regen and shouted at the top of his voice a demon's cry, "Damn you, you're stupidest dog I've ever known."

When Robin approached Regen, he slapped him again on the back of his head. Regen turned his back in anger to erupt and repeat the same ugly act subconsciously until the two girls shouted in one voice, "No, no, no, no, no, no." That stinking wind filled the huge reception hall and the scent spread around like wildfire, the controversy and discussion intensified between the visitors, and each of them began accusing the other of being the perpetrator, and so on until the voices of accusations rose between the workers, servants and visitors until the smell intensified and became like the explosion of a chemical element.

Then they hurried towards outside the hall and there was a catastrophic collision that aggravated the matter with everyone colliding because they did not see the road.

Priyanka said miserably, "There is no pact between us now. Damn it, Robin. You have deprived us today of all the joy we were planning for."

"Don't waste time," said Olivia, after holding Priyanka's hand. "Great opportunities only come when we light our own lanterns."

They slipped out of the hall, which they were not accustomed to entering, unaware that the guards had closed the other doors in order for the king and his companions to pass into Maya's room, while Robin behind them looked down one of the corridors, apparently empty of guard.

Then he released his hands, which were extended to the limit, to grab Priyanka's arm, who moved away from him and Olivia and they were disappointed after closing all the entrances to all the rooms and departments.

Then Robin silently gestured to her with his finger to the right to see one of the corridors leading to one of the corridors that none of the guards noticed because they were so preoccupied with the unexpected chaos.

And for the smallness of the place compared to the huge doors dedicated to the sections and rooms branching from the main hall of the palace, they were all for the first time entering this hallway.

Which was more like a piece of the king's room because of the splendour of the golden red carpet covering the long staircase leading to the upper floor decorated with murals of pictures of angelic fairies watering the warrior king with water during his great battle when the last of the seven kingdoms of the jinn was captured.

The place was considered an exit to the upper room, which was considered a meeting room, and as soon as they reached the end of the staircase, there was a strangely shaped wooden door, its colour faded and its sides corroded, divided into four sections, and it has a handle in the middle, not like the rest of the doors. It has the effect of a long life, as if it holds an ancient historical Archive. Perhaps if he spoke, he would have told many stories and events that passed from here.

But this old door remained tall, but it resembles the majesty of an old man whose back must have been bent from longevity.

Of course, it was not open, nor was it open, as they thought, after all of them tried to move the handle after dusting layers of dust from it.

But the result was the same, they could not move it even for an inch.

Olivia says, "Damn this handle is so strong, it was as if someone poured wet cement inside it until it dried out and became a rocky lock?"

I can't even hope to budge half an inch until Olivia said, "I'm so sorry, Priyanka, for being so overconfident in bringing you here?"

Priyanka said calmly and confidently, whispering to her, "You should not, smart girl, maybe the guards are gone now and maybe we can find another way out."

Oliva says cautiously, "They can't leave so quickly after this mess and we hear it from here, let's think of some way maybe..."

They were interrupted by the dog Regen, who had appeared out of nowhere and suddenly became among them, panting with his long, saliva-free tongue and wagging his tail vigorously in all directions.

Evidence of his happiness as he points back, Priyanka understood the sign, but Robin bit his face and blushed in anger, pointing at him, "What brings you, you disgusting skunk? It's all because of you!"

Regen stared at him with a blink of an eye and with pride and then grinned a little bit about his fangs until Priyanka got up and cleverly and courteously hugged him to avoid any further catastrophe that might be caused by Regen's anger and they are in more need of being with each other than being on each other.

Then she said with eagerness and optimism, "What a pleasure to see you again Regen. You seem to have good news like your sweet beauty?"

Then suddenly Regen vanished from her hands, he disappeared, but he came back in less than two seconds, but this time he stood in front of Priyanka on the stairs and looked back.

And he walked away a little to show her who had brought him this time, he was with him Foxy who was enough to make Priyanka explode crying from the intensity of joy like the one who found her child after a bitter parting!

Until she picked him up and cuddled him while he licked her face tenderly and said, "How much I miss you, my beautiful baby, thank God for your return. We worried about you so much."

And I took him shaking him as he spread his cute laughter as he licked the two girls' faces.

Soon, Robin had the idea of using Regen. Thinking, he said, "It's time to use Regen to address Priyanka, he hears you more now than I do. All you have to do is ask him to break through the door and try to open it from the inside.

"If there is no key, there will be a lock that can be opened from the inside, which leaves no doubt. The screws on this door show that it has been designed to open towards the inside, meaning that there is a manual lock inside, and this is easy for Regen!"

Priyanka said blithely, "How much has this been missing from my mind?" Then she looked at Regen with a wide smile and said, "You are really the impossible task man, and she grabbed Regen's head and put it in her hands."

And she says to him, "We need you now and our success depends on you. Can you do that? Regen bark confidence that there is no room for doubt!"

And she said, "So, come on, hero, go inside and try to open the door for us if you can, or bring us any key you might find, it might be the key for this door," and indeed Regen entered the meeting room and started looking for the key.

But without any trace, he continued looking here and there, and he was a little late, until signs of tension began to appear on them, and Robin was the most grumbling of all this, saying, whispering in a low, distracted voice, and he seemed angry as he was talking to himself, "I could not open the door, and now he will do it with this skunk."

But Olivia's curiosity made her search the door until she found a hole under the door handle. As she put her eyes to look through the door opening, her hand subconsciously fiddled with the door handle and moved it twice to the right and once to the left, and suddenly it hit them like a thunderbolt when he heard the creaking of the antique door.

Until Olivia backed away in fright, thinking someone had opened it from the inside? Then Priyanka raised her eyes to the scene of the door that opened and quietly advanced and pushed the door and found it opened more and that it was easier than they expected and it wasn't locked as they imagined?

Robin said in a weak voice, "What magic did you use, Olivia?"

As for Priyanka, I noticed her from the intensity of joy and said with longing, "I was really not disappointed when I chose you to be my friend, what a genius." Olivia said happily, "It seems that fear and confusion were preventing us from acting rationally, for we were imitating each other, and neither of us tried to try a different way from the other. If one of us tried to move the door handle

only twice, we would have succeeded the first time."

Even Regen in the room was surprised and thought they were making fun of him!

But from the first moment, they felt that the room was ready to receive a

meeting, as the candles seemed to have been lit for less than an hour, and in the middle of the spacious room was a large oval-shaped table, more than ten red chairs with gilded frames.

The entire table was covered with a silk sheet to the bottom of the floor so as not to cover its surface with dust. Suddenly they heard the sound of movement coming from the inner door of the room and the shadows of someone slipping from under the threshold until they crawled stealthily like snakes under that only table after noticing that the door had moved its handle for someone to enter!

Those who entered were only three people, two of them sat next to each other, in front of the other, who was none other than Chraklis, the unknown groom from the majority present for this party, and no one knows who will marry either, but this is not important for Priyanka and those with her until they heard

Chraklis asking nervously. In a hurry, in an angry voice, "What news, Counsellor Harulan, has her condition improved, or should I worry about such surprises?"

Counsellor Harulan was one of the king's most important advisors, but he had a strong relationship with Mr Chraklis, the most powerful military leader in the kingdom. Counsellor Harulan said, confused, "Until now, we don't know the real reason for what Maya was exposed to, but all we knew through the medical team that what happened to her was her exposure to incendiary energy. The jinn do not possess it except for some humans and use it as a guard for them to avoid being exposed to our harm. We are the jinn?"

"And how's that?" Chraklis said angrily, as he hit his fist on the table, which shook and shook, and those under it shook in terror, "How could this happen while I am here? How did people get here?"

The counsellor said, "Calm down, Mr Chraklis. We have ordered an investigation into this, and we will come to a conclusion and we will know the reason sooner or later. According to what I learned before I came here, Maya has passed the danger and her health is still stable."

Chraklis continued his words, "I swear, if I find out who did this to my wife Maya, he will pay the price!"

Talking to Priyanka and with her was like a thunderbolt! Maya, his wife, they looked at each other in disgust! Olivia whispered, the astonishment evident on her face, "It was all for Maya's marriage and we are the last to know?"

But until now, they did not know who the speaker was, but they were finally certain that he is the bridegroom of this party, and Maya is the one who will marry him as a wife, and not just an honorary princess for this strange party, as they thought.

King Barhout enters Maya's room with a pale face for the first time, after learning about his daughter's situation.

A chief of doctors and his team are still trying to mitigate the impact of the burning human spell. The king looks at his daughter's face for the first time after she was struck by the spell.

He puts his hand on her and gropes her face and says sadly, "Dear Maya, what happened to you and who would dare to do this to you!" The words of deep sadness got stuck in his throat and he began to be touched as he watched her angelic face.

The one who was overgrown and darker than those pale veins that covered her face became full of those frightening veins of blood clotting in her until he had the feeling that for the first time, he would lose his only daughter forever.

Mr Chraklis hurriedly enters Maya's room without asking where the king is, then stops behind the king while he is above his daughter, bent over as one who weeps over the past. Then he said softly, whispering near the king's shoulder, "We have arrested the perpetrator, my lord, she is in custody now and awaiting your orders!"

The king turned quickly and eagerly and said, "Who is he? You will know, sir, that he is in prison now, and it would be preferable for you to see him yourself in order to get out of your pocket and to be aware of everything from the criminal himself."

The king entered the prison to stand face to face with the one who is said to be the first accused of trying to kill his daughter, Princess Maya.

The king is advancing slowly towards the accused, who is chained, as if he were a wild beast. The place was dark until one of the guards came forward with a torch that lit the lamp that lit the solitary confinement of the accused.

Then the king saw the culprit, and it was a real surprise. The king felt that maybe something was wrong, but he controlled himself a little before he started the investigation himself. The accused was nothing but the human beautician, Mrs Ronat. In fact, it was shocking to everyone. He was expecting someone from outside the palace. He was sent, or one of the traitors, or at least he will be a man, but to be the human beautician that they brought specially from the human world for this purpose?

That is, she has no precedents and does not communicate with any suspicious party in order to do it, and this is what made the king be wiser when he looked into her eyes silently and said very gently and smiling, "What made you do this to a girl like Maya, who can't hurt a fly!"

He came closer to her, then bent down and sat on one of his knees until she moved away, her body trembling in fear, and her eyes filled with tears quickly, and she whispered with fear, "I swear by everything you believe in, and by Your Majesty, I have not touched her badly!"

Chraklis said excitedly, "Stop this cheap representation, O humanity, and answer your Lord, the king, why did you do this cowardly act and what prompted you to do this?"

The king shouted him in a loud voice and said to him, "Shut up, no one will dare to touch one of his hair badly, as long as I am the owner of the matter."

The king believed that Ronat had the thread of treatment in her hand, so it was necessary to use the method of enticement and reassurance, especially when he noticed signs of innocence and honesty on her.

Chraklis said, belittling the importance of the matter, "But, sir, it is a human creature, and lying runs in their veins, and treachery has been brought up on it, and you know that."

The king said mockingly, "Indeed! I doubt it, Commander, and now leave it to me, all of you get out now, and leave us alone. Let's go."

Mr Chraklis looks at the guards and orders them to go out, but he and the king remain. The king said to him firmly, and you too, "Chraklis, I do not want anyone here!"

"That's Your Majesty," says Chraklis, turning away.

And when they all left, the king said politely to Mrs Ronat, "Now there is no one but us and I am the king here. Your fate is now in my hands, and there is no need to be afraid, for I believe in saying first, what is your name?"

Ronat says, "As she wipes her tears with the back of her terrified palms, my name is Ronat, Your Majesty."

"You seem to be a good woman, and you do not seem to intend to harm anyone, but tell me, do you have children?"

Ronat says, "Yes, I have four sons in our village, and I came here after one of them offered me to work here for an attractive price, because I am good at beautifying the art of make-up and decorating. I was distinguished in my work, but an epidemic struck us in our village, and no one needed my work."

The king said, "Who offered you to work here, and how did you come here?"

Ronat says, "I was offered a job here more than once by a woman from the jinn who is told Alice. When she learned about my distinction in my work, and she came to my house, I returned several times disguised as many women, and I refused that because I did not imagine that I would leave my world and live in the world of the jinn."

The king repeats the name two and three times after holding the tip of his beard, "Alice, Alice! Are you sure of the name?"

She says, "yes, I am sure, and I know what she looks like too."

The king says, "Ah, well, go on, Ronat, and what happened after that?"

"When I refused her offer, she tried to harm my children and threatened to kidnap them. She came to me at night in frightening forms, once in the form of a black dog over the head of one of my children while they were sleeping, and once in the form of a very terrifying distorted monster watching my children playing.

"I had madness and obsessive-compulsive disorder and many times they came in the form of black snakes with more than one head or deformed children, and all of this was threatening messages which compelled me to turn to one of the chief monks in the village and tell him what happened, so he gave me a treasure to put on my necklace, bearing religious symbols, and taught me words that I always completed before wearing the necklace, otherwise the spell would not have any effect.

"And this score will be enough to keep her away from me and my house. Indeed, when I used it, I saw Mrs Alex in a dream one day, and she was approaching me, and when she saw the necklace in which the score was burnt, she was crying and saying, "Forgive me, I will not come back again. I will hide this score from me, and then it disappeared and did not return until after a long time." When our village was hit by the epidemic, our livelihood was cut off, and we were afflicted with poverty and misery.

"We did not find what to eat and nourish our children with, so that some of the villagers had to rent their children to work as slaves for others in order not to see them die of starvation.

"One day, someone knocked on my door, and when I opened it, there was a strange-looking old woman with so many bags of food that I was afraid of them, but she reassured me and said that she had brought great good to me and my children, which made me forget my fear of her.

"Due to my great need for anyone's help for my children, she told me that she had heard about me and about my wonderful work and that she needed my services and that the work would be in a place more than I expected, so she offered me a job as a dresser for the daughter of one of the great kings of the jinn.

"But I didn't care who she was or who that girl was, my only concern was that I would get the money that would satisfy the hunger of my children and our basic needs in return for that, so I agreed without even completing it, but she told me that I should not use that necklace at all, because it would harm me and harm me. Who will I work for?

"I promised her that, but when I went out, I forgot the necklace in my pocket and was surprised to find her with me, and when I was brushing Maya's hair, the necklace fell from me, so I muttered the words of the exorcism because I used to do this always and forgot its danger to the jinn, and I didn't mean that, Your Majesty, because I'm not evil to anyone and I didn't come here in order to cause harm to someone because I have little boys waiting for me, how can I do such a thing!"

Then she collapses in tears and laments with regret and sorrow for what she did unintentionally.

The king got up and then stood for a while after taking a long breath and realising that the matter was just an unintentional mistake and not an act against the king himself or an external conspiracy as the leader Chraklis was alluding to.

And in a surprising step from the king, he extended his hand to her, and she was astonished until her eyes widened, and she said in astonishment, "The king himself extends his hand for me? And after everything that happened to me for his daughter?" He nodded at her in response to her that yes, until she felt that she had escaped all that she feared, and a great worry had left her heart.

And he went to Maya's room with Mrs Ronat even if he arrived and said in a loud voice, "Let everyone, including the doctors and guards, go out and order them to stay outside. The king, Mrs Ronat and Maya remained on the bed as if she was a sleeping princess waiting for a kiss back to life from the awaited life antidote."

Then he said to Mrs Ronat, calmly and confidently, "Take out the necklace and put it on Maya and say the invocation upside down!" King Barhout was a great knowledge of the human world and its secrets.

Now trying to take advantage of his previous experiences to treat his daughter with the same weapon that wanted her bedridden, Mrs Ronat seemed confused while she was in the presence of the king, knowing that she was now required to treat his daughter.

The king said to her, "Don't worry, just do as I command you, put the necklace on the girl's chest, stand over her, and say the incantation upside down from the other to the first."

She gathered her strength and advanced and sat down next to Maya, all hoping that she would succeed to atone for her catastrophic mistake and put the necklace on Maya's chest after I took it out of her pocket and before she tried to remember the incantation from the horror she had gone through, smoke came out from under the spark that was covering Maya in the form of threads in the air and appeared as if the girl's body was burning, which confused Mrs Ronat, and she retreated.

Until the king pressed her shoulder and said to her firmly, "I am with you, hear and see my incantation as quickly as I commanded you," until the knot of her tongue was untied, and she bled, muttering the words of the magic spell, and continued to mumble until Maya's body rose from the bed and someone was lifting her from her waist.

Mrs Ronat panicked, and quickly read the murmurs, clasping her hands and clasping them to her chest and closing her eyes.

Until an angry wind stormed the windows, he turned off all the lanterns in the place, it made everything in the room scattered around them in complete darkness, and the window doors continued to hit the walls hard, as if the drums of fear were ringing around them.

But that did not frighten Mrs Ronat, who entered into a whirlpool of hidden forces. Then Maya rose from her bed an arm's length and in the midst of this confusing atmosphere, the smoke stopped, and those thick veins that ran from her face and hands faded, and the features of her beautiful face began to shine again, little by little, and the colour of darkness disappeared. She was completely faint, and her eyes were filled with tears, a sign that evil had left her body, and while Mrs Ronat was continuing to say the incantation, the room had calmed down from the state of frenzy, and the king's face rejoiced after Maya had fallen on her bed, as if she had been washed in heaven from every abomination and returned with a pure soul and body like the day of her birth.

Maya's lips moved and the first thing she said was "Archie" and she kept saying the name "Archie, Archie, where are you?" The king was very pleased and tears flowed from his eyes and choked him with a strong expression from the intensity of joy, Maya, my love, my dear daughter, then he hugged her tightly and did not care what she was saying.

Until Mrs Ronat opened her eyes after she stopped mumbling and saw everything she saw, Mr Chraklis entered the room after hearing all that noise and everyone behind him was curious to know what was going on.

Maya opened her eyes and her tears ran down her rosy white cheeks until he wiped. The king took her hand and wiped her tears from her cheeks and wiped all her face with his hand and felt the warmth of her breath. She remembers that first moment when he touched her for the first time after her birth.

Maya looked at him and opened her mouth after a long frown, with his index finger still touching her cheek, and this was the first time he felt that Maya was the only thing that could never be replaced in his life.

The guards and the workers rejoiced when they saw Maya well and she was finally surprised and came back to life, the king stood in his prestige and gestured with his hands and said with joy, "On this occasion, the wedding ceremony that was scheduled for an indefinite period will be cancelled and this day will be the day Maya returns to us all and let the kingdom celebrate everyone in it and to circulate this day and be an annual party."

Mr Chraklis was shocked when he saw his precious opportunity fly by.

His face shrank after this high royal order, and the world revolved with him in all directions until he almost passed out, but despite all this, Maya did not know anything about that all these preparations were for her wedding to Commander Chraklis, of course he would have gone crazy if she did not kill herself forcibly.

The servants and workers come out of Maya's room to inform everyone that the party has become public and not private, and that all these banquets will be spread outside the palace walls.

The double of what will be inside the palace will be for the general public, and that the ceremony will be open, and that the doors of the palace for the first time will be opened for all the sons of the kingdom, and it is not the preserve of the rich or the people of stature.

In the kingdom, Priyanka and Olivia heard the servants' talk, and they were glad with the news that the marriage had been cancelled and that the party had become a party of joy on the occasion of Maya's recovery.

This made them much happier than the others, but they were overwhelmed by curiosity. Olivia said sceptically, "It seems that we have missed a lot and we are the last to know. There must have been many things that happened that could change this matter."

Priyanka replied, agreeing with Olivia's words, "Indeed, it is a strange day, but the most important of all is that Maya is fine and that we will not be in a hurry to meet her after that. We have confirmed the news of the mysterious marriage cancellation, but we must reach Maya, whatever the cost. If we are not with her in these critical times, then when will Robin hit his hands together and say yes, you see, sister, but this time I am the one who will lead you to Maya's room.

"We did not succeed in anything, because of your poor leadership and the lack of sufficient courage in making the decision."

Here Regen barked in opposition to Robin, as usual, rejecting Robin's provocative style, then Robin responded in a cold, sarcastic voice, no one would blame me if I scolded this skunk again. Priyanka got up and hit Robin on the head and said, mocking him, "To experience the feeling of poor Regen when you hit him on the head like you did before."

Olivia did the same and slapped him on the forehead and said sarcastically, "And this is from me as well. You've hurt Regen before and you've disrupted our mornings and our unacceptable anxiety."

The dog Regen laughed sarcastically at Robin so that little Foxy jumped on Robin's head and tried to imitate what the others did, but his small hand was not enough to reach Robin's forehead because of his thick hair, which became like a nest for Foxy due to his small size, which prompted them to burst out laughing at this spontaneous situation.

Priyanka said excitedly, "Okay, come on, Robin. Go and show us your skills while we're behind you."

Robin says, "But you still owe me a debt that I won't forget. Plus, I want ten strawberry jam cakes."

Olivia commented as well and said, "Since there is a big event going to happen, I also want ten cakes, Priyanka, as your brother wants."

Priyanka replied, "If we reach Maya and tell her what we heard, I promise you twenty cakes for each of you, not ten.

"Wow," Robin said happily. "How much I knew that no one would beat my sister in generosity, so let's go."

After extensive and successful penetration of all those tight security barriers in the corridors of the palace, led by the young genie Robin, they arrived at Maya's suite, which was the most heavily guarded, then they stopped at the end of the paper while watching the decisive moment to seize the opportunity. It was difficult for them with such a number of guards, but without waiting long, there was a sign of some hope. Of course, hope must come to you sooner or later, if you seek your way with confidence only, do not despair, whatever your size and abilities, as long as you adhere to the rope of hope, you will not disappoint your expectations in reaching your goal, even if it is long.

The guards opened the doors of the giant wing after they gave the royal salute to let the king and those with him come out, and the escorts were more numerous than they expected from doctors, advisors and companions.

As he was in the interior of that evil that happened to Maya a great good that made her father decide to surprise her in a way that might fascinate her more than she expected.

The door to Maya's room consisted of two separate doors that opened wide so that the king and his entourage could come out smoothly and easily.

Robin realised that he would use one of his cunning tricks, as he kept small stones of soft texture, which he coloured in the form of gemstones of different colours in order to laugh at some sellers and in order to show them in front of others and play the role of an independent magician. His hand and his talkative tongue eased.

Then Robin said to his sister and Olivia, "Stay here, wait for my signal, and be ready. Except for those sent to it by higher orders."

Robin crept on his toes along the wall and groped his way until he reached the guard who was next to one of the two giant wing doors, where each door had a special guard standing next to him, not seeing the other guard.

And who was surprised by the presence of a boy next to him, throwing him a yellow smile, as if he had lost one of his parents! The guard asked him bluntly, "What are you doing here, boy? Did you lose your parents?"

Robin put his hand over his head and said, pretending to be impressed by the military uniform worn by the guard, and said to him, "Since I was young and I have been dreaming, I have acquired such a helmet that you wear, so I collected a lot of gems that he gives to my father as a monthly allowance instead of money."

Then he winked at the guard and approached him more and whispered to him very calmly, "You know the life of the rich and the extravagance in which they enjoy and do not like to show some of those appearances in front of others for fear of envy, my friend."

The guard replied surprised and said, minimising Robin's words, "What? What are you saying, child, let's go, before I catch you, and you might be beaten badly on your ass. You tried to disrupt my work. Go away."

Robin said, "Slow down a little before you regret it!" Then he took out the coloured stones in a professional way so as not to make you suspect for one moment that they were fake and poured them into his other hand.

He said mockingly at the guard in a seductive way, "If you knew that the value of one stone that I possess is worth the value of ten swords and ten spears! The guard's eyes widened and he was dazzled by what he saw before his eyes and salivated the desire to rob and seize the entire bag of this boy."

Then he looked to the right and left, hesitantly, then extended his hand, wanting to grab what was in Robin's hand, but Robin cleverly retreated back quickly.

He expected that reaction, which made the guard confused and hesitant. Should he stand in his place and keep his job, or would he catch up with the boy who has a big treasure in his hand that will make the guard rich throughout his life!

The bag contained more than thirty stones of different colours that had been dyed with a shiny substance in order for the trick that the feisty Robin had prepared to fool others easily.

The guard realised that he was facing a chance that might never be compensated, and then said his words and smiled foolishly to attract the boy who imagined that he was carrying with him his pink future that would make him live as one of the elites in the kingdom.

All of this quickly formed in the mind of the guard. Here, Robin realised that the guard had fallen into the trap and said to him impromptu, "Now I will make you an offer that you will not imagine, and if you collect all your dreams, you will not dream of it, and he is like this. If you bring it and I did not complete the number five, the bag will be yours!"

The guard's mind was distracted between standing in his place and the boy who offered him the dream offer, then Robin approached and said to him, "Don't worry, I have in my room such a bag, several bags. I don't think that being lost here in the halls of the palace to meet you specifically without anyone else is a message from God that this is your happy day, man. And now I'm going to start counting and I'm not a liar, just tell me that everyone is gone and I will put the bag and start counting!"

The guard says eagerly, "Well, but if you are a liar, I will stick this spear in your throat, and I will say that he was carrying an arrow that wanted to assassinate the king's daughter, so I killed him on the spot."

Robin laughed and mocked the guard's enthusiasm and said, "Don't worry, I'll be at the end of the corridor, waiting for you to signal." When all of the workers in Maya's room left, and made sure to the guard that no one else and the other guard behind the second door saw nothing, then the guard pointed to Robin in agreement and in turn Robin put the bag in its place at the end of the hallway from the east side, opposite the hall where Priyanka and her friends were.

Then the guard moved towards the bag of the counterfeit gem, and when Robin found himself between the two doors he pointed to Priyanka and those with her who did not hesitate to run between the halls, rushing like rabbits fleeing in the fields, as the guard of the other door of the suite did not see them, then they closed the door of the suite, and this was the idea of all this ploy, as they entered after the other guard was busy with the illusion of fake gems and managed to enter the Maya suite and indeed what they wanted was achieved.

Despite the difficulties they faced on this strange and wondrous day filled with contradictory events, the doors were closed behind them in the Royal Maya Suite, which has luxurious silk curtains combined in pink and crimson colours together and embroidered in an innovative way that does not occur to anyone. Silk curtains All that blew the breeze of the air from the balconies of the room suspended in the high sky of the kingdom.

When they came to Maya's bed, Priyanka asked and said, "I can smell Maya from here, unless you say I'm imagining it because I don't see her!"

Olivia said, "Yes, it is her scent, as rare as Maya among creation."

Robin said, "Don't worry that she is on her bed but she was covered well," and suddenly Regen stopped in front of Robin and Robin didn't notice it until he stepped on Regen's tail without realising until the dog howled with his voice like a wolf stabbed his voice all over the place made Priyanka jump on him quickly and put her hand on his mouth To make up for the situation, Maya jumped out of her bed in panic, and when she saw her five friends, like phantoms, they surrounded her bed from all sides, and they were at the top of embarrassment, and their faces froze from the embarrassing act.

Robin was scratching his scalp and he didn't know what he couldn't this time until they all made a frightened smile who had done a shameful act wanting to hide him from people's eyes and say with one voice but different words with different degree of embarrassment in each.

Priyanka said, "hello your dear majesty and bowed a little."

Olivia said, "How happy we are today to see you, my princess."

Robin said, "I am sad to sue you and happy at the same time because I saw

you after a long absence, beautiful Maya. As for Regen and the little red panda puppy, they were very happy to see the most people who showered them with the best kinds of food and pampered them so much that they jumped on her and hugged them with longing and enthusiasm, and they did not leave her bosom until she said in amazement. What brought you here and how did you get here?"

She resisted her fatigue and tried to get up from her bed, but Priyanka stopped her that you embraced and she said eagerly, "Praise be to God, you are fine, my princess, no matter how we got here there is no time to explain to you, someone may enter now and take us out of here, but we were saddened by what we heard about you and your illness, and we did not know anything about it except by chance."

Maya pointed to Robin and said to him, "Do you still steal strawberry cakes from bakers in the streets, Robin, or are you wise?"

Robin replied with a sly laugh, "The truth is not today, I was full, but I thank you very much, it was all because of you, sleeping princess."

"Because of me!" Maya said, wondering, "And how is that, Robin?"

"Robin, yes, because of your wedding, which you did not tell us about, which caused a lot of sellers this morning, especially my friend who sells strawberry cakes, and who a lot of their delicious pastries, and therefore there are many opportunities for free food!"

With knotted eyebrows, Maya said, "What? My wedding?"

Then Maya laughs a little while she is still almost lying on the bed, "What a beautiful boy, you still have a heavy sense of humour, come close to me, I like to put my hand in your thick hair, it makes me feel a kind of energy and a beautiful feeling."

Priyanka and Olivia exchanged looks of confusion after they breathed a sigh of relief, they did not want to tell her now that she is in this state and they were shocked by Robin, who never keeps a secret and concluded that she did not know anything about her marriage, not even about the husband to whom she will be married?

Priyanka said hmm then shrugged her shoulders a little and calmly Priyanka prepared to open the matter to Maya but in a gradual way without shocking her or making her afraid while she is still recovering and to tell her what they knew so that they had a clear idea of what they were facing or what might face Maya.

And what was cooking for Maya without her knowledge, and she said, "We have heard, my ladies, that you will be the queen of this party, and this is what made us hurry to see you before the crowds and see how our princess will be like the virgin pearls in the hands of the diver.

"But we got upset and later learned the news of your sudden illness for everyone, which postponed the upcoming ceremony, which as we long to see you and you are the queen of this marriage," Maya gathered her strength to raise her back a little on the head of the bed to focus more on what is being said and said, surprised, "What marriage are you talking about, Priyanka?"

Robin climbed into the bed and sat down next to her, boldly, and said with interest, "All we know, my lady, is that your wedding has been cancelled, and we heard a lot of pandemonium among the palace staff, most of whom were in this room of yours when your father and the doctors were here."

Priyanka said, "Yes, and then we realised it was your wedding to the captain Chraklis, and this is what made us rush to you to check on your health, when we heard that you were ill."

Olivia says, "Yes, my lady, and he repeated, saying 'my wedding' and saying 'my wife, Maya' several times and we do not believe that there is another Maya here, besides you and that there is no party but this party and therefore we made sure that this party is your wedding to Mr Chraklis, my princess."

Silence settled Maya's face and she relaxed a little and sighed the longest sigh in her life quietly, then returned to the sleeping position that she was in and rolled her eyes at the ceiling of the room, then quietly placed her hands on her chest after she tied them together and remembered her father's promise to her and realised that this was the expected news, but despite the horror of frustration that she felt With him she was optimistic when she learned that what happened to her from the exorcism was good and not evil, but was the reason that no one thought of to save her from the disaster of her marriage to the leader, Chraklis.

And this for Maya means that it had written on her secret misery and that her happiness after finding Archie was just a beautiful pipe illusion that quickly faded. Priyanka asked her after feeling that she had accepted it and that she was in a moment of contemplation, "But would you tell us, my lady, what happened to you so suddenly they said that you were between life and death at the time when

you were very healthy?"

Maya said while trying to go back to that moment while lying on the bed, "I

don't really know. It was like a dream. I actually felt pain. When Mrs Ronat was styling my hair, something fell out of her. I don't know what exactly. But I think it was a chain, and when she bent down to pick it up, she muttered words I didn't understand, and for a moment I felt as if someone poured me boiling water boiling in my ears, burning my body from the inside, and I felt my blood spurting through my veins in the heat, and my heart stopped and I felt a heavy weight in my head at that.

"I fell and didn't wake up until my father and Mrs Ronat hugged me over my head. I didn't know what exactly happened to me in the dressing room, but I had a feeling that there was something in those words that Mrs Ronat said because my feeling never lies, and I'm sure that something came out of that chain like a great beast tied in chains. He was released to devour the sacrifice, and I will never forget that feeling."

Before she could complete her words, she tried to get up and get out of bed, and found that she could no longer carry her feet, but rather thought that she was completely paralysed with that bracelet that was placed in her hands.

And he was limiting her abilities to hide and fly, but Maya is a stubborn girl, and nothing will stop her from doing what she wants, even if she loses her feet and legs.

And she said to them as she struggled to get her feet out of bed, "Please sit me on the chair that I have with you. I heard my father say that they brought me a wheelchair to help me regain my activity temporarily," and when they put her in the wheelchair, Maya felt that she was sitting on something she did not show that to anyone because the chair was covered with a rubber cushion to add more comfort. Then she looked with the tip of her eye below her thigh until she put her hand and pulled out what was under the pillow lightly, and behold, it was a necklace with a lobe of heavenly gemstone, like red veins, surrounded by an oval gold frame. A silver copper chain. She meditated on it well and said to herself, what is this necklace doing in my room?

Then she slowly raised it in front of her face, looking at her with some curiosity, and when Regen saw the necklace, his body hair stood up and fell back and put his tail between his hind legs and slipped quietly from in front of them and moved away and sat behind the bed looking at them half face, that scene did not pass on Olivia and she said with fear, "Look at Reagan, what it happened to him all of a sudden, so he showed signs of fear, as if he saw something we didn't see with our eyes?"

Priyanka laughed a mysterious laugh and said, "Come on, Regen, it's just a necklace, not a beast."

Then Maya said, "It's a rune necklace, yes, it's a rune necklace. I now remembered the colour of the chain, and since it was here, it seems to have been forgotten by the chaos and by the many people gathered in my room waiting for my death."

While they were busy talking about the necklace, one of the maids suddenly entered and said, "My Princess Maya, one of the guards wants to enter and says he has urgent royal orders!"

Maya quickly put the necklace back under the pillow, where she found it. She said, "Okay, let him come in."

When the guard came in quickly, he said, "Excuse me, my lady, for the inconvenience, but I came to you, with an order from Your Majesty, the king, your father, to look for the necklace here, it was lost! Has anyone seen any necklaces here?"

Maya says, "No, we didn't see anything." Then Maya asked the others, mocking the guard's question, "Did any of you see any necklace?" They said no. Then she turned to the guard and said passionately, "This room is in front of you. Look how you want." The guard stood in his place, his eyes looking around in confusion, and he felt embarrassed, and the girls' eyes turned him from top to bottom. Then he thought of making it short, and he could no longer bear those looks. He said with a shrunken face, "Well, my lady, thank you for that. We

apologise for the inconvenience."

when the guard was about to leave, Maya unexpectedly called him after she

got into the wheelchair and said, "I saw you and another soldier going out with Mrs Ronat, when you were in my room and it seemed to me that she was handcuffed! Why and where did you take it and where is it now?"

The guard said firmly, "She is accused, my lady, of trying to kill you, and she was in detention and under investigation, but now she is awaiting her fate in prison, and a final judgment may be issued on her within hours or days. Being executed."

Maya stood in the middle of the office and said with all force and threat, "I do not know how Ms. Ronat is sentenced to death and for what crime and where is she now?"

It was a strong and confusing entry for Chraklis and without any preliminaries, Chraklis stood up and said, "What do I see here? Maya? What a beautiful coincidence, and it never crossed my heart that it would be you, and if I knew, I would have laid the red carpet for you."

Maya gave him a hateful look while she was not concerned about his words and said, "I did not come to hear the words of flirtation, but I want an answer to my question?"

Chraklis face changed, and he said, "Well, it is clear how important that is."

Then he smiled a deceptive smile and added, "But I will not disappoint you, my dear wife. Ask what you want."

Maya went crazy when she heard that word, she couldn't bear hearing his name and she felt scum accompanied by severe cramps when she saw him, so how did he provoke her with this word and she said angrily, "If you repeat that word again, I promise you something that will disturb you greatly even while you are in your grave."

He made him even more belittle it and he said, "Oh, I'm sorry, I didn't mean to anger you, but it seems that the effect of what happened to you became clear in your behaviour, so I didn't promise you that nervousness. Oh princess."

Maya said in a soft voice, until he sensed the seriousness of her calm voice more than angry looks and slowly circled around him in the wheelchair, "It seems that my father does not know anything about the thousands of simple farmers whom she has deserted from their farms and taken over their farms and made them sign the waiver instruments while they are forced to do so under the threat of extortion. And that you threatened them that you will say that they want to spread the hatred of the king among the citizens and that the penalty for that is exile outside the kingdom!"

Those words were like knives in the chest of Commander Chraklis, who was silent for a long time, his face stained with all the colours of shame, wondering in frustration, what is this? How did you know that no one knew except me and Chancellor Gershom?

Maya completes the skin of sharks and said, "But that is not what brought me here but I had to return the word to the word and you are the one who started, I am not your wife and I will not be and remember this always put it between your eyes. But now I came to see Mrs Ronat, who you said was intent on killing me. I want to ask her about an important matter. I want you to send her to my room without anyone knowing about this, do you understand?"

Then she turned her angry face and turned the wheels of the wheelchair outward, and went back to her room, without Chraklis uttering a word on all that she had said.

And the minutes are very few until the guards knocked Maya's room.

Maya said attentively to everyone who was with her in the room, "Get out of that door, it will take you to a corridor that leads to a private road near the kitchen and back in an hour from now, come on quickly, then the guard entered and Chraklis was leading them and Mrs Ronat was tied and started crying when she saw Maya, "Praise be to God for your safety, my princesses, and may God keep you, the gift and light of this kingdom."

Maya said in a tone of command, "Loosen her bonds and leave all of them, including you, Mr Chraklis, and do not forget to say Your Majesty again when you address me!"

It was a heavy insult to Chraklis, who grabbed his hand and tightened it violently and said softly, hiding behind a vengeful volcano, "Well, Your

Majesty, and then they all left. Maya was like her father when it came to show strength. Do not hesitate to restrain anyone who thinks to abuse the protocols of office between them, whatever their position." She remains the king's daughter.

"Come close, Mrs Ronat, and sit on the chair, and do not be afraid of anything here as long as you are with me. You are immune from everything. Just trust me. I only brought you here to free you from what you are in, because I do not believe that you wanted to hurt me, and I do not believe that you wanted to do something like this before, Ronat. But let's go back a little bit to that moment when you were combing my hair."

Miss Ronat felt a great relief, relieved the tension that covered her body, and that Maya may have a different thought about what happened to her and what she thinks about her, and she is not like the others.

Maya continues her talk and said, "I saw you when something fell from you, but before you could pick it up, I heard you mumbling words and I can't hide from you that I have a strong feeling that those words you said were the reason for my fall, I felt that the words that came out of you were fire in my ears, will you tell me about those words and what were they?"

Mrs Ronat says, "Now that I am here with you and alone you should know that I told your father the whole truth and I did not hide anything from him and now I must tell you as well if your father did not tell you, Mr king."

Maya said, "No he did not tell me?"

Ronat said, "While I was combing your hair, I fell from my pocket a necklace with a magic spell that was specially made to be a guard against the jinn!"

Stretch the beginning of the speech Maya who listened carefully and did not know that there is something in this existence called score against the jinn and she never commented and continued her silence until suddenly Maya took the necklace out of her pocket and said to Ronat, "Is this the necklace?"

Ronat was silent and kept meditating the necklace with high concentration until she slowly extended her hand and touched it with her fingers, then decided to hold it after her thoughts were confused and brought it close to her eye and said with confidence, "It is my necklace, how is this and where did you get it? Or did your father give it to you the king? Because I didn't find it, and when your father asked me later, I told him that I lost it in your room when he used it to recite the invocation to you, and with great joy I did not know where I put it, and I thought that His Majesty, the king, had taken it because no one asked me about it until when they took me back to prison."

Maya says happily, "I found it under the pillow on this chair. It seems that you put it here without realising it, but tell me how this necklace can do that to me without harming others? How did it not work now while it is in my hands?"

Ronat told Maya all the details and the full story of the necklace, and then she reassured Ronat and said Maya to her, "Don't worry, everything will be fine, and she ordered them to take her and leave her room."

As soon as the door to her room closed, Maya pushed her wheelchair quickly towards the inner door of her room to see if her friends were still close to the room to return to her, and as soon as she opened the door, everyone fell on top of each other under Maya's feet!

Robin Priyanka, Olivia, and even the dog Regen and the red panda, Foxy; were eavesdropping on the interview in her room.

She said with a sarcastic laugh, "It seems that curiosity has been a trait that has accompanied you since you were created, you beautiful creatures. Well, let's have fun. Now I have a surprise for you. King Barhout had prepared a grand breakfast to open his day by hearing all that delights him, to prepare to announce joyful news from his point of view to the sons of the kingdom on the occasion of his daughter's recovery two days after the fall of Maya."

Everyone was present, except for Commander Chraklis, and the king noticed this and said sarcastically, "Where is Commander Chraklis?"

Then he was silent for a moment, after looking at everyone with disdain, and said to Mr Gersium, as he was eating soup, "Is everything all right, Counsellor?" The chancellor answered quickly, nervously, "Yes, yes, Your Majesty. We

are just waiting for when you give the signal to start the party."

The king said, with a little beard wet with soup, "I don't want to finish this soup until the bands have started playing the tunes I asked."

"And you know how good it makes me, right away, Your Majesty, everyone below they are all waiting for when they will be happy to receive your orders, and that will be without you asking."

Then the minister pointed with his hand to the conductor in the orchestra, and the classical royal melodies that were dedicated to the mood of the king were played.

And it happened that Maya entered in the meantime, as if the music was being played for her, so that she and everyone who was with her thought that he had already played the music for her, which made her proud as she entered her father and those with him, except for Robin, who was as usual looking for sweet cakes around the hall.

She was wearing a pink dress made of light silk, decorated with pearl beads from her navel to the beginning of the neck, and her hair was wrapped in four braids that fell from her shoulders to the bottom of her, for the length of her shiny black hair for the first time.

She was stronger than sitting in her bed for a longer period, knowing that she had things to be accomplished.

The king said with great pride, "For God's sake, isn't this a descendant of kings and the daughter of a king, but also his queen?" Then he struck his hand and got up and said with enthusiasm, as he was dazzled by the beauty of his daughter for the first time, he saw her in all her adornment, "For the first time in a long time I feel like I made a wise decision. Come close to me, my daughter."

Walking in her wheelchair to where her father is, shaking hands and kissing his hand, and he expressed great joy in her and did not stop praising her.

For the first time in his life, he says how strong you are, your father's daughter.

And he said again, bragging about her, "Look at the lady of this party," and he pointed with his hand and her hand was knotted with his hand, and said, "Now, come to the balconies, to announce this party. And that I have a big surprise for everyone," then he whispered in her ear, "It's you!"

He began to lead Maya's chair by himself to the balcony. Mr Chraklis took advantage of the busyness of the king and the rest in the upcoming party, because he had something more important than all that, which is curiosity. If he took advantage of this moment, he was alone with Mrs Ronat in her prison and entered her, arching his eyebrows, clenching his lips and standing in front of her, showing prestige in the face of her weakness and extreme misery.

Threateningly, he said, in a violent voice, as he beat the whip in his hand against the prison walls, "Now the sentence has been passed against you, accused, and it is a very hArchie sentence, as he deliberately stuns her and paralyses her thinking, so that she is completely subject to him and at his mercy."

Then he added, after he froze in place from the horror of the news, "But there is only one hope of survival, because you will not like what you will hear when you stand in court to face your death sentence and realise at that moment that you will not see your children forever and there is no moment of farewell, with dry lips and cold face and pale eyes she said like that breathe into the soul, "My execution?"

The tape of her life passed before her eyes as she uttered that word. She felt a great disappointment, and her heart almost stopped at any moment, as she was happy to meet Maya and did not promise her until she was devastated.

He said to her in a dry and hArchie tone, "Now you are starting to think better. First, I want you to tell me everything that happened between you and Maya without missing a single word, because you know that Maya will be my wife and that I am the second man in this kingdom and that whoever lies to me is never safe from my punishment." He blushed and smiled shyly to keep up with her situation.

"But now, I know everything about you and about your children, so I chose to do good for your children, for whom I have no fault in their mother's misfortune. For the sake of your innocent children, Mrs Ronat, come on tell me honestly what Maya told you!"

She tried to speak, but she got choked up and she said to herself, "Maya the king's daughter and at the same time I told her everything and that she could not break her promise and at the same time if she refused to reveal it, she would have killed her children with her own hands! It is really an unenviable position."

He frowned at her and said, "I don't think time is on your side now. When everyone finishes the party, the sentence will be executed without anyone noticing, because everyone will have drowned in the immersion of drinking, satiety and amusement."

Then he extended his lower lip with a strange movement, and said sarcastically, "Except for your children, who will be homeless when the owner of the house you live in finds out that they have lost the one who was paying the rent."

She said as she sobbed a lot, "My lady Maya, asked me about what happened to her and what she heard from me when I was combing her hair and about the pain that happened to her suddenly before she fell unconscious. Before I came here to protect my children from the threat of one of the fairies, I came here and forgot that the necklace was with me, and when it fell from me, I said the spell, and that was the reason for Maya's fall and what happened to her, and that's all."

Sir Chraklis began to be surprised how he would be after what happened. These are the characteristics of people who suffer from several psychological problems such as envy, domination, arrogance and love of possession, which are qualities that if they meet in a creature that will be nothing but a piece of evil moving everywhere.

He expressed his astonishment that Maya kept her as if they were old friends, as he was aware of the human spells that are used to repel the jinn from entering them in their homes.

He also knew that most spells caused the jinn to burn alive when they were cast on someone!

He asked her curiously, "Where is this necklace and how did it look?"

Weeping, said, "She has a metal chain and has an oval-shaped emerald, and she is with Maya now that she has got it."

His tongue stammered and said in shock, "With Maya? Does the king know that?"

The poor woman said, "Yes, he knows, and I told him that, but it seems that he forgot her when he saw Maya woke up from that coma, and when she summoned me, I told her about the necklace and the spell. To tell her and I was forced to do that in order to clear myself and the necklace is still with her, but she cannot do anything with it except with my presence because no one knows the amulet except me and the king himself!"

For a moment, Chraklis felt temporary reassurance that Maya did not get the spell, but Ronat was ready for his next question, so she kept him before he asked and said to him, after getting angry, "No genie has the right to learn it, otherwise he will be burnt immediately!"

And here Ronat has locked him up on what he will think or what he wants to do, and you will be aware, sir.

Then he went on, staring at her with contempt, and said with doubt running through his body, "But you didn't tell me what she said while cuddling you?"

Ronat was confused and silent as she rolled her frightened eyes between his shining eyes maliciously, then said after hesitation, "She didn't say anything, sir, she only said goodbye!"

He said sarcastically, "Just farewell? Are you sure about that, or is there something else you want to say before I also say goodbye to you and say goodbye to your last days of life?"

She couldn't say anything and then turned towards the door and she saw him moving away, as if he was taking her soul away from her with every step he took outside the prison door and she realises the extent of his threat?

And when he reached the door, he said to her coldly, "You did not pass the test, it seems that you preferred Maya to your children!" Then he left coldly without fulfilling his promise to her until she screamed at the top of her voice with a broken heart, "You promised me and now you are breaking your promise, why did you repudiate your promises after I told you everything you asked!"

But he did not respond to her with anything and went away, leaving her in painful torment.

By chance, it was Robin who had come late and was because he was looking for the main kitchen of the palace in order to ensure himself that he would be the first to try and taste all kinds of cakes and food prepared by the most skilled chefs in the main palace kitchen located after the south wing of the palace before the crowds.

And wading between the feet of the visitors in the expected ceremony, and the prison corridors all came from the bottom of the kitchen, where everyone who came out of the prison had to climb from the bottom to the top and meet the people who came out of the kitchen in the same corridor. He had just come out of the kitchen and quickly hid behind one of the statues in the hallway, until they left.

He was surprised that they were leaving this place from the palace, thinking that they were checking the food, and he was not aware of the prison order.

Until he returned to the kitchen and took a quick tour with his long hands and left nothing of the food except to eat a piece of it, even if he finished his tour and decided to get out of the kitchen, he hit a huge wet body as if it was a giant pillow that he had never seen before, and he fell to the ground.

And when he raised his head, he was surprised that that huge body was nothing but the stomach of the chief servant.

The giant Rarocha, holding in his hand a cleaver, with two huge blades, as though they were two ends of a mirror of sharp sharpness, with two equal faces. He said to him in a rising voice, "Or did you think that you would eat without a price, you thief? I have received your news from sellers, cooks and servants

that there is a little thief from whom no one has been spared!"

He grabbed the neck of Robin's shirt from behind and raised it up high with his hand until Robin looked like a feisty cat holding his owner by the back of his

neck.

Then Rarocha said with a hateful laugh, "Now where is the price for what I

ate?"

Robin coughed several times to make Mr Rarocha understand that he

couldn't speak until he dropped him to the ground, but he kept hanging in the air.

Until Rarocha lifted the cleaver in Robin's face, and Robin saw his face in the blade of the cleaver and saw in it the reflection of one of the cooks carrying on his shoulder plates of chocolate-covered pancakes until Robin said, muffled in a stifled voice, "Yes, for what I ate there behind you, sir, on the table."

Rarocha gave him doubtful eyes. Then he slowly turned his head back, his eyes not leaving Robin's eyes until Rarocha turned his head back. Robin took the opportunity to extend his hands as long as possible. Possibly to snatch a plate of oversized hot chocolate pies he saw in the reflection of the cleaver blade, and as soon as Robin got a plate of chocolate pies.

He said to the angry Rarocha, "Here is the price for what you ate."

So that if Rarosha turned to him, Robin made a plate of pancakes in the face of Rarosha, who escaped Robin screaming, "What a thief, a deceitful bastard!"

Robin ran away laughing like a flash of lightning and disappeared in a few seconds like a death run.

At this moment, the trumpets of the celebration had begun to blow, and everyone ran to crowd to see the balcony from which the king would appear, as usual, to give any speech or to open any occasion.

The place was buzzing with the sounds of royal instrumentals, and this was usually before any speech the king gave, lasting less than a quarter of an hour.

The melodies of immortality that the king enjoys on the giant canaries, which are more than two meters long and made of pure gold to be more heavy and beautiful, are called the giant canary machines, and on top of it is a statue of a boy with wings as if he is enjoying the immortal melodies and all the crowds lined up for the first time from all classes of society are heard in one place.

It is not hidden from anyone how the wealthy of the kingdom were clearly disgusted by the sight of the general categories of the people, including farmers, miners, servants of the palace, servants of storehouses, and coal collectors.

Even one of the farmers was accompanied by his seven children and she was covering them with some pieces called clothes.

Not a part of it is devoid of many patches with pieces that do not match the colour of the original clothing, which he used to say to his sons in good faith and joking in order to increase their joy and make them feel the most beautiful feeling that he could convey to them.

They were the ones who were deprived of these occasions throughout their lives when they saw dishes of food that they chose, drink of what they desired, meat of what they wished for, and everything that the souls desired and the eyes loved.

Also, from watching the luxurious palace of the kingdom with pillars covered with emeralds and rubies, "And the father said to his children, "Now, my children, live as if you own this great palace and rejoice. This is a happy day that may not be repeated. We must thank our great king for this opportunity. And do not forget the food, as this is a paradise opened to us today!"

Behind them stood a wealthy couple holding two glasses of fine wine in silver cups reserved only for these guests.

The couple stared at the farmer and his children in a disgusting way, as if they were watching a pile of garbage and not creatures that feel what they feel and wish like they wish.

And their hearts did not yearn even for these children with the simplest kind of mercy possible.

He said in a rude manner to the children of the farmer who were dazzled by the bliss they saw for the first time, "Well, you said it yourself, miserable farmer, that it might not happen again, so try to eat well because what you will find here you will never see in your life and never taste again even in your dreams?"

Then he turned his face with pride and arrogance and said to his wife with contempt, "I don't really know the wisdom of such a decision the king made. But it's okay to watch some of these servants and their children eat our food greedily for the first time, Ha-ha-ha."

He says to his wife, "Is not it, my dear?"

His wife looked at the farmer with a humiliating look, and she was the one who did not leave part of her arms without covering him with jewels and sparkling ornaments. She said, "Of course, my dear."

This is generosity from us and this is one of our traits, my dear husband, so it is okay to see them eating on this day from our food, so that they know why we live in a very different level, so that they do not multiply from those boring questions that we are tired of about the inequality between us and them.

Then she smiled proudly and gave her husband a false happiness like flies when they fall on the dirt and think that they have found the best food.

The poor farmer confidently said, "Well, my friend, who is sympathetic to others and is arrogant to those who are inferior to you because of their circumstances in which they have nothing to do with. Why don't you pity yourself when you have exhausted yourself with this comparison, which I doubt that the fire of blind hatred has burnt your heart and inside you there is nothing worthy.

"It is because of his abhorrent racism in yourselves that you created and made of it a way of life that makes you feel comfortable when you take out all your dirt on those who work day and night in order to make the luxurious cup from which you drink and what contains it of vintage wine! Neither you nor your wife would have made it, had it not been for our struggle in order to reach you with the most beautiful thing that the eye can see and the sweetest thing that the tongue can taste."

The arrogant man and his wife looked at the wine glass as if for the first time they saw its details, then they looked at each other stupidly!

Then they realised that they were embarrassed, so the man came back again with pride and raised his chin and wanted to respond to the farmer, but the farmer said to him strictly, "Shut up and tell me, Who makes these for your clothes? Did your wife make it for you? Did you make her shoes, big head? Who makes your underwear that covers your stinky private parts? Do you know how to knit clothes?"

The couple looked at themselves and their faces shrank and each of them saw the face of the other as if he saw the face of a donkey that lost its way back to its owner!

Then the disgruntled farmer added his stinging attack on them, "Who makes perfumes for you that cover the rotten smell of your racism?"

The angry farmer's words attracted the vast majority of the attendees, and most of them were of the same category and level of slaves, farmers and porters who were affected by his words and knew that he would not explode with anger in this violent image except when he heard racist and painful words from the racist couple, which was not surprising to them, as most of those present returned to treat this class of bullies with this inferiority.

From the intensity of his enthusiasm, he took the two glasses of wine from their hands and poured the wine on their heads until all their precious clothes were wet and they froze in their places from shock and extreme embarrassment.

Until they became the subject of ridicule by everyone, who filled the place with their laughter, mocking and indignant, as if it was a day of revenge against the couple who cast a disgusting look at those around them to feel the shame, and withdrew with their heads bowed to preserve what was left of their dignity and dragged the tails of racism with them to where they came and deprived themselves of such a rare party.

And that is because the people are arrogant, no matter what their affair is, but in the end, they remain captives of their sterile and frivolous ideas that no one can tolerate anymore.

The herald calls out loudly from the top of the palace balconies, after the trumpets are blown, "O people! O people! Now our king, the Great Barhout, will give his speech!"

The king overlooks from the high balcony, which was for those in it, as if he saw the end of the world from the prestige of his panoramic view of most of the city for the first time, his daughter Maya was next to him while she was in a wheelchair, where it was the first surprise that surprised everyone and diagnosed their eyes as they saw Maya for the first time next to her father, the king, and they knew that it would be an unusual party until silence fell.

Until one of the guards called out in a loud voice, "May God save the king and the kingdom," and the voices of cheers rose after him with a voice that shook the place. (God save the king, God save the king)

For the first time, the king's chest rattled and he was strangled for a long time, and he felt coldness in his heart as he sensed this overwhelming love from the subjects. The king, or the residents of the palace, as well as the people of the kingdom, were not used to such chants.

They were accustomed to the silence of the attendees in previous years, who were all from the silent elite class who consider attending such occasions as just a way of life to spend time between the looks of the king and his entourage to prove a false patriotism.

The king murmured inaudible. It is time for compensation, honest citizens. It is time for compensation for all those lean years until his tears rolled down his cheek and wet the hair of his white beard, and no one noticed it except Maya only. She felt the moaning of her father's heart as he felt his mistake.

But he hides it for his pride and for the factor of place and timing when he first felt that the real inhabitants of the kingdom really liked him on their own and without being favoured by them.

And it is not like a picture of his ministers and advisors around him that the people of the kingdom are just mobsters, thieves and thieves who want to stir up hatred against the king and attack the palace as soon as they get the chance!

And that they share the wealth of the kingdom and tear it apart like hyenas tore their prey, this misty evil thought was what the influential advisors and leaders planted completely in the mind of the king for a period of time, and they succeeded in that, but not forever.

The king raised his head to caress the air on his cheeks, and his hair travelled with the cold wind, then pointed with his right hand up to silence everyone in order to start until the crowd fainted until the king said, "O mistress, I really feel today that I am very lucky because I succeeded in making the appropriate decisions and here I am touching and seeing her in front of my eyes but I am very sad because I have not met you on such an occasion for a long time."

Mr Chraklis had come at last and seemed to stand behind, without anyone noticing his disappearance but the king continued, "I do not want to prolong you too much, and I know that you are eager for this party. This party will be for a whole week, not just today."

This was the second beautiful news for the attendees, and they seemed surprised and excited until they applauded enthusiastically.

And if the audience, all of them, repeated these patriotic chants in a very loud voice, from which the corners of the palace roared, and its echo reached throughout the villages around the kingdom.

It was excessive enthusiasm with pure love, the king tried to continue, but he could not, the crowd did not calm down, but more than that, if they all seemed to sing together, and the king could not interrupt them while he watched all those happy souls expressing the depth of their love on this day and this news until he laughed out loud.

It was very painful for some of the ministers, especially Chraklis, whose eyes shone with black hatred, and he was filled with anger, and he knew with his physiognomy that there was a great transformation coming for him.

A great fire begins only with a small spark that one does not care about until you burn it and burn everything around it.

The king added, after he signalled again with his hand to shower him to complete, and said quickly, "I really did not feel it in my first meeting and it is a pride for me to feel that I am from you and you are from me and that we each other will continue our mArchie for the prosperity of our nation, but now we have announced the ceremony and that it will be annually and not just once as some thought and the most important of all is what I decided and decided to hear it all, to share my decision, O sons of my kingdom."

Then he fell silent and turned to Maya while she was holding his hand and smiled a wide smile and reciprocated the same thing, not knowing what he wanted, but she realised that it was something that would please the king himself and said proudly, "I decided today that Maya will be the heir to the throne after me, and I will not wait fifty years until she grows up, for today she is older than ever, she will have the decision to choose her life partner, and no one will decide that! I appoint her from now on as the crown prince after me with full powers!"

The decision came as an astonishing shock to those present, who does not love Maya, the girl who is famous for her love of others and with an emerald reputation among most of the simple people in the kingdom.

Except for most of those behind the king who felt that this day was nothing but the worst setback they had experienced and thought that the earth had narrowed them down.

And the time for reckoning has come, and they have to change the rules of the game, or else the gallows are waiting.

As for Maya, she was no less shocked than the others, she did not turn her face away from her father as he spoke and gave the matter and completed his continuity in recounting the next steps of greater support for farmers and breaking the monopoly of traders and agents.

On all the productive and supportive sectors of the kingdom's economy, which seems to be the beginning of a worrying and painful cycle of transformation that will not satisfy some, and of course, they will not give up by watching all their wealth vanish before them and go to those who think they were created in order to be their slaves.

Yes, this will be the beginning of a very dangerous stage, the beginning of which was beautiful words and more beautiful decisions than the king, but there is a strong party that sees that the knife has been placed on his neck.

Therefore, he will not hesitate to do anything to save himself and will try hard to put an end to these decisions or obstruct them for the longest possible period of time so that they can collect all the stolen items before they are confiscated from their contaminated hands.

Because there must be consensus on Maya by the Senate, which in turn will become Maya after this decision is an important member of it.

Which is represented by the class of senior merchants and their agents in the palace the largest part of it and with this bold step the king joined him with an important member after the creation of the position of the crown prince, which is considered the strongest after the position of the king.

But it seems that this step is nothing but the wood that will ignite the fires of a battle that has been dormant for a thousand years, and whose scene will be this inhabited palace soon, as we expect or believe that it may happen after that.

There was great confusion, impromptu discussions and rumours of what might happen after this party, which was a strange party in every sense of the word.

But some of them are well aware of the far-sighted view of the king, and most of them do not know anything because of their ignorance of what is happening in the kingdom. The shallowness of the media controlling all parts of the kingdom and its monopoly by an influential class.

Maya threw her father from the side and said, "What is this, father? But I am still too young for this matter and I do not understand much of what is happening."

The king says, "From today, you will know everything, and you will manage everything in my sight and hearing."

She said, "But what pushed you, my father, to such a thing?"

He bowed his head and said, "Daughter, I was supposed to rearrange a lot of things sooner. But it seems that I am late, but remember well to do what you see fit, even if it is late, is better than not to do it at all," then he adjusted and said with a sigh, "I raised many dogs and left them to roam and have fun around the kingdom and when I realised my complete preoccupation with her, I turned into predatory beasts. I saw today what I had not seen before and I did not expect it to happen, but I do not know what inspired me to do this."

He turned his body to Maya and put his hands on her shoulders and said, "My dear daughter, life is more difficult than we can imagine, but what happened to you made me realise that I was oblivious to many things and that it was time for you to learn all the big and small things that happen here in the palace.

"Its impact is reflected on the kingdom and those in it, who considers the head and skull of the kingdom to be ruined and corrupted, the entire kingdom will be corrupted and we will all perish because no one lives in the destroyed land except the demons who will never have mercy on anyone."

Maya said politely after she realised what was behind those words, "Or do you mean those around you from the men of the kingdom, my father?"

He looked with half an eye at those behind him who were waiting for him to finish his announcement, then Maya stared at them sharply as if they were fools. Then he looked at each other again and said to her in a calm voice carrying a lot of warning, "Yes, these are the dogs of our world that are never satisfied. Do not be deceived by the clothes of chastity and wisdom that they wear, there is nothing more beautiful than the skin of snakes when you replace it with new skin, but the poison of killing remains between their fangs. They will not hesitate at the earliest moment to eat our meat while we are alive."

She said, "Did they hurt you, Dad? Don't think that these scattered people can frighten me even an iota. If I wanted to rid you of them, I would flay their skins now before your eyes from this balcony, and the crowd is looking to be an example to the rest of the dogs that think some of their master's hand."

The king laughed loudly and said, "I did not hate laughing in front of people like this in my life such a moment as you are your father's daughter, you honest and brave no king who has a son like you, Maya, will ever lose."

Then he hugged her while she was on the chair with force and everyone applauded after they were affected by this moment, especially after they had been overwhelmed by the joy of all those decisions that made them happy, except for the stray group that was behind the king.

Then asked Maya spontaneously and whispered in her father's ear, "What made you, father, think of marrying me to Chraklis, without consulting me?"

With great grumbling, the king said, "Oh, I wish you hadn't mentioned me. I was under the influence of anger, and the counsellor threw that idea into my mind in the form of a joke, so I grew up until it became an inevitable thing. I don't know what happened to me, whether he bewitched me or what! But after what happened to you, I prayed to God silently, then everything around me was revealed to me in the blink of an eye."

Then the king's eyes fell on his necklace on Maya's chest and he said with astonishment after touching the necklace with his fingertips and examining it, "What is this necklace, Maya! From where did you get it? Or is this Mrs Ronat's hairdresser's necklace?"

Maya said confidently, "Yes, and I deliberately wore it today so that you could see it, because I want to deliver a message to you, and I think you have received it now."

The king was silent for a long time, then raised his head after he understood the matter and told you that without asking you, because I know that you are doing nothing but the right thing.

And this is my pledge to you, then he turned around with his whole body and took two steps forward, then stopped and said, "Maya!"

Then he fell silent and turned to him and she sensed what he wanted to ask about!

And she didn't say anything, but said to herself, closing her eyes, "Not now, Dad," then he asked strangely without turning around and said quietly, "I didn't ask you about those boys you were with, so I say it again that I know that you will do nothing but the right thing!"

Then he completed his remaining steps to the balcony wall until the luminous missiles launched in the sky of the kingdom, marking the beginning of the celebration that lit the sky of the kingdom with sparkling lights, and everyone danced with joy and joy, and the servants came out with trays of food and drink to spread bliss on everyone on a happy day, it was like a group of dreams in waking time before the king left, Maya held his hand after you breathed a sigh of joy, not asking the king about Archie and those who were with him and said tenderly, "I promise you, my father, I swear that you will only see the good Maya, but I have a request that is not difficult for you, especially on this happy occasion and glorious night to be released about Mrs Ronat, and I knew, my father, how innocent she is of the charges brought against her, and that she should be returned to her children, as they have no breadwinner but her. And if you permit me and my friends to take her out before you leave."

The king smiled and said with his jokes, "As you conspire, Crown Princess, I don't need to go to her, because in fact I will not only release her, but we will honour her and reward her with a generous reward that will sing her and her children to extend her hand to anyone. Because she is the cause of this great event, after she was the cause of removing the mist from my eyes, and we will send her to your room enhanced and honoured."

Maya said with great joy, "Never before has the heart of anyone in this universe been manifested with great generosity and kindness like the heart of His Majesty, the king." Then she got up and hugged him tightly, crying hard. "How much I love you, Dad, and how I feel for the first time in this security in my life."

Even if she opened the door to her room with eagerness and great hope, and her father's words hit her eardrums hard, and that she would not reach her room unless Mrs Ronat preceded her.

Until her heart almost flew out of her ribs from the intensity of joy when she found Mrs Ronat in her room sitting on the chair waiting for Maya with great longing.

Ronat said while wiping her non-stop tears, "I lost hope of meeting you, my princess, thank God that you came. That angry man always came to me, and I don't remember his name here, and he threatened to deprive me of my children and that he would even apply the death sentence to me.

"After he defrauded me and asked me to tell him everything that happened between us and that I am sorry, I had to tell him everything."

Maya interrupts her and raises her head off Ronat's chest and says with frightened eyes, "Or did you tell him about the magical amulets?"

The lady says in a reassuring voice, "No, I told him what happened to you and how the amulets affected you, and he asked me to tell him about it, but I told him that she would burn him and burn those who were with him if I said it, and then he went angry and promised me evil after he had promised me that he would rid me of this judgment."

Maya said after the dryness that was her throat cleared, "Now you are safe, the pardon has come from the king and Chraklis no longer owns your destiny, you are now free and we will return you to your world honourable and you will see your children."

The greatest smile in Ronat's life was on her face, and her face shone again. Then she took out a piece of paper from her pocket on which she had written amulets.

She says, "I wanted to give her one of the guards to deliver it to you after I thought that I would never see you again. Except for the great jinn who are kept by your father in the high mountains, so this does not affect them because they have another spell stronger than this that only the great wise men of mankind have, and one of them lives in the kingdom whose name is Cayman."

Maya said strangely and bewildered as she looked at the distant mountains, the look of the one who wants to precede everyone with his steps more than the one who waits for the steps of others to think what he must do to keep pace with them, "And how are these jinn's apostasy!"

Ronat says simply, "Tell your father and he will teach you everything, my princess, because now you are no longer that ordinary girl, but you are now the crown prince and the matter is complicated and there is great harm to everyone."

Chapter 23

ISABELLA ALBERT

The doors of the windows slammed the walls of the room at the top of the fourth tower of the six palace towers that swim above the clouds from the cold north wind.

Like the evening's breath that breathed and the fingers of the wind turned the pages of the book of the novel, the girl sleeping on her silk bed with her transparent pink panamas, showing the sedition hidden beneath her, that everyone who sees her desires, caressing the softness of her pink skin, free of impurities, and the insomnia of a child's skin.

Until he whispered in her ear a voice with melody and nostalgia, longing absent at the length of parting, saying in a long whisper of letters, "Oh, what a beauty who did not find someone to hug him, you are the light of beauty and you are the sedition in itself, Isabella!"

Isabella felt those whispers reaching her heart before her ear until she opened half her eyes when she saw the book of the novel in front of her like a mirage, its pages turning until the pages settled from the movement on one of the chapters of the novel.

And the most important thing that did not come until she heard the same melody saying in her ear, as if the voice of a young man, "So, you are my girl whom I adore, what audacity you are, girl, now you have reached what I wanted you to reach!"

Isabella continued to slumber and slept around without getting up until she spoke to herself as if she was talking to someone in a dream.

This matter is inevitable, so you must drink from the cup of evil to protect yourself from it.

The voice of the invisible replied, "Do you think that he is able to do that, or that he will weaken in front of him!"

She said coldly as she struggled with drowsiness, "If he wants to reach, he will do so, even if he has to blow up his principles!"

The voice said, "How beautiful is your confidence in what you write, Isabella, don't you think that we must dance by candlelight before the sun of love goes out and we taste nothing of love!"

She said as if she had lost her will, "Well I did, I have been waiting anxiously for this moment, but promise me that you won't let me down like every time?"

He said in a happy voice, "Come to the balcony, Isabella!"

And when she got up from her bed and saw her clothes, she felt so ashamed that she covered herself with a thick cloak and looked around her.

Until she thought that she was walking towards the balcony of her room, that there was a man's shadow behind the curtain, and as soon as she rubbed her eyes, she did not see anything, and when she removed the curtain with her hand, the balcony was open with both doors wide.

She asked, questioning, "I remember that I closed it tightly, but..."

He said to her the same voice as if he was sitting behind her without turning around, "Did you think that I would dream about you when you made my enemy to escape several times, or is there another intention in the heart that I do not know?"

In turn, she said, "Why did you assume he was your enemy? Aren't we supposed to go along with everyone to walk what we planned after you instructed me to create imagination?"

He said, "Yes, and he is. Umm, do not worry, princess, let us leave this matter for a while. You know that I always sit waiting for those wishes and fill the place around me with roses, longing, love, and the sounds and melodies of happy songs, and I am waiting for that moment until the wax melts and the fire of wishes sleeps. And a voice inside me tells me that it wants you, and that longing that inflames and then subsides to a certain extent after realising that you are still far away."

Isabella laughed shyly and said, rubbing one of her braids hanging over her shoulder, "If my brother Alex finds out about something like this, he will go crazy, so you don't know how he is jealous of me, even those beautiful birds that come from the balcony and sing to me in the sweetest voice a human can hear."

He was silent for a long time, then said coldly as if he was calling Alex, "Alex, if he would have prevented me from you, you would not have made him move away from your thousands of leagues with your pen, not by my command."

Then she said while flirting with him, "Well, what are you doing after you learned that he was away?"

He said in a dissatisfied voice, "First get rid of your mistress who will knock on the door now and make her go away and beware of her because she will try to pet you?"

She said surprised, "My mistress?"

Suddenly, she heard someone knocking on the door of her room, in an intense and deliberate way until the invisible voice speaking to her disappeared.

Then she turned to see who was knocking and saw Sarah, her stepmother, Isabella welcomed her warmly after she opened half the door and said, half of her body was inside her hole and the other half was exposed to the unexpected visitor until Sarah said to her with a smile that concealed something the soul did not want to show, "I thought you would be asleep at this time!"

Isabella said, as if looking at herself with sly astonishment, "Then why did you come at this time and knock on my door if you thought so? Unless there was something important?"

Sarah said after biting her face a little, "No, no, nothing of the sort."

She had cast her gaze upon Isabella's body, looking at her like the look of a man thirsting for women, until Isabella noticed it.

She avoided her gaze and went behind the door, with only her head left outside her room until Sarah said, justifying her strange visit before her suspicious glances to remove the mist of doubt that fell on Isabella's soul.

"All in the matter, my dear Isabella, I felt a kind of boredom. Your father told me not to wait for him to be late, because he might lie in his office because he was busy with some meetings with the king and his servants. On the way, out if he had no one to occupy his spare time with!"

Isabella said after thinking a little and remembering the words of the voice on the balcony, "Aha, I understand you, Sarah, but unfortunately, I have some work to do in my spare time. This is not lying to you how hard it is to find time to sleep or time to write, and you know that I immerse myself in writing my novels."

Sarah smiled solemnly, showing the gentle face of the lamb, then reached out her hand and placed it on Isabella's cheek very gently, and wiped her cheek with tenderness and love, "So that I was ashamed of Isabella," after Sarah's hand continued to play with her face and went down to her throat. With looks that are not devoid of hidden sensuality and said in words lighter than a feather carried by a breeze, "I understand that, my dear, and you also understand what I mean." Until the voice called to Isabella in a tone that was not heard except on

Isabella's ear, "Shut the door in her face quickly?"

No sooner had Sarah finished her speech than the room door slammed her

face and closed with a frightening force until Sarah fell from the pressure of the air closing the door! Isabella's wristband fell from her hand, and she was confused. Did she close the door, or did the door close by itself in a strange way? She was not rude one day and did not understand how this happened?

As soon as Isabella turned back towards the balconies, the candles in the room lit up, and she put her hand over her heart from fear, and the voice from outside the balconies called her, saying in the melody of his melodious voice, "Forgive me, my princess, if I caused you some kind of embarrassment, but it is better for me to embarrass you than for someone's hand to touch your pure body with lust!"

Isabella said, "Are you jealous of me?"

He, in turn, answered her, "Departing from the familiar and intellectual and sexual perversions is an unnatural matter, corrupting the heart, destroying the mind and destroying morals. And if that happens, it becomes easy to control you, then you will become like a toy in the hands of others, moving you through your desires. And if you refuse to obey them, you will be deprived of it, and then you will feel as if you are eating yourself and will no longer think of anything in your life except those wild desires. Which will not end until you find yourself becoming an animal in human form.

"Therefore, as long as I am alive, I will not allow the infection of these diseases and sick thoughts to touch you, you have a great mission that you will not accomplish if you deviate into the world of lust and passion, so I will be your everything, my love."

Isabella said happily, "No one in my life has given me so much attention until my father, what an inspiration you are."

And before Isabella reached the balcony, the candles in her room went out all of a sudden, as if they were suddenly lit, as if a magical hand had suppressed her breath, and she heard the voice coming from behind her neck whispering lovingly saying, "Will you dance with me, my beautiful princess?"

Isabella did not turn quickly until she wanted to know where this feeling of love that emanated from the depths of seas of feeling that does not exist in this world of ours would take her. She realised that until she turned slowly after feeling a cold hand touching her heart, as if he had made a hole in it and put in it the semen of a great love that was only created for her.

And when she leaned her whole body back, the shadow of a man was taller than her until she raised her head to look at him, and she saw nothing but a black shadow from the top of his head to the soles of his feet, devoid of any features except the blackness of her body.

And a voice that was thick and soft on the heart, until she felt two cold hands in which were thick. She held the tips of her fingers until she felt while she was in his hands like a child or like a feather carried by the breezes, giving her bouquets of roses of love and the most beautiful melodies of speech filled with a cold fragrance for the most beautiful smell of perfume.

Her memory remains stuck in bottles carried by a herd of swallows.

Then he said as he danced her to the rhythm of timeless music she had never heard before, "You are my precious masterpiece, Isabella, you are more precious than thousands of stars, even if they were made of heavenly diamonds, and you are a treasure that no one appreciated, and you are the most beautiful of precious paintings I have seen."

Until she dazzled Isabella with all those words that she had forgotten about the discotheque and the steps, they were words that had a powerful magic effect on the girl's mind and heart.

She said to him with love, "For the first time, I feel that I am a real woman, you made me feel that in moments and that I am not just an ordinary girl."

So much so that she was so impressed she imagined that he built her a high palace out of an illusion that no one can reach and that she rises to the top on the steps of his sweet words who drowned her in it and said, "Show me look at you, handsome!"

He laughed gently and then approached her ear until she thought that she had seen the features of a human face.

Without saving anything from it, feelings have merged with darkness and when she got closer, she saw his eyes and said to him, "Why are your eyes yellow?"

He answered in a warm voice, "To see you well in the dark, you know very well that I am doomed to live in perpetual darkness until all that you write may be fulfilled, to see the light in your hands, and to put the crown of queens, on your head with my hand and he said whispering coldly, "Finish the novel properly, and then I will be standing at your feet to show me when you wake up!"

As soon as Isabella woke up, she saw the curtains of her room fluttering outward, and one of the candles still lit, struggling with the last thing she had before it withered away.

And the book of the novel was folded on the pen inside it until she put her hands on her face and said as she turned her face in her room.

Was it a dream or reality? Then she said, recalling after smelling the perfume of her breath that made her let out what was in her heart of love when she was dancing with that voice in a dream?

Then she got up towards the door of her room and before she opened the door, she felt a pain in her foot, even if she looked down. It was the bracelet of her hand that fell from her hand in a dream when she closed the door forcefully in Sarah's face and said, surprised by the matter, "No, this is unreasonable?"

Then she reached out her hand to open the door handle to look outside her room, but she didn't find anyone?

Until I heard the sounds of the pages of a book turning quickly and when it turned, the novel had opened and turned until it stopped suddenly, as there was no wind or even just a breeze to move these pages?

When Isabella came to see the book of her novel, it had been opened to a chapter, and she stopped at the last line she had written:

"You have become my vassal, Archie, and your life belongs to my hand, and now you will carry out what I command you to do of great killing in the kingdom."

Isabella paused, meditating, and said in astonishment, "When did I write that?"

Then she heard footsteps on the balcony and felt anxious and she thought that maybe a thief had climbed into the place until she came out of the room and happened to bump into Sarah while she was outside the room and Sarah said to her, "As if the devil is behind you, what happened, Isabella?"

Isabella said with fear, "I heard someone's footsteps on the balcony of the room and ran quickly before he attacked him until I entered Sarah opened the room door forcefully with an angry face and headed to the balcony and found no one?"

Sarah said, "Perhaps your over-writing, Isabella, is what made you think so?" Isabella sighed and said, "Maybe!"

Sarah said, "But is it not your habit to sit in the dark at this time of the evening?"

Isabella said hesitantly, "Actually, it's not like that, and I don't know how the candles went out."

Sarah turned to Isabella in the middle of the darkness of the room, and there was nothing between them but the moonlight that illuminated their faces and they sat looking at each other until Sarah grabbed the tip of Isabella's fingers, who pulled her quickly and said hesitantly, "I apologise frankly when I closed the door in your face a while ago, the truth was I wasn't completely in my mind. I felt like I was dreaming and I didn't realise it?"

Sarah said surprised, "When did this happen?"

Isabella knew now that it was only a dream, until Sarah said with a smile, "Didn't I tell you that the effect of your preoccupation with writing had affected your mind, so I find that this is a good and appropriate opportunity for both of us to get out of the deadly and boring routine, Isabella, don't you see that?"

"Of course," Isabella said cheerfully.

Then Sarah took a step she had wanted to do before in order to put Isabella in an awkward position and drag her into something she had previously planned to be a pressure point against Isabella after Sarah saw someone's shadow on the balcony and then kissed Isabella hard on the lips, but suddenly it seemed that what Isabella was afraid it was happening he was already spying on them out of the way they didn't feel it.

Where a masked man jumped from behind the balcony curtains and then revealed the cover from his face and the girls moved away very quickly from fear and Isabella said in shock, "Knight Schneider?"

Sarah said angrily, "How dare you, you thief, break into the room of the daughter of the king's advisor in the middle of the night? It's a serious crime punishable by death!"

The knight, Schneider, replied, mockingly, "It is not worse than the crime of practicing homosexuality with the daughter of the king's advisor, and betraying the wife of the king's advisor with his daughter, because her punishment is beheading...!"

Chapter 24

THE NYMPH AND FISH CURSE

Those terrifying moments that these brave boys lived through are still stuck in their minds, and it seems to them every time that it is in front of them running like a snake in front of one of your eyes.

Even if they reached an area close to the cave, these fantasies came to them and appeared to them as if it were a huge wall separating them from the dark cave from the severity of what they had suffered during the past days, especially the previous hours, which they thought they would be impossible to do without the space of hope and the collar of salvation that fate throws them from time to time.

The cave was lying under a round mountain without a top, as if a giant rock fell from the sky. It is said that the cave is the only way to pass this natural barrier from below, according to Alex.

The path would lead them to take the right paths to the bottom of the kingdom, and this made them seek with all their might to venture into the darkness of the cave.

It is easier than to jump on their own in the Mediterranean Sea, which separates the lands of the north from the south, which is known for the danger of its water currents and the creatures that inhabit it.

And they had given themselves up to that plan and it is that they leave the entire lands of the north for fear of Glister and the execution squad that roams the forests, valleys and hills in sears of them to liquidate them and not to hand them over to their families as they claim.

After the giant bear left them, the joy of surviving was great when they performed their famous dance, where they held each other's hands and moved in one row, then one of them came forward to demonstrate his solo dancing skills and returned to the class again, and so on until Archie tripped and twisted his injured ankle from the canines of the dopper.

He was not in his mood except that he wanted to share with them the joy they desperately needed, Alexander checks Archie and asks about his foot before they head to the cave before this afternoon how is your foot can you walk on it now? Or do we look to be healed?

Archie said, "There is no need for any more waiting, my feet have recovered a little, but I can walk, so you have to that the fangs of that animal did not fit well on my feet thanks to the shoes. But his weight caused the ankle nerve to twist a little, I think."

Alex says, "No worries, Archie, we have good Sebastian, he will be the king's doctor one day, and he will assess your case. Come and see, Sebastian, and tell us, will he be able to walk on it as he claims, or should he take a rest, not being indifferent, or pretending that there is no pain? It will cause us losses later. If we are destined to lose time, let us lose it here while we are safe. It is many times better than finding out that we need to carry a friend of ours on our shoulders while we are inside the cave. The place inside cannot bear any pauses."

Alexander said to Sebastian and he looked more interested, "You saw for yourself, Sebastian, that Archie was attacked by a dopper, but it seems that his foot was not crushed by the canine tubes of the dopper because of the strange shoes he was wearing, and this is a good thing, but it seems that there is an injury to his foot, I don't know what. Look for yourself."

Sebastian grabbed Archie's leg after removing his sole. Then Sebastian quickly covered his nose with his hand from the force of the stench that came out of it and Archie laughed loudly and said, proud of the quality and durability of his shoes, "It was my dear mother who made these shoes especially for me and my brothers so that we would not be exposed to snake bites when we go hunting with my father, and so that they would not be penetrated by thorns and pointed rock heads, and so that our feet would not sink in the mud.

"Also, even my father asked her to make one for him, and she refused and said only this is for Archie and his brothers, who are not more precious than them in this whole world, and that was the first time I saw jealousy on my father's face from me..."

Then Archie raised his head to the sky and said, "How I wish I could see my mother again to kiss and hug her. I really missed her." Without intending to Archie, his words were in the wrong place.

Until Alexander replied with a grumpy, "Really! Indeed, you are lucky with your mother, as many of us here do not have a mother, O Archie, so it is better if you keep your longing inside you!"

With his spontaneity, Archie provoked a hidden distress in the souls of those around him, most of whom had lost their mother in a different way, but what unites them is that they are orphans in this matter.

Either those who did not know their mother or those who did not see her forever, and some were adopted from a shelter after the death of their mother at a young age, and some of them lost their mother after realising her, including Alexander, Clementine, Martin Chubby and Luca.

When Archie felt that embarrassment, he made a scream of pain to distract them, reminding them of the pain of losing their mothers.

Before sorrows settle in their bodies, and the ghost of feeling inferior and the pain of deprivation of this blessing is removed from them after he realised that open wounds never heal except by forgetting.

Sebastian shuddered at Archie's fake scream and apologised and said, "I didn't mean to hurt you, but the canines didn't seem to hit any of the bones, and what's even more beautiful is that there's no rupture in the important muscles or veins. Your mom seems to have done a really good job, Archie." But it appears that you have a severe sprain of the ankle nerve and I will treat it immediately. Hold yourself a little and look at the sky and try to sing at the top of your voice and imagine that your mother is looking at you and she is very happy, then Archie twisted the foot hard.

Before Archie could even speak, he let out a so true and quick shriek as he who cried out of sudden pain of thorns when he was trampled upon.

Indeed, then he pulled her to him and put her back in place until Archie fell on his back as if he was passing out while looking at the sky in the midst of everyone's silence.

Then he moved the toes of his injured foot after feeling returned to it until he moved his entire foot with ease and then lifted his torso off the ground and said, unable to speak from his joy that his foot had healed so easily, "You're a magician, Sebastian. Yes, you're not a doctor. You're a real magician."

Then Sebastian grinned, splitting his face in half, bragging about that compliment. Which he will undoubtedly record in his autobiography as an important reference to save for the right time.

But Archie realised that it wasn't the right time to dwell on feelings until he shook them from before his eyes and left them behind him and didn't care about them.

He jumped up, then got to his feet, straightened himself, stood like a spear stuck to the ground hard, and started running to dispel doubts about the recovery of his foot.

Indeed, he started running like a graceful little deer that leaves his mother for the first time after birth.

While he was also in the midst of his joy, not knowing where his happy foot was taking him, until he found himself standing before the entrance to the black cave, which was as high from their position as a sloping hill, which was greater than he had thought.

He was deeply dazzled by his darkness, and if there was something that would attract someone's attention, it must be this scene of extreme fear and mystery. Then he whispered softly, asking those who thought they were next to him, "Oh heavens, how will we get here?" But no one answered him, then he turned to find that he had moved away from everyone who was around him, at least fifty meters away, and saw Clementine pointing to him from afar below the height and saying to him in a loud voice, "It seems that you have become better than I knew you, Archie."

Then he noticed that Archie heard a strange movement at the cave until he turned as if he saw the shadow of a human entering quickly into the cave.

And he tried to follow him, then stopped and slowed down and said with fear in himself, "No, Archie, beware, not every time you receive the jar." Then he turned and pointed to his friends and said in a loud voice, "What are you waiting for, come on over to me?"

Then he turned quickly to the cave to contemplate the view of the very black cave with great suspicion, but at this moment he felt as if the hair of his hands stopped suddenly, as if his body was electrifying.

He had a very strong feeling as if someone was staring at him in anger and waiting for him behind the darkness of the cave until he focused his eyes carefully in the middle of the darkness of the entrance to the cave.

Archie thought for a moment he saw a shadow of his yellow eyes that lightened quickly!

Archie fell back in fear until he bumped into someone's body from behind him and jumped quickly from the panic and looked behind him until he found Alexander.

Damn Alex, he said after he sighed hard, "You worried me!"

"Well, you seem to have outgrown us, Archieie," says Alexander, and so are the boys, whom none of them could even whisper in horror.

The cave and its dread, and everyone's mouths looked the same, trembling, exchanging words of fear and uttering the same thoughts that flooded their minds, which is anxiety about what might be worse than what happened to them.

"Are we really going in here?" Luca said, his face shrunken.

Fat Martin replied, repeating Luca's words, his eyes widened and his nose swollen to become closer to the nose of a gorilla and said as he retreated nervously, "No, no, it is impossible for us to enter this place. You seem to be joking. I would rather be eaten by that big talking bear or those black predators than to enter this place."

Alexander laughed gloatingly, "I knew I would hear these words and more, but do not be afraid and do not be deceived by this darkness. This is just a natural camouflage for the cave, like the camouflage of a chameleon, in order that no one approaches it, because there is a great treasure inside, so he will not get that treasure. Except he who was worthy, and he who was worthy is the one who will take the risk. As for cowards, it is written that they should wait for the pity of others."

Luca said, expressing his eagerness to know Alex's intent, which is like a puzzle, "Do I understand from your comparison that the goals have changed and we have become treasure hunters?"

Alexander showed no interest in Luca's question. He said calmly as he advanced towards the cave, "I understand your curiosity to know what I am throwing at, but the essence of the matter is that we are in front of the fait accompli and I don't mind taking some benefits that may unintentionally arise on our way after some wrong decisions led to us being forced to take more dangerous paths!"

Archie said with interest, "These are not wrong decisions, but how to deal with what we are in now is the real decision. It is fates that move us, but our decisions remain ours and we alone decide how to act with the place and situation in which fate puts us."

Alexander avoided looking at Archie and continued his conversation, "This cave has many properties that no one, not even me, knows, but I had one experience that was like a journey into the world of dreams that made me realise that this is the right choice for us and the best. Despite some difficulties that we will encounter so as not to exaggerate that we entered the cave, it will not be a passing picnic.

"But at the same time, it is the exaggerated fear that will make what you imagine of negative things turn into reality, especially when we ride the narrow waterway inside this cave. And it actually happened to me, when I used to fantasise like I see ghosts. For example, you will definitely see them in front of you, and I hope that they will disappoint me."

Clementine asked fearfully, "How is that? Do you mean that if I imagine that huge bear who saved us and the daubers, I will see them in front of me again?"

Alexander laughed, belittling the matter, "Don't imagine too much and you will be fine that the cave wants to expel everyone who enters it. Therefore, he has the amazing ability to make people imagine everything they wished to see, but frighteningly, even if you imagine that you see your father or mother or someone you love, you will see him here as an evil spirit. She wants to hurt you in various ways, but in fact, it is all an illusion that does not exist. If you close your eyes and ignore him."

Clementine was silent for a little and rolled his eyes at everyone, then laughed a fake laugh and said, "It seems that it will be a very beautiful adventure."

As for Archie, he listened carefully to Alex's sudden words, which he had not shown them before, and his eyes were still on the entrance to the cave, and he was talking to him about many things.

Then he said sarcastically, "Didn't your experience tell you that there are yellow eyes watching us?" Then he answered himself and said, "It doesn't matter what happens to us, in general, we have one choice but to do it. Alexander or any of the others did not comment on Archie's words. I thought he might match the sarcastic conversation between Alex and Clementine."

Then the feet moved to the cave in steady steps, and they were feeling for the first time a strange curiosity that they had not felt before, not once in their lives, in front of this situation.

Then Alexander stopped in front of the cave gate, from which cold, fast- flowing air was coming out. Then the air suddenly stopped and became there as if a giant magnet was attracting them very strongly. It sucked everyone who stood in front of the cave and made him feel as if he was running into the cave without him doing that?

Until Alex said, "Now the plan is for you. We will walk in a straight line, the first of which is me and the end of it is Archie, because there is a strong gravitational force. When we approach a distance of five meters from the cave, it will cause us to be thrown inside hard, but do not worry, the first thing that will confront you is a swamp that does not exceed a meter in depth and there is nothing but frogs, even his water is clean."

Then he said in an inaudible voice, fearing embarrassment, "This has been many years, and I hope nothing has changed."

Then he continued his speech to them, "So, hold on tight to each other so that none of you is thrown away and we run in search of him and then we get lost. We find ourselves in a labyrinth of a cave that you will never get out of. There is a steep slope after the swamp that leads to falling into a river with a strong flow of three branches, and it penetrates the cave for a very long distance until it reaches us to one of the ends of the kingdom, and from there we will ascend together to safety and we will have passed the greatest rehabilitation course that other knights in this world went through!"

Clementine said excitedly, "Come on, then I am more excited about this adventure than I feared."

As soon as Alexander released his feet into the cave and broke through the barrier of darkness, the others flew over Alexander as if they were hollow puppets from the force of the gravity of the cave and the cave threw them into it before Alex entered, including Archie, and a great whirlpool devoured them like a black hole devoured galaxies, stars and planets.

Archie pulled his head out from under the surface of the water to find the others in the middle of the swamp, he looked through the cave at its walls, which were lit by the sun's rays that penetrated the wall of great darkness, and the place inside was rather luminous.

Contrary to what they expected, until he saw the face of an angry lion engraved on the wall of the cave surrounded by inscriptions with strange incomprehensible letters, then he looked up to see what made his heart jump from between his ribs.

He saw the face of a human being who did not have any features, as if the painter wanted to send them a message that they should understand from now before something terrible happens.

Where you don't see in the face if you look with high concentration only two yellow eyes! Which Archie thought that he saw this face before entering the cave, but he still thought it was a phantom of imagination and continued to stare at the drawing silently. It was as if she was talking to him until he thought for a moment that it was the eyes of the cave that would start watching them and their movements until Alex called out in fear for Clementine, of course, because he is his brother and he is the youngest of them and said from behind him, "I'm behind you," then he turned to see

Clementine, with the leaves of the swamp on his head, and being mastered by a frog that seemed to chirp loudly.

She seems very angry at the intruders who broke into her kingdom and disturbed her sleep and her young and then began to jump on the heads of others as if she wanted to tell them to get out of my land at once, you strange invaders and the frog continued to chirp until it got into Martin's pants, who jumped out of the swamp while running and screaming, "Oh my God, what is that in my pants!"

Clementine said to him, sarcastically, "It looks like a snake looking for warmth, and of course it will find nothing more than the grease collector you have ha-ha-ha-ha."

Martin took off his pants and continued to run with a loud scream, and his appearance seemed funny and pathetic, until Alexander said to Clementine sharply, "This is not the time for ridicule and laughter, and then the frog fell out of Martin's pants."

She squatted again in the swamp, then jumped back on a rock at the edge of the swamp, and this time was even more angry and shrieked like a scream.

And she looks at them with her huge eyes with malice, which is no longer hidden from anyone, and she says, "Have you not finished sitting in my house yet, your homeless people?"

Sebastian said, spreading a smile to everyone, "Come on, people, we seem to be unwanted guests here. This lady seems to have more to do in the swamp than we do."

Archie said to Alexander and looked at him from the side, glaring at him, "Would you not tell us a little about these drawings, which seem to have not been

drawn in vain and that they have an important significance from my point of view, or were they not drawn when you came here, as you told us?"

Alexander turned his body towards the wall and contemplated the two carved drawings a little, then put his hand and wiped it until it became clearer and said, surprised and almost stuck his face to the face of the carved lion as he contemplated, "Yes, she was here when I came with my father but! But!" Repeated it several times. "The lion's face was not like this, but the face was calm and it was not as angry as it is now?"

Charlie said sarcastically, "It seems that the one who drew it has changed his mood from that era to these days, so even we were shaking in fear a while ago. And now we can't stop laughing because of his frog."

Alex continued, "The story says and the credibility according to the writer's, that this lion was not a lion one day and that there is another prophecy talking about him, as well as this yellow-eyed face is nothing but!"

Then he fell silent and did not complete, and said, "But I don't remember it now, but I will tell you many things that you must understand us related to what we are coming to, but let's finish this issue first and reach our destination in peace."

(Archie remembers Isabella's novel with him, but it is in a bag that is wrapped and closed tightly and time does not help to read)

Not everyone cared much, but the effect of the speech was horrific on Archie, in particular, who felt a strange thing. These may be the signs of his beginning.

Then Alex added, "No more of these legends now. All that matters to us now is that we strictly adhere to every step we take, fighters, because we will lose this element of sunlight after a little while, even if it is simple. So please leave everything going on in your mind because what you will come across now may be the worst we will find here.

"Now we will have to go down to the slope. On the edge, there are rocks in the form of stairs, but they are very small, and whoever falls will be swept away by the water current to no end, and we do not know where, but if we reach the bottom in peace, we will walk a little and then we will enter a tunnel in which a water branch is the one Our way will be under the walls of the kingdom, but now, carefully, just follow me. I will be the first one of you. Just watch every step I take. Hold each other's hands. And let's continue walking in a straight line and imitate my steps, and now tie the rope to the waist of each of you, starting with me."

Alex took very careful steps ahead of them, everyone behind them as if they were a shadow with pale faces and knees dancing after each step they took after they tied the rope all over their waists as they watched that dangerous slope, it was as if the hands of death were pulling them together from below.

The waterway was cutting the floor of the cave in two and running with such great force that they could not even hear each other's words because of the roar of the water.

Alex said after they all reached one of the banks of the narrow stream, "Now we will walk on the edge of the stream, but with caution, it seems to me that the water level is rising more and more and it will continue like this every half hour. This means that the sun and the moon will perpendicular to each other on this day,soIdonotknowwhatdayweare,soIamnottoblamemyself,andIdonot blame any of you after what happened to us, but this means that the water of the watercourse that will bring us to the kingdom, if we reach it quickly, may be at its lowest levels, and therefore it is now continuing to rise, and this is good news, which will reduce the risk rate in the event that one of us falls into the water."

Archie asks, "How long will it take for us to reach the water junction that will connect us to the bottom of the land of the kingdom?"

Alex says, "Maybe four hours or more if nothing hits us!"

"What? Four hours? The two ends of the watercourse will be filled and we will not have the ability to resist this current!"

Alex said confidently, "Don't worry, there's a place I know full of rickety boats?"

Archie looked at Alexander in disapproval, "Are you kidding? What are rickety boats?"

Sebastian interrupted them and asked, annoyed, "Sorry, people, for my intrusion, but I don't know it according to the laws of human physics and cosmic geology. If we stay in a place like this for more than two hours, it will cause us shortness of breath, which means that we are at risk of this lack of oxygen, if we assume that we reach our destination quickly and without any delay. But if it happens and we stumble a little, it will become tragic!"

"You've passed this place before, right?" Archie asked Alexander in an angry voice.

Alexander said, looking shaky, "True, but the truth is, I did not go through the tunnel, but went with this current when I fell into it, and while I was trying to escape, I hung on a tree and then followed a dim light source at the top of the ceiling of the cave and climbed until it brought me to the middle of the forest in which we sat when we got out of the camp!"

Archie interrupted him in anger, "And how do you tell us that this tunnel will take us to the bottom of the kingdom, and now you say that you have reached the point from which we started? Is this another lie?"

Alexander felt that speech had been imprisoned in his stomach, "No, I did not lie, but I did not tell you the exact story. The truth is, my father was with me, and he threw me into this waterway in order to survive, because someone was chasing us, and this is another story. Then my father continued to the tunnel, and then told me the story later, and that this is the stream that he took to me. kingdom directly as described."

Archie asked, "You and your father were stalkers? Of whom?"

Alex said, trying to escape from the answer, "But what Doctor Sebastian said is true, we will not get there unless we are in a bad condition, but I want to assure you that we are on the right path so far when I learned that this time is the timing of the sun and moon perpendicular. Thus, the lowering of the water level in the watercourse leads to a rise in oxygen and will not rise to the level of danger unless we have reached our destination, and this will not prevent us from experiencing shortness of breath in any case, but its impact will be limited. And you know that we don't have a choice."

Archie yelled at Alexander for the first time and said, blue in colour, "Rather, we had the option to rug and reach the kingdom as quickly and with less risk and as for the danger of the guards of the walls of the kingdom, we were able to sit and plan and help each other, we had Maya and the magic carpet."

Alexander let out a sarcastic laugh, and said sarcastically, "Did you say Maya and the carpet?" Then he turned and said to Archie, after raising his hands in the air, and pointing at them, "Where are they now? Look around you! Where are they now? Did you forget that she threw you from the top of the magic carpet and ran away on her own? And left us alone to face our fate like we did before? We succeeded without it and we will succeed now too, then you don't know anything about the Knight Schneider, the leader of the sniper squad? You are really poor, Archie, you do not know what is going on there in the kingdom, so we will try to help you to get back there as soon as possible to take many lessons and learn more than we learned!"

Archie became more excited, and yielded to the demon of his wrath, so that he drew nearer to Alexander, grabbed his shirt and pulled him tightly, "You have caused us to lose the most important thing we had on this trip because of your thoughts in order to make us risk our souls to take a path that you don't even know how your father took?"

Martin whispered to Charlie sarcastically, "It seems we were brought here to die because of these idiots."

Charlie said, confirming Martin's words, "I had a doubt about it, and now my hunch is right."

But Clementine was standing next to them, as if he were their consort and he quarrels to them, "Shut up, you idiots, no one forced you to come here, you came of your own free will."

Martin responds to Charlie, "Look, my friend, who is talking. Look at this tramp who is now giving us orders and even threatening us."

Luca intervenes and says, "No, Martin, you and your friend are already so angry at all of us, as if you had come with us just to sniff every trouble we get into. Why didn't you go with your master, Nathan, if you didn't like it!"

He also added in a sharp tone, "Indeed, if you do not like what we are doing, we are still at the beginning of the road. Go back now and go back to where you were and we will help you with that. It is your longing for your authoritarian leader that made you flatter everything that happens to us we are one group and our destiny is one who doesn't like our behaviour go to hell."

Charlie said, indignant at Luca's words, "So that's it? So, at first, we felt we were not welcome here but only because you needed us so you tricked us into joining you!"

Then he stepped back and took out his dagger, and so did Martin, who gave them a mean look and said defiantly, "Come on, you idiots, show us what you will do more than the screaming of women!"

Clementine said contemptuously, "How dare you raise your arms in the face of your friends and we who embraced you after you were slaves to Mr Gambley, the blacksmith? This is how relations deteriorate when leaders are preoccupied with their personal problems at the expense of the affairs of the parish, as it seems that the matter has worsened at an unexpected moment in place and time, and things may escalate and that the breaths in the chests have narrowed to each other before the breaths narrow in the tunnel."

Alexander and Archie turned to the position behind them. Alexander said, denouncing Archie's behaviour calmly and reproaching him, "This must happen.

When one of the leaders reaches out to the other, the others must imitate him, and if he goes further, they will go too far."

Archie realised the greatness of his mistake and that he went too far in his reaction and could not control himself, although the situation did not call for that, especially since Alex had never seen anything wrong with him before except for his bad habits of excessive drinking and the lack of clarity of his plan that brought them here without a well-thought-out plan when they were surprised Not knowing fully the corridors of the cave, as previously claimed.

Archie shouted at them, threateningly, "You seem really just a boy. If you weren't like that, you wouldn't have raised your weapons in each other's faces just because of different points of view."

Continuing in the conversation, Martin said, "Likewise, when you extended your hand to Alex's dress, and he was the one who rescued you from Nathan's hands."

Martin deliberately used this term to stir up a dormant sedition in Alexander's mind, especially after discussions escalated and raged between them. But Archie hid his anger in himself and did not want anyone to feel that these words were a slap to him to avoid the development of the situation.

Archie had to respond quickly so that Martine's seditious words wouldn't get stuck in the minds of others and said to him, "You two are evil to us, and if I had not taken a vow to myself that I would protect you more than I would protect myself, I would have gotten rid of you now."

Alexander cut short the incident of disagreement and proceeded to the walk towards the forked tunnel and said in anger, "We are still in of danger, and he who slips his feet has no one to blame but himself!"

And as soon as they entered the tunnel, they found a dense group

and overlapping wood, as if it was an old carpentry warehouse, as if

was preparing to use it for something after he collected it, and an urgent matter happened that made him leave it.

And so, it became like rubbish of worn wood. Alex said, "Come, let's pull these blankets and weeds off this boat."

In fact, no one would have guessed that under these piles of grass and wood they would find a boat until Archie and the others pulled everything that covered that thing which for them is an important means of achieving their goal of crossing through the mysterious waterway.

complete the midst of weeds someone

Until the boat appeared from under the pile of worn timber as if it was one of the oldest eras of mankind and that the shrivelling and shrinkage of the wood of the boat because of the water and the dampness between which he lived for many years and the sun never touched him, it was a five-meter boat made of solid oak, and its width did not exceed the first meter less, in order to be smoother with the narrow waterways in this place.

Suddenly a stench spread among them, which made them quickly turn away after covering their faces from that stench. Clementine jumped out of his place like a stung cat and screamed.

Oh my God, what is this mould? He saw the skeleton of a complete human, then put his hand on his nose like the rest. Alex took advantage of the situation and said coldly, "This is an obvious matter. It seems that this miserable lost here and did not find anyone to help him get out!"

At this moment, the eyes turned to each other, wondering about their fate if they got lost. Indeed, it is not worth wasting a single second in a talk that is not related to getting out of the cave at all, or else the end will be like this unfortunate man.

Alex asked them sarcastically, "Will you keep looking at me cleaning this damn boat by myself?"

Before they threw the boat into the fast waterway, Archie said, "Wait, hey, didn't you say, Alex, that the waterway was going to split into three sections? Wouldn't you explain to us how we can control this boat and make it run, the path we want, and we don't have oars and no rudder to control? We will be at the mercy of the force of the flow of water and may find ourselves lost forever in this cave?"

Alexander said in an accent that seemed to be grumbling and indignant, "Don't act like a child, Archie."

Archie replied quickly, before Alexander could catch his breath, and put an end to any insult coming from him to his jealous temperament, "That's what everyone agrees on. I'm not like a child, Alex!"

Alexander paused for a moment to calm himself before emerging from his nostrils, carrying an axe of wrath on Archie and he came back and said after sighing in his misery, "I have planned everything and I know what to do, as for the rudders and the oars, to reassure you more, I will be the rudder and I will be the oar, and you don't ask me how it will be, and now let's push the boat like the hand of one man and let's jump in it together before the water steals it from us."

It seemed like the beginning of a challenge between Alexander and Archie, both of whom were very angry with each other, as Archie sees Alexander starting to be moved by Martin's fat, seductive words.

To his feeling of failing to lead in front of others, and this caused jealousy in his chest as for Alexander, he believes that Archie has begun to take his place from him with his own merit, and not with the honour of anyone, but Archie went further than that for another matter.

Maya's words were ringing in his mind like temple bells from time to time when she was telling him. You were created for something great and what awaits you for something greater than you can realise with your feet.

Until he began to realise that his confrontation with Alex might be one of those challenges that he was destined to face, but does he believe his belief in that, or is he just an obsession from the unknown cave spirits?

The one he felt before he entered the cave and that it wanted something to happen between him and Alex!

The rickety boat sets sail, cuts the waves of despair, and breaks the rocks of fear, as long as hope is the oar, and the quest of every seeker will not be disappointed.

Alex said and the rushing water hit their faces, "The stream will start to narrow a little and as expected the oxygen will go down so don't worry if you feel your souls wanting to come out of your ears just talk less and breathe as slowly as possible until we reach the water junction."

And this very disturbing and uncomfortable thing happened, as the faces turned blue and the eyes drooped, and each of them thought that the other was breathing.

The place was covered in complete darkness until the sounds of the flowing water calmed down and the speed of the boat suddenly and quickly decreased until all that disturbance disappeared.

And the place became one of the quietest and darkest places that they passed by, as no one could hardly see the palm of his hand, and there was no sound for any echo, not even their voices.

And their intermittent whispering subsided automatically without them being aware, because of the geographical location of the place, as it is at the bottom and middle of a deep cave in the middle of a very hard rocky natural chain.

Inside a mould of intense fear, the sense of hearing in each of them seemed to work automatically, like the ears of a bat, because there was no glimmer of hope to see anything going on around them.

Apart from hearing each other's breaths, the place has already become like the darkness of the sea on a very dark night until Alex spoke in a calm, cautious tone and said, "Now you must bring out your swords or daggers or even your hands and extend them as far as you can reach to the right and to the left to the outside to see the distance between us and the walls of the cave.

"Because then the stream will branch into many branches, and I will try to slow down our speed until we stop completely over the water to control our direction over the water."

Everyone kept trying to find any trace with the tips of their daggers and their hands on the walls of the cave until they heard the sound of rubbing the blade of one of them on the rocks and said Archie with joy, "I found it, I found it on the right of the boat."

Strong, but those daggers were not pierced into the walls because the rocks are smooth and very solid Luca said in a stifled voice, "Damn it, I'm starting to feel that my breath is starting to cut from the many attempts that didn't work."

Alexander tried to excite them before their worries cooled and he said to Luca, "This will not be a reason to stop our resolve, Luca, go on, comrades, and try to make your daggers like brakes, so that the boat does not drift us into the wrong branch. The middle branch is our goal. If we enter it, we will have successfully passed the task, and only time will separate us from reaching the kingdom."

Charlie said, looking very tired, and his tongue could barely carry the words out, like someone vomiting rocks because of shortness of breath, "I feel claustrophobic, nothing more."

Suddenly Charlie screams sharply, like a woman screaming when she sees a rat between her feet. Everyone shut up and stopped after they were terrified and no one dared to ask him as for Alexander, he murmured and bowed his head and said he had had a hard day, he knew that what he had warned about had begun to fall, except for Archie, who put his hands on Charlie's shoulder and said nervously, "What is wrong with you, boy, what scares you?"

Then Clementine screamed at the same level as Charlie's scream, but more and more and he continued screaming and moved his hands in front of his face as if he wanted to repel the attacks of hornets from his face until he fell into the water on his back until the fat Martin grabbed Clementine's hair and raised his head out of the water, then Clementine repeated with trembling lips and screamed like a girl in Martin's face.

What is it! It's Martin without eyes until Martin freaked out and threw Clementine's head into the water, Martin felt his eyes and thought that he really did not feel them, despite his feeling of their presence, from the power of the effect of panic on the soul, and started screaming and running in the boat shout, "No, no, tell me you joking?" Everything but my eyes and he bumped into Sebastian until he too fell into the water, Alex was calmer than everyone else.

He said in a desperate tone, seeing the deterioration of the situation, "I told you before that this matter will happen, just remain silent and calm."

Then the place became more and more narrowed, in addition to the loud screams of the children that were attacked by the evil phantoms of the cave.

Feeling his face, he said, "It's Sebastian, but without eyes, and his face is like a monkey's. What's going on?"

Archie took out the spear and forgot what Alexander told them. They are just fantasies released by the spirit of the cave found by an active act and not from nature itself to distract everyone who begs himself to enter here and enter a kingdom that is perhaps considered one of the most secret kingdoms in the world.

Archie rolls up his sleeves on his forearms, thinking that an enemy of a different kind will try to tear them apart and single them out in this suffocating place, and that he has chosen to play with them in an unexpected and eccentric way.

But soon, signs of panic appeared on Archie's face, and the courage was absenting from this position, as usual, until his colour turned yellow from what he saw, and the spear shook from his hands, and his feet fell back until he slipped off the shoulder of the boat and fell into the water.

But he quickly pulled his head out from under the water, fearing for the lives of others, and said in horror, "Oh my God, what did my eyes see! Everyone looked at him more shocked than they were, I saw my father and my brothers as if they had fangs and demonic shapes and they opened their mouths like the mouths of wolves wanting to cut me!"

Archie watched everyone crouched in the boat and shrank like a worn-out rag so that the wave of terror wouldn't hit them.

Alex stared, eyes brimming with astonishment, and there was nothing he could do with his hands until he helped Archie back to the boat, in the midst of that panic, falling back into the water, with a lot of movement on top of the boat.

They started talking and talking in order to be encouraged and overcome what happened. The water had pulled the boat to the right opening, not the middle one, which they were very keen to enter, and no one felt that.

Until they slid down a steep slope that quickly threw them into an inner fork.

Steeper with little increments like little stairs until Alexander screamed and his hair flew with his words into the air from the speed of the boat set back. It was as if it was plunging them to a deep bottom, and he said with emotion.

Damn us, we drifted. We weren't afraid. Hold on with all you might. We seem to be going downhill. Hold on until the boat settles down. There must be an end to these damn cliffs.

After a quarter of an hour of tension and dread, the darkness gradually began to diminish and was replaced by a dim light, which began to increase as the speed of the boat slowed, until some of the features of the Great Cave became clear to them, and they were more like hand-carved hollows than they were natural!

Of course, no one cared about anything other than the safety of their arrival, and the boat stopped in any way for fear that it would enter them into another dark tunnel that might be their last grave.

It didn't stop there only when Clementine felt something soft and wet slip between his feet smoothly and softly until he plunged into an unexpected relaxation at such a place and time as if he was in a royal massage!

He closed his eyes to forget everything that happened to him and live a moment of pleasure that he would never have dreamed of, even if it was in his subconscious mind.

Then he said with relief and in a cold voice, "I do not think that I have tasted such pleasure in my life as this soft feeling, then the curiosity inside him pokes him to look under his feet and investigate the source of this comfort that suddenly descended upon him!"

And behold, an anaconda, a very giant, bright yellow, had stretched along the length of the boat. From the force of the shock, he did not scream. Rather, it circled along the snake, looking for the location of the snake's head. The snake's body was suggesting that its neck and head had returned from the bottom of its feet, and that it was standing next to it from the other side, then turned its head from. However, he moved his body as the owl turns its head to see the snake standing beside his shoulder smiling with yellow eyes shining maliciously until he gave a hArchie shout at the top of his voice. It is a huge anaconda.

However, Archie caught them and quickly caught them before they jumped and hit the head of the snake with the tip of the spear to cut its head, but the blade of the spear crossed the neck of the snake and passed it without cutting it, as if it hit a passing cloud of air until it suddenly disappeared and turned to them in anger and said, scolding them, "They are just illusions, you idiots! We have repeated this many times. You are now learning from your mistakes. We will perish at any moment."

Archie has discovered a way to escape from these terrifying fantasies, although for the first time he encounters them, and it did not happen that he passed by such a thing, he only found out from Alexander's words the solution.

So, he decided to repeat it between him and himself throughout the past period and succeeded.

Which is that if you close your eyes and open them three times in a row, you will never see those evil spectra again. It is the method of experience that happened to him by chance that made him know the way to get rid of this matter, but the time was too narrow for him to explain to one of them that method to protect them from what they are in from embarrassment and fear.

Archie looked at Alexander, who was sitting in the first boat this time, and his facial movements were like a crow whose head hardly stopped moving when it sensed danger.

He kept staring at a high concentration to see any hope, and it seemed to him that he was very surprised and often turned to them and forward to tell them something.

Even Archie wanted to reassure his heart, even for a little while, after they passed the terrifying darkness and corridors of the cave.

Alexander said, with his face shrivelled with reproach and disappointment, "It seems that the good news will be delayed, my friends. I do not hide from you that we have lost the way, and I do not blame anyone, but I blame myself. We swept the slope to a course other than the one I wanted to take, after those evil spirits occupied us, and the water swept us in a completely different direction from the path that I came with my father! It was the only way to get to the bottom of the kingdom!"

Archie felt nervousness in his tongue and said, "I understand from your words that we are walking into the unknown, Alex?"

Alex smiled the smile of the miserable loser and said, "It is worse than that, young man, that this path is not only an unknown path."

Then he became silent as he contemplated the drawings of the cave, and as soon as he did not complete it, his chest became tighter until he turned to Archie slowly, and there were looks of intense anxiety in his eyes and he did not comment.

Then he turned again forward with eyes devoid of any glimmer of hope that made Archie and those with him realise that they had entered a very dangerous turn and that they had already reached the stage of fatal loss.

And he felt great sorrow over what might happen to them, then said to Alex coldly, "Say what you have left. It does not hurt the sheep to flay it after slaughtering, because we live in disappointment now."

Alex said trying to find a thread of hope even if it was without hope, "According to my father's words, both ways except the middle way. He'll lead us right into the middle of ogre land if we don't encounter some ogre scouts at the bottom of this cave before we reach their lands. This is what I fear. We will only have half a day left, and we will have no way out except by penetrating their lands and getting out of it to the kingdom. Because the way back to the entrance to the cave is to go back against the watercourse, and this is impossible to happen due to the speed of the water currents in addition to the steep slopes.

"And the lack of time, and our presence here for a longer period means our inevitable death, so I would rather face the ogres than die of suffocation. It seems that every experience these boys go through appears as a journey of jumping from a hill to a hill higher than it and between them is an abyssal bottom. If you fall, you lose everything. This is what happened and is still happening to them and each time the height of each hill increases with each adventure they take on, but will they succeed in reaching the desired hill while they are full of their number? Or who will survive? Or do they not reach all of them forever?"

The two looked at the others, and they began to complain about the horror they had been through, until no one was asked to ask Archie or Alex, they only drank the doses of disappointment little by little, until it became on their ears that it was not a shocking thing, and they became empty from the inside of everything.

The way of the watercourse was about to come to an end, and before them a golden glint appeared that drew all eyes to him and revived them as the sun greets the morning flowers.

How can this bright light be in a dark place unless it is evidence of the presence of the sun, and this means that they are close to finding a way out?

Until the boat approached the exit from the narrow watercourse to a wide space, until they realised that they had entered a wide lake with clear water, pure and very white and clear. Its bottom was seen and there were no shells of bright phosphorescent colours, but they were in their hands more than it was at the bottom of the lake, and they imagined that they were looking at the furniture of a palace. Luxurious and spacious due to the high ceiling of the lake, as if it were the dome of a giant palace.

Happiness seemed to everyone more than their happiness at any time in their lives, as if they had emerged from the narrowness of a deep well to the extent of the world.

There were openings of running water pouring out from all the walls of the granite cave and from all sides into the lake as if they were jugs poured by the maidservants into the bathtub of a luxurious king.

The sun's rays penetrated the place from everywhere from the high ceiling, as if they were panoramic openings that reflected light across the lake.

It reveals a dazzling beauty that feels to one who looks at it that everything around it sparkles, as if everything is man-made and not an act of nature.

For the sake of accuracy, the drawings surround the place from all sides, especially the drawings of nymphs, whose bodies are half fish and the upper half is human. They were drawn very carefully, and in the middle a giant chair was drawn as if it were the throne of one of the kings, but it was of a strange shape, as it was decorated with jugs pouring water or whatever. That liquid that comes out of it in the tubes surrounding the chair in a spiral shape, and this is not familiar to anyone who has increased their confusion and fascination, but not until now.

Because of the beauty of the place, everyone forgot what they had gone through of psychological torment, as if they had never been sad or afraid.

So, Archie took off his clothes without saying anything and jumped into the lake and dived into it. Alex turned to the boys and said, smiling with eyes shining with happiness, "If you don't swim in this magical place now and enjoy it, you won't enjoy anywhere else again. Look around you at this beauty. I have never seen anything like it in my life. I don't think you will see a lake with this beauty. Do you think that if we get out of here, we will risk entering here again after all we have seen? Come on, take off your clothes and jump!"

Everyone jumped for joy before Alex completed even his words, indifferent to what might happen or happen to them, nothing inspires fear at all like the one who encounters a treasure, so the first thing he will do is jump on it and embrace it other than his father who owns it or who guards it.

Clementine and Luca excelled in jumping from under the water to the top as dolphins on the first trip to learn to swim, and everyone continued to express his joy in his own way in the lake, which did not exceed four meters in depth.

Others were busy collecting those snails of beautiful and flashy colours, whose beauty you think that they are pieces of candy wrapped in glass, and the soul desires to eat them more than to examine them, which they have not seen before. Some of them were transparent in colour and contained pearl beads, some of them were of natural colour, and others were very black with an unstoppable gloss.

As if it reflects the eyes of those who look at it and the other in green and blue colours, as if they had entered the promised Gardens of Eden, and not just a lake in an unknown land that kidnapped the souls of everyone who got lost in it.

But Clementine and Luca, because of their speed, skill in swimming, and their enjoyment more than others who did not leave the perimeter of the boat standing in the middle of the lake.

Curiosity prompted them to go deeper into the bottom of the lake, where there was a rocky slope that did not see what was below.

For it was lower than the bottom and the height of the cliff rocks, which were like a visor behind which something was hidden?

And when they reached the edge of the cliff, they saw what surprised them and opened their eyes to something that they thought would be the best luck in their next life?

They saw luxurious wooden boxes, open and some of them were broken, and their number was innumerable.

She took out what was in her stomach to the bottom, and it was all about jewellery, diamond necklaces, bottles of gold, and a lot of accessories that radiate beauty, and also many golden statues piled with different shapes of creatures and humans as well?

Some of them were placed on a face at the bottom of the lake and mountains of luxurious furniture that did not look like furniture that had been made before for any type of human being, and part of it is not devoid of the luxury and wealth of those who owned all these sunken treasures until they thought that what their eyes saw was nothing but an exhibition of precious antiques. Collectibles rarities. Its lustre was mixed with the light of the warm sunshine reflection on the surface of the lake.

They breathed a sigh of relief from the joy of what they found and went back down to complete the second campaign.

To explore the great treasure and they chose not to tell anyone to compete with them for their supposed share, as it seemed to them in a moment of weakness that they had found something that belonged to them and no one could share that with them?

Without even verifying things from several aspects, before they become the cause of a disaster that may not have occurred to anyone before.

Clementine thought, after he came to his senses, that it might be better if they told everyone that any agreed course of action would be better than that they acted alone without the knowledge of the others?

But Luca had another opinion, and he said sharply and seriously, unusually, "No, Clementine, let us first take what we can take, and then tell them, because if we tell them now, we will not be able to own anything, even if it is crumbs You know Archie and his never-ending philosophy and his reprehensible lectures on morals and principles and all those trifles that will not enrich us and will not fatten us from poverty, O clever one!"

Clementine was silent a little and exchanged those cautious looks with Luca, who was like a possessed devil who would not stop until he lured you into the trap.

Unfortunately, this happened as the devil made their work attractive to them, and that they are more deserving of whoever owns this treasure, even if it is just a handful of small jewellery they hide in their pants.

If it happened and they did not get anything and asked them to back off, they would not regret much, as they would have hidden something of it that might benefit them one day without anyone realising it!

Suddenly, Clementine received a slap in the back of the head from Luca, "What is wrong with you, where did you go? Huh! Oh no, I've thought about your words and already realised that it's better to take something, even if it's small, to ensure that we find something that will please us when we return, who knows, maybe it will be a reason for us to be rich, you and me, Luca."

Luca smiled maliciously and said appraisingly, "This is the clever Clementine I know." Then he quickly sank down and took off like little fish in the river. You don't know if she swam away or just disappeared.

Until the two of them disappeared from view again.

Alexander was left alone on the boat and didn't get off, he just sat on the boat and rolled his eyes around the place thought deeply and quietly, meditating in a very strange way, and said to himself, "There must be a way out, and everything in this place suggests that it was settled by humans. So, this place must have an exit like it has an entrance for those who drew all these drawings and created everything around it without anyone hearing about them before!"

Then he said, regretfully, "Oh, how did you bring them here, and what to do now?"

This amazing and mysterious place in the depths of the belly of the earth, pregnant with surprises will only be reached by those who have a mighty strength. This place must have been carefully chosen, and that there must be people who frequent it, but where do they come from and where do they return?

It seemed more than just a puzzle with those winds blowing in his direction and coming out at once as if it was coming from a big door. Until he closed his eyes and entered into a silent meditation as if his soul left the place and all the sounds around him faded, trying to sense a thread of any hope from his imagination, even if it was weaker than the thread of the spider web.

Luca and Clementine released their hands to grab everything that was lighter and more valuable and hid it in the stash of their pants as if they were professional thieves. Until Luca caught his eye, a violet emerald in the form of a tulip was attached to the head of the statue of a young woman until he attacked her with his hands, trying to pull it out, but it was tightly attached to the head of the statue.

As he tried his best to catch his eye, giant air bubbles appeared from behind the pile of luxurious furniture piled next to them.

Until he felt great fear and shivered in terror. Then he ran after poking Clementine and pointed at him. Then Clementine looked at a look more frightened than Luca and hurried after his brother too, and they went up to the top.

Thinking that he must be the treasure keeper, the ancient legends they had grown up hearing were more present in their midst than ever before.

As soon as they reached the surface and took a deep breath before one of them shouted at the others, they were surprised that the entire surface of the lake

had turned into a festival of bubbles whose sound was about to explode in the air of those who heard it.

From the loudness of the explosions, then the two boys ran away to the boat, and everyone had preceded them to ascend after the situation hit them with panic and extreme tension.

Watching the exciting scene, Alex warned, warning, "I may feel that there is someone living here, but we hope it is a human being. We can no longer bear the frightening and frustrating shocks to our bodies and our hopes, for our weakness has reached an unbearable level."

Then he instructed them to take out their weapons, take a position of readiness, bend at the level of the shoulders of the boat so that their heads do not appear, and cling well to the floor of the boat, perhaps something sudden will happen to the boat that causes it to capsize.

There is no land or place to sit in it except this boat. The lake was surrounded by a smooth rock formation that made it like soup inside a pot of broth, and this is what everyone thought.

It will also get a large percentage, or at least the most frightening thing they expected to happen was that the expected thing would capsize the boat. An alarming silence fell over the place, as if a cloud of fear overshadowed them.

The eyes were turbulent and the heartbeat accelerated until it almost reached the throats, and at the same time the sounds of bursting bubbles increased as if they were beating the drums of the upcoming battle of the unknown.

Which comes to them every time uglier than before until they thought they had heard a human voice coming out through the bubbles but it wasn't clear yet until the boat started to shake. It was above the crater of a dormant volcano that was about to explode, which came at the wrong time, until Archie and the ghost slowly raised their heads to watch with half their eyes the lake, its surface covered with half huge bubbles emanating from the bottom of the lake, even the rest of the children were curious and their eyes began to spin in their place, contemplating that truly amazing panoramic view.

It was a sight that looked like an antidote to the eyes and soothing to the scattered soul. Indeed, it is worth watching, but the human instinct makes him fear everything he does not know.

Even if he liked what his eyes saw, the feeling of dread at the unknown did not leave them to continue enjoying the beautiful beauty of nature while they were in its midst.

Suddenly, while they were waiting for something to appear from the front of the boat, they felt something strange happening behind them!

And no one dared to look back because of the severity of their tension, and each of them said to himself to the other (Look at you first)! It was laughable and pitiful at the same time, and they exchanged anxious looks, and in the meantime, a strange event had already happened behind them.

He does not need to know this matter but to pay attention to him and peace be upon him.

Behind them I cracked a bubble on the surface of the water, but it wasn't any bubble. It was like a huge pearly egg and it continued to swell and rise until it was over ten meters in length and a little more.

A light radiates a bright glow and does not see what is inside it, everyone turned back at the same moment and looked at the look of one man, slowly and very carefully!

To witness that scene that astonished them so full of prestige that their weapons fell from their hands while they did not realise.

Archie said, wisely and calmly, "Freeze and I hope none of you will think of escaping and throwing himself into the lake. The boat is the strongest place on which our feet may rest at this moment."

Alexander said, with a shrivelled face summarising the situation, "I hope the gods surprise us better than we expect!"

And in the midst of all these feelings, the light of that great bubble stopped, and all that huge mass turned into a cloud, from which drops of water fell, and the bubble vanished, to show an unexpected strange thing, as the snow melts and shows what it was hiding from the views below it.

Until they saw a man of huge build, six meters in length, in the sky, naked, to the navel, muscular, half the body of a man and the other half the body of a fish with a long, twisted tail ending in a transparent fin resembling the fin of a shark's tail, a glossy green colour covered with scales like shards of very sharp shards of glass.

As for his head, he had thick and long white hair that reached half his back, and his beard was white and thick, as if he was an old man who had reached the age of eighty years, with the body of a young warrior holding in his hand a stick with a head resembling the head of a dragon with two yellow horns and between the two horns a ball of emerald sapphire in the shape of a crescent. The creature is a nymph of great prestige and majestic dignity.

He was staring at the boys with great anger, as if he was looking for something that had been taken from him more than he recognised the new arrivals.

Alex whispered, "I heard about this creature, but I did not expect to see him one day in my life, and to stand in front of him, face to face, but rest assured, he will never harm us. He appears to be angry because we entered his kingdom without permission. This is what I think and I hope there is no other reason!"

The giant lowered his head from the boat until the distance between him and the boys was no more than two meters. Then he said in a calm and rough voice, "If you knew that wrong was punishable, why did you do what you did if you did not have the courage, my children?"

Everyone was close to hugging each other as they watched those giant hands, thinking that he would have to use them sooner or later.

Clementine and Luca exchanged looks of doubt and concern, and they realised the giant's words that it had something to do with what they had stolen! Luca looks at his pants with the blink of an eye and his feet are trembling so

much that he urinated in his pants, as well as Clementine.

And they were convinced that it was time to pay the price, that nothing would

go unnoticed, and that every right holder would come to claim his right one day, no matter how long or short the time.

Archie rejoiced when he heard those kind words despite the suddenness of the situation and the prestige of the male nymph that left in the soul hesitation until he took a step forward and said gently to the male nymph, after assuring them that they were in front of the master of this place, "Permit me, my noble sir, to speak?

"My name is Archie from Kling Ling village, and these are my brothers. We admit that we made a mistake, me and my brothers, by storming your land or your kingdom without asking your permission, but we did not come here of our own free will. Rather, it is the place that brought us to your beautiful lake, gentleman, and I will not hide from you that we only felt safe for the first time when we saw you and you spoke to us with such great kindness despite our inconvenience to you. Your house. And we hope that we will only find generosity and hospitality from you. Otherwise, who is like you who will honour the hungry little wayfarers lost in your kingdom, my lord?"

Alexander whispered in Archie's ear, "What a sad story, I don't know how you drew it, but I hope it works!"

The giant turned his head back after listening to them and moved away a little and tied his arms together to his chest after it became clear to him briefly who they are and their story and said thinking, "Hmmm, nice words, eloquent boy, but that's what I always do with all our guests. I welcomed you without you knowing and illuminated the lake for you to enjoy its warmth and tranquillity on these cold nights after I had been dark before you entered it and you were well- hosted and I intended to increase you my generosity but!"

Then he looked at them, furrowing his eyebrows. He said in an accusing voice, "But how can I do that when I see that the one who honoured them has bitten the hand that treated them kindly and even went too far and asked themselves to steal the king of this cave?"

Everyone's feelings froze and they were surprised by that, except for Clementine and Luca.

Here, Archie quickly concluded his intuition that something wrong had happened or that there was confusion. The giant approached again, but this time much more, until his giant head became attached to Archie's face, "Is this how he returned the favour, my son? Tell me, is that how you return the favour, people?"

Then he said sadly, "In fact, I was not surprised or surprised too much, because a person did it before you, and what I did to her had a very painful impact on me, but when I saw you before you reached the lake, I and my daughter, Ella, rejoiced for you."

Archie said doubtfully, "But what are you talking about, sir? And what theft are you talking about? Damn us if we come here to steal and that's not our thing, my lord?"

The king turned with angry eyes to Luca and Clementine and said to Archie, "Look with your eyes at your two thieves and say what you see! Until all the pieces that Luca and Clementine stole from their pants fell in front of everyone's eyes, which shocked everyone from the horror of the matter. To steal from someone, even if he is their enemy"

The king said in a very sharp sarcastic tone, "Now what do you think this is, boy?"

Archie felt that one of them had tied an iron knot on his tongue, and he did not understand that such a thing would happen between them, especially from a boy like Clementine!

Alexander was no better off than Archie and the others, but the event was to him as a disgrace to them.

Clementine reproached him, "Are you stealing, Clementine? Is this how my father taught you? How did I teach you?"

Alexander bit his lips forcibly. Then he looked at the king with a broken heart and said sadly, "O king, we are your children and you are our father here and if you want to be punished, do not punish except those who have your possessions, they deserve that and we bear witness to them and if you pardon, it is from the honour and generosity of kings, and you are their master, but I beg you not to wrong us, for we have no power to bear more than what we are in from stumbles and losses."

Suddenly two words came forward and fell on his knees before the king, and clasped his hands together, weeping, "Your Majesty, please forgive us, for we were so drawn to her by her beauty, and we also asked ourselves."

Luca shouted unexpectedly and said accusingly, "But you, Clementine, who slandered himself, I have nothing to do with you, but I did not steal, I found a treasure without his guards, and so will everyone who was in my place."

Alexander replied angrily, "Damn you, I didn't see a thief so impudent." Luca quarrelsomely said, "I saw Clementine the thief and did the same!" Alexander was angry and wanted to strike Luca, but I Archie. Hold his hand

and said, "Hold himself, Alexander." Then Alex turned to the king, addressing him kindly, after he had collected all the things that Luca and Clementine had taken from the king's treasures and put them before the king, "This is your treasure that was taken from you unjustly, we will return it to you and we will not be satisfied to take something that does not belong to us, especially from those who have honoured us and are serious about security in his kingdom, without asking him to do so. So how if we ask him for forgiveness and you are more generous than Your Majesty to punish us?"

The king said with pride, "If corrupters are found in a country, they will destroy it, and if they mediate a group of creatures, they will ruin it. And what this young thief said among you is the biggest proof that whoever is safe from punishment is bad manners, and he has asked himself to make stealing an inevitable matter. As for my generosity and the honour of kings, it will not change my judgment on you now, and that was before these thieves did what I did, but now I will not call you until you fulfil my conditions. Otherwise, you will never get out of here, but worse than that, I will cast a curse spell on you and make fish and frogs from you, and you will never get out of this lake.”

Alexander raged with anger, his heart pounding hard, and said violently, angering the king, “Where is the generosity in such punishment?” Archie quickly intervened and said coldly, so as not to give the king a chance, that he had put them in an ambush to carry out his conditions, hoping that the king did not mean what he was saying or that he wanted to test them.

Archie said to him, “Hey, Alex, take it easy.” Then he looked at the king and said to him, smiling despite his sadness, “Your Majesty, we are all ears, we are under your command, because I know if you wanted to harm us, you would have done without any preamble.”

The king replied, closing his eyes, “Unfortunately for you, you have come to days in my kingdom that are not beautiful, and if you came many years ago, you would understand what I mean! This is the law of my kingdom. It applies to everyone without exception, even to my daughter.”

The water gurgled again with the sound of air bubbles that came out from the bottom of the boat. When they saw in the lake, they heard the voice of a girl behind them saying, Hello, Dad!

Then they looked from different sides until they saw a dragon’s head coming out of the water advancing towards them and they were terrified and thought that the king had sent him to lick them in it until they almost fell from the boat on the other side. Then the king laughed when the dragon stopped next to the boat and on his back a beautiful nymph sitting on the back of the water dragon on one side!

They were amazed again when they saw that beautiful nymph above the frightening dragon until Archie said with certainty, “Now I am sure that we are part of the world of wonders that they thought were just legends and stories in books and novels.”

Ella, the daughter of the king, was a mermaid with a soft face and sweet beauty, with red-brown hair, as if she had descended from the sky, and she had never been under water. The most beautiful thing was that she was not the size of her father, but was the same length as the boy, and of course she was not bare- chested. She covered her chest with green bras, as if they were tree leaves grapes, she introduced herself without introduction and said, "I am Ella, the daughter of the king of this place."

She pointed to her father as he looked at her proudly and added, "I am very happy to meet you, strangers. It seems that you have made my father happy, as he is eager to see any visitors for a long time!"

She was a girl at the top of literature and beauty of speech, but the poor girl does not know that her father has honoured them well.

Until Alex said with high attention and interest, "Oh heavens, you are the most girl I have ever seen that looks like my sister Isabella. What an extraordinary coincidence that the days turn us around and cram us into the caves and pits of the deep earth to bring me together with the person I have longed to see since I left the kingdom and the most similar to her."

Clementine said, "Yes, Alex, it is a copy. Who is sister Isabella?"

Archie said to himself in a whisper, "I missed seeing that Isabella," then he said to Alex cautiously in a whispering voice, "It's not the time to flirt now, Alex. Help me ask this monster what condition he wants from us so that we can get out safely!"

The king laughed loudly and said, "You can take your time to speak, but you must hear my conditions first, or else we will gladly welcome you all in your new appearance as fish and frogs in our kingdom!" Then he let out a sarcastic laugh in the air.

Alexander whispered nervously, "Didn't I tell you; he seems determined to do so. I lost my enthusiasm after he assured us, but I still hope he was nothing but a liar."

Archie said to the king confidently, "Well, my lord the king, say what you have, whatever your condition, it will not be a heavy burden on our backs." Then he looked at Ella with a look of admiration and added:

"You and your beautiful daughter will not be satisfied that your guests come out disappointed despite what some of us did, and that was a great offence from them to us before they offended you."

He hit the king with his stick in the lake and the boat shook violently until they all fell inside it, then he pointed with his hand high to inhabit the lake and the lake calmed down immediately and the king said with a sharp gesture, "Well, boys, so that I am not unjust and do not like injustice, even though I have been unjust. Listen to this story, so that you will find out later that I am right and that my conditions have a valid reason so that it is not said that the King of the Cave is stealing children:

"I had a guest a long time ago, a century before you and my daughter came into this life. He was homeless, miserable, poor, frightened, humiliated, carrying the whole world's worries, and a condition that made the rock cry for him, and with my kind nature, I pity him until I honoured him above generosity. He would

not have found an equal for my generosity, even from his parents, and he came to me when I needed him, and I thought that he was a reason from God to be kind to me after I separated all creatures, so that the walls of the cave failed to respond to me with one word when I was speaking to her!

"I wanted someone to talk to me like I talk to myself and when that guest came with your arrival, and I was overwhelmed with happiness more than the happiness of the thirsty land with the arrival of the rain, to the point that I made him as a member of my body that does not leave me in my kingdom because he is the only creature that comforted me in my sadness and I swore to make him my right hand in everything.

"I had a great throne to sit on over the lake, which I made in fifty years. Your minds have no ability to imagine what it looked like as it shone like a shining moon to turn the darkness of the cave into day and lasting joy from which no evil was seen.

"I strove to resurrect the soul of my father's mortal kingdom after a long death, and I told him about the importance of this matter and the value of every piece that covered that great throne, especially the pot of the magic potion.

"Which I had carefully placed at the top of the throne in a safe place, as that magical jug contained an antidote that has no equal in the entire universe, as if it were the antidote for life that does not exist on earth! He had the ability to turn everything mixed with it into pure gold that will never return as it was. Then I made the magic jug pour into the tubes of the throne from above, as one of you pours a teapot with a very genius thought.

"My thoughts to him inspired me from the imagination of the gods, and I made him pass over each piece, turning it into real gold. That fake friend was very impressed and told me that he was impressed by the horror of what I had done with my hands and from everything I decided to create so that this kingdom would become the promised paradise.

"He showed astonishment on his face, who collected the wickedness of all the creatures of the earth and told me that this made him decide to pledge his life to be my faithful servant who will serve me forever. And I thought it was like that, as he showed me a lot of sincerity as he started telling me many things outside my kingdom.

"In addition to bringing friends of his, he told me that he and everyone with him would be at my service and my army, which does not disobey my orders. Which made me so much happier I hosted them as if they were my brothers, and all that rapid development led to my marriage to my dear wife, Verne, Ella's mother.

"But I didn't know that he was trying to reassure me to blind my eyes to what he was secretly planning, and indeed he did, and he blasphemed all those vows and stole everything I worked on for the years of his death until I thought that my soul was the one who stole me and I entered into a psychological disaster that made me not care about anyone around me from the horror of pain and breakage until I forgot my wife who got sick after the birth of my daughter Ella, I didn't feel it until I left life!"

Then he fell silent with great sadness and looked at his daughter and said, "Forgive me, Ella, for what happened to you because of me." Then he turned to the girl in anger, raising his voice, "Since then I have demolished the throne and drowned it at the bottom of the lake with these two hands that I made it with. But these two boys, by their actions, blown into the ashes of memories and ignited the fires of hatred and revenge in my chest.

"Which will never subside this time, and they have repeated what that treacherous friend did, so I decided that I would not allow anyone to rob me after that day, and that whoever did so would be punished severely. So now I ask you to bring me that magic jug or else you will turn into fish and frogs in a short time and if you try to get out of the water you will die instantly and become food for birds and worms. It is up to you that is the condition. I judged you and it's over, boy!"

Archie turned his head to look with eyes of blame and sorrow for both Clementine and Luca, and he carried within him a great hatred for them and said to them, "This is what your hands did when you followed the whim of your souls."

Archie tried hard to use all soft and emotional methods to discourage the king from his decision and the unjust police against them without provoking him more than he had provoked himself by reminding himself of the horror of his wound that did not heal during that long period.

Until the king decided on the matter and said his word with certainty, "This is a right that I made upon myself, and I will not back down from it, for one day you will know what you have done to me, and now the countdown to the time has begun. You may be shorter than the blink of an eye if you hesitate to think. Either you agree, or else you will accept the punishment of disgrace and continue enjoying the warm waters with the delicious and varied meals of algae in this lake."

Then he took a step back and said quarrelsomely to them, "Do not approach Ella, or else the condition will be immediately cancelled, and you know what that means."

Then he turned around and dived into the lake, repeating, "I'm coming back in a little while to take the road map to the magic jug. No one uttered a word, despite the horror, as the presence of the nymph, Ella, in front of them robbed them of the core of their hearts after each of them felt for a moment that he had left her alone!"

And the minds of teenagers in imagination drifted away in the world of teenage whims until Alex screamed and shouted them out loud and said, "You fools, your lives will be taken from you while you are in the absence of your childish dreams."

Ella finally spoke and said with her innocent face, "If my father's matter has disturbed you, I hope you can imagine how much he suffered and broke his pure heart from the tragedy of betrayal and the bitterness of loss! You will thank him because the condition that I don't know is what happened. It would be just a nice walk in this vast world in exchange for it not happening to you like what happened to him."

Archie looked pityingly at Ella and then turned and looked at Alex's face, who hid his laughter in himself, and Archie did the same, and said in a gentle voice, "You are as pure as your face, Ella," until she started to get confused.

And she saw all those eyes staring at her until Alex approached Archie and whispered to him what Archie was not expecting and said to him, "Isn't it fair that we take her hostage until we get out of here with the swords in our hands and the girl in front of her?"

Archie said angrily, "Are you really what you're saying to Alex?" Alex was silent and shook his head at the sincerity of his intent. Archie looked at him and said excitedly, "Does it satisfy you to see Glister take your innocent sister Isabella hostage in return for your innocent actions?"

Alex said, "We have returned to him what the fools stole, and the charge of theft is no longer charged, but Your Majesty, this king has sentenced us hArchiely. Do you find that justice, O Archie, son of Abraham?"

Archie answered in turn, "Your words are sound in terms of comparison, but this time I feel that the matter is very different. You have told me something that I do not know what it is, but there is something in me that I did not feel before, unlike the previous times when we met fate with its ugly face. I have a feeling inside me like a revelation and hours like a creaking sound since we got here pushing me to accept the king's condition. Because I am almost certain that there is something that will change everything in our lives and this adventure, so I decided now without hesitation that we agree to a condition as long as it will help us get out by himself. This is a point that shortens the time and we are safe as well. And if we seek to retrieve his lost precious treasure, it will be in our hands, then this is another matter that only a wise person can understand."

Alex said with two greedy eyes, "What a cunning fox! So, we will be partners in making his kingdom that was lost from him, and we may be the masters and partners in ruling with him."

Archie said, "I like you when you read my thoughts without explanation."

Alex turned to Ella, noticing her admiration for him, and said in a low voice, "Likewise, I will have with her more than the tales of a thousand and one nights. Everyone remained in anticipation and curiosity of what the king might bring, and wondered where the destination would be, how to retrieve that lost jug, and with what, and who is that cunning thief?"

All these questions ran through everyone's minds without asking one another until the corners of the boat shook and the king came out of the lake, shaking the water from his hair, but this time the king had something surprising in his hand.

He was carrying a golden sword radiating a bright flicker. He forced everyone to cover their eyes for fear that they would be blinded by the power of its brilliance. Then the king stretched out his hand and said cheerfully, "I see on your faces the happiness that must be."

Archie said with satisfaction, "How not, my lord, when we know that you will be the main mastermind of this adventure and the financier as well, and this is reason enough for happiness, then Archie finished the conversation with a wide smile that did not come out of him before and then decided to resume his talk."

And he added, "But, my lord, you have a very small request, and I do not think that you will refuse it in exchange for your precious treasure, which you are looking for, O great king."

Archie did not say to anyone that he would ask something from the king, and this made the others confused by his words, but they were all confident in Archie, as he was the most tactful of them in speech and the most skilled in negotiating.

The king turned and stared at his daughter for a short while before saying to her, thinking, "Did you hear what he said, my daughter?"

She said, "You are the noble king, whom no one else can ask for, because I see that they are very friendly."

Then she looked at Alex with great admiration without her father hinting at her and said, "Is there anything else you would like to add? Just make them leave and they wish to come back again because of your generosity, Dad."

He shook his head with him as if he was saying, "I will not return a request to you, my only daughter." Then he turned to Archie and said to him, "Tell me, boy, what you want to say!"

Archie approached and put one of his feet on the shoulder of the boat and said sarcastically, "We want a promise from you that if we take back the magic jug that we will have a wage that you did not give to any of the worlds, nor to that thief who betrayed you!"

The king said without thinking, "If you can return the magic jug, you will become the closest people to me, and you will have what yourselves desire in my eternal kingdom."

Alexander began to be very puzzled when he saw the exciting sword in the king's hand and concluded that the king would send them to a land from which it would not be easier to get out than enter it!

Then he took out what was baffling him and said, asking the king, "But you did not tell us, my lord the king, about that thief, how he looked, where he lives, and how we will find him, specifically, and what his social value is in his homeland, and how do you know that the jug is with him? Could he have sold it since he was a thief after finding such a treasure?"

The king said excitedly, "Do not ask until you hear the end of the talk. If you waited only a few seconds, I would hear the answer to these questions of yours, and I advise you, young man, to have long patience and deep silence in all matters of your life. Perhaps a word will come out of you that you do not realise its size until when the answer comes to you in the form of spears and arrows that will silence you forever!"

Alexander felt a strong slap that shook his confidence in front of others. Then the king said to everyone, his eyes did not leave Archie, "Listen carefully, if you miss any of my words, blame only yourselves, and you will be destined to live like shells alone at the bottom of the lake, but her beauty did not help her to help her speak or express, even in one word, what is inside it of beauty to others?"

Then he pointed his index finger at them because of the importance of his words, which are similar to his sermon on death, "Do not forget that you have only seven days before you are completely mutated."

Then he was silent for a while, closed his eyes, and added sadly, saying, "I do not hide from you that even in the process of transforming your skins and changing them into fish scales, there will be pain, meaning that you must carry out the task as soon as possible and not at the last moment."

Ella noticed that Alex was sad and sad as well as the others. Then she wanted to calm the sour mood a little and get rid of that panic that might precipitate their failure and then early loss.

She said she showed her love for them, the truth was her words were directed at Alex and they don't feel my father is very generous, and he would only do this when he saw your courage and ability to carry out his condition, which no hero like you can't.

Then she fell silent and said, her face reddened, making up for her mistake, until her father breathed mockingly, she said, "Your faces are not the faces of those who are destined to remain a captive or a slave. Rather, I see the moment of victory in your eyes, even if you have floated on seas and on seas. Even if your sorrows grow."

Alexander interrupted her after her admiring glances at him encouraged him even a simple thing, "If something bad happened to us, would you allow us to become non-human beings and allow your father to take our lives for something we did not do?"

She felt very embarrassed to speak about something on behalf of her father and he looked behind her until she gathered her strength and turned to her father and said, her eyes shed tears, "My father never wronged anyone and did not accept him against himself even when he was alone and he was in his hand. So how now he taught me to love life and preserve life the others."

Archie realised that the girl exposed her father to embarrassment, but he was afraid that this would be the case not their favour. He just thinks that the king has nothing to lose. He is a wounded king who is looking for his strength that was taken from him. He thinks that there is no other way to do that than to take advantage of others and their need for life in order to restore to him what revives his kingdom. Archie hastened to remove the embarrassment from the king, and said, "Is it possible to get our lives back, my lord, if we do not succeed in the journey to retrieve the magic jug?"

The king laughed with his mouth full, and he put his hand over his heart from laughter and said, "My daughter told you a little while ago that I do not accept injustice because I realise that your return before the deadline expires, that is a fantasy, but I see in your eyes the ability to do so. Therefore, if you can come back here, you are my family and my guests. As for the condition that you see as unfair, this is an obvious matter. Who is safe from punishment betrayed the covenant? This is the covenant between us, my children.

"Everyone has good tidings after the chances of them avoiding punishment increased, whether it was success or failure. The important thing is that they return here as soon as possible. And this would be easier than for them to return only with the magic jug, or else their fate would die in both cases, and this talk had a profound effect on Alex's soul."

Who completed his conversation with Ella, saying with love, "Do you think that a day will come when I see you with bare feet like ours, walking on them like us?"

Martin said sulking, "Is this really the Alexander we know? Look how he woos this human fish like a princess? Oh, if Mr Albert had seen you, so tarnish his reputation, arrogant Alexander."

Suddenly Martin felt that his head was shaking and he saw the earth and everything in front of him as if it had been repeated before his eyes twenty times in a confused manner.

When he was slapped from behind him. She is indeed a princess, you idiot, that you say this because she did not pay any attention to you, I swear to the whole God that if the nymph looked at you only, your pants would fall off your fat from the pleasure of it!

That was the voice of Sebastian reprimanding Martin for the curiosity of his often-unsuccessful tongue. Clementine said softly:

"My brother deserves to find someone who suits him, he has been deprived of tenderness of love and affection since he was young."

The king heard Alexander's words and said to him, reprimanding him, "If you liked Ella, then be that legendary knight who was never created. Because Ella will not be taken by anyone. Except for the one who found only one copy of him in this world. And don't just be a foolish boy, you deserve it, your arrogant boy, if you want to promise to her while you are carrying the magic jug. As for speech, even liars, charlatans, and deceivers can recite the most beautiful poems and sing the sweetest melodies. Do not think that with your sweet tongue, you may have pierced my daughter's heart with the arrow of love.

"Do you know boy? That even the thief who robbed me came here to ask for my daughter Ella's hand in marriage? He became a king of a great king and offered to help me rebuild my old kingdom and throne?"

Then the king laughed sarcastically and said, "Can you imagine how that happened? That damn thief who robbed me came to marry my daughter Ella after all he did to her father? And when I asked him why he did the ugly thing, he said stupidly that the healer, Masa, had ordered him to do so, and that he had made him a great promise. And I know that the healer, Masa, is nothing but a myth made by humans and jinn to steal from each other and to kill each other. In order for each of them to raise the slogan (the healer masa), which they say when he leaves. Will he reward those who helped him to achieve his goals and will make them rule all worlds with him?"

Then he said with a laugh that contained a lot of irony, "What foolish human beings, how happy I am that you are not a human and not a jinni to live within those worn-out myths."

The story was very surprising to everyone, except for Ella, who tried to hide her face, as it seemed that something embarrassing related to this story had happened to her, not just because the one who asked for her hand in marriage was the one who burnt her father's heart and made him drink betrayal, but for things that may remain buried for a known time.

Even Alexander whispered to himself and said strangely, "Could she have agreed to marry the one who stole her father? Is it impossible for Ella to do it to her father, the king? Looks like there are things to know, but not now? I will know the news and that I can smell something unfriendly going on in secret, and I hope he does not believe the magic of my intuition!"

Then the king approached Alex suspiciously until Archie and the others thought that the king wanted to swallow Alex and said in a whisper, and the hair of his wet beard was touching Alex's face:

"It is better not to waste your time by asking too many questions, because time is counted on you, minutes are like dead people, if they are gone, they will never come back, what is the point of enjoying the beauty of the feet of my beautiful daughter, Ella, as she walks in bare feet, followed by all the creatures of the earth and trees, in the hope that you will favour them with the scent of her sweat that surpasses the most beautiful perfume made by mankind? Aren't you because in fact you will have become a fish?

"You may not wish to see Ella at that time because she will have come to hunt you and cook you, not to eat you, of course, but to give your stinky flesh to the beasts of the earth who admire their princess and mistress."

Those words angered Alex for the second time, and he was mocked by the king in front of everyone, but he preferred to hide his anger for a few seconds than to show it in public and regret it for the rest of his life.

"Do not make your name more expensive than your looks!"

The king was astonished by Alexander's boldness against him, and he was the one who had his fate in his hands so, Archie jumped before Alexander and said to the king's astonished face with a yellow smile, "Ha-ha, this boy is good at delaying time and loves riddles very much, Your Majesty. Now let's finish what you were saying, we are all in great eagerness to hear the rest of the plan!"

The king frowned for a while and realised that a little mercy at this time is okay, given the predicament they are in and the matter they are approaching, which may quickly end with a bad end for them.

The king turned his back and said mockingly, pretending not to understand what Alexander had said, "Oh, really, I forgot what you came out for, then he coughed hard to draw attention from the structure of the plan, which would be either a lifeline for their necks if they implemented it, or a pit from the pits of hell if they deviated from it!"

He said in a dry voice, while showing the exciting sword that he brought from under the lake, "This sword in my hand will be the key to every closed matter that will come across you on your journey. This sword will be a reason to help you. Because I know that that thief has made a kingdom of gold and he has surrounded it with heavy guards that you can only penetrate with this sword, which is made of the same material as the antidote inside the magic mug. It is a valuable treasure, but it is a deadly weapon, and no one will ever have the ability to reproduce it."

Then he raised the sword high, and behold, it became brighter like lightning that grabs the eyes, until they thought it was a spark of lightning.

Archie says, "Oh gods, I've never seen a sword like this in my life."

Luca follows him, expressing his admiration, "It's just a fantasy!"

The king replies, "Take him, Archie, and do not hesitate to cut off the neck of

anyone who tries to stand before you! This sword is a shield for you and a strong shield for all kinds of evil. But beware not to lose it, and if you lose it, I fear that you will never return.

"As for the land on which the stolen jug will be located, the sign of your presence on it is that the sword lights up in a blue colour that is not harmful to the eye.

"As for the thief, he became a king crowned with money that is not his money and a land that is not his land, so warn him that he is a bald-headed dwarf like the head of a snake, his tongue dripping with poisoned honey.

"You will see in his kingdom various things that will impress you, and you will think that you have not lived before in this life for the awesomeness of bliss that you will find there. So, you say to yourselves why don't we live here?

"Beware. As for the magical jug, it was placed on his throne and tied with iron chains on which molten rocks were poured, until it became an integral part of the mountain on which the throne rests, and no one can save it except with a blow from this sword, which I told you, is the key to everything in your journey never let go of your hand."

King Gabriel moved the sword from his right hand to his left hand, then pointed his hand up in a semi-circular motion to the lake sideways and silently extended his left hand holding the sword to Archie and nodded, "Head to take it and as soon as his hand stopped, successive waves appeared from the end of the lake, the place they had not seen, which they were obscured by a rocky twisting with natural colours of multi-coloured from top to bottom, other than the colour of the rock formation that surrounds the place as if it were a gate separating two places. The waves were as if someone was pushing them with his hands towards the boat, not natural waves."

The boys did not fear that, but they felt its excitement and longing to know the beauty of what those waves might carry. They knew that every surprise was in this place.

More beautiful than the other, despite some disasters, as if their minds are preparing an album of special memories for these anecdotes that did not occur to anyone, so they will have beautiful memories for the end of their life.

There were murmurs and whispers between the boys and Alexander turned to Ella and called her in a whisper and said hissing, "Hey, you beautiful, at this dreadful beast, look here."

As soon as she turned to him, she gave him a radiant smile that resembled hidden pearls.

Even Alexander felt a gentle chill in his stomach. Then she increased on him and sent him an air kiss that caused tension in his feet and made his heart beat so hard. She forgot what he wanted to ask. Then she said with a sign, "Be patient and you will know shortly."

And before those soft waves crashed into the boat, they saw what they had never expected in this particular place when they saw those many fins like those of great white sharks. Then they broke off from each other and jumped to the other side of the boat until the nymph Ella laughed loudly and said and they hold their breath, "Do not be afraid, they are the wonderful dolphins of the lake, and they are very friendly, more than you are familiar with a brother."

They were surprised by the presence of dolphins in this place, in this large number, and in this unusual and comfortable way to look. It was a herd of white rhinoceros dolphins surrounding the boat from each side, jumping over the boat, in front of it and behind it, and their number exceeded fifty dolphins, shouting, the air expressing their happiness. Welcoming these children with childlike features, everyone in the boat smiled again when they began to caress and caress the dolphins, which did not stop for a moment to jump over them and try some of them to climb the boat for fun.

The king said with an unexpected sadness in a faint voice, "It's time to say goodbye, my children. Then he leaned over his shoulder to hide the features of his face." He continued saying, and he was choking up, "Come on, ride on these dolphins, and they will lead you out of my kingdom to the widest oceans and the vast land to be the beginning of your journey, and I wish you good luck. Come on, let each of you ride a dolphin and go to glory, and don't look back, and I'm sad to leave you."

No one focused on King Gabriel's features except Archie, who marvelled at the king's sadness over their separation, as if he was already that kind father who bids farewell to his only son, forever!

While everyone jumped on the backs of dolphins, they were happy, as if they were in one of the winter amusement parties that are held every year in the kingdom.

However, Archie who kept staring and staring questioningly without batting an eyelid was certain that there was something he was hiding from them!

Otherwise, why would he punish them with such a punishment when he is aware of its consequences, and then shows grief over their departure, eating what is left of his heart?

The dolphins lined up in a very tidy way, as do the horses of the military parade, and more beautiful than that. Then Ella said, "You, Alex, ride with me on the dragon, and we will advance them, and I will be with you until you reach safety."

And, of course, that pleased Alexander, and his heart fluttered with its wings from the sheer amount of happiness and joy that recounted his old grimace.

And he says to himself with optimism (This nymph is nothing but a compensation for the seven goddesses for all my emotional failures in the past and for repelling that fairy who did not accept my every look, even if I accidentally fell on her, as if between me and her there is grudges for all human beings).

Someday luck will be on your side, there is no permanent sadness or everlasting happiness in this life, and after the passing of crying comes joy.

The dolphins moved, carrying on top of them the little adventurers who hurried to bring out everything that they had hidden inside them during the past days.

Until they were stripped of all fear, anxiety, and waiting for another unknown, not knowing where it would take them, and they continued throwing the water of the lake at each other.

Until they reached the place from which the dolphins came at the end of the lake at the rocky cavity with colourful mountain walls between red, white, black and other colours that they had not seen before. They walked with them along the channel, which was like a long groove.

In which the colour of the water became more like the darkness of the night due to its extreme depth, after about three hours, they saw the sky as if it had risen to them from the bottom of the mountains, and their faces had shone with light after they had been in the ground for difficult times.

So that their coming out from inside became like the exit of a new-born from his mother's womb when he sees light in him after the darkness of nothingness. The sky had turned red with the redness of the setting sun, and the glow of its rays had been extinguished in the sunset, as if they had breathed a sigh of relief after what they had gone through.

Starting with the herd of doppers and the strange talking bear, and ending with the king of that place, who was the best they have ever met on this journey, and the truth is that he was indeed a noble king, but unfortunately for them, the mistake of the gentleman committed by Clementine and Luca was enough to strip him of the nobility and give them a cruel curse befall them There is no escape from it except by implementing the unfair condition, or they are satisfied with the result and bear the consequences of the wrong hands of some.

The end of the gully led to another sprawling lake. They almost thought the most important had reached an ocean or a vast sea.

Until Ella said, "I know you think that we swim in an endless sea, but in fact it is a lake and it is called the Lake of Kings. It separates our miserable kingdom (she said it badly) and it was a strange thing about her, no one understood what she meant?"

Then she continued, "And the kingdom of bliss, or what is called the kingdom of the dwarves, in relation to the one who rules it."

Alexander said, "You mean the dwarf, the thief who stole your father?"

The beautiful nymph replied sharply, "I do not like these descriptions, because Mr Prakshim has now become a king and has made a kingdom that no one has dreamed of, and no one will imagine that one person can do all this alone unless he deserves to be a king with a unique mind."

Alex turned to Archie, who blushed with anger when he heard the mermaid's words that contradict her father's brokenness and deep sadness!

Then he linked intelligently and cleverly between the story of the dwarf king when he wanted to marry Ella and the sad looks of King Gabriel!

He realised that there was a missing link between the nymph Ella and the king who stole and betrayed her father and stole them!

And that King Gabriel seems to have cut that missing link, but Ella wants to get it back, but she must find who will be that broken ring!

The fear is that Alexander will be the scapegoat (the desired link) around whom the mermaid weaves her nets to fall into a link with a thief king who wants her as his wife to eliminate what remains of her father's property and then she prepares for Alexander and then we live with the curse of King Gabriel if we go back and find that King Gabriel has been eliminated?

These were just ideas in Archie's imagination that were revealed to him as a warning message that may not have any physical evidence proven in reality, not even any approach to the worst expectations, but Archie's mentality in analysing the simplest words and the way they came out from between the lips was enough to draw these imaginations as an exit map and take an approach that might happen at what time.

And as soon as they approached the bank of the coast, the size of the huge thick fog was like an impenetrable dam, and he did not see what frightened him behind him.

And he who does not see its end and behind it the heads of a mountain range do not know the extent of its extension inside, it had covered the thick clouds above dolphins stand on the shore of the lake, which was filled with white boulders, free of impurities, as if they were scattered pearls, not just rocks.

Until Sebastian said, feeling a great happiness that he had not felt for a long time, "Indeed, it seems that we are in the land of bliss, why have I never seen a beach so clean, this beauty, and this wonderful symmetry?"

Ella said in displeasure, "This is what my father was afraid of. You should be fascinated by what you will see, but remember that you are on a mission to save your lives and not to save anyone but yourselves." Then she whispered to Alex, who was behind her on the back of the dragon, "You will be sure when you enter this kingdom that whoever rules it is someone who is not normal and worthy of respect!

"And now it's time to say goodbye, you feisty guests, and I hope you are in good health. Everyone went down except Alex, who continued with her on the back of the dragon, who did not catch up with the others. He was not satisfied with spending all that long time talking to Ella while he was guarding her from others like a duck guarding its young and leaving no room for anyone. To approach them."

He did not leave her, even for a moment, until they reached the shore. He said eagerly, as if he were not with her, "I have been talking to you about everything. But the most important thing on my mind I forgot to mention is, can you really be like us and have two feet to walk on, i.e., a body like ours?"

She gave him a look to the side with a wicked smile and said, "I understand what you are aiming at, your lustful person, but if that happens and you see me walking with a body like your girls, what are you going to do to me then?"

Alexander said with great happiness, "You will become my queen, and no one will separate us except death."

I interrupted him quickly and said firmly, and whispered it in his ear, Archie watches the scene with great suspicion, "If that is really the case, if the task is accomplished, come back to us quickly, and I will be waiting for you in the form that satisfies your desires."

Then he turned and dived into the water with her dragon and called her. Alex, "No, wait, wait!"

Until a herd of dolphins became among them and completely disappeared who thought it was the water of his life that he found after years of thirst!

But the truth seems to be that it was a trick a female is cunning to make him relate to the mirage of meeting her more than his eagerness to free himself from the curse.

Chapter 25

GOLDEN CITY AND THE LEGEND

On the cool breezes and showers of early winter, next to a burning fire inside an antique oil tank that surrounded everyone around it with a deep warmth that was enough to make everyone who woke up on this beautiful morning think that he was still asleep on his warm bed in his mother's calm lap and that he was also waiting for her voice to start a meal, a delicious breakfast in front of the fireplace whose blazing fire glows under the window.

Luca was the first to wake up and overcame the pleasure of a comfortable sleep for the first time, and as soon as he stood on the shore of the lake, the new world they had reached, he dipped his hands to sip from the lake water to wash his face.

Then he saw something strange in his hands and kept turning it around, not believing what he saw, then he quickly washed his face and wiped his eyes hard again to make sure of what he saw!

But he was shocked when he saw that the skin of his palms from the top had turned half into thin golden scales, closer to the scales of a small salmon fish, closer to the scales of some reptiles.

To add to his certainty even more, he examined the skin of his palms from above, but in fact the skin of his palms had turned to scales, and then turned back with a terrified face in disbelief after hearing the sound of someone's feet on the beach pebbles he saw Charlie and Sebastian come to wash their faces too, as he glimpses the palms of their hands, they had already covered with scales before they noticed this, and he continued silently, waiting for the reaction when they noticed that disaster, and to feel somewhat safe when he felt that someone shared his misfortune.

Until he noticed the frown, contraction and yellowing of their faces at the same time, and he began to look at them as surprised and terrified, and whispered to them and said, "Don't worry, I am too, it happened to me like what happened to you two."

Then Sebastian hurried off to Archie, who had risen early, to cut the branches of the young trees to make breakfast, especially the tea he had kept in his bag and which Charlotte had given him.

The tea (fern leaves), which was considered to have a tonic effect, was popular in Kling Ling village. It is considered the first drink in the village, but it seems that they are not destined to taste it this morning, as the boys came to Archie rushing with yellowish and pale faces after they realised literally that they were on their way to turn into fish and that the effect of King Gabriel's curse had begun!

Archie turned attentively and said, "What about you, and the lions were chasing you?" Sebastian stood, panting to catch his breath, then raised the back of his palms in Archie's face to see what happened to them, until Archie bowed his head to see his palms too, and he found them, half of their backs turned into scales?

It did not take long for Alexander to appear with a frowning face, and raised an eyebrow, and said, "It seems that what brought you here so early is the same that brought me here?"

Show me all your hands. Then he looked at the palms of Archie and Luca and found them like his palms. Then Archie said in a desperate tone, "I did not imagine that this would happen so quickly, but what happened to us was expected. But we had incomplete doubt until we saw it now with our own eyes.

"What happened is enough to make each of you realise what we are in, so do not blame but yourselves if you find yourselves have turned into fish, so none of us would have thought that his end would be such a shameful end! It is now up to your resolve and how strong the survival instinct is in each one of you and so am I and all I can do is I will struggle to reach the goal of survival and to lead you to the path of salvation. Either you help me to do that, or you face this painful fate, and I can no longer do more than that, and I will not hide that from you."

Alexander stuck his fingers into Archie's shirt ripped from his shoulder and pulled him tightly, smiling, and said, "Don't worry, boy, if we die, we'll die together. And if it happens, and if we succeed, we will succeed together, and now it will not help us to talk and reflect on what happened to us, but I think that this is a sign of more haste, and that the time on this journey is different from any time we have gone through before, my dear Archie."

Archie felt a moral impulse that removed the locks of despair from his mind until he said excitedly, "Alex is right and you are, my friends," until he said sarcastically, "But I swear to you that this will not stop me from making this tea, as it is one of the most important drinks in our village and one of our most important traditions that we are proud of."

Clementine says, "Will this tea stop the curse?"

Sebastian replied, laughing at him, "Rather, it will speed up the transformation of your head into the head of a carp."

The long-muscled Martin laughed stubbornly, as did the others, but this time the laughter was filled with hidden fear that copied its threads on the lost souls who thought that any other unthoughtful move like what happened in the course of the cave would lose them the time counted on them every fraction of a minute and that they are very close to becoming mutant creatures and that they have to live as jungle animals and even worse than that!

Archie bravely said, "Our fear of what frightens us will never prevent us from dying, but it will spoil our time, which we can live, because it is in our hands now. And we should sing instead of crying until we reach our goal, and if none of you can sing, I will disturb you with my ugly singing. The important thing is that one of us should sing."

Everyone laughed this time with joy after the fears gradually dissipated.

"Now come to the fireplace and enjoy the most beautiful tea you will ever drink in your life. It is the tea of angel (Charlotte), that beautiful and childish love."

Clementine said, "You seem to have great luck in women."

Alexander said after taking a sip of tea, "This tea makes me feel a kind of relief and the moments of victory are approaching. Then he continued taking a sip on both ends of his lips to avoid his heat."

He said, with the steam of tea coming out of his mouth, trying to sharpen the resolve in the frustrated souls, "I will tell you something you have not heard before!"

Everyone was silent about the whisper and the side talk, then continued his speech, "The nymph, Ella, told me exactly where the thief was from the magic jug!"

Then he said cheerfully, "Between me and the day of my betrothal to Princess Ella, the question of our return only to the cave while we were carrying the magic

jug for which I will be crowned prince of that lost world. But I promise you to look into your matter and your requests."

Martin replied with joking, "Of course, Your Highness, you will need someone who is responsible for the food cabinets and has a high taste in food, laughter rose."

"I didn't know you, Alexander," said Sebastian, "That you had such a good sense of humour."

Suddenly, a large shadow descended on the beach, and they were not able to lift their heads up to see the source of the shadows. They were the bright sunlight in their eyes, even if the shadow covered the sun's rays, it revealed to them that dear guest who came at the right time and without anyone expecting him to be the magic carpet that Maya brought him from her magical world.

It was a gift to them, but how did this happen? Did not King Barhout invalidate his abilities?

The magic carpet landed on the ground and was surrounded by Archie and those with them, as if they were welcoming their parents with joy and welcomed him with the most beautiful welcome they did in their lives for many reasons, including knowing what happened to Maya and those with her after they separated over the river.

Including that they desperately need someone to shorten their time more than they need all food and drink, Clementine said whispering to Alexander, "Is this the magic carpet we were on with that witch's fairy and her two fairies?"

Alexander said, "Even if it wasn't him, we were facing something that seemed beautiful, and we wouldn't even dream of it."

"It's a strange place to meet your beautiful magic carpet, and I had no doubt that you wouldn't leave," said Archie, overjoyed.

The rug said in his huge voice, "And I do not abandon those whom I entrusted with their service, so I had to find you and I found you."

Then Archie asked him quickly about Maya and those with her, and what happened to them from the cloud after they were left alone on the magic carpet? And where are they now?

The magic rug says, surprised by the response, "Excuse me, it is not permitted for me to speak about what is happening between Mistress Maya and His Majesty the king. I was created like this to listen and obey, and I am not a news reporter, and I am now at your service, sir."

Everyone's eyes turned to benefit from a piece of information, which is their knowledge of what this rug is and how it works. Archie said, "What a powerful perfume, Maya. I smell as if she was standing in front of me?"

Alexander said winking Archie, "You know the perfume of whom you hug every day!"

Archie ignored him and continued his words, saying firmly, "But now, my brothers, this seems to be another sign of rushing to move towards our destiny, interrupted by Clementine, "But tea?"

Archie gave him half his gaze and said, "I would rather be deprived of drinking tea today than not drinking it for the rest of my life. So, let's hurry up, let's break into the place and find what we're looking for. Indeed, they all hurried after putting out the fires they lit, and they flew with the magic carpet, looking for the kingdom of the dwarves.

"And those who are on its shores, and while they were on the back of the rug in the midst of a clear and refreshing atmosphere, the forest appeared to them from above, which was not like the rest of the forests they passed through and which they saw in their lives only. A giant in the middle of all the amazing nature in the forest, which will only be enjoyed in rare opportunities, and they live in one of them now, but they lack time."

Clementine said, dazed with happiness, describing the beauty of what he sees and feels, "How beautiful is this breeze, despite its coldness, and my eyes have not seen such pleasure as what I see now. I feel indescribable, as if I were to fly soon."

Clementine got excited and rose to his feet at the front of the flying carpet, while everyone was on their knees and spread his hands to one side like a dove spreads its wings.

Archie said, staring at Clementine with joy, addressing his words to the others, "If you all had this feeling that Clementine has now and lives inside him, believe me, we will never lose."

A person will not reach his dream unless he lives his dream in imagination first in its smallest details and he is sure that he will realise it in reality, then it will not separate you from reaching your dream except what was destined for you only time.

It appeared to them from afar that on the ground, among the many trees, and following between them, there was a long wall that did not see an end, as if it had the arms of an octopus embracing an endless land, walking up and down from both sides over the topography of the green nature that it passed through.

Behind him, the misty mountains appeared, and in front over a distance that was not far from them, and it was longer and more misty and darker as they approached, and it was as if the sun had to seek permission first from the owner of the land to let its light enter these lands.

The flying rug lowered a little and its front bent down hard, and for a while they thought that they were passengers of a ship that plunged into the depth of the sea from its front suddenly and even the hair of their heads flew back violently from the severity of the landing, to bring them down the flying rug in a deep valley after realising something they had not noticed.

They passed over a dense forest with overlapping branches that resembled nets, until a strong glow appeared in front of them, like the glow of the sun.

Until the rug came down behind the giant wall and said eagerly, "Archie, "Is this the desired place, magic carpet?"

"Yes, sir, this is the land of the dwarves and their kingdom. There is no land and kingdom for them except this one!"

Then Alexander asked strangely, "But I do not see any evidence of the existence of any trace of any human settlement, and there is not even a bird of birds, as if it were the land of nothing?"

Archie said, "Hey Alex, don't hurry." Then asked the magic carpet while they were still lying on his back after he landed on the ground, "Why don't you take us to those mountain baskets, maybe we will find a settlement there, then that kingdom must have a beginning and an indication of its existence!"

The magic carpet said, "I can't, sir, go further, your matter and mine will be revealed, and I see what you don't see?"

This pulled Archie and Alexander to the point where they felt the ground shake below them, so Archie didn't take his eyes off his feet until Sebastian shouted, "What is this heap of dust heading towards us so quickly?"

It was already a huge pile of dust approaching them, accompanied by a violent ground shaking with a huge crashing sound that made them hug each other on the rug from fear and anticipation.

Until Archie said, "Damn it as if the earth is going to swallow us!"

Then the matter was slowly revealed until Clementine said to Alexander, "Here you have the answer!"

It was a military legion they had never seen before, as if they were in the middle of the battle of the great kingdoms of prestige, led by cavalrymen on heavy iron chariots with armoured armour pulled by giant mammoth elephants that Archie and his companions had never seen for their lives.

Eleven chariots in each chariot were six soldiers armed with spears with two blades on both sides and shields full of irregular nails like the back of a hedgehog, preceded by a golden cart from the top and black from the bottom, pulled by one of the mammoth elephants, who covered most of his body with bronze shields with long needles that seemed to be part of the bones of his body.

Martin cried, "Oh my God, why are you stuck in your place like this? Shouldn't the rug escape us from those who seem to be cannibals!"

"Don't let that worry you," said Archie bravely and remember that we did not come here to escape, but this is what is required and this is what we want now! Everyone retreated behind Archie, except for Alexander, who is still contemplating these very large and suspicious creatures, not believing that they are real, but that they are coming to him with their feet, both good and bad.

The Knights of the Legion besieged the rug of magic and those who were on it, and all the soldiers of it, raising their spears in the face of the young boy, empty hands, and the innocence of a baby was drawn after he broke his precious mother's pottery at their faces.

The leader got out of the golden vehicle after the soldiers opened the doors to him, and the boy was notified for him that this is the king of the dwarves.

The most attention after seeing the largest creatures they saw in their lives is that the leader of this majestic corporate and the guards who were with him were almost throughout the height and they were not a dwarf in addition to their inauguration of these solid war cure clothes with steel breasts and metal shoulders that made them seem to be larger than any giant person. They have seen it throughout their lives. As for Archie, he did not care about all of this, because he has a goal in the very importance.

Towards the leader, who was a huge with a red beard, specified in the corners and corners, and with a thick red moustache, and this raised the surprise of the leader who gave his soldiers in his view, doubt and question.

What makes a boy like this in this position his fear does not appear and he appeared before them as if he were a small rabbit.

The silent leader looked at one of his guards in his view of it to act with the boy, as he thought that this is much less than his rank.

And he asked Archie with a very powerful and strong voice, "First, I am sorry, sir, we did not intend to enter this way, but we lost the way and something dangerous happened to us that could have caused our death and the loss of the message for which we came to the king of this place, and the matter is very dangerous!"

Archie's words were enough to change the commander's view of them and that they were not what he thought when it came to their king and their kingdom, the commander said doubtfully, "Come closer, young man. I mean, come closer, Archie Abraham. Isn't that what your name is?"

Archie said, "Yes, sir."

Then hurries to complete his speech before the leader asks him. It is better that you initiate the dialogue to anticipate the type of questions that will come to you, than letting the other person initiate the question to you, then do not be surprised if you put yourself in an embarrassing situation under a barrage of questions that may embarrass you and take you out of the ordinary.

Then Archie continued his words and said, after thoughts raced through his mind, "We came from our country for the sake of the king, and I have a matter that I should not tell anyone except for the king himself."

The leader turns his head back a little and slowly when he hears those words and that the matter seems important but he had to make sure of it himself, not everyone who said such words should be honest unless he has concrete evidence otherwise everyone can say such words and more the leader, who was wise and discreet, says, "Well, Archie, I believe you and what you say, but you know that words remain words and that the tongue is empty of the bone and each of us can say what he likes or what he dreams about as well," with a sarcastic smile.

Archie put his hand on his arm and said, "You are right, Commander, but if I show you the evidence will you believe me?"

The leader says eagerly, "Yes, yes, but I have a promise that you will be under my care and protection, as long as I live." Then he turned to the guard and said defiantly, "Did you know before that I broke my promise to one of you?"

The guards all said, "No, sir, no, sir. You are a man of speech and a position."

The clever Archie took advantage of the situation to his advantage and said with joy, "It seems that we have agreed, sir?"

He extends his hand to the commander to greet the commander with his hand, and this was a strange thing for the commander and the guards, until the commander marvelled when he saw that slender boy whose height did not exceed the commander's thigh.

Archie repeats, saying, "You promised me and your sword, Commander, that I will be under your protection and care, me and these friends of mine, as long as we are here."

(That promise caused embarrassment to the commander in front of his soldiers and to himself as well. He did not expect that what he said would become a debt to his neck. This is the promise of the legion commander in front of his guards. It will not be just a word, but a word of honour that must be implemented.)

Archie walks in a way (take everything you find in front of you to fight over it, and do not care whether it is small or old) he said the commander with a scornful face, "Well, boy," then he extends his giant hand to Archie and greets him and says to him, "As for the evidence, this is Archie who raises the back of his palm to the leader and shows him how the back of his hand has turned half of it into scales!"

That scene aroused the commander's astonishment and astonishment, and he bowed to see closely, and so did the guards behind him, not feeling to see for themselves.

What is this strange evidence in the boy's palm? Then Archie turned to his companions and ordered them to come closer and said to them, stretch out your hands so that the commander can see it.

The commander took a careful examination of their hands for fear that it was just a contagious disease or something, and he held his breath in shock, then said with great sorrow, "I am sorry for what happened to your hands, but what is this in the name of the gods, boy?"

Archie says this is the proof sir that if we don't reach the right time to the king and tell him what message we have otherwise tomorrow everyone in the kingdom will turn like we are and it will spread until everyone is just freaks and then they will die quickly. It is a curse cast by one of the magicians, and we must reach the king to inform him of the matter before the sorcerer reaches here and remedy the matter before a great destruction occurs that will destroy everyone, including your family and loved ones, O Commander!

The commander stammered and was so confused that he forgot what he had in mind from asking his intelligence, so he ordered the soldiers to take all the boys as soon as possible and head into the kingdom immediately.

Archie winked at his friends as they were riding to the wagons, and was late to return to the rug amidst the noise of mammoth feet and the wheels of the wagons as they turned.

He said to the magic carpet, panting, "We are now in great trouble and we do not know how things will turn out to him with these soldiers or the king that we will meet! I want to deliver this message to Maya. I don't care how you will reach her or how you will reach her. I don't know the ways you communicate.

"But we are in a very serious matter. Just tell Maya that Archie and those with him have reached the situation that they are close to being eliminated. And that we may never meet again. Just tell her that I miss her so much and that if she doesn't find me again in this life, we will meet again in another world. Now I will leave and you will not move until we all leave and these people disappear from your eyes, and I do not know where your eyes are? Goodbye, sincere carpet, and it was a pleasure to meet you. Thank you once again."

Then Archie turned and joined the others in the guard carriages, and they set off to their destination.

As soon as the feet of the mammoth elephants stopped shaking the ground from under their feet, after about an hour of walking, one of the elephants sounded a loud, trumpet-like shout.

Suddenly, a giant door opened in front of their eyes, as they looked out the windows of the carriages. The door was covered with thick vegetation.

To the extent that no one knows if there is a door here or just a barrier of water trees, dense and flowering at the same time.

The height of the wall was three times more than the height of the giant mammoth elephant, due to its height and height, and the gate opened wide, and the boys looked suspiciously in astonishment from the dread of that great gate.

It consisted of two thick iron doors, one of which was decorated with inscriptions in the form of a three-headed snake, and the other door was a sleeping black lion, not agitated for those snakes, as if they were in an unexpected confrontation!

The size of the two doors was slightly less than the size of the wall, but for those who saw it for the first time, it was surprising and admirable to see such a wall and such doors of such huge sizes; which indicates the greatness of what it hides behind it, for everything has a face that indicates it, and these giant walls and the ambiguity of what they hide indicate the greatness of this kingdom.

It seems that the kingdom of the dwarves is completely different from its name so far. They have seen only the largest creatures, the largest humans, the highest walls and the largest iron gates. So, are there really dwarves, or was the name only metaphorical?

Boys stick their heads out of wagon windows to explore the new world, as moles stick their heads out of a hole in a burrow.

After the land expanded before them as they saw the long streams piercing the meadows of the vast land on which they walked, everything seemed to them completely different from any country and land they had set foot on, from the guards' weapons and their huge animals to this solemn reception.

The road was paved with great care, they did not feel any disturbance in the cabin of the car as usual, the road widened gradually.

And there was a junction separating the paved road into two lanes, and this was never the case for them to see a street from two different directions for each lane, and this was indicative of the high level of organisation convex.

The various colours between white, red and green, tightly aligned beautifully and wonderfully, as if it were a very beautiful rose garden. As for the chimneys, it was as if they had been built of silver blocks due to their intense lustre, despite the waning and shining of the sun. The frames of the Arched windows were a real decoration for the house with golden colours, indicating that beauty. It is an integral part of the culture of this kingdom, and it bears a very high standard of life here.

Every house had a small garden in front of it, which did not have any types of trees except for roses and various flowers, and the viewer of the place in general imagines that the neighbourhoods from afar are like logo games because of their similarity and the clarity of their colours that delight the onlookers.

But the strange thing is that there was no one in the place except birds, horses and some pets such as cats that sit on the walls of houses or roosters that stand on the pillars of the walls of houses as if they are the guards of those quiet houses that seemed to be neighbourhoods devoid of residents, or that the neighbourhoods are modern and were not handed over to their owners?

Which made Archie to get out what was on his mind from asking him and said to the commander from the window, "But where are the people of the city, Commander, I don't see anyone here?"

The commander stared at Archie a little in astonishment, then said, after remembering that they were strangers:

"Today is an official holiday throughout the kingdom, and everyone is sleeping or spending family time in their homes, and no one goes out until after the afternoon.

"Where everyone goes to the markets after they open their doors until midnight for three consecutive days. Today is the day of the founding of this great kingdom, and it is the day of glory that transformed this kingdom from a land of misery and misery to a land of immense wealth and singing."

Archie says, emphasising the words of the commander, "Yes, I felt this richness from the beauty of these houses, despite their smallness, and from the cleanliness of the streets, which are cleaner than me and my clothes. Even the sidewalks of the streets shine and as if they were made of gold!"

The commander laughed sarcastically without a sound and said, "Your analogy was innocent, boy, but in fact it is really pure gold, didn't I tell you that it is the land of obscene wealth! This day is the most important day of the year and celebrations will be held all over the kingdom but it seems that your news may worsen the face of the king today, so I advise you to wait until tomorrow!"

"No," Alexander said in a loud voice, looking at the commander, "And he confused the others with him, so they did not know what the commander's reaction would be." Then he added, "We will not be patient until tomorrow. We told you the importance of the matter and you saw for yourself what happened to us and I don't know, maybe the situation may get worse and we don't know how we will act if it gets worse than it will be. Time has been lost and you will put your king in an embarrassing position."

Archie put his hand to his face in disappointment after Alexander's violent words, the commander stared at him sharply, but the commander was wiser, he did not comment on Alexander's violent reproach on his spontaneous answer to Archie's question and then signalled starkly to stop, they stopped right in front of the king's palace, this time.

It was clear that the palace was isolated from the city, with a distance that was neither short nor long, exceeding ten kilometres at most. In fact, the palace was an integral part of the mountain adjacent to it in the back, which embraced all the corners and outskirts of the palace to be more fortified than any invaders or penetration Which category is rogue?

So, any attackers of this kingdom will first think of how to break through the fortification of this fortified place before they can break through the walls of the kingdom.

Because the closed door of the palace was more solid than the mountain itself.

The commander asked everyone to get out of the cart and follow him, and advised the guards to stay in their places, and as soon as they crossed the gate, he showed them the accuracy and skill with which this palace was engraved as they entered it.

Luca, expressing unprecedented astonishment, said, "Oh, greatness, this building must be one of the wonders of this world!"

And every step they took amazed their minds more and more as they swim in a space of multiple decorations and domes that adorn the ceilings and inscriptions in which the craftsmen and painters excelled so ably; the eye quickly notices from the seduction of elaborate engineering creativity.

They all stopped in front of a huge courtyard in the middle of the palace with a crimson glass dome with panoramic design in the middle of the mountain that surrounds the palace from all directions except from the top. Nothing is above it except the sky. It has several entrances. Each entrance leads to a pavilion.

Each suite consisted of several sections, and each section was considered a private palace with a miniature version, containing everything the guest needed and more.

The commander turned around silently and said, "Now, boys, you will go to the guest suite, and Mr Gongora will take you to your rooms, and you will rest in it until I go to see if I can meet the king today or not, and tell him your story. Then, you will receive an answer by setting the time to meet the king, because the king's schedule is very full and full of important dates usually. Also, given the particularity of this day, I do not hide from you that it may be very difficult to find an appointment, but I will do what I can because of the importance of the message you are carrying."

The commander stared at Alexander, who was frowning at the commander's face and said to him with a smile on his face, "Calm down, angry boy, you will not change anything in your anger, and everything will come in its time."

For Alexander, the words were insignificant, and nothing seemed to have any importance either from Alexander's point of view, after he knew that their meeting with the king might become in the knowledge of the unknown and in the hands of waiting, which no one likes.

Then the commander's eyes turned between the boys and settled on Archie, and he said with a yellow smile that was hiding something, "Now

Mr Gongora will come to take you to the guest suite, do not worry, he is kind-hearted, contrary to what his appearance suggests!"

These looks were not strange to Archie, so he felt fear in himself and thought that he might be an ambush, but he did not unleash the phobia of suspicion, but rather he waited and improved the thought. The clever young man responded and said, "No worries, sir. I don't think there is a safer place than the king's palace, nothing will frighten us."

The leader smiled with glee and said, "A smart boy, then he left and took the boys to contemplate that panoramic roof and the sun's rays penetrate some of its parts made of mosaic and reflect drawings as if they were animations on the floor of the hall as the sun increased its rays or dimmed. Welcome, guests of His Majesty, the King!"

It was a thick, slow voice, with a slight hoarseness that penetrated the moment of contemplation overwhelmed by true imagination until they were shocked by what they saw and hearts flew until their souls almost flew from their bodies and thought that they had fallen into the trap.

He was a huge polar bear standing on his feet and his head was almost touching his head to the ceiling from his greatness. Martin cried out in fear from the depths of his heart until he fainted and everyone stumbled backwards so fast that Alexander stumbled his feet and fell to the ground. Cloth behind his shirt and put it in front of his eyes in a position of readiness for combat.

(Curse, is it possible that we fell into the ambush) To come from behind them reassurance in the form of laughter that filled the place echoing from the mouth of one of the palace cooks and said after he approached, "Calm down, calm down, calm down. And in the whole kingdom."

Embarrassment was evident on the bear Gongora's face after he thought he had caused a deathly dread to these friendly boys. He descended on his fore-legs and said in a sad tone, "I apologise to you, dear guests, for this heinous thing that happened to me unintentionally, as I thought Commander Regrid had already explained to you in advance, and I was also supposed to stand a little further away from you just as a precaution."

The bear was very shy and very polite despite his huge and very fierce prestige, but Archie was still staring at him and even stared at him for a long time until the bear noticed those sharp eyes watching him and gave him a quick look and then turned his eyes quickly as if he had not seen Archie.

If everyone forgets, Archie will never forget, he remembered that talking brown bear that he rescued from the savage doper creatures that nearly ripped them alive.

Until he quickly linked them up and told himself that this bear has the same colour as the eyes of that bear in the cave, so their eyes were green, and this feature is not one of the characteristics of the bears, but is this also a coincidence.

To find another talking bear! But does it have the same eye colour as well?

Gongora softly opened the door of the royal suite and said politely and in a very low voice, "Your Majesty, guests, and I hope you will accept my apologies once more. This is your suite where you will be staying. The maid will come to you every hour to ask about your needs and I will come back to you again when the news comes from my master."

And when the bear wanted to leave, he glanced again at Archie's scrutinising and hateful looks in his eyes, but he looked away from him and ignored him for the second time. With great admiration Alexander said after he passed the threshold of the door of their private suite, "It seems that this is the paradise that the gods have promised us."

Sebastian remarked with an ironic eagerness, "It is indeed that it is necessary for God to tell us only who this wing is."

Martin replied jokingly, only to wake up from his coma, "But they told us that in heaven there are many foods that come to you without you asking for them."

Then he shrugged his shoulders sarcastically until Luca replied, mocking him, "Heaven without food is better than sleepless fire, your fat idiot, don't you see how much we have suffered for so long for lack of sleep?"

Martin replied angrily, "I'm a moron, crow's face? A slap on Martin's forehead from Luca was enough to ignite the fuse between them and made Martin like a smashing tiger to pounce on Luca's neck and quarrel like two hungry wolves amid the clamour of others who were entering into an overwhelming joy filled with dancing and childish singing."

Alexander insinuated that there seemed to be a blue outside scene behind the transparent curtain covering two glass doors, as if to conceal something from them shyly, like a virgin girl who shyly hides her legs.

And as soon as he approached, he revealed with his hand what was behind the curtain and saw a large balcony overlooking a lake swimming from behind the balcony that overlooked it!

He opened the door hurriedly and advanced to the edge of the balcony, and it was already a shining lake from the intensity of the reflection of the light on its calm surface from behind the pavilion, as if its surface was pure crystal from the cleanliness and clarity of its water. Clementine said cheerfully, "Wow, it is really a miracle. Is it possible that we will leave all this beauty and think of stealing in order to escape and leave all this beautiful paradise behind us?"

"Yes, this is true my friend!" It was Archie's voice. "If you are watching now, what is the sedition that King Gabriel warned us about, whoever was deceived by it will perish, and you are the best example. You must always remember that you should not make pleasures forget your priorities in life. Our priority now is to save our souls, not to search for its pleasure. The pleasure will be found sooner or later. As for our lives, if it goes, we are the losers.

"If you do not realise that you will turn into a monstrosity soon, make sure that you are a frivolous person who has no value for your life, because the origin in life is to live as a human being first, and then comes the stage of searching for pleasures!"

"Take it easy, Archie, we need humour at these times to kill the heavy burden that we carried because of a mistake that was not taken into account." Alex's voice was contemplating the beauty of the scene with great sadness and turns his palms with grief that they will leave this place soon.

Martin's belly rumbled with an open voice, and he said in a loud voice, "How long will we be here without food? Is there an answer? Philosophical advice?"

Clementine said in support of Martin, after he was able to hunger, "Yes, Martin's words are correct, we will not be able to enjoy more of what is around us, even if we are in heaven, if we do not find something to fill our hunger with, then we cannot be in this luxurious palace and this generous land, and if we do not find the simplest things, which is food!"

Charlie said intently, "Exactly, we haven't eaten anything since poor yesterday's dinner. It's been more than half a day and we haven't eaten anything, but you know what?"

We did not search well in this luxurious place. They must have put food somewhere here. The wing is large and has many boxes. Perhaps we did not see well.

Luca said lightly, "Do you think they will hide it so that the guests can search for it? Stop this nonsense. No. Of course, I don't think that there is food here in

the first place, otherwise it would have been placed in a clear place to make it easier for the guest to find it."

Clementine poke Archie in the waist and pointed at him with his finger to the edge of the lake. They were two boys, dressed in white uniforms with a belt in the middle and bonnets over their heads, and they were on the deck of a thin boat.

They were calm and smiling, they weren't dwarves of course, but they were normal young men who knew themselves that they had come to ask the guests to go down to the meal and then they pointed their hands down the balcony, but they didn't see anything, only the balcony was a little ahead over the lake and the boat was just below it until Archie came forward To take a look, he tilted his head a little over the edge of the balcony to look down and saw that there was a boat bigger than the two young men were on.

It was filled with food, and its appearance was delicious, increasing their hunger twice as much, broadcasting within them the return of life again with the return of the hope of abundant food.

The boat full of food was ready to sit and eat.

More than floating above the lake, it was surrounded by expensive pillows filled with the finest types of rare feathers for comfort equivalent to the luxury of the place and those in it.

After swallowing his saliva, Archie said, "It is the most beautiful place for comrades to meet." Then he turned his face to them and said, "Here is what you needed, my brothers. He has come to you more beautiful than you imagined." Then he said to the two children, "Is this for us alone, or is someone going to join us in these feasts?"

Before one of the boys could speak, the fat Martin had already had their tongues out and jumped into the boat to devour all his hands of roasted lamb, roasted and mashed turkey with potatoes, carrots, and sweet buns with all kinds of pleasure and endless pleasure. A few weeks ago, Alexander let out a hysterical laugh and said, "By gosh, you're fat, boy."

Then Archie said gently and with a stupid smile, "Excuse us, young men, if you knew what he went through, you would have turned a blind eye to his rude behaviour," and laughed as we laughed.

And in a crucial moment while everyone is busy filling those empty bellies to make up for their lost.

Luca noticed that the feet of everyone around him had turned to scales after they took off their shoes and their eyes did not leave that table that blinded them from seeing any expected transformation in their bodies until he stopped eating after seeing the two young men giving them suspicious looks, he wanted to distract them before they even noticed it. He threw each one of them pieces of meat, and the two servants were surprised by this unpolitic and disgraceful act.

Then he said to them, "This may seem strange, but in our law, it is shameful that you eat while people look at you. Either you eat with people or people eat with you, so I did it by force, and it was not impolite on my part. So, accept this from me, please. The two young men looked at each other and then turned away with signs of dissatisfaction on their faces."

Alexander looked angry when he said to Luca, "You are so rude, boy, how do you treat people with such villainy?"

Luca replied, "Don't be in a hurry to judge, all of you look at your feet!"

Sebastian said, "Oh, my God, why do you want to grieve over our joy?" Until they all realised that silent death was in their wake, and that it was approaching every minute of their lives.

Clementine said, "Listen to me, whether we eat this food or not, and whether we are happy or not, then this curse does what the king ordered it to do, and nothing will change, and so is our date with the king. Eating is the solution and nothing else, it is the cure and it is comfort."

Archie said cautiously, "Silence please and calm down!"

So, they all fell silent while they watched his eyes, "What happened, Archie!" He said, "I heard a knock on the door of our room!"

Indeed, there was someone knocking on the door, and it was a heavy and

unusual knock, so Archie rushed to see who was knocking, perhaps the bear or the maid that the bear had talked about.

As soon as Archie put his hand on the door handle until it opened by itself, he finds himself face to face with that giant bear (Gongora), the two of them froze, their eyes spinning in each other. Then the bear says (Gongora), "I am sorry for the inconvenience, but they told me that you need help, so I loved being at your service. Is there anything you need!"

Archie says, starting a little hesitant and surprised, and said, "So far, it's not all right." Then he fell silent for a while and suddenly said, "Actually, yes, I remembered after that long journey we made here, not all of our shoes were cut off, but you know it's funny when one of us walks with one of his shoes cut and torn, and you know that we are Mr Gongora. Is that your name?"

Bear Gongora says, "Yes, it's my name and it's good if someone memorises my name from the first time."

Archie said, complimenting, "Oh, don't worry. Pretty names are memorised the first time."

Gongora said with a sarcastic laugh, "That's an exaggerated compliment! Hey! Hey!"

Archie said quickly, "My name is Archie."

The bear said, "A beautiful name, boy, and very suitable for your shape and beautiful personality. Thank you, Mr Gongora, but in order not to take us too much, I want to continue what I was telling you that we need shoes, but not with ordinary shoes, but with long necks, because most of us have suffered various injuries in one of our feet due to thorns and rocks, so it is better to wear high-top shoes to protect the wounds are from mosquito bites and hurt by flies, and you know, Mr Gongora, that we are about to meet the king. It is not good to meet him with legs full of pimples and boils."

"You are right, Archie, in what you said. Don't worry, I will send a cobbler to take your measurements, and then he will make new shoes for you, one of the best you can imagine."

Archie says, "No, you know that the king may meet us at the soonest time, and that the cobbler may take time to take our measurements. What do you think that I take all the measurements from my friends and give them to you and you tell the cobbler about them and start making them right away, so we have gained a lot of time!"

Archie realised that he must not give any room for any creature in this palace to watch their feet and what happened to them, otherwise it would be reflected in the false story they would write to tell the king.

Bear Gongora says, "Well, good idea."

Archie said hesitantly and, in a hurry, "Then give me just a minute and I will come to you with the measurements." Archie rushed to his friends, but he had made a mistake that might expose him later without realising that he forgot to put his shoes on, and this made Gongora notice Archie's feet after he stood up and turned, which aroused the curiosity of the bear about the presence of those scales on the boy's feet, who sat thinking about the strange thing in a different way usual?

As soon as Archie hurriedly returned with a piece of paper in his hand, in which he had recorded all the measurements of the boys' legs, even before Archie had reached the door, Gongora had entered the room of the suite where the guests

were staying and saw Archie the bear staring at his feet with a question like the one who says, "What is this I see?"

Archie bitterly realised the fatal mistake he had made and felt as he was heading to the bear with his bare feet as if they were slapping him hard to chastise him for this mistake!

And that the bear had seen everything Archie was trying to hide from him.

Even slower than he walked, but he did not look at his feet, but his eyes remained in the eyes of the bear, whose eyes did not leave the feet of Archie with fish scales.

The bear says in the voice of the all-knowing, sending an indirect message to Archie, "If you have a secret that you want to hide or are ashamed of telling me about it, make sure that I did not see anything, my dear Archie, and if there is something you want to tell me, I am the best who keeps secrets."

Then he raised his eyebrows to the top, indicating the meaning of 'Archie' (Will I wait for an answer or should I be satisfied with this paper?)

Archie felt frustrated and that he was at a crossroads, either to venture and tell him the truth, and then later discover that Gongora is nothing but a spy for them! Or does he tell the truth and gain an important element to their side, especially when they are in dire need of someone who works for them as a trusted

guide at this particular time and in this important place?

In both cases, Archie's belief was realistic, especially that they are in the cold

war phase with their unknown enemy?

Archie thought quickly, does he consult his colleagues as usual, and this is the

origin of Archie's personal orientation, or does he decide for himself according to what his conscience and intuitive planning dictate to him?

He is in fact, and the matter is not likely to bear reprimand more than Alex and the rest? Then he said quickly, after taking a step that involved a lot of risk, and said with concern, "How can I reveal my secret to someone I do not know?"

Gongora furrowed his eyebrows and said, "I have no interest in hurting the king's guests, but it's good that you are so careful and intelligent, boy, but I'm afraid the curiosity that killed the cat will kill me too. When I first see a man with fish scales covering his feet, don't you see that this is strange and makes me wonder?"

This is all there is to it, and I am an honest advisor to you. If you suffer from a disease, it is better that you do not hide that, as your health is more important than other things, no matter how big they are.

Archie sighed with a long exhale, then looked back to make sure that there was no one but them, then said to the bear with apprehension, "I will tell you because I knew from your eyes that you never knew malice and treachery, bear, and this covenant will remain between you and me."

Gongora interrupted him, saying, "A promise without fulfilment is enmity without a reason. There is no reason for me to be hostile to someone like you!"

"Well," said Archie, with a good soul, "The truth is sometimes stranger than fiction, and..."

Gongora interrupted him again and said coldly, "Is it true that you see a bear talking like you do?"

Archie wanted to say "Yes" and tell him the story of the brown bear, but Gongora interrupted him too and added sadly, "What happened to me in the past made me believe anything said to be stranger than fiction since you entered this kingdom, consider that you have entered the realm of fantasy."

The bear heard the clamour of the boys as they came and said, "As long as you trusted me, I will hurry first to the cobbler to ensure I get your shoes as soon as possible before he too gets busy taking his family to the celebration, then I will not guarantee that you will do what is required."

The bear left and Archie returned, but did not get down to the food boat until he rested his elbow on the front of the balcony wall and put his palm on his cheek to wander away in his imagination, and he said grumbling, "What happened to me? I no longer distinguish between fantasy and reality!"

He felt great distress and annoyance inside him, not knowing how to get it out, and his thoughts were scattered between wishes, reality, fantasy and what awaits them!

Then he found nothing but to return to his reality to prove his feet again and then calmly set out to break through a storm. Obsessions and fear of the worst things that made him confused and a great void.

Then he felt Maya's hand arranged on his shoulder and raised his head with lightning speed to turn to her and then found Alexander saying to him, "Do not overburden yourself with too much thinking and do not worry, for I heard everything that happened between you and the bear and you did the right thing and I would do the same as you did because we need someone who works with us as a guide and a safe source of information to help us to gain time and not to make any mistake that may lead us to doom. And since the first time, despite my extreme fear of him, I saw in him a kind of kindness and kindness that I had never seen in a predatory creature in my life."

Archie said, "Really? Do you think I should tell him everything I'm going to do about the magic jug?"

Alex said, "It is much worse to tell the truth incomplete than to lie, since you are convinced of this whole idea. Didn't you say that it is better for us to die the death of the brave than to live the life of cowards? Suppose he's a spy? What's new, they won't even be able to interrogate us because we'd be lost from this curse? If it is true, then we are the winners."

Archie said happily, "Your words are literally true, Alex, but hey, didn't you say after the mermaid Ella left us that she handed you a short map to get to the magic jug?"

Alexander bit his face, and a yellow smile appeared on his lips, causing me to become suspicious! Hmmm, in fact, yes, but let's wait after meeting the king and what will happen to the situation, and then I will explain the plan to you.

It did not take long, for more than five hours, until the door of the royal suite was opened without any knocking or permission. Gongora returned faster than they thought, with a chest, and said to Archie with a frowned face, "Will this be our partner in secret?"

Archie answered, "This and I are a person, and we are all one group, and we are not different from each other in everything, except that we are the two of us, the oldest and most responsible. So yes, he is our partner, Gongora, oh sorry, I forgot to introduce you to Alexander."

Then Alexander looked at him and said with pride, "This is our new colleague, Gongora."

Alex said to Archie in a whisper, as he stared at Gongora, "Did you ask him if there was any kinship between him and the bear who rescued us out of the kingdom? Do you have a relative outside this kingdom?"

The bear wondered at Alexander's question until it bit Archie's face, and he shrank from embarrassment, and that the time was not right for any personal questions, so that the agreement would not falter over more trivial matters than anyone expected.

Archie replied after being silent for a while, "Alexander means that you look like another bear we saw when we were far from the shore of your kingdom!"

Then Archie turned to Alexander, winked, and bit his lip vigorously, in a sign of him changing the question, "Didn't he, Alexander?"

Alexander replied with confusion, "Oh yes, yes, it doesn't matter," after he tried to make him surprised and said, "Now, Mr Gongora, I don't think Archie has told you the whole truth."

Gongora said, "This is not what I came for, but I came to tell you that the date of the ceremony will be soon and that it will be an opportunity for you to get an idea of the place to enjoy watching the land of the kingdom before your meeting with the king, which we do not know when. So, I will come to you after erect tomorrow morning in new shoes and I will be the official who will supervise your tour and this will be a perfect opportunity for us to reveal secrets and there will be an important entertainment event that I will have to bring you to and it will be a great opportunity to explore the landmarks of the kingdom."

This morning, a knocked on the door, and when Archie opened the door, he found no one but a luxurious medium-sized wooden box, and when he opened it, happiness flooded his face as if he had found the magic jug until everyone noticed that in his face.

They sat around him, eagerly asking what made him happy, until Archie took out a pair of shoes from among a heap of straw that filled the box. The eyes were drawn to him by his beauty, and on it was written the measurements of thirty- three.

And he says with sincere feelings, "Thank you, thank you for this gift, bear, how happy I am to see happiness on the faces of my brothers. Thank you to those who left us with this feeling after we thought that life and everyone on it do not want us to be good."

In the midst of that, Archie stopped for a while, after everyone was busy with the shoes, and went to the place where the sword was hidden, the holy sword of King Gabriel, while talking to himself while his hands turned the sword over it after he raised it, contemplating the beauty of its craftsmanship and the splendour of its charming colour.

He said in a whisper, after he had a great feeling like that of a moment of revenge, "Is your appointment time near." Then his enthusiasm was cut short by a quiet voice behind him, "Will you take him outside with you?"

Archie gave him a half smile, "Clementine, I don't think it's time, but that's where I think this sword was made for, so I hope our tour around the city will be useful and brief. The sword will be doubtful, or rather will hasten the failure of our scheme if we even show it to anyone and if our friend, Gongora, is the good bear."

Clementine asked logically, "But what guarantees that someone will enter to search behind us and then find the sword and flee with it, or report it to the palace authorities?"

Archie put his hand on Clementine's shoulder and said calmly, "I am Archie, the son of Abraham. Now go get your new shoes and let me see what you look like handsome."

Suddenly the mouths stopped talking after everyone heard the sound of a strong door slam and their heads turned around as they looked towards the door until the huge Gongora appeared to them and looked at them in astonishment after seeing their appearance completely different when they put on those luxurious and luxurious shoes and he said, "And your beauty hiding behind your old shoes woke up." So that he smiled at their faces for the first time and said jokingly, "I think that everyone who will see you with me on this tour will think that you are the sons of the nobles of the kingdom, freaks!"

Alexander did not like this joke of the bear, and felt that it was heavier than his size, and replied coldly, "I think you came to take us to the expected picnic, didn't you? We are ready now."

Gongora felt their gazes focus on him to hurry their way out to the picnic.

Until the bear said, "In fact, I could not understand you until now, but it seems that the picnic will be full of excitement with you, you weirdos. Come on, now follow me."

The rickshaw driver waited for us, apparently very angry, that we were so late, and before he turned, he caught a glimpse of the sword with Archie.

Then he straightened and slowly walked towards Archie, and his eyes did not leave the sword! Even Archie was confused and put the sword behind his back. Gongora, furrowing his eyebrows, said, "Is that a sword?"

Happy Archie said, "Yes, it is a sword to protect ourselves, and what is strange about that!"

Then he showed him from behind to see the bear, who was so astonished, and stood on his feet and astonished everyone with him, and said in a terrified voice, "As if it were the sword of King Gabriel?"

Archie was silent and everyone was silent. Archie answered him without any hesitation, despite his astonishment, "Indeed, it is the sword of King Gabriel, but how did you know?"

The bear said, "I was present myself when that battle took place in which King Gabriel invaded this kingdom, but he was defeated badly, and this sword was the sword of battle, yes, he is sure of that as I am sure I see you in front of me?"

Feelings grew dull and their faces turned dark after they heard a paragraph from a novel, they believed from the beginning that it had many missing episodes that they did not complete the rest of them, and Alexander said hesitantly, "King Gabriel invaded this kingdom? This is a strange thing that we have never heard of, and we have not learned about it, neither from the king himself nor from his daughter, Ella?"

The bear replied quickly, before the dialogue hurried up and turned into a question, her answer would be long, "As I said earlier, it seems that this tour will be full of excitement and information, so come on, follow me outside and you will know everything in due time."

Luca grumbled, "I began to feel as if we had entered a whirlpool of puzzles and we had to solve them."

Gongora said, "Just rest assured and don't talk too much, boy, now come on, follow me. Ride quietly in this carriage without provoking any kind of eye- catching movement so that the driver does not catch you, because he is very bad- tempered."

Gongora was advising the boys before they got into the carriage, but he didn't finish his words until that dwarf, who actually looked like a damn dwarf from his face, came out to them.

The one whose bread was like burnt bread was thrown into the water until it shrank and broke from the severity of the wrinkles on that ugly, slashing face.

The one who greeted the bear and the king's guests with the most awful words while raising the whip in his hand, and this was their first meeting with one of the dwarves, and he shouted, "What is this delay, your fat bear? All this delay for those rats? Who seem not even worthy to ride an old, three-legged, lame donkey, and even too much for them!"

The bear felt a kind of embarrassment and did not get angry because he was so used to it that he pushed Gongora and Clementine with his hand to ride after they stopped with exclamation marks from so many insults and curses and they did nothing until Alexander said jokingly, "Finally, we saw a dwarf, but it seems that we are happy because he was not greeted by us, or I would have cut off that bald tongue for him."

The dwarf was not satisfied with that, but even raised the whip to the faces of the boys and said angrily, grinning, "What are you looking at, you bastards? Come on up, you've wasted my precious time."

Martin cried out from the carriage window to the dwarf, "Why all these dirty words when we are the king's guests! Aren't you ashamed of yourself when you're at this age to speak these bad words?"

The dwarf said sarcastically, laughing at Martin's words, "For the first time in my life I saw a ball of fat talking, hahaha." Then he continued, "Hear, you fat pig, if you say another word, I will shove you in the ass of this idiot bear who has brought you here and caused me to delay my return home until this time!"

Archie said quietly, "Ignore him and excuse his old age. Let's go. Archie did not know how to deal with this sharp-tongued dwarf, as he is an old man, and in addition to that he does not know what the truth is, and the dwarf may be right despite the dirtiness of his tongue."

However, Archie understood that they might have already disrupted his day without intending to. The old dwarf may have some right to be angry and not curse? This was Archie's belief, despite those hurtful words that came out of the old dwarf's mouth that caused Charlie's nerves to convulse as he heard those curses and raised his voice in the cart, "Why all this silence on this ugly dwarf, why are you silent on his insulting you like this! We did not come here to bear the insult of a wretched old man without doing anything to him!"

Archie angrily replied to Charlie, "Take a deep breath, Charlie, to calm down, and keep your calm. If it is, it is not polite to speak to someone who is older than you like this, even if something bad happens because of him, we don't know what his circumstances are. And whoever speaks in this way, make sure he has pain inside him, we don't know the type and amount of pain. And what damage we inflicted on him!"

Even if we didn't mean that, then Archie came out of the front carriage window that separates the passengers and the driver and surprised everyone with his reaction and said to the dwarf, "I apologise on behalf of everyone, sir. I reiterate my regret and apologies for everything we have caused you, and I thank you with all my heart for waiting for us and for being patient with us."

The carriage with its horses left the confines of the palace until it was hidden from view and the bear was walking next to it like a fierce bodyguard guarding important figures.

They felt a deep eagerness to see this solemn festival, as described by those who told them, and they seemed very satisfied with the new situation, despite the tragedy they are in.

The rays of the sun were still shining on the city, its neighbourhoods and its markets, until they saw a large crowd of people they had never seen before, from the large number of souls teeming in it. They are followed by men and women, some of them carrying their children in cradles, and boys dressed in clown clothes, and the shapes of different animals were drawn on their faces, and the crowd was very noisy, as if it represented a farce aimed at something from the heritage of the kingdom that the stranger boys did not understand until they became like locusts of their abundance.

The carriage found itself in the midst of this crowd, which made the guests express their annoyance after their thoughts were confused while watching these indistinct nonsense thoughts until the city bells rang and the music and melodies increased closer to the melodies of the dances of the barbarians and gypsy savages.

The dwarf, the driver of the carriage, was shouting and shouting at everyone who approached the carriage, and spitting on others in anger and hitting his whip, and saying, disgusted by those celebrations, "Fools, idiots, petty habits. A gypsy must end immediately. If I had the power, I would have ordered you to be burnt alive, you miserable impure—"

And as soon as he was silent, some of the quarrelsome boys threw eggs at him and ran away laughing, leaving the dwarf to eat each other from the intensity of his anger.

Until Archie, watching that painful scene for him, said, "I am afraid for this dwarf that his heart will explode from the intensity of anger that I have never seen a man in my life with such a miserable soul! O God of heaven, have mercy on him and ease him, for he has no control over his affairs."

Alexander said jokingly, "Why do you show so much interest in this idiot as if he were your father?"

Archie replied, "And why are you overpowering him, even praying, as if he had killed one of your family? Praying for the good of others is free and will not cost you anything except that it shows the beautiful side inside you."

Alexander said indignantly, "Do you still believe in these things, Archie? I thought that those in the villages live in an intellectual situation that is very different from us, as we, the inhabitants of the kingdom, have been plagued by these shabby religious ideas that have no origin except that the priests transmitted them to us from their false ancestors?"

Sebastian said, Archie, "Do not worry, Archie. Alexander is inclined to the thought free from the rules of religions, which he sees as the cause of all our social problems, individual grudges and eternal wars!"

Archie said excitedly, "It is a good thing to be proud of your thoughts and belief, as long as you have the evidence for that. In fact, I also share Alexander's idea on the one hand, which is that following whoever says he owns religion among others and that others should listen and obey his orders because of his claim that he has the unique divine right to speak on behalf God, no matter how many and wherever they are."

Luca said, "I think we are on a tour to know the city and not in a synagogue to discuss your religious and theological ideas!"

Gongora knocked on the window of the carriage after they reached the parking lot for carriages, which was filled to the brim due to the large number of guests who flocked from all over the kingdom to participate in this great feast.

Archie felt a cramp in his stomach and depression in his heart when he saw all those huge crowds and the loss of time with the bear and their distance from the place of the goal for which they came, and continued turning his palms and contemplating them with great sadness, knowing well that a time had passed and no plan had begun to restore the magic jug.

Except that he grabbed the first thread that might shorten their time. Then he said sadly to himself, "Perhaps it is good, after realising why King Gabriel could not retrieve his precious treasure from this kingdom."

And that it was not as easy as I thought Archie, he realised at that time the offer of King Gabriel when he said just that you only come back, he will celebrate with us even if we don't bring the magic jug!

It seems that he wanted to use us as a message to his enemy King Prakshim and tell him that he had penetrated his kingdom and his palace, this is what Archie understood and concluded through what he discovered so far in this kingdom.

And when they set out on foot, Gongora was walking next to Archie, and after raising his voice sharply, because of the loudness and the people's closeness, he said to him, "Let me tell you that you are a beautiful coincidence in my life and at this time, oppression has reached me a great thing. I can no longer bear what I am in, but I believe a lot that relief always comes at the end and I think it has come."

At this time, Bear Gongora started talking and telling his story from the beginning, and went on to describe his disastrous life story, which was for Archie, as if he had heard someone's description of a frightening nightmare full of tragic events that he never understood what he heard! The green bear's eyes sparkled with tears.

And he said regretfully, "And that is only the beginning of what you will hear in order to know what is happening in secret in this kingdom, in which no one sees except beauty, money, pleasures and lusts that make you doubt that there is a paradise other than this paradise we are in!"

And that all this was only in the eyes of those who did not realise the truth of what is happening here from behind the scenes, and my story is nothing but a small thing that is hardly mentioned in front of the rest of the tragic stories.

Gongora briefly tells Archie about his past and his beginnings with a very important benefit that illuminates the thought of Archie lost in the mists of strangers' land and it's really worth stopping by, as the bear Gongora and the bears that live here and will meet her on their way later are only humans before this unique kingdom becomes for everyone who doesn't know it!

They were living a normal life. They lived in a very small village with a small number of dwarves, who were among them the family of the King Prakshim, and this was a very long time ago, dating back to more than a hundred years, where they lived a simple and quiet life despite the poverty and extreme destitution at the time.

Where they depended for their livelihood on the harvest, which was quickly damaged in many cases due to the great drought that ravaged most of the lands. Sometimes herds of migrating animals would come and pass on the farms of

the people of the small village and make them ruins and don't leave it for the people until a dry tree, talking to himself.

Until one day, they made an agreement with one of the kingdoms to shake off the dust of humiliation and humiliation that the kingdom that was called (Kingdom of Hemyaros) would be established.

As soon as the name was mentioned in the ear of Archie, he stopped walking at the sign of the name, and Luca bumped into him from behind, and said with grumbling, "Stop looking at the beautiful girls, for you have the most beautiful of them all together, Archie?"

Archie apologised and continued walking, unable to claim that he had stood so as not to trample on those pigeons that collect the corn kernels scattered on the ground. Then Gongora continued his interesting speech to Archie, "They agreed that the Kingdom of Hemyaros would finance them with sufficient food in exchange for the dwarves to make artistic sculptures and make statues and decorate and decorate the walls of the palaces public squares and the front of important state institutions throughout the kingdom."

Whereas, King the Mar, King of Hemyaros, had entrusted himself at that time to make his kingdom the pioneer of work and arts in the entire globe, to create landmarks that the eyes had not seen before, to be proud of when he showed them in front of others.

Especially in the field of making statues, and this is what the dwarves of our village excelled in, and no one has ever surpassed them. It is even said that the jinn also relied on them in making statues and sculptures. Indeed, that happened and the people of the village rejoiced, and we lived a period of time in a comfortable life.

Gongora paused for a while at the honey store. He couldn't bear to watch the hanging honeycomb cells dripping thick golden honey until he felt the feeling of a hungry bear from quickly swooping on the cell and eating all the cells with one bite, which angered the seller and his emotions in a hysterical way. He shouted sharply, "If you don't put a price. You ate, old bear. I will cut open your belly at once."

Without further ado, Gongora burped at the honey seller, then roared wildly, opening his huge jaws like the biggest jaws of a predator living on earth. He saw nothing of the seller but the dust of his escape, and so did everyone else run away.

Thinking that he had regained his animal instinct to eat someone, then Gongora turned to Archie and tried to seem innocent and whispered as lightly as he could and continued his narration, "Until the day came when King Prakshim stole the jewellery of King the Mar's wife, taking advantage of his work inside the palace and stole one of the most important, king's wife's jewellery which was considered a very precious gift.

"It is a blue diamond emerald called the Dragon's Eye Emerald with some jewels, which provoked the madness of the king who erupted like a very explosive volcano and who ordered a comprehensive war on the dwarves who were an integral part of the inhabitants of our village.

"Unfortunately, the king with his army attacked our small village and destroyed everything in it. We fled to the plains and valleys from the king's oppression and accompanied us in great misery. Many of the villagers saw their children dying in front of him from starvation, and he was unable to do anything because of the inability to do anything.

"The king took everything, they took all the livestock, burnt the carts, houses, and crops, killed the horses, and took revenge on our village for no reason."

"But only because the thief in Prakshim was among her," said Archie, astonished, "Oh damn, it is true who said if he knew the reason, there would be no wonder.

"Now I know why Prakshim betrayed King Gabriel after he trusted him. It seems that he was a natural thief, and I will not be surprised by any other bad thing I will hear about him in the future."

Gongora pokes Archie and said to him, "Wait, boy, to hear the rest."

He was sharp-witted, narcissistic, and always had a sense of grandeur, even as a boy. He coveted supernatural powers and loved tricks and deceptions. It was very difficult to deceive him, but unfortunately, he used that genius to spread and ignite the conspiracies among the people of the village in order to be himself. Owner of the word, he was helped by the treasure he stole to use it as a carrot on a stick for the residents of the village to owe him obedience, everyone was in desperate need of food and he succeeded in that and then resolved to take revenge on King the Mar, but, very maliciously!

In addition to all his possessions, he also had an amazing ability to be patient and wait, and this helped him in his gradual ascent until he rebuilt the village again.

With the stolen treasure, but he would not have succeeded if he had not made another agreement, this time with King Gabriel, and that agreement was the one that would change the features of the world and kingdoms later, and no one knows how he got there. King Gabriel had a great treasure that no one on earth had. Very generous and kind.

Archie continued in his long silence until all the crowds and disturbing activities around him did not distract him from the talk of Gongora, who completed the story and said after wiping his lips from the remnants of honey, "As soon as King Prakshim arrived at King Gabriel, he told him their story and what happened to them from King the Mar, who destroyed their small village, dispersed their dreams, and killed everything in their village unjustly and coercively, only because they demanded the king to pay their financial fees for the crafts they accomplished. And therefore, he decided to get rid of them at the

lowest price, which is to kill them and destroy them completely so that they would not ask for anything again. This was the false story of Prakshim to King Gabriel.

"This was the story of King Prakshim from his false point of view, and King Gabriel committed a big mistake, as he gave his kindness and good thought to others in an exaggerated way at the expense of investigating accuracy and trying to reach the truth of the other party's doing this not insignificant matter.

"King Gabriel has a strong principle that does not easily budge from his thoughts, even if it is against his family and himself. At the same time, the interests of King Gabriel intersected here with the interest of Prakshim, who realised that King Gabriel wanted to establish a small kingdom, but extremely rich and luxurious, after knowing the most important secret in his life!"

Prakshim realised this quickly because of the strength of his intuition until he lured the kindness of Gabriel to him to be close to them and considered them among the inhabitants of his future kingdom.

Prakshim and those with him were able to create multiple statues and a great throne that dazzled Gabriel's imagination and tickled his dreamy feelings, who was very excited and trusted Prakshim more than anyone else around him, especially his daughter... It is said that Prakshim wanted to marry her, but they disagreed later and it does not matter to us. Right Now.

Until the promised day came that Prakshim had always dreamed of, to see the magic jug up close and know it's working mechanism in front of his sight, which did not stop shining maliciously until he laid the malicious scheme for the most important theft in his life.

"A magic jug," said Archie, claiming ignorance of not knowing anything about this story. We were there and we knew nothing!

Do you mean a jug in the sense that we understand, that is, it resembles a teapot, or is it just a metaphor and a noun only? Gongora let out an innocent and sarcastic laugh and said, "I know it seems strange and strange to you at the same time, but in fact, yes, the magic pot is nothing but a teapot."

Which you know and I know but when Prakshim was able to find out the secret of the power of this magical jug and its financial value in particular.

And that this is the opportunity to obtain the nucleus of power that he dreamed of obtaining one day to create his dream on the ground to ignite the fires of revenge with the wood of his grudges throughout the universe until the appropriate opportunity came to pounce on this great treasure when the wife of Gabriel, whom he loved so dearly, died. Building statues of gold surrounded by Roman columns of marble boulder.

He ordered that all her jewellery and clothes be collected and placed inside the throne on which he sits, and that this throne should be a great throne to immortalise her memory.

The order was given to Prakshim to accomplish this historical task by using the magic jug himself, after he taught him the secret of its use, as Gabriel at that time could not bear to see anyone or even talk to himself, and chose to live in solitude and alone, involving in his deep sadness the extinguishing of the candle of his life.

At that time, Prakshim had tightened his grip on the secret and key of the jug, after knowing his strengths, weaknesses, and the extent of his ultimate ability.

Prakshim was well represented in the role of the faithful and faithful servant while he was hiding the fact that he was a wolf breathing treacherousness and betrayal his conscience did not dissuade him from even any shame or the simplest branch of chivalry from his ugly act, and he prepared a solid plan to keep everyone busy by making the workers sing during the works of sculpture and painting to be a tight cover against any eyes that might insinuate smuggling operations.

He transported and smuggled most of the golden statues through a large network of spies and cheap labour who hired them to cut the gold that he obtained from the golden statues after cutting them in a store outside the cave, which he established to launch his criminal operations consisting of a network of hired mercenaries and they had already transferred all those stolen goods. They had already transferred a great reward to the village, where he worked to employ the people in it in building and forming an army and security guards to take over the task of managing the stolen goods from the land of the grieving king, who left the rope on the boat to discover later that the boat had sailed away with all the hardship of his life. He tried to retrieve it; the titles were gone forever.

After the vision became clear, Archie said, "Now I understand why King Gabriel was angry with us and linked us to that curse. He was betrayed by a friend and tasted the bitter taste of loss at the same time. This made him harden against us, thinking that this might ease him or remove heavy worries, damn this evil Prakshim!"

Gongora replied, thinking, "Ah, now I understand the matter of those scales in your hands, but let me continue for you so that you can hear the rest of the tragedies, which are the most important. As for us, we knew nothing but that we were surprised that the dwarves started running an army in the village of people that we don't know whether they are from the earth or demons?

"Where security guards were being recruited in strange military clothes, and the headquarters was this palace, which you were inside and you saw how large and wide its area, while originally it was a fortified castle, almost abandoned and dilapidated."

After being attacked by the king, The Mar, it took its share of natural growth until it became a well-established and inhabited palace, the like of which has not been seen.

As for the security soldiers who were brought by Prakshim to be the nucleus of his army, they were called the Hopis in order to work as a strong guard who had no loyalty except to those who paid them more. What his eyes see and wish for are piles and tons of pure gold.

One day he had a diabolical idea that had never occurred to anyone before, until he decided, in the height of his terrifying anger, to provide the soldiers and guards with weapons that would terrorise the villagers to submit to him by force.

When he brought to the village for the first time the predators whose presence is not familiar in our lands, he brought some of them from my land thousands of leagues away from us. Of the most dangerous and evil ones are those black lions!

Then Gongora was silent for a long time and bowed his head down until Archie thought he wanted to pick up something from the ground in the midst of the blazing festival. Then he asked him, after seeing him otherwise, "What is wrong with you, Gongora?" He slowly raised his head and continued telling that hateful tale, and added:

He brought some other creatures from the distant and frozen lands of Siberia, such as the mammoth elephants, which turned into a deadly weapon that no one dared to try to stand in its way, but because of Prakshim's love for money and gold, he felt that he must change his way in the matter of spending on soldiers and weapons and because of his usual intelligence he used the method (Drown the feet of your opponents in the mud), instead of engaging in war battles with opponents, drains the treasury of the kingdom, which will cost its treasury a lot of money.

Where he decided to take advantage of the circumstances of his opponents to his advantage and to lend them money in exchange for long-term benefits through what they own of assets in their kingdoms or outside in return for not raising the interest on them, and this is what made many villages and kingdoms panting behind what they thought was the cake of a happy life and they agreed to these deceptive terms and they are they laugh!

But without realising, he supported the villages that had enmities with the villages he lent him with more tempting and generous offers to sharpen their fangs and claws in order to make wars with the borrowers to ensure that they defaulted and that the borrowing village would not repay the loan.

Thus, he will demand from them the assets they agreed upon, otherwise he will support their opponents in their war against them, which in turn will undoubtedly eliminate them, because they know for certain that Prakshim standing with any party means the other party's loss.

The news of the rising power of Prakshim reached the east and west of the earth.

Thus, the fall of the other villages continued between my hands after their inability to pay the debt to him, until Prakshim collected the residents of those villages and enticed them with money and even lavished them on them, not love and generosity, of course not.

But in the hope that they would follow him to climb on their backs and fulfil his wish to establish his unique kingdom that he dreamed of.

This is what made many small villages request to be affiliated with him and to enter into his possession in exchange for the hunger of their stomachs to be silenced after they witnessed the residents of other villages and those who changed their situation from poor villages that depend on limited resources that they do not obtain until after their suffering, to luxury villages where each family was spent. All the requirements of food and clothing without any effort, in exchange for their children to work for Prakshim and for each of them to sign a contract for life.

And if one of them violates the terms, he is sentenced to death or exile, and this is what made everyone abide by the terms of that unfair contract.

On the other hand, I will not hide from you that Prakshim did a great job when he first competed with himself to establish a real city for which he gave every precious price.

Without being stingy with it when he brought the distances between villages closer by paving and paving roads and building residential neighbourhoods between the distant villages.

To turn those villages into one city, separating the neighbourhoods only short distances, and when the thorn (Prakshim) became strong and the moment of revenge on King the Mar came, King the Mar had died!

This news was a shock to Prakshim, who heard the news while watching the completion of his statue, which will be one of the greatest statues made by man, and which you will see shortly on the battlefield, the aquarium building.

Archie said attentively, "Battlefield?"

The bear said, "I will not talk about it because you will see it soon and we will have a story in it, my boy, because what you will hear now you will see with your own eyes on the ground of truth in the aquarium building, but now I will tell you how you were and became a bear, and perhaps this will explain many of the things that made you in confusion."

Gongora said happily, "It seems that your friends liked the festival. Perhaps this will make them forget something that made them sad before."

Then he removed with his hand the curious pigeons that crept under the intertwined feet as if they were sewer rats and not birds, and they searched very eagerly for the falling corn kernels, because this holiday only happens once a year, and she knows it well.

Until Charlie said calling Martin, "Look, Martin, for this juice shop. We need to cool off our miserable hearts after this fatigue and suffocation in this suffocating crowd. Let's have a cold drink anyway."

Luca said to them, "How are you going to buy it when you have no money?"

Martin looked at Gongora maliciously and smiled, "We are now guests of Gongora. Just as he ate honey for free, he will buy us cold drink for free too. Otherwise, what do you think, Gongora? Don't your guests deserve a cold cup of fruit juice formed to quench their thirst after this fatigue?"

Gongora grumbled, "If you were to turn into a bear, your fat one, I'm almost certain that you would eat the inhabitants of the kingdom one by one."

Then he hurriedly continued his conversation with Archie, after he hinted that they had approached one of the important landmarks as they were walking with difficulty in the midst of crowds.

And he said to Archie, "My family owned a group of acres, and it was located on the outskirts of the kingdom, precisely the area on which part of the eastern wall of the kingdom was built, where the king issued an order that no family could own more than four hundred acres.

"The rest is confiscated to the financial treasury without any compensation? This angered my father and those with him, and they refused this matter after they presented a statement to the king explaining to him their historical ownership of these acres."

However, Prakshim refutes all those historical arguments made by my father.

It was not from my father and all the landowners who were heads of other families and declared their categorical rejection of any appropriation of their lands without compensation, whatever the pretext.

As this law was disruptive to the conditions of landowners, including my family, and will make us at risk of bankruptcy at any moment due to the shrinking of the cultivated areas allocated to them.

And they will be at the mercy and extortion of these new landowners if they do not become their slaves. My father and his friends discovered after investigation that the confiscated acres would go to one of the great contractors in the kingdom, who is famous for his long hand in stealing other people's property unlawfully and without the slightest mercy to the real owners.

That is, he was another king in the kingdom.

Meaning that he was running a state within the state because of these dirty deeds that he was doing and in full view and hearing from the king.

Two days later, my father and those with him announced the rebellion against the unjust decisions of the king, and I was a young child, not more than three years old, and since that moment our lives turned forever and we are no longer like we were.

They threatened my father and those with him by crushing them under the feet of mammoths clasped with all kinds of armour, which no one is able to stand before them except for those who created them.

But my father's experience in agriculture and wildlife helped him temporarily to stop these barbaric threats, as he coordinated with other farmers to collect the largest number of rats that they were using as a weapon to fight the pest of earthworms.

Which was a source of great concern to the farmers, as my father ordered them to put as many rats as possible in bags and that each of them carry a bag and they ascend to the tops of the trees that remained on both sides of the road, and when the mammoth hordes approached, my father whistled the beginning of the war, and they rained the appearance of the invading mammoth corps with bags of rats, which were like stones from hell falling on them from the sky it caused the earth to shake under us from the intensity of the mammoth herd's panic, so that I remember that night when the wall of our house fell from the force of the earth's panic from the weight of what was on it, so that the mammoths crushed those who were on their backs under feet while fleeing, fleeing.

And in the midst of this conflict, which led to the opposite result, as these criminals were desperate to break my father and his companions, they had a great impact on revenge in the most violent and bloodiest way.

And they found what they wanted when they used those black, deadly and mighty lions in their brutality, which were not like the rest of the other lions.

Where they ambush my father and his friends, and they knew the plan of my father and the rats, until they sent only one elephant to occupy the focus of my father and the warriors who were with him, and then released their ferocious beasts that surprised all those who were high in the trees and killed them more than one can imagine until we did not recognise my father's body and who with him.

In a moment of anger, Gongora pulled out his fearsome claws and stuck them to the ground hard and pressed his fangs with the utmost force as if he was sticking them in the body of his enemies to extinguish the fire of oppression that had perched on him all those years until Archie's feet shook, but he quickly and wisely understood that until he stood on Gongora's hands and hugged the head of the huge bear tenderly. It's like he's embracing his love, Charlotte, not a beast.

He said calmly, "One moment of anger may steal from you a hundred. Years of joy."

Meanwhile, the snow fell as if the white visitor that everyone was waiting for on this happy occasion, when heads rose to the sky to make sure that it was really snow and not the drizzle of some events until the voices rose with joy and as if peace had enveloped the place suddenly until the feelings of the rebellious Gongora cooled, and the snow was falling as well. His time.

Archie excitedly said to him, "Have you ever heard that grief saved its owner or returned absent? No, of course, Gongora."

Then Archie remembered that he had not seen Alexander all that long, who was supposed to be with him, even if he turned back and found him behind him, just like the shadow of the absent, smiling and said happily, "I have not left your shadow, and I have heard everything, and I am excited to hear the end."

Gongora continued his speech steadily after the signs of anger faded from him, "The last time someone hugged me was my mother after my father was killed, and since then I have not seen her!"

Archie said strangely, "Why?"

The bear said, "Where the damned cavalry leader ordered Haguin at that time to imprison everyone in the village and in order that no one would know what they had done, and they brought a cursed priest who was not less than them in crime it is said to him (the eye of the cat) was one of the most powerful magicians and the most dangerous of them evil.

"But he was only allowed to live in a maximum-security prison so that he would not use his magic against any of them he was considered a joker card to be used only as a fatal blow to their dirty goals.

"They brought him to the village in handcuffs in exchange for feeding him and not dying of starvation. This was the way they force him to do what they wanted. They brought him to our village after they gathered me, my mother, my sister, and everyone else who remained in the village, where the men who were among the resistance with my father were eliminated and then they instructed the magician. Cast a spell of madness on us!

"But the unexpected happened. The wizard (Cat's Eye) took advantage of this temporary freedom in order to escape from their grip forever and cast a spell on us different from what was asked of him or expected of him.

"We were suddenly transformed into bears, as you can see, after the spell was cast upon us, and the released magic words gushed out of the crypt of his ancient mouth. We fell into a coma accompanied by severe pain, but it did not last long. We woke up as a result of which we were bears of different colours and shapes!

"The reason for this was a tragedy for Commander Haguin and his soldiers, and at that moment the instinct of fear in the bears had taken control of us, and then my mother attacked Commander Haguin and pulled his head out of his body in front of his followers who froze in their places and their legs could not carry them from the horror of the shock, so my mother completed finishing them as they had prepared On my father, this was justified justice from the justice of heaven, which ruled as just as possible and as quickly as possible."

As for the sorcerer, he ran away and we know nothing about him since that day. Alexander said with great regret, "What a tragedy!"

Archie replied, "But that means that if we find the wizard, he can bring you back as evil as you were, right?"

Gongora grumbled, "This is in distant dreams. If there was a trace of this cat- eye wizard, we would have found it a long time ago. My mother roamed the wasteland and vast lands in search of him until she was killed by a hunter.

"I don't think it unless it vanishes in the air like smoke vanishes, and when they wanted to oppress us, my sister and those who stayed with us fled, but we didn't know that they were luring us into a tight ambush that ended all our dreams and my sister could not save us and we were sold at a cheap price to one of the contractors and contractors of the aquarium theatre to fight."

"Ummm," Alexander said and pressed his lips to Archie.

Archie said in a low voice, "Black Cave Bear, Black Cave Bear!"

Ah, then Archie turned and offered his condolences and condolences for what

had happened and said to Gongora, "I am very sad to hear this and because I reminded you of something you don't want to remember but may I ask you and excuse me for this question but I think it may be a thread to find your sister!"

Gongora stared at him strangely, "What do you mean?"

Archie said, "Did your sister turn into a white bear like you, or was it a different colour?"

Gongora replied, his eyes rolling between Archie's eyes, "Rather, it was a grey colour, closer to brown, with a necklace on her neck..."

Archie interrupted him with confidence and continued the words of the bear saying to him excitedly, "She has a red rope like a thread of silk, and she has green eyes, right?"

Gongora shook his head in astonishment, then added, Archie, "I saw her, yes, yes, she was the one who saved me from the doppers while we were there."

She was a brown teddy bear with a red rope on her neck. "Yes, she is your sister, Gongora, and she spoke too!"

Gongora rose to his feet, tense and agitated, and said angrily, "I never knew you were such a young man to play with the feelings of others, Archie."

Archie said, swearing, "God of heaven, we saw her before we came to your kingdom in the lands of Hammerut, at the black cave in the forest."

"Isn't that so, Alexander?" Alexander said, confirming Archie's words, "Yes, Gongora, we saw her as we see you now, there is no doubt about that, and it is not possible for two bears to have these qualities at the same time, and that is a coincidence! Unless she is your sister! The bottom line is that we saw her at the entrance to the black cave and that we all owe her our lives, Gongora."

Archie said, "Now the truth has appeared, Gongora. The real reason for our being here is only to get back the magic jug, the treasure of King Gabriel that was stolen, and since our interests have intersected with each other, we are now one hand. We want to get our lives back and you are too."

For the first time in his life, he sees Gongora, sees that he has found someone who cares for him, and feels what he feels. He remains silent for a while, then ponders, "Now I understand, my friends, what a coincidence. It seems that what brought you here was not a coincidence. It is clear that it is very difficult for you, although it seems You are enjoying this experience."

Alexander joked, "Of course, no matter how you are on your way to search for your new life, do not forget to live and enjoy, at least, if you do not find in your life what you wish for, then your past life will not be wasted for nothing. I do not hide from you how much I feel now that I am lighter than before for the first time. I feel very happy when I told you the details of everything, despite my fear that my relationship with you, my friends, will be exposed, okay guys.

"Now we got into the serious matter, but before I draw any plan, I want to tell you that I have a brother and friends at the amphitheatre and this day will be a day. Decisive for them and most likely that the king will attend the show as usual, unless there is a change in its dates! But this is not mentioned in most of us until now, at least, so it is better for us to hurry to get them out first to save their innocent souls that are wasted in vain to make those filthy sadistic and thirsty souls thirsty to see bloodshed in the squares in order to satisfy their sick lusts. And secondly, to have us at noon to retrieve the magic jug because it is not easy for us alone because I know the place very well.

"So, something needs strength and numbers, just as it needs intelligence and politics, because when the king goes out to the aquarium, the security guards are less than the times when the king himself is inside the palace, and therefore this day will be a precious opportunity that we may not find like it except in the next year if we are alive, of course. Are you ready to start now? So, let's change direction to the aquarium theatre," said Archie excitedly.

Then Alexander yelled at Sebastian and Luca who were petting the dog of one of the girls lied to make up an opportunity to talk to her.

Alex said, "They all gathered here." Then he said in a softer voice, it seems that we are going to go through a terrifying adventure again. Gongora addressed him, advising, "If you did not encounter Radenback in this adventure, you did not know the meaning of horror at all!"

Archie replied, "To this degree, Gongora? Even more, Archie, it is evil in itself, if we must liberate our brothers. So, we have a date with Radenback tonight."

Archie looked at Alexander with pale eyes. Alexander's eyes widened as he turned his face away. He looks at the rest of the boys who are approaching him at the top of their happiness and says sadly, "How much it pains me that this happiness does not last long, my brothers, and I fear death for you tonight."

Gongora stood in front of the royal horses that were pulling the chariot in which the king's strange guests came on board while the old dwarf was going to lunch time in a restaurant. After removing the saddles from their backs, Gongora stood staring at the horses with eyes shining maliciously, until the horses groaned in fear of him.

Her hooves seemed turbulent and turned back and purred from her noses as she looked at each other in tension, and Gongora gave Gongora looks of panic and suspicion as if she knew the intention behind the actions of the bear who suddenly roared in her in a frightening, hysterical and violent manner.

With all his might, the birds flew at the suspicious sound and scattered through the sky and the horses ran around, not knowing what was going on just to escape with their skin from this beast who laughed loudly at the exciting and funny situation for him hahaha.

Gongora laughed until he put his hand on the ground so that he wouldn't fall from laughter, then put the saddle on his back and when he saw the boys staring at him in amazement at his behaviour and said to them, "I think you understood the point of my doing this! Speed alone is not enough, but it also takes strength to reach the aquarium. Come on, stop staring and get in the carriage, we are all racing against time before his sword cuts us off while heedless. And the bear sped away, pulling the cart running away with it, like the one who ran away with the stolen treasure, racing against time to catch up with his brother before he was killed in the arena, and to catch up with his sister to reunite what was left of his family before finding death one before the other."

Gongora stopped the royal carriage at the entrance of the VIPs, where it served as a transit check, to make room for her to the main entrance that leads to the cabin into which the king and his entourage will enter, so that he may know the king's news from the dignitaries who know Gongora well because of his service in the hospitality of the king's guests and their accompanying servants who they will come soon, but here.

Everyone inhaled the air and took many breaths of air the moment the carriage stopped, after their hearts almost flew out of place due to the speed of the bear as it made their way towards the aquarium amid all those crowds and narrow roads full of street vendors and the general visitors.

Until Clementine muttered, watching the bear remove the saddle from his back, "I don't blame you for that speed, but do you need some help?"

Alexander said, "Sorry, little Clemento, for he was too busy to think about your strong feelings."

Gongora replied firmly, "I thought I would at least appreciate you for my effort to reach as fast as possible, or we would still be stuck in the midst of that hateful crowd!"

From Gongora's enthusiasm, his soul glowed, and he forgot the rules of the place where the arrivals had to observe the special regulations of the aquarium to enter.

Especially if one of the officials working for the king will be blamed more than others, and because of his excessive enthusiasm, he did not care about the instructions of the guards and the reception staff.

Where there was a long line of nobles and their wives waiting to enter the grand aquarium amphitheatre.

But this did not deter Gongora, who bypassed the pride of the queue of rich guests standing and raised their social status while staring in disgust at the bear and the boy!

One of the guards stopped them and said, confused, "Excuse me, but you must stand at the end of this queue and no one is allowed to pass the other?"

There was a girl accompanying her parents at the age of Clementine among those who stood waiting watching what was happening attentively. Then she looked at Clementine from top to bottom and whispered to her father, who was angry about the behaviour of the bear, "Why do they want to overtake everyone else? Is this not evidence of a lack of literature and taste!"

The father said firmly, "Well done, my daughter. The question is yes, it is a lack of literature and a lack of upbringing, and you should know very well that in every family you will find garbage, and it seems that these are the garbage of their families!"

The girl looked at her father and said in amazement, "But look, my father, at those shoes that these boys wear."

The father replied in disapproval, "Not all that glitters is gold, my daughter!"

The girl said intelligently, "And not everyone who disagrees with his family should be bad in our eyes, Dad! You do not know, perhaps there are things that we may not know that made them act in a hurry, especially since that giant bear that precedes them seems to have been sent by a responsible party to help them reach their goal quickly. Forgive me, father, but this is what I concluded without being hArchie in judging them without knowledge."

Clementine heard the conversation that took place between the girl and her father until she smiled on her face silent, but she did not pay him any attention until his face shrank from disappointment.

The girl had a good opinion of them, unlike her father, who added with great pride, saying, "You do not know much of what is happening around you, my daughter, that many rich people take advantage of their position and reputation at such times to spend their needs at the expense of others."

The girl replied to her father with genius and said, "But what is the important need that made us come here, father? Is watching these poor creatures brutally killing each other something worth standing for?"

Her father was stunned and her mother's face turned red in shame and embarrassment, so they could not answer her!

Then she continued, "If they have the right to break this queue and do whatever they want, the whole thing is shameful, and therefore all those rules, ethics and principles that you talk about fall when our presence here basically has no moral or human principle!

"You were angered by their lack of commitment to standing in line and you do not know what their reasons are, but you did not get angry for yourself and you want to watch the principles as they kill and slaughter each other in front of your eyes just for fun!"

The father could not keep up with his daring daughter and bowed his head in sweat after they were eaten by all the eyes around them and he is exposed to this humiliating amount of embarrassment from his daughter. He whispered to his wife to leave until they were already leaving after his conscience woke up at the last moments.

As for Clementine, he was impressed by the girl's physiognomy and the depth of her thinking, as he left his colleagues and followed her until she and her parents stopped her and said to her boldly, "If the matter were in my hands and the days turned around and I found you again in front of me, girl, I would choose you as my wife!"

She blushed and didn't know where Bog was going when Clemento surprised her with his feelings until the chrysanthemum rose became very red amid her parents' astonishment until he said to them politely, "Pardon me, parents, what your daughter said should be written in gold. For a girl to say these words, this indicates your rare manners and intellect, and the good upbringing of your parents who mistreated us and considered us to be rubbish. If we know what we are going through, we would be excused!"

The girl was very happy, but her mother bit her face and turned to her father and said, "I saw them, I told you that we must excuse them."

Clementine bowed down to introduce himself, "My name is Clementine, I came here with my friends on an urgent matter and I was pleased to meet you. A beautiful name, Clementine, and my name is Lisbeth. What a wonderful name. Until the voice and the name rang in Archie's ear and disturbed him from the strength of memory?"

And when Archie turned to the girl and the first time, he laid eyes on the necklace she was wearing on her neck?

It almost flew by the beauty of the surprise! It is the girl who was attached to their luxury carriage pulled by six horses when he got lost in his journey at the beginning, and opened for him a bag that contained the boxes of biscuits that were in the back of the cart and she was wearing the same necklace of the unknown girl who kidnapped her from her in the village and she was in the end what was only Maya's necklace? And the women or who is supposed to be her mother was Charlotte's aunt, Catherine?

But she did not recognise Archie, because she got married when he was seven years old and left the village and has not returned since then, but Archie recognised her from a birthmark on her neck, so this girl is Charlotte's cousin?

It was a coincidence that never crossed his heart until he passed by her without anyone noticing, and while her father was leaving, Archie whispered to her in her ear, thank you for the box of sweet biscuits, Elizabeth, and by the way, the necklace is beautiful on your pure chest.

And when she turned around to see who was the speaker, Archie was holding Clemento's hand and dragging him and whispering in his ear, "Either you follow us, or else you will never see another girl in your life!"

The girl says, "Hey who are you? And signs of admiration and amazement on her face!"

Archie looked at her half-showingly and smiled without uttering a word!

Gongora cleverly asked the guard and said, "It seems the king won't come tonight!"

The guard said surprised, "Who told you this? Rather, on the way here?"

Gongora said, "Sorry, I did not mean the king, but I meant another person, and I slipped my tongue because of the pressure, the intense preparations for the king's arrival."

Then Gongora persuaded the guard to enter after he made him see the boys' shoes and whispered in the guard's ear, "They are the sons of the queen's sister, and the king does not want anyone to know about them so that they are safe."

The door in front of them leads directly to the top of the amphitheatre, where there is the hall of the king and the dignitaries, and then directly in front of it, after five stands, facing down, an emergency exit and at the same time leading to the lower floors of the aquarium building, specifically to the headquarters of the predators that will perform the fighting shows for this day.

"Now wait, the queen and her family will come, they will all be watching over them, and it will be our chance to go down to the emergency exit after we go up to the main cabin with them," said Gongora.

Suddenly, there was a great commotion. Gongora said, "Oh, how fast is destiny, that's the queen and her family!"

Where it was surrounded by tight security guards and everyone stood to salute their queen.

"Now, now, follow me," said Gongora, in a decisive tone. "And they ran like reptiles towards the emergency exit until they hid in the corridors of the aquarium, which seemed very strange and remote, contrary to what it seemed to suggest, and far from their expectations."

Clementine says, after affixing his back to the wall from fear, "Oh, dog it, what a difference between the appearance of the aquarium and what is behind its decorated walls."

Charlie said to him, mocking him, "Do your shoes look like the bottom?"

Clementine said, "I wonder, O wise one, and I did not ask for an explanation from you!"

Charlie continued to provoke Clementine and said quarrelsomely, "We also did not ask you to ask."

Charlie laughed and replied cheerfully, "It seems that that girl has taken your mind and started talking to yourself a lot."

Clementine looked at him sharply and said, "It seems that jealousy will blind your heart. It is none of my business if you are ugly, Charlie, and you never find a girl in your life to talk to you."

Unfamiliar clattering interrupted them, until Gongora stopped walking and waved, "Shut up, teens!"

Then he looked at them and said firmly, advising, "No matter what frightening sounds you hear, remember well that nothing will reach you because the place is very secure, but I cannot hide from you that you may get some dread."

Alexander whispered, "I don't think so!"

Archie answered in a more whispered voice, "Neither am I, as long as we are with the brave Gongora, we are safe."

Gongora says, "Let's see if you are brave! Then they continued walking with unsure steps through the corridors that seemed to be short of breath, and the hands of this place were slowly suffocating them."

The walls shook again, but this time with the sound of a terrifying and frightening roar of a group of lions, with a great echo, as if the sound was coming out of the spaces in the walls that surrounded them.

Until they crouched on their knees on the ground in fright, Gongora said after his worried face faded, "Where is your confidence that you bragged about, a little while ago? If you continue like this, I suggest you go back to wait for your disastrous fate, and I will continue on my own if you do not have any confidence in my words!"

Archie sighed of relief when he realised that there was indeed no danger to them, but the soul was still tense from the inside, knowing that there was something unpleasant they would face, but he did not know what his form would be and how far fear might reach them!

Until Luca said in frustration, "How long will we be from fear to fear greater than him? He has given up since now."

Alex rebuked Luca, "We fled with knowledge, knowledge, strength and courage, and we did not flee from humiliation, and we were not terrified by the tyranny of everyone we encountered, and we were not frightened by the fluctuations of the events of the day and night. So, stop complaining, all of us, for what we are in is a temporary pang for the birth of our new life full of all your dreams."

Archie asked, "How long will these lanterns continue to light, Gongora?"

The bear's response was not comforting when he said, "This will be the last lantern you will see here. We will continue the rest of the way in the dark. All you have to do is follow each other's breaths until we reach," he said.

Alexander with a confused face, "Are you really what you're saying, or are you mocking us?" The bear stared at him sarcastically, then turned and continued, and said, "See for yourself."

Everyone looked at a place they had not thought, and behold, in the dark, he stood right in front of them, as if he were the guard of the place, who had come to perform his mission.

The terrifying roars fell silent, and Gongora whispered, "The lanterns and saddles are extinguished to the end of this fortified trench because this is where the black lions, which derive their energy only from darkness and can only live in the light for a very short time, their genes are hybrids and derive their energy from the coldness of darkness that absorbs energy." He turns it into an inner force that turns it into a mass of pure evil.

After a period of time, the hanging lamps are lit against each prison to curb their growing power. If they remain in the dark for a long time, unless they are exposed to light or sunlight for a period of time, they will surely die.

Martin grabbed Alexander's shirt from behind and pulled him hard, shivering from head to toe, "I don't see anything I don't see anything I want to get out of here now quickly get me out?"

Alexander turned and put his hand on Martin's mouth and said to him in a low voice, "Shut up, you coward, you are going to scare us all."

Gongora said, "Walk behind me in a row, and don't pay attention to any sound you hear if you want safety." And when they went further into the corridors of the aquarium, they seemed to have gone too deep, and the walk had taken them long in the lonely darkness, until all of them were surprised by a thick voice laughing maliciously around them, then quickly fell silent?

They froze in their place and no one was able to move, thinking that there was a strange creature in their midst in this darkness.

When they heard the sound of exhaling hot air, it left no face but slapped him.

Until it seemed to them that what they were afraid of, and the majestic voice of fear spoke to them behind their ears, and it was enough to make them urinate in their pants and said mockingly, "It seems that my food for the first time in a long time will be human meat and I think it is very soft this time, but I also smell the smell of a wild animal among them Do you think Is this a gift from the king? Or is it another bribe?"

This was the voice of the lion Radenback, the leader of the black lions, and a legend engraved in one of the immortal novels, but this time he addresses them from behind them directly and not in the lines of a novel!

And between them were separated by very strong iron barriers and the killer of Gongora's father, Gongora answered bravely, "Not this time, Radenback, they are the sons of men who made you their slave and those with you and do whatever they desire and you are servile because you are only a servant, contrary to what your outward appearance suggests!"

"Oh, that sound sounds familiar to me!" Radenback answered coldly. "Let me guess. Ummm... you are Gongora, son of Nayzak!"

This provoked Gongora, and he felt that someone had lit a fire in him from the inside, which he must put out quickly before she eats him from the severity of the pain.

Radenback continued his intended disdain, and his eyes gleamed slyly, "Oh, poor Gongora, I saw that tone on your father's face when I pounced on him as he hid behind a tree like a frightened little chimpanzee with a sack of rats in his hand. I enjoyed tearing him up and hearing his screaming repeat under me. 'Save me, save me, ha-ha-ha-ha-ha-ha-ha-ha.' It was a very good moment, though your father's flesh was stinky and I'd like to repeat it with you, Gongora, so look at yourself I've become like a fat ram, even much bigger. Then he laughed even more lightly."

The lion continued his frightening speech:

But not before I taste some of what you brought with you, Archie put his hand on Gongora's shoulder and pulled his hair hard and whispered to him, "It's Gongora's trap, don't bow to your anger, and that's what this monster wants. Humiliate his pride with silence and disregard, and he will eat himself as a bundle of anger."

Well done, Archie, Gongora almost lost his nerve and attacked the iron barriers separating him from the bully lion, then moved away a little and then said angrily as he moved forward, "Come on, guys, we have a job to do."

Archie felt as if his little wolf HArchieey was sniffing his clothes behind him, so he was curious at the same time to see what this Radenback looked like until he pulled a socket from his pocket and a piece of cloth and tried several times until it caught fire and revealed to them the cover of darkness that was hiding under the face of that terrifying predator who showed great anger. When he lit up the place and revealed the features of his fearsome face, he launched an imaginary attack on Archie from behind the iron bars, to slay them with his very huge size, those two sinister sunken yellow eyes, and the density of his hair different from the rest of the lions.

They fell to the ground stumbling from the severity of his fear, which angered Gongora, who in turn also launched a very fierce counterattack on Radenback from behind the walls to restore the same fear to him, but who had no effect on that lion.

The two met face to face, separated only by these thick bars. Gongora's eyes were piercing Radenback, but Radenback gaze had more energy and force that subdued Gongora's wrath as he looked into Radenback eyes higher than him.

Until Gongora moved away a little after he felt Radenback super power charges burn his skin from its heat, and the boys were astonished by the size difference between them.

"May the gods have mercy on us," cried Sebastian, "What a beast!"

Gongora said, "I always see your head rolling in my dreams, and I knew that I could not have fought you one day, Radenback."

Radenback said sharply, "Then do it now, or you won't be able to, your mutant child!"

Archie said firmly, "You will not take your revenge as long as you live, Gongora, if you listen to this beast"

Radenback replied coldly and whispered to Archie, "What a beautiful voice, boy. I long to meet you in private, so that we can have a conversation and enjoy the sweetness of your vocal cords as if they were a royal harp on the day of eternity."

There was a long silence, then said Archie, to prevent any feeling from Radenback from appearing, "Radenback promises you that we will meet and there will be no barrier between us, and I will play that royal guitar for you in the tunes you wanted."

They all went away, having failed the beast Radenback, to shake and defeat them inwardly, until he let out his fierce rage and roared loudly with the utmost of his power, until the place roared with a voice like no earth had before.

Until they hurried, thinking that he would come out from behind the barriers after the earth shook from under their feet and the rocks of the walls shook, which shook dust from between their folds.

Until the rest of the other lions in their cages echoed the same pace as their leader's roar, declaring their loyalty to him.

"Boy, I promise you, my voice will be the last you will hear in your life," said Radenback, with his eyes sparkling with evil audibly.

Then he let out an evil laugh that frightened the rest of the lions, and their voices subsided and cooled the heat of his burning heart.

And as soon as they reached a crossroads with a number of entrances and exits before the end of the dark corridor, the bear stopped and stood on his feet and stuck his ear to the wall and was hitting the wall with his hand and continued like this until he said eagerly, I found her!

Alexander said what did you find! The bear pushed one of the wall's rocks inward in the belly of the wall until they heard a sharp creaking sound, and a piece of marble below them moved as if the elves had opened the door to the secrets of the place to reveal to them an opening that they did not know of features, because it was part of the ground on which they walked.

Until it became like a hole created out of nothing without introductions, it was the size of a door with two sections that did not see what was inside!

Gongora walked into her dark interior silently, then suddenly the place below lit up with a lamp, then he waved for them to follow him until Martin came forward with curiosity, but slipped and rolled like a ball until he bumped into Gongora, who tried to muffle his laughter.

Then he said, "We were too late before the guards came here in order to open the prisons of the executioners?"

Archie says, "Executioners? And the gladiators?" The bear said, "Do not ask about every word, because you will soon see everything your ear hears with your eyes."

And when they reached the bottom end of the aquarium, it was an open space as if it was a large rectangular room surrounded by large cages that stuck to all sides in the room, the number of which exceeded eighty cages.

However, Gongora knew what was inside, in fact, the cages were the prisons in which all the fighting animals were placed, and they were the sons of the skin of Gongora, including his younger brother, until he ran faster and with high concentration towards the cages and called, "Ganthum, Ganthum."

The eyes of the bear rolled between the cages as he called eagerly for his brother Ganthum, until Alex said, expressing his astonishment at the bear's behaviour, "I fear for this bear that he has gone crazy?"

Clementine replied, "It is longing, my brother. What a poor thing. I hope he finds his brother, but it seems that they are too late."

A sad voice called him from a prison, and there was the voice of one of the white bears fighting in the arena of the aquarium, saying, "They took him a little while ago, Gongora. I am sorry to tell you that it is too late."

They took Ganthum to fight with my brother, Spartex, then the bear wept from worry and helplessness, and what would happen to his brothers who were forced to kill each other.

Then Gongora went crazy, his face turned pale, and he started spinning around, not knowing what to do?

He repeats in confusion, "Impossible, impossible, no, that's not true, no, no, they didn't go."

The bear said to Gongora, "It's the truth, my friend. We lost them forever. They will fight to the death like we lost our brothers before."

Archie felt his stomach cramp as he saw Gongora's condition after they learned of the disaster that had befallen him.

The nervous bear could not comprehend the idea that he would lose the only remaining brother of his family, which was torn apart by the oppression of their village by King Prakshim and his soldiers.

Archie heard quick footsteps coming from the top of the stairs they came down from and knew that the soldiers had found out about them.

And he said to his friends, "It seems that he has revealed our matter," then he issued an order to prepare to clash with the coming soldiers and said, "Come on, let all three of us stand on the edge of the entrance, and when they enter, we will attack them!" Before Archie finished speaking, two soldiers had already entered and they said violently, while raising their weapons, "All surrender, you thieve, we have been watching you well!"

Before he finished his sentence, Archie shouted loudly, "Attacking!" until the two men were distracted and confused as they watched these boys pounce on them like hyena's pounce on their prey without leaving any room for them to catch their breath. The two soldiers did not expect this quick response until they found themselves submissive and easily by Archie and his comrades and stripped of their much-needed weapons.

Then Archie turned to Gongora and shouted loudly, "Your brother is waiting for you, Gongora, it is still too early for the crowds to raise their voices so far, and this is the proof that your brother and his companion are still alive. Supposed to the ring from the inside the approximate number of soldiers and their locations so that we can avoid the arrows of snipers!"

The anxiety from Gongora's face suddenly melted away, as a clove of salt melted and intensified, and he smiled after a long sadness, and his ears rose up after that enthusiastic paragraph, he cast a spell on the defeated bear from the horror of the catastrophe after the rapid dramatic change that made them an advantage in attack, as they now possess the element of surprise, even if it is temporary.

As Archie and his companions became more prepared after fate handed them the appropriate tools for this particular operation, as if fate did not work unless you acted on the causes, then it would do the rest.

Among the weapons they looted were two swords, two long, medium-sized daggers, and four bows, with four bundles of arrows, which they shared among themselves, and in the twinkling of an eye they became an unarmed soldier until a broad smile broke the face of the bear.

He said hastily with his plan, "First, we will open the cages of the bears, and then some of them will climb to the top to get out from where we entered until they reach the stands, which will be filled with a large number of attendees. Where security guards abound there, and we will have killed two birds with one stone."

Thus, the bears' exit to the surface will cause great panic among the attendees, which will distract the focus of the snipers and the rest of the guards who were dedicated to monitoring the aquarium circuit.

Then the alarm will sound, and chaos will reign, and we will have our chance to save my brother and his friend Spartex. As for me and the bear (Kodiak) we will launch a sudden, sweeping attack on the guards of the main gate, without any mercy and without stopping. On all the soldiers who were placed inside the arena itself, which is surprise and speed.

This will save us time and of course my brother Ganthum and Spartex will have either started fighting among themselves in the ring or they haven't started yet and I hope that they have not killed each other and that our work is in vain!

Gongora continues his urgent plan, "After we break into the main gate (Kodiak and I), the snipers from above will be surprised by our presence on the battlefield, distracting their focus for a while due to the noise, hustle and screams in the stands.

"Then you will go out and shoot arrows at the sniper. After you leave the gate, you must count ten meters, then turn back over the gate. Four snipers will be at the top and their focus will be misplaced, and here it will be easy for you to target them easily.

"As for the other snipers, they are far away, and their arrows will not be able to reach us unless we approach the gates that are located below the VIP amphitheatre."

Archie interrupts him as he heads to open the cages to get Kodiak and the rest of the bears out. Gongora says, "No, it would be no more dangerous for them to climb above the arena than to cross the arena, because their exit from the gate at the top would cause great chaos in the stands where the queen is, and this will distract us from our presence in the arena, and it will be a cover for us and them as well, because after we penetrate the arena and liberate all the bears, the soldiers will follow us from the same gate and also from above they will try to close the gate thinking that we will get out of it. This will give us and the other bears time and space to escape as far as possible."

Alexander says, wondering, "But how will we meet them when they will leave one place and we are from another? We all know the size of this building!" Archie murmured and said, "Don't put the cart in front of the horses, Alex, because in this way you will frustrate yourself and those with you. We must focus on the main task, which is to rescue Ganthum, Spartans, and those with them, so that they can have our back. If we think about the obstacles and how to get rid of

them, or how difficult they are, we will not move forward one step."

Gongora answered Alexander and said, "Don't worry, I didn't lose sight of this, and now I will tell them where the meeting will be, and it will be a semi-

safe place for a while until we meet again."

And we arrange ourselves in it to continue Archie together, at a steady

pace, because I know that we will run a run that we have not run in our lives before.

Then he turned his face to the remaining bear, and they were ten bears remaining among the eighty bears who died in the battles of the aquarium, and he advised them, "Our sudden entry into the arena is the most powerful weapon we have now. My father will meet soon, I promise you friends, now let's move and go to freedom, and we are waiting for the screams and wails of these fools. Let's do our part to save Ganthum and Spartex."

Not a few quick minutes passed after the liberated bears set out for the exit gate at the top, until they heard alarm bells ringing from the top of the aquarium building. The exit from which the bears came out and spread terror and terrorised everyone who had a soul.

Gongora said the bears did it... Archie said eagerly with a bow in his hand, "I will climb on Gongora's back and the others will be behind Kodiak who will pave the way for you after storming the gate of the plaza and you will protect his back."

And as soon as they set out, Gongora took off the door of the main plaza, and he saw nothing between his eyes except his brother. The first thing they met in front of them were three guards who were astounded by the rebel bear with one slap of his hand that was enough to shut them up forever.

As for Archie, he was sitting on Gongora's back in the opposite direction to the bear's head.

He turns his eyes like a hawk to catch snipers above, when they spot Gongora penetrating the arena, Archie stuns them before they let out their arrows until they fall dead from above.

At the same time, the conflict between Ganthum and Spartex had begun, and they were forced to wear armour with iron thorns in order to shed as much blood as possible between the wrestlers to excite the public thirsty for this sadistic pleasure.

Gongora roared angry when he saw his brother and his friend fighting, "Stop you idiots, it's your chance now to escape forever from this kingdom of criminals and its people. Follow us and don't ask about anything else the arrows of the guard will pierce your skulls and you will die like two stray dogs."

Then Archie said, "We will return now from the same place to reach another corridor, but outside the arena before the soldiers open the doors of the black lions' rooms, or else our end will be inevitable because we can't fight Radenback alone, so how can he lead a whole squad?"

Meanwhile, the other bears had succeeded in getting out of the darkness and oppression of the aquarium to the sun of freedom for the first time in years of slavery. No one likes chains, even if they are of gold.

After the chaos that they left behind them and made the stands as a battlefield, in which they are the victors, all those crowds poured out all their anger on poor organisation and poor security.

Until the corners of the stands erupted with cheers and shouts of anger at the police and guards, as if they were the ones who released these monsters to wreak havoc on lives.

Some of them even threw their shoes and spit on them, complaining about this catastrophic failure to protect them and their queen before the arrival of the king, and this will make the matter worse.

As soon as Gongora and the boys crossed the place of residence of Radenback and the other lions, they did not realise something dangerous, for they were lost by the darkness of the place and the danger of what they did to snatch the bite from the fangs of the hungry lion.

Isn't Archie sure for a moment that there is an unjustified calm and silence in the black area at all at a time like this in particular! "It's scary," Archie said.

This time they did not ascend to the secret gate through which they entered, but went to reverse direction to another gate that leads to the main vaults of the aquarium below, where the stores of oil and gunpowder are, said Alexander, "I have never walked in my life in such darkness, without kindness or caution as I am now!"

Gongora answered him, his breath racing, racing his steps, "Do not be afraid with me, boy."

Clementine said thinking after they saw the dim light of the stores, "It was the same wine barrels that were in the palace stores when my father took me there!"

"It is, boy," said Gongora hurriedly, "But these barrels hold wine of a very fine quality. It is the poisoned wine that the most evil of creatures will soon gulp down."

Suddenly, a loud roar sounded, as if right behind their backs, as if they were uttering all kinds of insults, the worst of all. Followed by the sounds of a collective roar chilling!

At these moments, Archie realises that Radenback and his companions have been released until he is fed up with himself and feels as if a mountain has fallen on him.

Because there is no other place for him and those with him to go than under the ring after the bears closed the door leading to the upper lane, in other words, they became a target within Radenback's reach!

"Sounds like that's Radenback's voice?" The Bear Ganthum said, frightened.

Archie answered, "Yes, it is he, and it seems that he has been released, and it is impossible if we do not find what we can protect ourselves with, Gongora!"

"It seems that I will taste the torment twice in this miserable place," said Spartex in frustration.

Gongora's mouth exploded with angry words at Spartex, and he reproached him with anger, "Perhaps we are fools, Spartex. If we had not come, you would have rotted in your blood in the middle of the aquarium, and the people around you laughing, groaning, and disgusting at the sight of your stinking carcass. If you want to die, we will never dissuade you."

Then he went to a group of barrels filled with oil that had been placed at the end of the hallway, and next to it were a group of boxes filled with Bardot mixed with a chemical substance to have a powerful explosive power, and a barrier of ropes separated them.

Then Gongora pointed to Archie and Alex, "You two light as many caps as possible at the end of the ropes, the rest of you have to roll the drums so that they are in a long line, and we will light the gunpowder drums and put each next to each oil drum to the entrance of the warehouse after we spill one of the oil drums to cover the entire floor of the store!

"The plan was to detonate the entire place the moment the lions entered, which will be a great trap if the plan succeeds. The bottom, and the quantity was sufficient to pass around the corridors of the arena at least twice, and as soon as he finished discharging the explosive gunpowder."

So, he said, "Come on, run through that door, which leads straight out of the aquarium." Gongora turned to them, and they were all staring at him like they were stupid idols!

Did they not understand? He said, astonished by their looks, "Why do you look at me like that, you idiots? I told you to run and not to look back, and if you ignore the roars and everything that goes on behind you, you have won."

His brother Ganthum replied, "I will not move without you. Gongora either sit with you or you go with us?"

"Who told you that I'm going to sit down?" Gongora said furiously. My concern is that I must preserve your lives, as I am the one who started this matter and I am the one who will end it now.

A violent voice shouted from above, with rapid and earth-shattering steps, which fell from its trembling between the walls and some barrels rolled, "Gongoraaaaaaaaaa!" I promised you that I would taste your blood like I tasted your father's blood before!" Then followed by her malicious laughter carrying all evil.

Gongora raised his head confidently and said softly, "I am waiting for you, my dear."

Alexander shouted at him, "No, Gongora, please light the fuse and go with us, this is not the time to settle scores remember your sister and brother and they need you the most!"

After understanding what Gongora was thinking, Archie said wisely, "Don't argue with him, Alexander, we'll waste our time. Gongora knows what he's doing. It's his battle, and I'm sure he'll catch up with us soon after he does what he wants!"

And now they ran away without looking back, and they all slipped away, not looking behind them through the door until they found themselves outside the aquarium for the first time since they first entered it until they found themselves in front of a semi-deserted garden with only a few trees and some chairs that broke some of their legs and covered with algae.

As for Gongora, he lit the fuse of his farewell wine when he watched Radenback's error slip slowly from the threshold of the storeroom door until the grooves of the pits were filled with oil, and they ran like a river flowing with force in all the galleries of the aquarium, bearing with it the spectre of death and people in heedless people.

Gongora's heart was so heavy that the death knell surrounded him on every side until Radenback peeked out at his huge and majestic head until his bright eyes rolled and Gongora's reflection passed through them when the fire caught on, and there was a long silence except for the sound of the crawling flames until the bear said with a yellow smile, "Good evening, you bastards!"

Then he threw the last wick in his hand into the ground filled with exploding oil, and lightly and quickly jumped aside to the door to run behind the boy.

When Radenback's eyes shone with the fire of a great explosion, she flung him into the road from which she came, to fall on top of those behind him.

The roof is collapsing more than he expected.

The roof collapsed under the building in a catastrophic manner, as if it were dynamo stones, and Gongora quickly moved away before being crushed under the walls of the outer building, which was heralding the beginning of the end of one of the chapters of the novel Injustice Does Not Continue.

The crackling of the sky with frightening sounds, and there was nothing but the sound of the corners of the arena falling apart in a breath-taking scene. The explosions that still occur in all corners and pillars of the aquarium, whose explosions shook the happy kingdom and turned the glorious day of celebration on them to what will become the day of great disgrace.

That edifice, which was a pride for the history and present of the kingdom of the dwarves in the architectural, cultural and sports art for them, and it represented a slaughterhouse and an altar for bloodshed for the other category of the original inhabitants of the kingdom, who are mutated into bears.

But the justice of heaven refused, except to break the back of every mighty and arrogant person on earth, and to serve as an example to others if they were bitten.

And here is the great edifice collapsing in front of everyone's eyes and on those in it of the criminal soldiers and some groups of people with hardened hearts.

But wonder what happened to the family of King Prakshim? Did she die in the collapse that they fled before that and survived?

The news reached all parts of the kingdom, and it did not leave the ear of a creature except and entered it against his nose, until King Prakshim went crazy and descended from his throne while he was barefoot, as it was his habit that if he sat on the throne, he took off his sandals.

But for the horror of the catastrophe that is occurring for the first time in his kingdom, in addition to the mystery surrounding the situation of his wife and children, he was running and the guards and advisers were running behind him, not knowing what to do to remedy the tragic situation.

Clementine said, his teeth chattered from the cold, "Although we survived that ordeal, we were in great warmth."

"Oh, man," said Spartex murmured, "I'm ready to die of cold than to be a slave in the most beautiful and warmest place."

Gongora said, "We've come halfway, guys. I see the moment of our liberation has come."

They strengthened their resolve and did not insult them.

Archie says, "You seem to be thinking like I am, we have escaped from a hornet's nest!"

Charlie says mockingly, "Share with us this idea that you discovered in the midst of this huge devastation we have caused!"

Bear Ganthum agreed to Charlie's words and said, "I don't know what you have come up with, but I know for sure that there is a huge army that will come out to search for us in various ways and they will get rid of us in the most horrific way possible."

Spartex said, "What I fear is that all this effort will be wasted if we are caught unless we move and flee quickly instead of talking and petty arguments."

Then Kodiak says, sulking, "What I really fear is not all of this, but that Radenback will be alive, although I doubt that, but whatever the outcome, you must show us your next step instead of watching that destruction as if you were those foolish tourists watching everything!"

Gongora said, "Everything you said is true and everything you assumed may be true, but there is a promise I made to myself to Archie and his companions, the goal and destiny are the same. Just as we seek freedom and salvation, they also seek the same thing."

Then he directs his words to Archie and says to him, "My friend, Archie, you know that my brothers did not know your story, and they also do not know that if you and your friends were not here, we would not have done this thing of saving my brothers and ridding them of what they are in."

Then he turns to his brother Ganthum and their friends, Spartex and Kodiak, and says to them, explaining, "You do not know what I know. This boy has great merit in what you are in now. Therefore, we must return the debt to him. He rescued and liberated us from slavery. Is to head to the dragon tree to meet the rest of the bears and going to the palace, which will be the lightest guards after the aquarium incident, which will draw the eyes towards it, and it will be our chance to recover the magic jug!"

Kodiak said in a stifled voice, "The magic jug! Are you crazy, Gongora! It is in the king's palace, specifically at the top of the throne, and whoever thinks of reaching there is a madman or a suicide, and you know that armies will be mobilised in order to find us. Instead of thinking of escaping out of the kingdom, you want us to go back to the lion's den again?

"Gongora says you are right, but I don't think there is anything that will surpass Archie's ability to analyse, think and deduce to find his line. As for getting inside the palace, it will be my job that one of the leaders in the palace wishes this opportunity more than any other creature to take revenge on the king who left no one he loved, and he is to run the palace guard squad and will not hesitate to help us!"

Kodiak asked, "But everyone in the arena saw you, and the news must have reached the king, and that all the guards knew about your storming of the arena?" "Don't worry about this, Kodiak," said Gongora confidently. "I can make them lose their focus with my shyness and my tongue, because I was the one

who was carrying out many secret missions outside the palace!"

Archie murmured, surprised, "Secret missions?"

The bear was silent a little embarrassed, Archie realised that Gongora was an

accomplice in some of the crimes that the king might have committed against his people secretly, but it was not the right time for research, questions and investigations that might negatively affect their way towards their goal that brought them together.

Ganthum said to his brother, "It seems that there are many things you have been doing, my brother, and I am afraid that there will be nothing wrong with us hearing them!"

Gongora replies, "This is not an important matter now. The past will not return. We are the children of this moment, and we are not the children of yesterday. Every event has a recent conversation, and our talk now is freedom, only to have no voice louder than that voice now. Come on, go to the place that no one will think of visiting. Go to the ruins of the arena from the side of the gate we came out of, because eyes will be around the main gate in order to search for the queen and her children, if they have not survived. But now I will go and come back as soon as I can to complete the trip."

Archie's heart broke and he felt his stomach contract so hard when he learned that there were children who might have died in the collapse of the battlefield, and they were not responsible but that they were accompanying their parents only until they bite his face and paint in all the colours of the spectrum, and he imagines that they are his brothers, mother, father, Charlotte and everyone dear to him. They were crushed by those mountain-like walls.

Destruction and nothing but destruction? The king was angrily repeating those words, his teeth grinding each other out of the tragedy of loss.

After his men and senior commanders, including a man named Edward, who is the commander of the Special Palace Corps, entrusted with all the special tasks that come out from under the fingers of the king personally, gathered his men and senior leaders.

King Prakshim appeared for the first time, sad and severely broken, and said sadly in a low, trembling voice, "It has hurt me so much, just as all the inhabitants of our precious kingdom suffered from all of us what happened in the aquarium and how it was destroyed."

Then he was silent for a while and leaned his hands on his staff after placing it directly in front of him and added in a stifled voice, "Until now, I do not know what happened to my wife and children, but I still have hope of finding them, because I know that the gods will protect them just as I have preserved this kingdom from the futility of the abusers and made it a beacon of light among the nations that will not be oppressed. Someone and that what happened would not have happened except by the action of an evil doer who does not like good for anyone, and this would not have happened without the failure to perform the tasks and that whoever made a mistake must be punished, but this is not what you agreed on, but because you know that there is an enemy in his heart, a disease that roams and roams the city.

"And that if he is not caught within the next hours, I will not hesitate to tie you all by your feet and hands to two elephants and then order them to part to cut your bodies to pieces in front of everyone to be a reminder.

"Others will be crushed under the feet of elephants alive, and some will be thrown to food for the black lions, which I don't think are alive, but if so, this is no more a threat than a reminder of the punishments for complacency in the security of the kingdom.

"And I will never be lenient in this matter. I did not appoint you here in order for you to stand before me like helpless women. As for the person responsible for penetrating and stabbing our backs with such a crime, he will suffer a painful punishment from me."

The trumpeters came forward, announcing the start of the military campaign that the king would lead himself against those who were accused of the acts of violence and terror that took place in the aquarium, and he said threateningly and threateningly in a loud voice, "I myself will clean the kingdom of everyone I

suspect, even if he is innocent, I will order his crush, I will not let anyone today in this kingdom or outside it, but he will know and hear about my doing this to be a warning that reaches their ears and eyes that they will die of fear and everyone who thinks after them of betraying us again, or hides any information about any spy or mercenary hired!"

Indeed, King Prakshim and the guards around him are equipped with huge mammoth elephants and the armoured carts they pull. This time, chariots of a different type than the ones used in the missions of observation or reception. It was a terrifying battalion for everyone who saw it. It was the King Prakshim battalion. This battalion, if it moved, would not return unless bloodshed in the roads of the kingdom, and this matter was deliberately happening, so the king resorted to these brutal and barbaric methods to terrorise everyone who opposes him, and he did it several times.

And it caused a catastrophe on the roads of the kingdom, where many innocents died as a result of the running of those elephants and the carts that were drawn with serrated arms, that were cutting everybody they collided with in half for no reason just because the king was angry?

What a tragedy that the sons of this kingdom have lived through and are still living through, completely bound by the chains of oppression and terrorism.

Commander Edward knew that a massacre would happen after he saw the king's eyes devoid of any mercy or tenderness, but he had no choice but to pray and hope that nothing happens to anyone.

After a long wait, more than waiting for rain on hot summer days, which may not come most of the time, Gongora and those with him met the rest of the bears at the dragon tree that they had agreed upon. The site was three kilometres closer to the palace than to the aquarium, until they saw the military crowd leaving the palace until Gongora learned it is the king's personal legion of elephant shields, which indicates that this day is a difficult day that will not end except with a massacre, the extent of its horror!

Gongora said with great eagerness, "I did not expect the king to come out with all his personal strength under the leadership of the palace corps, the presence of the queen and her sons in the destroyed fighting runway must have made him go out of his way and that the palace in this case will have many loopholes. He acts on behalf of the king in such cases, if there is no change, then this will be in our best interest."

When our interests and Guard have intersected in the king's palace and this opportunity will not be repeated every day, not even every year.

When they seized the opportunity, which was rarer than the most precious metals in their eyes, and at this time in particular, and headed to the palace, Gongora said, "We will now launch the most important stage, which is the stage of decisiveness and escape.

"We have a will of iron, so listen carefully, now we will split into two parts, I and the rest of the Bears, and you, Archie and your comrades, and Ganthum and Spartex will be with you as strong support for any emergency."

"But until now you haven't told us about the plan?" said Archie, recalling.

Gongora said, "How curious you are. I wanted to say it, but you prompted me to ask your question as often."

Alexander said with a laugh: "It's Archie Gongora who won't leave you until he analyses every word you say."

Archie said, "Right, I remembered the sword! King Gabriel's sword."

Clementine hit his forehead in exasperation. Oh heavens, how did we miss this?"

Gongora replied sharply, "Everything will happen as you planned. Just listen quickly. Stop wasting time. Trouble getting us in, and then rushing like the wind to your suite to notice the sword, and the boys and I will be waiting for you, pretending its lunchtime for the guests."

Then he mumbled, "Of course, there will be no lunch and no time for food due to the state of emergency in the palace. This is another advantage in our favour, as there will be no doubt that we are the serpent that they themselves have brought into the rabbit's hole.

"As for the rest of the bears, they will not move from your place until you hear the horns of emergency. If you dare to try to enter by force, you will be eliminated before your feet cross the threshold of the palace door, and now we will pretend that we are panting from fatigue to tell them that we fled that terrible massacre that took place in the city."

Until the place is ready for us without there being any investigation, Archie said, "Let's do it if I'm excited about it."

When they entered the palace, Archie and his companions went to the pavilion to fetch the sword, but Gongora went to the office of Lord Edward, rushing with force, as if on a hunting mission in the wilderness, until the guards stopped him and said, pretending to be confused, that he had an urgent message from the king to the commander until he stormed the office of Commander Edward after he passed them in amazement and astonishment from Edward, who expected anyone but to enter Gongora!

And he was the one who spread the news that he was the one who broke into the arena and that he was considered one of the wanted traitors, then Edward pointed with his hand at the guards to leave and leave them alone and they didn't say a word. At the height of anxiety and tension due to the involvement of those who entered the office, who is considered the first suspect in the aquarium crime.

He whispered angrily, "Are you really the one who broke into the ring, Gongora?"

Gongora quickly replied with an outburst of anger, "Yes, I was the one who broke into the ring and I blew it up, and I was the cause of the downfall of the era of evil and injustice from this kingdom, so that the whole world could rest from this criminal forum that spilled the blood of my family for the sake of entertainment.

"But I didn't come to you to check with me, I came to ask you, Edward, that this was the opportunity that you told me would never come, and she came to your office herself!"

Edward was confused and stuttered and said with anxious eyes filled with doubt and bewilderment, "What chance are you talking about?" The bear explained the situation to him quickly until Edward understood the matter and threw his back on the chair and sat staring at himself and talking to her from behind his lips.

Gongora continues his talk and narrates the plan, "Our partners in this revolution will come in order to take the magic pitcher from the throne, which you will accompany, and I do not think that you will not have clients that you trust through your strong relationships here and trust you with full confidence as you trusted me to carry out some dirty missions for the king without anyone's knowledge!"

Then he winked at him with half an eye and said, "You are an inspiring and wise person and it is time to use your tools to implement our agenda, which is also yours. Guard, I will send someone to the main gate in order to ask permission to enter and the password will be (Archie) and when you will know that it is from us and here. You will change the soldiers and put other soldiers who you trust or owe allegiance to you and therefore the agent we will send will give us the signal to enter the palace. And here we will break into the throne room and seize the magic jug."

Edward said, "And how many are you?"

Gongora replied forcefully, "Enough to annihilate all of the king's guards left in this palace!"

Just help us to penetrate the throne room and leave the rest to us without you having any direct military intervention to support us and then we promise you that you will see the freedom for which we were created and to a world free of this sadistic Prakshim and his bloody regime that enslaved us for his lusts and made us mere puppets to die in order to one of their children laughs at us as we eat each other in the arenas.

Edward said in frustration, "My fate is now dependent on yours, and I am very confident that you will not disappoint Gongora. Otherwise, you will bear the guilt of my family, which will lose those who support it in this life and who protects it, if this man does not take revenge on them in Prakshim and his army. This man does not shy away from doing everything that does not occur to me." The heart of a human being is a hideous revenge method.

Gongora says confidently, "I did not come here to take you out of the world of misery to a world more wretched than it, and I see in your face the face of my brother, and I will see in the faces of all your family members, the glory of all my family, you have this promise, Edward, I will leave now and see you soon. Be ready, loyal fighter."

The bear returned outside the palace when the rest of the bears gathered and said, "It is time to rip the heart of evil from its roots. Commander Edward has agreed to join us and will be waiting for us as soon as possible to arrange entry into the palace, but Ganthum and Spartans must camouflage themselves in order to remove the suspicion from them." Everyone knew that there are bears fleeing throughout the kingdom, so we will not approach the palace gate unless we receive the signal from one of Edward's clients.

Less than a quarter of an hour later, a man in military clothes finally appeared with his banner waving as a sign to enter from the main gate and here Gongora and the rest of the bears set off until Gongora said to them, "You will be like guards here to protect our backs when we storm the throne room, and you will have less than half an hour or less if we do not come out."

From the throne room, set out on your own to the port. Follow this road, which will lead you directly to it, without deviating from it even an inch. You will find us there, otherwise we will come out for you here if we can, but I doubt that.

As soon as they arrived at the gate, those who were receiving them were from the guard's other than those who had been before, so Gongora understood that Edward had done his job to the fullest, and they headed to the headquarters of Commander Edward, where he was with two guards who brought with them several weapons of shields and arrows and said to them with great certainty, "These bows. They are your weapon here. They are very accurate bows with super light blades, but they are very strong and fast, with heads that have special diamond blades to give weight to the arrow to hit the target with greater accuracy. It was specially made only for the king's legion."

Then Edward said, "Now, tell me, Gongora, who you trust in his abilities and competence to be trusted to carry these special arrows and has the speed of shooting!"

He must carry two bows at once because the mistake will cost a lot, for I know the security guards of the throne room, no one shoots an arrow except that a soul flies to the sky, if there are no souls, these guards are not like any guards you may hear of in your life! Because they are well trained for this deadly task.

Gongora pondered the man's words well, then said in a calm tone, "I trust them all more than I trust myself, for these are the ones who insulted King Prakshim in his own home thanks to their intelligence and courage."

Edward interrupted him and said, "This is a foregone conclusion. But one of them must be better than the other, and this is self-evident in any group."

Gongora quickly said, "I recommend Archie, he did it a while ago and we left the aquarium with our skins safely thanks to his remarkable skill."

Edward looked at Archie with an admiring eye after contemplating his facial features well and said, "From the face of your face, I knew that you have a talent for something, and I don't think except that you will be a knight in the future and I hope so, but I do not guarantee that the world will seduce you and divert you from your path, my son, as it has seduced many young men! But not before we finish our battle first.

"Now you and I, Archie, we'll go forward, and you'll be just like my shadow and I will be the guide to reveal to you where the guards are stationed, and you, Gongora, and the bear will stay behind, and the rest of the boys are completely behind us to prevent any disaster. If we fail to hit the gate guard, we will have put ourselves in a mousetrap. Then you must put all your weight on your ears to

carry out every letter I say, and there is no excuse for anyone to delay in carrying out his mission. We are the ones who have the element of surprise. Whoever misses something of what I say does not blame but himself."

Seconds before they could move, there were quick steps and a voice shouting from afar, "Sir, Commander!"

It was one of Edward's agents warning in a broken voice until he stood in front of him and bent down and put his hands on his knees to take a deep breath, then raised his head a little and said with a broken breath, "Sir, the commander, the king and his soldiers are returning to the palace! I'm sure what you said!"

Yes, sir, it seems that someone has slandered us, otherwise the king could not return so quickly with that legion that accompanies him and the emergency mission for which they went!

It was really frightening news, and at a very inopportune time, until the eyes turned sullen, and Martin grumbled, holding a bow longer than himself, "We have come to death by ourselves. Save us, O God. I don't want to see that monster dig out my guts while I'm looking at it!"

Luca quarrelsomely said to him, "Guess that the lions like to start eating the ass of the prey first, until Clementine stops laughing and puts his hand to his mouth and walks away a little."

Then Archie, decisively, said, "In both cases, we are dead. If we retreat or leave, you have no choice but to run forward and follow me now. Come on, Edward, let's go as we planned."

As for the rest, they felt pity for themselves like sheep being led to the slaughterhouse until Gongora said silently.

"It was the sound of the feet of the soldiers coming from inside the throne room. And this will shorten us a lot. Now hide behind the corners of the columns and the hallway, and when they approach, kill them all without pity, so you do not know if someone catches you, your eyes will come out of your skull, they are criminal soldiers! Indeed, the soldiers approached and they were five carrying huge batons with them."

He did not finish talking until one of them saw them shocked and froze in place, seeing Commander Edward and the strangers around him, all of them carrying weapons?

He quickly understood that it was a betrayal of the leader, Edward, against the king, but before he retreated and screamed, a killer arrow in his neck from Archie killed him at once.

Until that dazzled Edward, and Gongora said to him, emphasising his previous words, "Didn't I tell you this, Edward?"

They ran towards the gate of the throne room after they jumped over the body of the soldier and Sebastian said in his hate, "I hope I don't see that their day comes to jump on our bodies!"

Alexander said sharply, "Why not, if we do not carry out the task with courage instead of words!"

The three bears, Gongora, his brother Ganthum, and their friend Spartex were a little late, and when Edward and Archie approached the huge gate to find it, it opened a little unusually, which aroused suspicion in Edward's soul until four guards surrounded them from behind, and Alex shouted, "It's a trap, it's a trap!"

No one was able to raise the arrows, for the guards were raising batons, waiting for the signal from their leader to destroy them with one blow, until one of the guards said sarcastically, "We were aware of your news, you traitor and thieves, as for you, you traitor commander, you will have a different kind of punishment!"

Edward said to them with a yellow smile, "Me too?" Then their eyes rolled at each other, thinking about his mockery of them while he was in this situation? Then they were silent for a moment, and one of them burst into laughter, followed by the others. Their leader did not complete his laughter until his skull was pierced by the fangs of Spartex and he smashed his head with one bite, as if he was eating a modern biscuit. As for Ganthum, the other guard was surprised

and his stomach gnawing until his intestines came out of it.

As for the others, Gongora crouched on them and took their lives with his

huge weight without having time to get the last word out before their souls were taken by force.

Guards said the Luxor Archieers to go forward.

So, he grabbed Luca, Martin, and Clementine, and said to them, "You, boy," meaning Alexander, "And you," pointing at Sebastian and Charlie, "Will be right behind them, but you three bears will go quickly to the edge of the wall. When we push the door hard, there will be a stairway to the north and right of the gate, which will frighten the shooters of no more than twenty and distract them and change their position then the shooters will advance and snipe them like you snipe birds.

"As for me and Archie with this great sword in his hand, as if I see him holding the key to victory, we will go straight to the throne where the magic jug is." Then

he turned to Gongora and said to him, "Come on, kick the door hard without breaking it to make a sound like a great explosion and then I will close it when we all enter so that we delay any possible support for the protectors of the throne."

Gongora slammed the door that slammed the wall of the hall hard and dropped some fine pottery pots that were shattered and Archie and all who were inside the throne hall became restless.

Until Gongora went to the stairs to the right of the door, and his brother Ganthum and Spartex went up the stairs to the north of the door and let out a very frightening roar and shout that confused all those guards at the top and lost control of themselves, so that the boys carrying the arrows quickly grab them from below and get rid of the sniper's obstacle. More than expected until Archie raised his sword high and shouted in a proud voice, "Here we are, O pitcher, and ascended the throne stairs with Edward, and his eyes did not leave the magic pitcher."

Edward told him, warning, but remember that he is tightly tight and tried not to break the pits from which the golden water comes out to all the gutters of the palace will become like a volcano erupting in our midst.

If he did not dissolve us while we were alive, Archie did not realise that danger, and he believed that the jug had been installed on the throne like a teapot when it was placed on the table, and that it was easy to take despite his knowledge before, when King Gabriel told them about this brief information about the magic jug a loud voice shouted, "They are traitorous thieves, kill them."

They were guards and watchdogs, which Edward apparently did not reckon with. They came from the throne's back gate, the gate for the king's entry and exit.

Until the months of Archie the sword, he pointed with his flick at them and confronted the six soldiers. As soon as the swords were fused, a strong flash came out. When he struck Archie with his sword, he smashed two swords with one blow without noticing.

Their eyes revolve around the sword, when Alex urgently comes to them with several deadly arrows that eliminated them. Then Archie completed the task and quickly climbed very lightly above the throne to take off the magic jug and try to remove it from its place, but he was very tight and while he was, until one of the snipers who claimed death rose to avoid the bears' blows and aimed his arrow in the direction of Archie, but Charlie hit him well, but it did not prevent

that stubborn sniper from shooting his arrow that hit the catch, which was covered with full glass covering the gutters attached to the jug to all the other gutters that pass through the palace!

Which caused the exit of the golden water, which was chemically reacted and had a high temperature, as if it was lava from a dormant volcano.

The matter did not stop at this point, but the escalation of the incendiary substance continued, causing the melting of the glass that protects it from the outside, which was coated with a heat-resistant substance from the inside that makes it resistant to the most severe types of heat.

Archie noticed this while holding the magic jug, as the place became very hot and the place became unbearable for any creature after the spread of the poisonous chemical smell, the most deadly of the poison of the royal cobra, which causes a kind of headache accompanied by nausea leading to entering into a long coma, which made Archie hasten to get down and shout out loud. His voice was for Gongora, but as the other Royal Guard Corps intervened from the West Gate, everyone was busy fighting with them.

While the glass of the gutters began to break in succession from both sides of the throne, and Archie feared that this would cause them to lose the magical jug, which represents their lives.

Something had to be done before that. Then he realised that he had to use the sword of Gabriel's possession in his hand until he stuck it under the magic jug in the base to which he stuck the jug of layers of marble, but he decided to hit both ends of the catch that hugs the jug and then jump quickly so that the gases wouldn't kill him and indeed he carried out his plan bravely and shouted at Alexander and threw the jug at him and threw himself until he fell on his back over the corpses of soldiers lying on the ground and then the gutters turned into fountains and fireworks until some of them ignited a fire that burnt the entire throne and the angry lava flew out, throwing its sparks and poison everywhere as if it was anger that poured all the curses of heaven on them!

Archie ran away after crawling away from over the corpses, stained with their blood, shouting, "To the door, all to the door, Edward, we've got the jug, and you, Alexander, come before me to cover you.

Until Gongora said to the bears, they covered the boys to slip to the gate, and then they all followed Edward, who stood with his pale face at the gate from which they came, waiting until they all entered, and soon they were surrounded by fire from everywhere and from every side.

As for the throne, its upper pillars began to melt after the smoke of toxicities turned into a sticky liquid resembling lava.

And before Edward closed the door behind him to run away quickly, a killer spear pierced his back until it came out of his chest and fell behind them until Archie felt and his heart had fallen from between his ribs to the bottom of his feet from the horror of the catastrophe after he saw Edward fall in front of him.

Edward said to Archie, with blood gurgling from Edward's throat to his lips, "It seems that he did not write for me to see those smiling moments, but I am happy because I will end my life and I am striving to fulfil a dream other than me, and this is what I sought and it has happened now, but I recommend you, my dear Archie, you and my friend Gongora, don't forget my family if you find them honour them, for they do not have anyone but me to support them. Then he closed his eyes on my thighs. Archie and his soul overflowed with the rest of the souls to her world in peace, after he struggled and turned from a pickaxe for evil to a life ladder at the end of his life."

Archie cried, burning him until his tears soaked the ground, and the souls of others were embarrassed by this painful situation, but Gongora seems to have gotten used to it and the other bears until he winked at Alex to carry the body of Edward and put it on Gongora's back because there is an enemy in their tracks whose purpose is to tear them apart like the people who ripped his kingdom that he built on the ruin of another king.

And as they approached the gate, led by Edward's remaining friends, the sound of a strong explosion shook the place violently until the walls cracked, as if an earthquake on the Day of Resurrection had hit the palace from the front of the hall!

And when they came out of the side gate of the palace wall, it was a very big surprise. It was one of the mammoth elephants of the royal legion, the king's legion, who returned after some soldiers slandered Commander Edward and learned of the plan of the intruders, then the king decided to attack the hall from the outside to ensure the dispersal of the thoughts of the intruders in order to slow their movement as long as possible maybe.

Until the place turned as if they were in the middle of a sandstorm after some walls collapsed, and this was in their favour, contrary to what King Prakshim had expected, as the dust became a barrier between them and the king's soldiers, who were revolting in anger, knowing that their souls would be lost if they did not arrest those most evil guests. Their view.

The two teams stand face-to-face, with only a small distance separating them. Then King Prakshim, a passenger on the chariot of one of his leaders, steps forward until he stops in front of them and makes a malicious and sarcastic laugh until he stops in front of them, and he did not have signs of overwhelming anger at what they had caused from the devastation that the invading armies left behind with all their might in which village and city did they invade?

Rather, it was more coherent and balanced and he said, "You are the most foolish people I have ever seen in my life, you thief. You did that and thought that you would get away. You believed by spreading death and terror throughout the kingdom, and then stealing the jug, that you would flee like this so quickly?

"Whatever your skills and those stolen weapons in your hands, tell me the truth of what you worship, who will save you from me now, and I own this land that you are on and everything in it, and I own this great legion and a great army capable of occupying other kingdoms with ease!"

Then his eyes turned and settled on Gongora and his features were well studied until his eyes pierced Gongora's eyes from the severity of the hatred and hatred that he had become for this bear after what happened because of him.

Then he gave him a sharp look and said softly, bearing all kinds of anger, "Well, well, you, your vile bear, who saved you and your brothers from the black-tusks of lions, when they almost killed you when you were weak pups, you fur hater, useless, and now you reward me, after all that, by conspiring against someone who is better to you, and you have done what you did. Heinous with these traitors! Damn you traitor, you will meet your fate as those who were before you met their painful fate!"

Gongora said, his eyebrows creased, "Would you believe me that you enslaved me and my brothers, killed my family, robbed our human life and made us beasts? As for the reason, why you rescued us from the fangs of lions, not out of concern for us, but in order to make us puppets in the monsters of your palace and victims of your sadistic instincts, nothing more, O tyrant."

Archie came and said with confidence, "It is a great honour to meet you, O king, and we hoped that the meeting would be in a better situation than this, but it seems that you have chosen the dishonourable situation yourself. We came here of our own free will, not to steal or to move even a rock out of its place in your beautiful country?

"Everything that happened was the result of your actions and your injustice to others, and not the result of our planning. We came to restore what is right to its owners. You took the magic jug from the man who honoured you and did good to you. What happened to you today is heaven's justice, which is stronger than you. Whatever your strength, I advise you to stop chasing us and do good in Your life for once and allow us to return the jug to its owner immediately and without any conditions?"

The king applauded warmly, then turned to those behind him and said mockingly, "Do you hear?"

Archie said, "Or do your followers know about your past, your betrayal of King Gabriel, and your stealing the jug?"

The king smiled, his face turned pale, and he was sure that the young man knew everything about him and realised that what had happened was the arrangement of King Gabriel and that these were nothing but his agents.

And if they succeed in returning the jug, Gabriel will not hesitate to plan a devastating revenge!

Until Prakshim said to Archie, belittling his words, "What a wonderful speech, young man, but it seems to have come at an extra time. If you had come to us before, I would have made you one of the riches of this kingdom, and I would have been saved from engaging in a life of meanness, humiliation and meanness which you make for a miserable creature. He lives in a cave full of megalomaniacs and thinks he is a king.

"But it seems that you are unlucky, and you have no choice now but to die, then he bent down a little and put the horse bridle on the cart, then said, "By the way, if you hand over the magic jug now, I will look at you only! As for the others, their fate has been settled, but now I will give you a few seconds to breathe in just one breath, and then give me your answer."

"Now we have only one chance," said Gongora, whispering to Alex. "They think they have surrounded us, and that will make them feel at ease. Look with half your eyes at the mammoth drivers and don't raise your head so that Prakshim will not notice. Most of them were busy eating when they saw the king approaching to be engaged."

And now we will launch a surprise attack, and you prepare all who have a bow in their hand, to get ready to cover my back, and when I go, do not think about what will happen to me, for I am sure of what I will do.

I will make a rift in their ranks, and it will make a great commotion among the elephants, which must have reminded them of the attacks of rats, and besides, there is an important matter that Commander Edward has put in your horse, and then the bear put his hand on a bag tied tightly over the horse's thigh!

Alex's body shivered when he saw the bag shake and thought it had a snake.

Until the bear reassured him and carried it in his mouth and said it was a survival bag and now just follow me and give the signal by throwing a volley of arrows at all the chariots and the elephants then I will hit them as I run towards Prakshim and do not take your eyes off me and follow me with all your strength.

King Prakshim said sarcastically, "What kept you, boy, did you hold your breath?"

Then he let out a sarcastic laugh that made Gongora take advantage of the opportunity. When Prakshim turned to join his soldiers, Gongora had launched a fierce attack on the king, who fell to the ground after frightening the horse, which started to kick in fear of being preyed upon by the huge bear, and Gongora made his way between the feet of the mammoth. So, huge that the bag was thrown between the legs of a terrified mammoth and then a flock of rats came out, climbing the legs and feet of the thick-haired mammoth, thinking that they were tree trunks, until the mammoths became mad from the intensity of panic.

Then Prakshim realised this clever movement of the bear and shouted angrily, "Crush it between your feet!"

But before he could complete his crow-like scream, a barrage of arrows rained down on them from the top, until everyone on the backs of the mammoth fell and fell to the ground.

Gongora said to the king sarcastically, laughing, "Suppose you can, loser. A group of boys have insulted you and sprayed your nose with mud, and your strength has not helped you, and will not help you from the arrows of heaven's justice."

Archie and his companions took advantage of the explosion of the situation in the midst of the king's legion and told all those who were with him on horseback, "Get off your horses and hit the rear, you will make the same path that Gongora made behind him."

And they slipped with a terrible speed between the intertwined feet of the mammoths, running with their legs behind their horses, which were making their way with great skill amid the collision and head-throwing of the terrified bodies and heads of elephants, crossing the barrier of fear and panic until they found themselves having passed the obstacle of the legion without realising and as soon as they crossed Prakshim and his gang, they appeared before them from the bottom of the hill that separated their position from the port not far away, the banners of the ships and their white sails looming in the horizon.

Until their hearts beat with hope and joy as they prepared to accompany the travelling wind to smash the waves of the lake to its destination, in the meantime, the snow had covered the entire place and he could only see the whiteness of snow and the clouds were insisting not to sleep on the ground.

Gongora says, talking to himself with strong eagerness, as he runs, "It is the door, it is the door, the door to exit from this hell, so that God and those in the heavens help me to reach the exit."

And there, King Prakshim murmured and shouted in anger with the defeated loser's voice, "They surrounded them from all directions before they escaped, you idiots. Damn you, how could they bypass a legion with all this equipment?"

And when they arrived at the port, and the seagulls were filling the sky of the coast, revolving in rings and flocks around the ships and the coast of the port, and the snowflakes did not leave a face but stuck to it.

Gongora said to the sailors with a sharp tone and evil eyes when he arrived, "Which of these ships are ready to set out?"

Panic seized the sailors and one of them said while pointing at one of the ships, which was the only civilian ship among the three wArchieips, "This, sir? Where is her lord?" The one beside him, who was calmer and more stable, said, "I am the captain, sir. The ship is ready to sail, but we do not have any flight for this day, and because there are some daily routines, we must always be ready to take any requests."

Gongora said decisively, "Now you have the order to move, we will sail as fast as possible, and we will pay you your weight in pure gold. When we reach our destination, what you will earn today will save you for life from this miserable profession!"

The captain of the ship turned to his followers in astonishment, and they were ten, and their eyes turned to each other, then Archie said to them excitedly, "Rather, we will pay you the weight of each one of you in gold, not just the captain!"

The captain turned his head towards his followers again and their tongue said I accept without conditions until he was silent for a little then one of them said before the captain decided with happy eyes, "We don't have time, boy. Let's go up quickly."

He said it again, and their faces were filled with laughter from a light he had never seen because of the sudden offer, which he never refuses.

They felt that they were in a dream, and they did not express their joy except by silence, which was a great surprise.

Once again, a shout of anger and a voice roared violently in the air, echoing like the roar of lightning, interspersed with a sharp roar, calling out in exasperating anger, "I have fulfilled my promise, Gongora, so get ready for confrontation?"

That was nothing but the lion, Radenback!

Yes, it is Radenback, who seems to have miraculously survived the collapse of the arena. It was a cruel and frustrating shock for everyone without exception, and they realised that they were doomed.

This time, no barrier or walls would separate them, unless a very painful sacrifice took place. Indeed, a sacrifice should have taken place.

No one can stand up to this monster, it's a killing machine with advanced genes, super powerful and brutal, never created before.

Gongora shouted at Kodiak, his brother Ganthum, and Spartex, "You three, stay with me, so we can push the ship away from the berth, so we can hurry away from Radenback's line, and the rest to board the ship at once."

He pushed Gongora and the poor bears to hurry away from the dock. He didn't care about anything but the survival of Archie and those with him. Then he said to his brother and his friends Kodiak, Spartex and the rest of the bears, "Come on, jump into the ship quickly before you move away."

But Ganthum refused and said, "I am with you, brother, and I will not leave you, this time no matter what. Either we die together or we live together, and I told you before, and it seems that you can no longer comprehend the words, brother."

But that did not like Gongora, who grabbed his brother by the neck and threw him into the sea and said to him as he struggled with the cold water of the lake, "If you are my real brother, board the ship, but I have an account that I must settle with Radenback."

To which Kodiak and Spartex responded enthusiastically, "We too, Gongora, and now the time has come to avenge our blood!"

Clementine said, "I wished that we would live as captives to the king, or that we would turn into fish, then to see our bear friends die more horrible than we imagine this if we did not catch up with them!"

Alex said sadly, "It won't be long before Gongora may be killed and we will be slaughtered after him!"

With the determination of the beasts, the bears forgot the vast difference between them and Radenback, and launched a counterattack on Radenback, and both Kodiak and Spartex shot out like two arrows on fire.

If he hit the leg of a giant pine tree with his hand, he would have split it in half, taking advantage of the force of Radenback's momentum towards them.

But he was stronger and more powerful, even urgent, with a blow that knocked them away from him, as if they were two weightless vibrations!

Until the decisive moment came and the way was cleared for him and he was now face to face with a lonely Gongora. Showing his huge fangs, Radenback said, "Your father's screams still ring in me every time I see you, and I think that I will make you cry together in my ear."

Then let out a malicious laugh and his eyes pierce Gongora's soul to kill him. From the inside out of fear, while Gongora was so focused on Radenback's feet to investigate any reaction from him to decide how to attack him and to distract him from Kodiak and Spartex. Then Gongora let out a strange laugh and surprise to Radenback, which was intended to distract Radenback mind from feeling any danger until the bears Kodiak and Spartex managed to bite In his feet fiercely to lose his most important element in the movement, he turned to them to rid his feet of their strong jaws and quickly took advantage of that opportunity, which is difficult to obtain at this time and jumped with his entire huge body to pounce on the head of Radenback and planted her fangs in his large hairless forehead and he had become Radenback. Now surrounded by three white bears determined to kill him at any cost until Archie and all those on the ship rejoiced and rejoiced with great joy about the imminence of the death of that beast.

But Radenback's abilities were far above the abilities of the bears, as he was not just a large lion, but he was even great in his supernatural abilities, and this was what others lacked.

When he took out all his anger in the form of a ray of fire that came out from between his ribs with great sparks, the three bears were thrown into the air as if they were dolls that flew with the wind.

Then Radenback headed to all of Spartex and Kodiak, and Spartex was the closest of them. Burning injury until Radenback jumped on the back of Kodiak and broke his back from the first bite and then grabbed him by the neck to make sure he was completely destroyed and he was not satisfied with that, but to cure his jealousy more, he separated the poor bear's head from his body in front of Gongora's eyes, in his worst tragedy.

They suffered a deep psychological breakdown, and as soon as Radenback went to Gongora holding the head of his friend, Kodiak, between his jaws in the most tragic and heart-breaking scene that one of you may pass in his life.

As soon as Radenback approached the place of Gongora with steps dripping with blood, suddenly the place rained with flaming arrows as if they were meteors of anger.

But at the moment of anger, the mind becomes a hollow box devoid of anything. Radenback dodges all those arrows and retreats towards the back until he decided to coalesce with the king and his soldiers before they eliminate him. The soldiers were terrified while they watched the looks of the lion bearing death between his eyes, Gongora retreated crawling in the meantime, Archie had jumped out of the ship and swam towards the pier, where he slipped into Gongora, and after him came his brother, the Bear Ganthum, amid the turning of the Lion Radenback against his master, King Prakshim; who launched a deadly attack on soldiers and armoured mammoths.

This was an opportunity for Archie and Ganthum to drive Gongora out of danger, and they saw the attack of Radenback on the king's legion!

Archie said to Ganthum, "Let's draw him to the lake quickly before Radenback returns."

Ganthum said, "I don't think he's going back.

Archie quickly replied, "We don't care who wins and who loses, they both look at us as if we were precious hunting, let's jump now quickly, cold water will relieve the pain for enough time."

On the other hand, the lion Radenback had committed a massacre against the king's legion, where the rocks were stained with blood and scattered on the ground body parts and human heads.

But the largest of the mammoth elephants surprised the angry lion and grabbed him with his huge trunk from the middle and threw him hard, hitting Radenback's head against the mountain wall.

Then the remaining soldiers took out those sturdy nets as if they were fishing nets to catch one of the ogres, and they brought them for the moment of arresting the fleeing bears, where the elephants fixed the ends of the nets under their feet after they were thrown at Radenback and he wrapped around him tightly while he was unconscious and Prakshim said sharply, "I will have an appointment with you for chastisement, your hybrid cat."

Then Prakshim shouted forcefully from his depths, "Come on, catch up with the escaping ship, and bring me the jug. As for those scumbags, burn them alive." He shouted with hysterical laughter from the intensity of what he hides of oppression and great hatred behind that bloody face.

The two wArchieips set out following the small ship in which Alex and his boys and bears remained, intending to sink it and close the file of the intruders as soon as possible, and kill everything in it mercilessly after they retrieve the magic jug.

It was good for Archie and those with him that the soldiers and the king did not notice their presence in the sea, so what happened was enough to make each of them forget even the name of his mother.

Then Gongora said in a gurgling voice from the water of the lake as he was swimming with Archie and his brother Ganthum, "This man drank hate as a thirsty drinks water to bring him back to life. But I resolved to kill him today, whatever the cost, so that by death I would have done something that would benefit all humanity and everyone who lives in this universe. I see the real devil in this creature."

Then his body shivered and suddenly rose up and said with his teeth chattering from the cold, "Oh, how cold this water is, I feel like I've lost my organs!"

Gangnam also said to him, "It is not worse than the pain of burning, my brother."

Then Gongora said, "I cannot describe to you how overwhelming I feel that if I hit the ship with my hand, I would have drowned it despite all the sadness inside me."

Archie from behind the water said, "It is enough that you rid us of this dwarf villain, and then you will cuddle yourself with joy before others notice you.

"Don't worry, it's a matter of time," said Gongora. "Now listen to me carefully. We will hold onto the stern of the ship that the king rode before they reach our ship, and when the two ships reach our ship, I will board this ship to single out Prakshim on our own, because he has nothing left of the soldiers but like the number of fingers.

"Either you will board the other ship and blow up everyone you meet or capture. Either I trust in you, Grantham, and you, Archie, with this sword that you have, you can take their lives, or they surrender to you and they are obedient to you, for you have a tongue that drips honey."

Archie said, "He will know that his departure from the palace will be the beginning of his exit from this life forever, and I hope that he will not leave it, unless I am carrying his head."

Meanwhile, the soldiers on the two wArchieips were sharpening their cannons to ram the small ship to stop it, and then kidnapped the magic jug before it sank and whoever was in it, while Prakshim continued to shout out the strongest and hArchieest words of threat and threat to all those in the ship at the top of his voice, "You will not return to your homes today except for the bodies if they escape, these criminals and those who follow them are traitors and when the two ships surrounded the small ship and those on it, the ship led by King Prakshim shook strongly as if it had hit something, but in fact this shaking was only due to the weight of Gongora, who landed on the deck of the ship after he succeeded in climbing from the back that was above the bow, and the many white sails were between Gongora and the others are like a barrier."

The bear descended quickly to the stairs that lead to the bottom of the ship, where the cannons and stores are, where he was surprised and thought that he had entered the snake's hole with his bare feet when he was surprised by a number of soldiers preparing and sharpening swords and untangling the nets to catch him without knowing that he had come to them with his feet!

On the other hand, the entry of the bear on them was shocking to them as they saw this giant fleeing bear overlooking them himself!

Until one of them shouted and scared the others and said, "It's the fleeing bear, it's the traitor bear, it's Gongora!"

Another soldier ran to ring the alarm, but from the tragedy he forgot and went up from the other door to warn King Prakshim, who was disturbed and hid behind his guards.

Even in the worst-case scenario, Gongora had never expected to reveal his whereabouts so quickly, nor would Prakshim ever have thought that he would infiltrate the ship, which was the last place he thought of heading to the escaping bear.

Because he knew that it was very difficult to control or even kill a monster the size of a Gongora in a confined space, as there was no space for soldiers to shoot them with their spears and arrows at once.

As for Archie, he went up and hid in the stern of the other ship, behind some crates of provisions, and in front of them the sails that had been lowered to half the mast to slow the ship down so that their guns could hit their target more accurately.

Archie relaxed a little after contemplating the white cloth of the sail of the fool swaying in front of him as if it was Maya's shimmering dress in the first meeting that happened between them so, he went too far in his imagination and extended his hand to take the end of the sail despite its distance from him until his lover heart imagined that Maya had wrapped that sail and then began to take it off her naked body.

She dances with the wind breezes carrying the leaves of spring roses flying all over the place until she is completely stripped of the sail that wrapped around her body.

However, the health of the soldiers from the other ship disturbed a moment of contemplation by a witch who almost ascended with a spirit of brilliance above the layers of white clouds.

Archie found himself in front of the same door that Gongora had found on the other ship and he went down from him to the bottom of the ship, but Archie was more careful, and he was not in a hurry in his matter for fear of his case being exposed, so he did not see anyone at the bottom except some of the empty barrels. To me that the captain and crew and that of their clothes!

Archie took advantage of the element of surprise and the great sword in his possession until he reached the front of the ship, where the captain and soldiers were, their number was four, and they were preoccupied with fear of knowing the source of the sound that came from a ship commanded by King Prakshim.

"It's your chance, Archie," said Archie, sneaking up on tiptoes, and he took out his sword after waving it with a quick movement, then put it beside him.

He raised his sword in front of his face, pointed with his pointed tip at them, and said violently behind them, "Who among you would take any step without me asking him will see his head roll in front of his body? Who wants that? Huh? And you, captain, I command you, captain, to stop the ship at once and to throw yourselves into the sea now, without any hesitation or discussion!

"It was a somewhat reckless and urgent request, but we don't blame Archie, he didn't have time to ask them about their conditions, health and intentions. It's a fight of a murderer or a murderer. There is no choice but that and there is no place for mercy when your enemy tells you that, so why not take your sword before his sword overtakes you."

The captain was a wise person in his work and had a great experience in sailing and in fighting pirates in particular. There is no doubt that such a situation was not strange for him until the captain said with his wisdom, "Well, son, we do not know who you are, but it seems that you are one of those fleeing who we are chasing, right?"

Archie says nervously, "Yes, a thief is one of the thieves you are chasing, and this is a useless talk."

The captain said coldly, "We also did not go out in order to talk to you, but in order to stop you at your own after what you did in our great kingdom of devastation and destruction after we honoured you, welcomed you and sheltered you, and this is sufficient evidence of your bad intentions!"

Archie answered, "I told you that I will not come here to talk to you and tell me about your tragedies that you have made with your own hands."

The captain kept dragging Archie to speak and delaying it, so he did not seem afraid at all, but it seems that he was hoping for something to happen by making the conversation long, and unfortunately that happened?

There was a person up in the watchtower watching Archie and he didn't notice his presence until he jumped with the rope from the top over Archie and threw himself over Archie from behind and fell over him and grabbed him after the sword fell from Archie's hand but soon Archie was able to escape from the attacker's grip and as soon as he wanted to get up he found His sword was in his face after the captain caught him and he was rubbing it on Archie's cheek until he bled and the captain said sarcastically,

"Didn't I tell you that we had no time to talk to bandits and rogues like you, young thief?"

Archie said angrily after the captain had provoked him, "Do not repeat this word again..."

The captain interrupts him and put the tip of the sword on Archie's lip. He said to him in defiance, "You are a thief, son of a thief?"

Those words ignited a fire that could not be extinguished by the waters of the whole lake until he bared his fangs in anger in a way that had not happened to him in his entire life, and his face became like a vampire with long fangs dripping with blood.

Damn it, he turned into a demon! And his heart almost jumped out of his place when he saw with his own eyes that beautiful face turns into a vampire's face. As for the sailors, they jumped into the lake from the fright of fear, and the captain turned around, calling out to them, where did you go? And when he turned to raise the sword in the face of Archie, Archie pounced on the captain's face and killed him and ripped off the flesh of his face, and the captain fell dead in the blink of an eye.

As soon as Archie returned to his senses after he felt a severe dizziness in his head and saw himself crouching on the corpse of the laying captain, he wiped his lips with his hand and saw blood and said what is this?

Blood? But how did this happen?

Then he heard a clanging at the bottom until he remembered as if he was in a coma and that he had to go down to the bottom to restrain the steering of the ship to prevent it from catching up with the small ship.

Then an idea came to his mind that he had not considered, as he thought that he would use the entire ship as a big stick to hit the other ship and thus he would have hit two birds with a stone!

Archie found workers under the ship and they were responsible for the movement of the ship and said decisively, "There is no one on this ship but me and you, and I am the new captain."

Then he put the sword in front of him and leaned on it: evidence of possessing control and strength!

The signs of exclamation were imprinted on their faces. The sailors in this ship were not soldiers but slaves, unlike that ship in which everyone in it were from the king's war squad and who would not leave their king with anyone else.

Then he added, whoever did not believe my words, let him go upstairs. You will not see anyone but the dead body of the captain. As for the rest, they fled and left you facing death alone. This sword will be an answer in the neck of everyone who refuses. Either you hear my words, and as for death now, there is nothing else, O slaves?

Their eyes rolled at each other and misery covered their features. After using the method of intimidation, Archie said with confidence, "Opportunities do not always come. Either you are with me to become free like me and everyone else."

The free people in this world, or you reject my words and die as slaves as you lived!

Come on, hurry up. I want an answer now. I don't have time to spend with those who are willing to be slaves forever. It was confusing and scary for them.

But they have no trick until one of them said with joy, "I am with you, sir. We are all with you. If what you say is true, then I guarantee that if your words are true, we are all with you."

Archie says, "Show me, what are you going to do? All I want from you now is to divert the direction of the ship to make it collide with the king's ship so that we can get rid of them and bury the king and his army together in this lake."

One of them said, "But we will drown with them, sir, if we do that."

Another said, "There are lifeboats and we can swim in it too, and the lake is not big!"

The third of them said, "Why all this, sir, we will drown it with the cannon we have!"

Archie looked around and inspected the place after turning his head like an owl in every corner and said, "But I don't see any cannon!"

The sailor says, "Yes, sir." He took a few steps until he reached the corner of the ship at a group of covered barrels, and when the cover was pulled from above, among the barrels was a gigantic pure gold cannon, whose nozzle was coming out of the ship's hatch and in full readiness to fire until Archie said inquiring, "Oh my God a pure gold cannon? But why are there no cannons here but this cannon and why has it been covered so far while you are at war!"

The servant said, "These were the orders of the captain, my lord, he is the one who ordered to cover the cannon and not to use it because he wanted to confiscate it for himself and sell it in another place, but he was surprised by the emergency situation we are in now, and then he ordered us to transfer his place to the other direction and to tell the king that we do not have a cannon in this direction from the ship and he asked us to break the wheels of the cannon and to install it on the floor of the ship in order not to move it in order to be an excuse not to use it and he was afraid that using the cannon would cause the loss of some of its value!"

Archie said, "No wonder that when the king of the country is a thief, his followers must also be thieves."

As for Gongora, still thinking about a solution to his predicament under the ship, he found himself trapped among a flock of hungry wolves from all sides, waiting for the opportunity to eat him alive.

Until they were surprised by the voice of Prakshim personally speaking to him directly through the communication slot designated for communication between the headquarters at the top and the base leadership at the bottom.

It consisted of two holes at the top and the bottom, connected by a copper tube that emits a kind of high echo to communicate due to the high sound of waves or strong winds.

Until Prakshim said, "I admit your courage, Gongora, which made you come here by yourself, but I also admit your intelligence and wit, and I knew how to survive your life, because life is too precious to be wasted for the sake of some funny boys! Having you here at my mercy will give you one last chance, and if you were on the ship with the other thieves, you'd be getting ready to take a shell full of nails. It will make you wish that you had been dead for a long time and this is a confession from me personally, King

Prakshim of my greatness and majesty and my great king I confess to you and not only that, but I have a very big offer for you that you will not be able to return unless you have already determined your fate and the fate of your brothers with disgraceful perdition!"

Gongora replied coldly, "Thank you, you have saved me many options and a lot of talking. If trees and stones uttered, they would say the same as I say this, no one will tolerate your presence in life, so how about someone who is at your mercy, sick sadist!"

And while Gongora was talking at length to empty what was inside, Gongora heard the sound of a door creaking. When he raised his eyes, the upper door was quietly opened until the bear became silent and backed away, thinking that they had taken an order to attack him!

At the beginning, it was like what he expected when he saw six soldiers descending, aiming their arrows at the defenceless bear, and behind them three others armed with shields and long, double-bladed spears that drip poison, and behind them King Prakshim, who did not seem afraid or worried, not because he had all those giant guards armed with the strongest types weapons, but because he has something else, he knows very well that he will force the bear to change his mind.

Until his eyes flashed with confusion as he watched what the cunning Prakshim would pull out of his sleeve this time?

These are the tricks of Prakshim that no one can outdo him in.

Prakshim stood confidently without uttering a word and looked at the victor's gaze, then turned around to the top of the stairs and nodded his head to those above the guard, and behold, a shadow appeared on the face of Prakshim before his companion shadowed them.

Gongora's eyes roll into place and his heart beats faster, as if he knew it wasn't in his favour.

That heavy surprise confused Gongora's mind, distracted his thoughts and scattered his priorities after he despaired of finding the magician (Cat's Eye) who cast the spell on Gongora and his family and turned their hearts from peaceful humans to savage bears!

Where Gongora considered him the owner of the biggest crime committed against him and his family, so much so that he considers it greater than the crime of killing his father at the hands of Radenback and because he killed them without killing them and made them suffer every day since that fateful day until this moment when he deprived them of their humanity and made them animals used for killing purposes and amusement.

Gongora stared in amazement to himself, "Is this true what I see?"

So, he asked hesitantly, "Are you a cat eye?"

The magician trembled and the heartbreak was clear on his face when he

remembered the cries of women and children while he was casting spells on them until King Prakshim took hold of the magician's hand and said to him maliciously, "Calm, my friend, and do not be afraid of the words of this bear, you are a nice person who did nothing but what your master commanded you and you have done your best interest."

Prakshim stared at Gongora with murderous coldness and continued, saying, "Although the result did not appeal to some and they did not like it, and I will not hide from you that it did not like me either, but it was necessary and that this happens in order for the kingdom to live. There is no harm in harming a few of the local residents who are of no value in order for the others to live in lasting prosperity!"

Then he followed his words with evil laughter and murmured after that and that it was time to surrender, Gongora, and it was time to return what you stole so that your lives could come back to you again?

Gongora replied with a hidden hatred, "Damn you, what made you mad after everything you did to us and happened to us because of you and the loss of so many innocent lives and your conscience still doesn't blame you for what you did, as if you were made of rock?"

"Oh ooh, try to calm yourself down, Gongora, didn't you ask yourself why I myself came here to you? I gave up my lofty pride and went down to the dirt of this ship for what? Didn't you ask yourself why now I brought you the cat-eye wizard! Do you see how much you are worth to me? Should I leave you thinking or do you want me to answer you myself, Gongora!"

Gongora raised his eyebrows as if he understood the intent behind his words and said, "No, whatever you say, I don't believe you because I know that you will never do anything good to anyone unless you have humiliating demands behind it."

In the absence of a quiet dialogue between them, cries were heard and feet ran from the top of the ship until the king raised his eyes, looking at the ceiling shaking and the dirt falling on his face.

What mobilised everyone, Prakshim shouted at them with tension and fear, "What is happening, you cowardly scum?"

And as soon as one of them climbed to the top to investigate the matter, he shouted loudly, "Run, my lord, the king! Flee quickly!"

The bear rejoiced and thought that perhaps Archie had come to the rescue and invaded the ship and those who were with him until Prakshim took a sword from the sheath of one of the guards and went up himself to fight after he told the soldiers, "Do not let your eyes be absent from this bear. And he still does not know what is happening."

King Prakshim was weak in body and short in stature, but he was also characterised by courage and aggression.

Even before he climbed to the end of the stairs, a very strong and violent collision occurred that shook the ship and shook its pillars with a great earthquake until one of the masts fell as if the ship was a toy with the hand of a child shaking it hard.

Until everyone in it rolled together with barrels of gunpowder and wine, and likewise Prakshim fell from the stairs and rolled like a ball over his soldiers.

The bow of the ship in which Archie was in the middle of this ship was pierced until it was divided into two halves from the top, but the ship remained welded from the bottom and a little in the middle.

Gongora shouted to Archie, "It's our chance that he's in our hands with the cat-eye wizard. Heaven has given us the most beautiful gift and we will never lose it."

Gongora tried to get up, but the section he had fallen on was tilted towards the water and heading towards drowning. And he ran like the wind up towards the door, where Archie was in the middle of the ship, and the angle of view didn't help him to notice Prakshim fleeing.

When he said to his guards while holding the cat-eye wizard and never letting go of him, "Kill them and do not call any of them, or I will flay your skins while you are alive."

He continued dragging the magician behind him as if he were a lame dog.

As he considered him a trump card, if it was lost, he might get lost too. Without Archie noticing, he was surprised by a barrage of arrows from the bottom of the ship that almost pierced his chin from the bottom, fired by the king's guard until he climbed over one of the boxes and shouted to Gongora, "Where did Gongora go, I didn't see him?"

Gongora, without being asked to do so, made all his focus and his only goal at this moment was to catch the wizard (Cat's Eye) more than Prakshim, for he considered his loss to be like sentencing him to life.

Archie noticed that the deck of the ship began to crack, as the ice on the surface of the frozen lake was cracking, which predicted that the ship would split in two and thus sank directly. And they left their king alone to face his fate after realising that the ship was sinking for his destiny.

Archie witnesses Prakshim holding the magician (Cat's Eye) behind him with a knife on his neck and in front of them Gongora shouting violently threatening the magician after he twisted his hand on his neck from behind and put the sword on the neck of the magician until the sharp blade of the sword sank in the skin of the magician's neck, "Come on, magician. The damned one turned this lazy bear into a blind, deaf and dumb handicapped ogre to be a ball of meat and bone for no use except for crows to eat from it and then put their droppings on it."

Archie had managed to slip into the stern of the ship without noticing the mad king and when Gongora saw that Archie was behind Prakshim, Gongora tried to keep Prakshim busy by talking to give Archie to do what he could do.

At last, Archie stood directly behind Prakshim and Gongora was silent, and so did the king when he felt that something uncomfortable was going on behind him!

Until he loosened the knife from the magician's neck after he felt suspicious.

Archie was convinced that he had reached for the first time the most important goal he hoped to reach in the journey of his amazing adventure, and that he was just around the corner to save all of humanity from the evil of this man.

Until Archie slowly raised his sword up until the king saw the shadow of the sword in front of him wanting to land on his head from the top and realised that he was dead in his power, then he turned quietly to Archie and looked at him with pitying eyes as he wanted to utter his last words before the guillotine came down on his neck!

Until Gongora yelled "Kill him, Archie, kill him before he utters a word!"

Gongora was afraid of the treachery, malice, and malice of King Prakshim, his charming eyes that could turn things around in his favour in seconds, and he knows him better than anyone in this place.

Until Archie said coldly, "It is your misfortune, O king, that you have not met me before, or else you would have convinced me of something!"

And when Archie decided to cut off the king's head so that he was surprised by a high wave hitting the ship, it was to sink the doomed ship and dismantle all the wood of the ship's body except for a few and when that wave went and that moo disappeared, more afraid that it was carrying the lion, Radenback, to the deck of the ship until he stood with all his weight on the tip of the middle of the dilapidated ship and behind him was Gongora and in front of him.

Archie and the king separated by the water, which began to swallow the dead boat actually, the king took advantage of this surprise and paid Archie away with a very violent movement threw Archie to the ground and jumped into the lake and disappeared completely like a fish escaping from the angler's hook.

The matter was not welcomed by the turbulent and convulsive souls until Gongora exhaled a smoke more intense than a dragon's fire after all that tragedy upon them, until he said, "My suspicions were corrected that you would return, your mongrel cat."

Before perishing, "No worries, my friend. I have prepared well for all shocks and surprises. They no longer affect my resolve and determination to confront everyone who stands in front of us."

Radenback shook the water from the hair of his body up to his tail and splashed the face of Gongora, who was standing behind him completely, feeling awe of Radenback, who was at full strength. The supernatural geneticist, thinking from where he will start with him this time, it is not easy to pounce on a monster like this, the magician did not wait for the Cat's Eye for long, the doors of survival opened wide in front of his eyes until he jumped as the fugitive king jumped after the failure of Archie's attempt to grab the end of his robe, but he managed to take it off quickly and slither his slender body in Archie's arms was like his little limbs.

Gongora couldn't stand the sorcerer's flight until he jumped into the lake to follow the wizard, forgetting that he had left Archie alone in the face of Radenback in an absolutely unequal confrontation.

Archie cried, "No, Gongora, and this was something he couldn't comprehend, but Archie did not think for a moment that it was selfish from Gongora to think about himself, but he had the right to put priorities over everything else." He jumped on Archie, who lost his balance from the swaying of the ship's body heading into the depths of the lake until he jumped on Archie, from whom fell the sword that was the shield, the hope of overcoming any danger after losing the support of Gongora and becoming devoid of anything to protect him except his bare hands.

The lion put Archie directly under him in a position unenviable to any creature and said, with his hot saliva digging furrows in the defenceless boy's face, "I promised you, boy, that we will have a date that we will never leave, and here I am, and I will keep my promise, and I would never break the promise, O..."

Before he completed, his words pierced two arrows that tied together Radenback's foot and they came out from the other side until he jumped away from Archie from the severity of the injury that injured the ankle of the foot.

Archie grabbed his sword and pressed it hard to get everything out of his power until the blade of the sword turned red and became like burning embers. He could make him disassociate himself from the sword and jump away, then he turned and turned to a snarling Archie and said, "I seem to have underestimated your abilities, boy, but it seems like a good attempt, but I promise you it will be the last!"

Unfortunately, once again, he lost his balance due to the approach of the weight of Radenback, which hastened the sinking of the ship under the water, and before Radenback launched his second attack, another arrow hit his left ankle, causing him to kneel in place like a camel!

Then Alex shouted at Radenback, "If I had known that these arrows would kill you, I would have pointed them at your huge head, devil."

But the injury to the feet of the lion will ensure that his strength decreases rapidly in catching up with them.

But this did not dissuade Radenback, who looked at the source of the arrows and saw Alexander standing at the end of the other ship, holding one of the masts carrying him and his friends behind him.

Alexander realised that those looks of terror were nothing but the language of a savage attack that the wounded lion would undoubtedly launch upon them.

Until he screamed as he retreated back, get down to the bottom of the ship and stay near the cannon holes, and if this monster enters you, jump into the lake quickly.

Then Radenback decided to strike his blow and end the matter quickly because it was the perfect time to reap the fruits of his decision to take revenge to jump from the sinking ship that was completely covered by the waters of the lake and to secure a place for himself above the water to have the advantage and superiority to launch his raids on everyone who remained alive and the extermination of everybody pulsing with life above the surface of the lake!

As for Archie, he did the same thing, as he dived with the wreckage to avoid the eyes of Radenback, who landed on the weak ship and hit the huge cuff on its deck until he fell on it, unfortunately. Strongly. "Jump."

Until a voice from above interrupts him, saying, "Do not jump!"

It was Gongora who jumped from above on Radenback's back and stuck his claws and fangs into his back, trying to break his back. It seems that he understood that this was the weakness of the Radenback monster, to break his spine and immobilise him.

But it seems that this battle will be at the expense of the ship's destruction, including those in it, when its floor collapsed with them, and the two sank together in the lake whose waters jumped to the top of the ship, as if a great flood swallowed everything in front of it.

Alexander called everyone in panic, "Climb to the top to gain as much time as possible before the ship sank."

The fat Martin said weeping, "The two ships sank and our ship is on its way to drowning while we are in the middle of the lake and I don't know how to swim and the black beast won't leave us!"

Clementine grumbled to him, "If he suggested that we throw you into this beast, so that we might escape, if you really admitted that it was useless for you, at least if we offered you to this beast, you would have provided us with a benefit for once in your life!"

Martin answered him, biting his teeth, "If it weren't for this, we'd have given you a lesson, girl."

Clementine laughed sarcastically, and said in a surprising voice, "He's behind you, the black lion behind you."

Until Martin throws himself into Alexander's lap, who grumbled, "You are still like chickens pecking each other every minute until we are facing death, you idiots? Stop this, because we don't know who will die before the other."

Suddenly they heard a weak voice calling from the bottom of the ship and when Alexander lowered his head, he saw the magician (Cat's Eye) clinging to the bottom of the iron bow of the ship.

Oh my God it's the magician (Cat's Eye) I thought you were vaporised in the air Luca said sharply, "Take the rope, Alexander, before he drowns and then we lose Gongora's loyalty and then we are alone in the face of our destiny. No, we won't be alone Lucca, Gongora didn't just go out with us for a wizard but for the same purpose that expelled you from the kingdom."

Archie's voice from behind them after he ascended from the gap created by the conflict between Radenback and Gongora under the ship. Oh heavens!

Clementine gleefully says until he almost flies with joy. Archie said, "Don't move too much before that ship reaches us. Fortunately, they didn't move all with that crazy Prakshim. Then he waved his hand high to the ship coming from the port."

Sebastian said happily, "You have come with hope, Archie, how inspiring you are."

Alexander said, "Thank God for your return, my friend. But now I feel that a heavy burden has been lifted from us, even if temporarily, so that I can no longer feel my leg."

Archie stared at the wizard and said scornfully, "I wish I could see Gongora looking at you, what heart you had to do your ugly deed!"

The magician said coldly and confidently, "The same reason that made you run and run to escape what you fear also happened to me, but everyone wants others to bear all his mistakes and fear. It's okay, everyone feels that he deserves to live in peace more than others, and this is what you think, so you do not want to understand or to put yourself, even for a moment, in the same place and situation in which you were previously placed. Whether you believe my words or not does not matter!"

The wizard had a good soul despite his bad reputation until he touched Archie and then Alexander said to him, "Now what is the plan, Archie? We're going to the next boat, then what?"

Archie said, after he was silent for a while, "Then we wait for Gongora."

Alexander said, "God's right on you, Archie. I saw what happened to Gongora and Radenback, after they fell into that whirlpool and the blood that the water left after them.

"I think he's still alive! It's enough sympathy, Archie, to save ourselves first. Radenback is on his way, and he may come out now at any moment and kill us all before the ship arrives and you're still thinking about waiting. Are you crazy?"

The ship shook violently and suddenly, as if it had collided head-on with a mountain while it was speeding up.

Until they all fell into the waters of the lake, floundering among the water and some remains of the wreckage of the other ship.

And when they knew that danger was coming again, a loud voice cried out from under the rescue ship as it was sinking into the depths, "Swim quickly to the next ship, as fast as you can."

He was trying to hold on to the remains of the ship, which had turned closer than a beaver's nest in the middle of the lake. The boys had swum before they heard Gongora until they reached the ship coming from the port, until Archie remained in the middle between the wreck and the oncoming ship, hesitating until He watched blackness from the bottom of the water growing more and more and thought that it was nothing but a group of flocks of seagulls that gathered around them to wait for their meal that the battle will leave behind.

Archie noticed many bodies floating on the surface of the lake, and realised that the passengers of the ship and some of the other bears who were with them had died along with the rest of the soldiers of Prakshim.

Until he realised at the last moment that the blackness below him was nothing but Radenback, then he threw Archie himself and jumped like a dolphin after Radenback opened his jaws as if they were the jaws of a giant shark below him.

"I don't know how long this situation will last with this Radenback, but if it is, I must finish what I have started, no matter what," said Gongora miserably.

Archie fled quickly and was able to swim and cling to the ship until Gongora said, calling Radenback violently, "Leave these boys, for your battle is with me and not with these, you bastard!"

Radenback did not care, but, contrary to expectation, Radenback realised that he would increase the suffering of Gongora and break his promises and dreams of revenge when he eliminates his human friends to destroy him morally and thwart his plans.

Radenback continued swimming until he climbed the ship, and the boys and their crew fled to the stern, and now Radenback is the master of the situation, and he is the king of the lake and those on it unchallenged.

Gongora hurriedly boarded the ship behind Radenback, his heart almost jumping out of his place in fear for the boys, until he stood behind Radenback, angry at everyone, even himself.

"I know you want me, Radenback, and if that's fine, here I am in front of you this time, I promise I will not resist, and do to me as you wished and promised, for we admit that we lost before you. Just leave these boys alone and that's my policeman, otherwise chances don't always come back like this, Radenback!"

"Oh, it seems to me that you've grown so confident that I don't trust you!"

But for you to know that I am the one who creates opportunities, and you have escaped from my grip so far twice, and this third will be the end, and you must understand before your death, because you will not exist soon and that the laws of your world do not exist in my world!

Archie whispered to Alex and said, "We are dead and we have no hope but to try to stab him with this sword, for it is our solution to the last."

The hugeness of his body means that the rate of our injury to him will be great if we plan well in any way, and all I want you to run next to him quickly towards Gongora, then he will raise his fear and confuse him, and then hope will have opened his doors for us to give him a fatal blow with the sword, perhaps that will succeed this time!

Alex said, "And if we fail?"

Archie said sadly, "And if we fail and at least kill us, we will be dead trying better than devouring us like sheep one by one!"

Alexander looked at him with a look of farewell, but with enthusiasm and courage, and said to him, "So, death is calling for us, my friend."

Archie said, "Yes, it is the call of death, my friend? Let's go without planning, I promise we will succeed."

And in a blink of an eye, before Radenback straightened himself and turned to the boys, Alexander ran on the side of the ship until his movement caught Radenback's eyes, and he quickly gritted his teeth and wanted to cut off Alexander, who was planning to reach Gongora.

Archie took advantage of that moment in which the weak point of the injured Radenback in his back was revealed, which is that he could not protect his body from both sides unless he was ready to confront. Archie and if he faced the whole of Radenback's palm, he would have killed him at once until Archie hit one of the masts that broke and half of it fell in an unexpected way while Gongora launched a sweeping attack on Radenback's back again.

This time, Radenback could not easily get rid of Radenback's fangs because he was unable to jump due to the injury he sustained in his feet from Alex's arrows.

And I lost him part of his abilities, but unfortunately again when the sail column completed it fall and fell on Gongora's head completely and hit him with a concussion that knocked him unconscious and fell from the back of Radenback and fate had written for them not to defeat this monster at all!

Then Radenback turned quickly and put his hand on Gongora who was lying on the ground and roared in a loud voice that shook the wide lake and everyone fell as if they had been struck by lightning until Alexander said desperately, after his tongue was temporarily paralysed from the bad situation, "We are close to the end!"

Radenback replied, "You are not close, but it is your end O miserable man, I will break your bones while you are alive, so that you may taste the error of your choices."

Martin shouted in horror as hard as he could for the first time in his life at Radenback and said, "Don't do that if you believe that you are the strongest and the master of this place and every place you walk! You got what you want, this is the bear under your hands, do with it what you want, we never had any revenge between us and you except that our misfortune brought this bear on our way, so the curse be upon him We absolve you of all his actions that angered you"

Martin's words shocked everyone, but everyone knew that these words would not have come out of Martin except from the horror of the situation and his extreme panic, so no one argued with him until Radenback said with amazement that hides great malice, "Hmm, very smart boy, but come closer to me to see you closely and to hear the rest of your tactful speech. More!"

Alexander scolded him and said to him, "No, Martin, do not approach him, for this beast is not safe, even his malicious soul."

Then someone's voice shouted in astonishment, and it was Clementine, "Look, look at that cloud!"

It was like a black cloud piercing the white of the snowy clouds towards them, and when it got closer, it was a cloud of a very huge and majestic swarm of bats.

Until cries of supplication and chants of hope erupted from the boys' mouths and Archie heard a buzzing in his ear saying, we will not forget you!

All eyes gasped in horror at the size of that frightening swarm of bats, and so did Radenback, who left Gongora and walked a few steps towards the edge of the ship with his head up watching that strange scene with anxious eyes and said as if he knew something that no one else knew, "This is nothing but the work of the jinn!"

He bared his fangs, showing fear of the matter, and in a decisive moment that no one imagined, even among the most faithful in miracles and optimism in the midst of a stupor that swept the faces of panic, the rest of the sails were fluttering so strongly that the swarm of bats covered the ship from its abundance, even if Radenback found himself rising in the air hanging from his tail. And his head down like a lion doll of wool and cloth in the hand of a child who grabbed him by his long tail and raised him high in the sky?

He watches the ship and those on it look at him from below while they are getting smaller because of his height from the ship towards the sky and he hits with his claws and his feet in the air until he plunges his claws into the sails of the ship roaring with fear and terror for the first time and he says terrified, "What is happening to me! What is it? What is going on where am I!"

Until everyone saw him for the first time, as if he was a small black cat of no value!

As for the reason for that, and the force that turned the scales in the last moments, it was only the horse Barbora! Yes, it's Barbora, the talking horse that Archie meets in his first meeting with Maya.

But this time he came like an angel of mercy with white wings spread in the sky with all prestige and beauty, as Radenback grabbed his tail with his teeth and threw him away from the ship in the middle of the lake, saying to him in a loud and sarcastic voice, "You beast have sinned against my friends, you will not be able to harm them anymore."

The horse, Barbora, was different from the one that was the first time. It had two giant wings, and with it a herd of winged horses, until it landed on the ship's land, welcoming Archie, saying with joy, "It seems that we have come at the right time!"

Archie said in a stifled voice, "Is that you, Barbora?"

He said with joy, "Yes, it is me, my friend, how happy I am to see you again, my friend. I expected everything but to see you again, especially in this difficult time."

Clementine said, opening his mouth from the strangeness of what he saw, "Is it true what my eyes see, or am I in a dream?"

Luca pinched him and said, "After what we've been through, I think we live in dreams and we haven't woken up from it until this moment!"

Archie said while wiping his tears with his sleeve, "It doesn't matter how you found out about our location, we are now on a mission, every minute that passes by it will kill an innocent soul."

Barbora said, "I came here only to help you. You only have to point to me by the name of the place, and you will find yourself there in the shortest time. As for your friends, the bears, they will remain in the ship, and the rest of the horses will drag it behind us, and we will go forward now. Come on, my friends. Take these boys and the rest, and let them drag the ship from behind us to where we fly!"

And they all went off in disbelief, shouting joyous expressions from every side that they had succeeded in getting the jug and snatching it from the lion's den.

This would not have happened if they had placed all the obstacles in front of them, but their determination and belief in the justice of their cause was a reason to overcome matters that an armoured army with the most powerful weapons and the strongest soldiers would not have overcome.

Archie looked from above at the kingdom, and the smoke of grey ruins was mixed with the whiteness of snow, and all those fires that they left after them, and how it turned from the icon of the kingdoms of the world in beauty and perfection to a heap of ashes!

And they went back to the black cave to restore their lives again, until Archie wept with his burning and his eyes red from crying and said to himself with burning and pain, "You are an idiot, Archie, you have caused all that pain and harm to many innocent people in this kingdom. Because you came for something that didn't belong to you even though you were forced to, in order to get your life back again, or you will die.

"What a cruel adventure to end with joy and tears, you don't know which of them you will turn, but the fact remains that you have triumphed over all your fears only because you believed in your just cause, even though everything around you say otherwise."

Chapter 26

DEMONS GAME START

The sun disc began to fade at the end of the lake on the side of the mountain canyon, announcing the beginning of darkness, and before it, the thick snow stopped falling on the lake, which became of two beautiful colours, white and blue-white.

They had a feeling and a dreamy feeling free from any blemish of fear or anxiety, and they were alerted by a beautiful refreshing feeling. Luca said happily, "For the first time, I feel like I am drinking from fresh, cold water from the coldness of this cold air."

Charlie said, "What is this beauty? I do not hide from you my feelings, as if my heart was refreshed with pleasure and happiness. Look how we were and where we became. Who would have believed while we were running from that monster in fear? That in a few minutes we will be on the backs of winged horses? I do not think that if we gathered to dream the most beautiful dream, we would not dream of such a reality. Look at the beauty of these horses and the beauty of this feeling that I cannot describe to anyone.

"They have the right to express happily their sense of the amazing and unexpected victory that ended with the most beautiful and expected end and crowned with comfort and safety that they did not expect, not even in distant dreams."

The sounds of flapping soft wings of horses caressed their ears with real peace of mind. It was like an antidote to give them the hope of returning to their normal lives after not long moments. Rather, they will reward the most beautiful reward that will spare them from returning to the kingdom. Rather, it will make them partners in the new kingdom, and they may become its princes and kings if they do well. Estimate or if Alex's hunch is true in King Gabriel.

With great curiosity, thoughts swarmed in Barbora's mind right and left until she suppressed what she wanted himself to show about how Archie was in this far country, and what was the story of that terrifying, very big lions, and who were these boys? And those bears?

And what did they do to scatter the bodies of soldiers and sailors over the waters of the lake, and what battle took place here and why and for what?

But he knows that he was sent as a messenger and not of his own accord to ask all these questions, and whoever sent him here must have known their story and their misfortune that almost hid them forever.

Barbora wanted to calm his friend's mind better than silence and hear him cry all the time and he said to him while joking, "Didn't you ask yourself what brought me here and how I knew this exact place of yours when I hadn't heard of it before?"

Archie said eagerly, "Yes, but what we were in was more than I had time to tell you about the joy of and how you knew where we were."

Then he hit Barbora's neck with his hands and grabbed the long hair of his neck and pulled him to him and said excitedly, "How beautiful you are now, if I saw you somewhere, I would never know you, but I don't mind you telling me. But she was the one who asked for help from me and told me where you were and described it to me as if I saw him in front of me until I came to you without making a mistake in the place, as if I grew up in it since childhood?"

Archie silently thought, but inside him there was a double happiness that he had never felt before, as if he saw Maya directly in front of him, taking him in her arms with great love after that long absence until he hid the features of his face to know it from others.

Then Barbora added, "The truth is that I have not met her since the last time I saw you with her, but a messenger came to me from her in a hurry and told me that she was asking me to go to the kingdom of the dwarves, so that I was astonished by that. Archie is in urgent need of help.

"I did not hesitate even for a moment about anything Maya was asking of me, and when I arrived at the port, I saw what I saw and then realised the wisdom of Maya's request."

Archie thought and said to himself, without saying a word, "If she really knew I was in danger, why didn't she come by herself like every time! Why do you think! Did something happen to her or was she imprisoned after the incident of that cloud?"

No, no, since she knew about me and sent a request for help for me, she must be fine, then he wanted not to deviate the course of the dialogue to distract them from their main goal, which after moments will determine their fate forever until he said to him, "But you did not tell me how you and all the wings got these wings while when we met you had no wings and I saw no signs of them!"

The sword that was hanging behind his back lit up until he felt its heat, and as soon as he raised it, it was lit up sharply, and then he knew that they had approached the land of King Gabriel.

Then he interrupted Barbora's words before speaking and said, raising his sword in a loud voice to his friends, "We have arrived and we are close to salvation. Come on, get ready to enjoy the joy and dance of this victory and the sweeping achievement, until he indicated to Barbora to go down the groove at the end of which the entrance to the cave will be waiting for them."

In fact, it is calculated for them that they have reached the cave before the appointed time for them, and this is an achievement above the achievement of the unexpected victory that they achieved with their great determination to survive with their lives, no matter how hard it may cost them, until they achieved miracles in their adventure.

Before the hooves of the flying horses touched the surface of the calm gully water, a group came out.

The rhinoceros dolphins that carried them to the shores of the former Pygmy kingdom.

"Look," Luca said with his mouth full. "Look. Aren't those the same dolphins we rode with Princess Ella, the daughter of that fearsome king?"

"Yes, yes," with great happiness, he said, with two words, eyes rolling everywhere, happy and floundering with happiness, almost escaping from their eyes from the intensity of joy as they watch the group of rhinoceros dolphins receiving them by dancing and jumping from under the water in an astonishing display of grace as graceful ballet dancers.

And when they all descended on a rocky shelf from the side of the gully before the opening of the cave, a sweet voice called out to them, as if it were a hymn of love and peace from dreams.

Until Princess Ella came out on her dragon, which suddenly changed its colour to red, in contrast to its grey colour? If anyone notices that except Archie?

And she welcomed them, as if she were shooting arrows of love from between her lips, "Welcome to the heroes."

Her eyes did not leave Alexander's face as he held the magic jug in his hands, and she had been staring at him with spinning looks since the last time, until Alex felt like a clove of salt would melt if she continued to give him those very charming looks.

Alex advanced towards Ella until he stood at the edge of the cliff, completely enchanted, who had apparently lost the feeling of himself from the power of Ella's magic, until Archie grabbed him by his shirt from behind and said to him in a loud and indirect way, addressing his words to Princess Ella, "Calm a little, dear Alex, Princess Ella has come. To come here to receive us and take us to her father and hand him his long-awaited treasure?"

Then he put his hands on the magic jug and dragged him out of the arms of the demented Alexander, and that was like a slap in the face of Ella, who changed her face.

Now, come, take us to His Majesty the king, to fulfil our promise, so that he may fulfil his promise to us, and also remove this invocation from us, which it is no secret to you that it has hurt us a lot, and we will not bear more than we could bear.

She turned her face away from him and said, "In the name of the Lord of this place, you dolphins, take the king's guests to where the king is, for he is eager to see you."

Then the tenderness of the nymph, Ella, Archie was very maliciously unlike what she was, and here I felt Archie, an uncomfortable doubt in himself, until he felt a constriction in his heart and tingling as if he sensed something innocuous arranging against them. Signs of drunkenness, wandering and out of mind, and they staggered and were close to losing their balance while they were standing in their places, like those who were subjected to a collective curse, except for Archie?

It was suspicious and surprising, as if someone had cast a great magic spell on them. Their minds took them for a short time, but after the nymph Ella preceded them and moved away from them, Archie felt as if an evil energy had disappeared from the place and with it what was controlling their minds and they returned to their full consciousness?

The boys jumped for joy on the backs of dolphins, caressing them by their horns and fins, as if they were riding horses, and they were not marine animals that they did not know their behaviour.

As for Archie, he ran quickly to the horse, Barbora and Gongora, and said in a frightened whisper, "If it is midnight and none of us has come out to you, make sure that we are in great danger and tell Maya about the matter and I will not hide from you that my intuition is never wrong.

"But I hope that I will make a mistake this time, because something will happen, and I hope that it will not be evil. The looks of this nymph do not suggest good, and I am afraid that we will get into another trouble.

"As soon as the dolphins entered the dark water cave tunnel until no one could see the palm of his hand, then a bright blue light appeared, walking with them in the same direction as them, from the walls of the cave from all sides of the rocky road, as if it were spider webs painted on the rocks.

"The darkness of the place was dispelled with its enchanting light, full of deep romance, more than just a light that brought joy and pleasure into the souls. "Except Archie, who was obsessed a lot with a pale face, collecting ideas from here and there, riding them and untangling them like the knot of an old puzzle, then remember King Gabriel's sad looks when they left him as if he was saying

this is the last time you see me?"

Alexander said in a tone that he could guess what was going on in the

turbulent mind of Archie, even in this darkness, "I know that there is something that troubles you about your turbulent movements, Archie."

Archie did not want to say a letter because his soul was in a world other than the one in which his body was, as if someone had lost his mind.

He continued to think, struggling with his thoughts, which aggravated his tension even more after he had imagined that King Gabriel had incarnated in front of him and was sad in a way that aroused both pity and fear, and his beard withered and his strong and muscular body was emaciated and said with his head down in great sorrow.

"I'm sad, my son, I am sad, my son!" He said it in a heart-breaking voice from the severity of sadness and sorrow for what happened?

Then he vanished suddenly and quickly until Alexander noticed the rapid backward movement of Archie's head as if he had awakened from a nightmare.

Alexander put his hand on Archie's shoulder, but the dolphins scattered and moved away from each other, and now they entered the vast lake in which they were, but it was for them as if it was not the lake of crystal clear and crystal-clear waters, and as if something had changed in their absence?

Suddenly, light appeared from below them, phosphorous shells, until the surface of the lake appeared in completely different colours. It carved the darkness of the place and illuminated it, but in a completely different way from what they were in until Princess Ella came out sitting on a giant shell with human legs?

As for the dragon, it became larger and had the body of a snake that turned from behind the boy and closed the exit with its huge body?

On the other hand, Ella was wearing revealing clothes after lowering her bras a little so that only what was left was covering her nipples? Like trying to seduce someone?

This aroused Archie's discontent while others salivated. Here, Archie realises that something is being hatched against them and that this mermaid wants to play with them a game that is never clean, and what the nymph is hiding must be revealed early so that he knows how to act. Until Archie asked her sharply and earnestly, "Where is Your Majesty, girl?"

Without calling her name this time to make her understand that what she is doing is not normal until he laughed out loud with a lot of temptations, then she fell silent and said, "Would you not go up on the wooden pier first to rest our beautiful dolphins?"

The dolphins took them on their own to the wooden pier that was connected to a rocky cliff. Then Archie jumped up and said again after he advanced to the tip of the wooden pier and asked the same question with an angry face, "Why do you answer me, where is the king? We came for the king, and since you knew of our coming, it is better that he knew too, or is there something you are hiding from us?"

She smiled maliciously and approached quietly with her hand on her breast and did not leave her eyes Alex, and she meant what she was doing for a need in herself. Then she said while extending one of her hands towards Archie, "Hand me my father's jug and his sword!"

Archie looked at Alexander and the others, puzzled. Then Alex said, smiling happily, "Hand it, Archie! We've gone to get him!"

Then Archie turned and said more sharply, "No, I will not give you anything, for the sword is in trust from your father, and the jug is a trust to your father, and I will not hand him over until the curse is lifted from us, or else?" He fell silent and sat down looking at her closely while she stared at her with hatred. Then he continued with nervousness and improvisation, after he put the jug on the ground and took out the sword and raised it in Ella's face and said, "Otherwise I will break the jug and make it scattered for nothing."

Fearfully, she put her hand over her mouth and backed away and said while pretending to cry, "How dare you do this after my father did good to you and gave you hope to get out of our land after you tried to rob us!"

Archie argued, "Would you be so kind to us when your father sent us to hell to punish us for something we didn't do?"

Clementine said in confusion, "Look, look there, Archie. Isn't that the king's shell on which he was standing?"

"Yes, it is itself (the king has gone and gone with him to decipher the spell he cast on you, and the key to your survival has become in my own hands)?"

A familiar voice from afar, as if it was close to the other side of the bank, it was like a shadow, but as if it were two shadows?

It was a great tragedy for the boys as they see again who had escaped from his grip hours ago? It was not only King Prakshim, but also the sorcerer (Cat's Eye) whom they left captive in the hands of Gongora and the rest of the bears outside the cave?

Archie said in amazement, "What's going on? How did Prakshim get here and how did Cat's Eye get to Prakshim when we left him with Gongora and the others captive outside the cave? Where is Gongora and the rest of the bears and Barbora, and where is King Gabriel?"

Ella said to Archie with sly looks, "You haven't seen anything yet? Are you going to give me the magic jug and the sword, or are we going to have to take it our way, smart boy?"

Alex replied heartbroken, "What's going on here, Ella? Do you know this ugly? He's your father's thief, and he's the one who ventured to get the magic jug back from him. What's he doing here and how did he get here?"

The nymph Ella laughed sarcastically and turned back, and Prakshim was above King Gabriel's shell, and with him the cat-eye magician had arrived near the boys. Then she said, placing her hands on the shell on which Prakshim was standing, "He does nothing, Alex, but he came to make a promise to me and to make me his wife!"

A shocked Alex said, almost out of his mind, "What? Do you make yourself a wife to your father's thief? Where is your father?"

Prakshim said, "You have taken enough time to ask the question, although it is not important to what will happen to you, and you should know, boy, that your

method is not the way it works anymore, but before I start with you to go into the details of the new situation, I would like to thank you for your deed, without which I would not have things came to him when you see them now and when my influence expanded and I became the possession of the kingdom of King Gabriel and his beautiful daughter, Ella!"

Then he looked at her with malicious admiration, and their gazes began to roll at each other, until Archie said angrily, "I felt from the beginning that you are a dirty girl, but I gave good thought to my good opinion of your father, and now tell me where is King Gabriel, what have you done to him. Otherwise, I will break this jug."

Then he raised the magic jug with his hands above his head and said angrily, "Now we will see if you can take it from me!"

Alex said frightened, "No, Archie, don't, if you do, we'll have lost the last bargaining chip we have!"

Prakshim said coldly, "Do it if you are able to do so and we will see who will lift the spell from you?"

Archie, in turn, said, "Yes, we will see who will lift this spell from us until he returns by himself and we see him in front of us, or your dreams will be in vain, and you will rule a cave that contains nothing but ancient ruins, and a malicious girl will need to waste an entire budget to extract what is inside this damned cave and you know that you are no longer what you used to be, after what happened to your kingdom of destruction and that the population of the kingdom turned against me, it is only a matter of time."

Suddenly the place shuddered from the water of the lake to the ceiling of the cave as if an earthquake hit it, and as soon as all that stopped, a caller called out as if the voice of the cave said, "You have done well, Archie, and I am a fan of you, boy!"

It was the first time that Archie was called by his real name, Archie.

Everyone was surprised by that voice, except for Prakshim and the nymph. They did not seem surprised and surprised, as if they knew very well the truth of the sound?

No wonder they both know the truth about the disappearance of KING GABRIEL of this place, if we do not suppose that they had a hand in the mysterious and frightening matter? As for Archie and the boys, he did not stop staring around them as they searched for the source of the sound that came to them from all sides! It is as strange and confusing as the confusion of the situation they are in now!

Alex said, "Could this be King Gabriel?"

Archie said, "No."

Charlie comforted himself, "For a moment, I thought we had survived, and I

wish I hadn't."

The voice continued, saying, "I know very well how worried you are about

the effect of the spell and the disappearance of King Gabriel, but the matter is wide and safe, but it is associated with you, especially you, Archie. As for the spell, it will be invalidated.

"As for King Gabriel, it is none of your business, his daughter is more deserving of him and she is the heir to her father's inheritance. As for the covenant between you, it is that you bring the magic jug and the spell will be nullified at once, and you have done what was asked of you.

"As for the role of King Gabriel in the casting of the spell, I will perform it on his behalf for his own reasons.

"But his daughter, on behalf of her father, will receive it from you, and thus you will have completed the task and achieved what you wanted and freed yourselves from what you fear and you are free to go, except Archie!

"Your liberation from the spell remains dependent on you and your flexibility and acceptance of what I will ask of you, otherwise you will lose yourself and others as well! What did you say now! Do you dare?"

Archie looked behind him, and everyone was astonished and worried, like the one who looks at the exam paper and was surprised that everything he studied was not mentioned in the questions, and he felt like a failure from the first moment!

Archie turned his head and said softly, "Yes, I dare say what you have, but show us yourself so we can see you!"

The source of the voice said, "Look to your right! When Archie and those with him turned, as if the scene became slow, until he saw, beside a dark corner at the end of the lake, the shadow of a man with defined features of the body, but he did not see anything from him, as if it was a real shadow of the body of a person who refused to progress further so that he did not see a face or a mark!"

And when he spoke, the voice was like that of a young man, in contrast to his voice a few seconds ago, until he said, "How happy I am to see you, Archie, face to face."

Archie said, "I don't see any way to say that we met face to face?"

Alex said with interest and confusion, "As if you! Like a healer?"

The shadow answered, "It may be true, or it may not be, Brother Isabella!" Archie said firmly and confidently, "You are the healer we hear about!"

He said very calmly, "Yes, I am him, and he is me. I have been watching you

from afar, after I was the one who supervised your movements, and I found in you may need that I was looking for. In fact, you are my soul that will represent me before humans. And you will be my hand with which I will move the chess pieces!"

"I don't like riddles because my mind doesn't understand them quickly," said Archie curtly.

Prakshim interrupted him after he broke into the discussion and said, arguing with cunning eyes, "The great master gave you an initiative of goodwill without you not realising and without wishing you, of course, look at your hands, all," then whispered to Archie, "Except you, the leader of the band of thieves!"

When they turned their paws, and took off their shoes, their skins were back to normal and all those disgusting scales disappeared until they almost flew from the joy of intense joy!

Except Archie it still in his body, nothing changed, but the pain increased until he saw his skin transform quickly and fish scales swept most of his arm until he pooled on his knees from the severity of the pain and the golden jug fell from him and rolled until Ella picked him up quickly and with great attention!

Clemento shouted, "Catch up with Archie, and he seems to be in great pain?"

Luca said, confused, "Look, the mermaid took the magic jug as if she was a thief, not a princess!"

Archie said, writhing in pain, "Say what you have and give us what we want, so that we can finish it quickly and end this chapter that has exhausted us."

Archie heard a voice in his ear that no one heard but him saying to him, "Commander Glister is heading to your village to take revenge on your people and eliminate them, and no one will stop him but me, the ogres will submit to you, and you will see your love, Charlotte, so happy to live with her as a prince and princess, not as a farmer. And I don't think you will be satisfied that all your family die, Archie.

"Just accept my offer and you will be my messenger to the kingdom and I chose you because you are a descendant of the house ruling Himyarite family. It is only through you that what I seek will come true, and we will judge together, and each of us will achieve what we wish for, Archie!"

The healer, who did not move a finger from his place, calmly and coldly said, "You have become one of my followers from now on and we will finish this chapter of the novel to open a new chapter and it will be the most important chapters of the novel!"

Archie felt his heat in his throat, and when he put his hand, Maya's necklace had shone as light as the sun's rays until he put his hand on it so that they would not see her.

Then the healer asked a question that was not directed at Archie or any of the attendees, and he said with confidence and coldness, "Is that true?"

Until the cave suddenly rumbled with a violent roar like angry thunder until they became tired while they were tumbling on the ground and as if the earth had thrown them high in the air and then the sound swept them into the sky and they knew very well who the owner of this voice was!

Alex said with worried eyes. "Couldn't he be back?"

The healer said, "No, it is not what you think! But he is our other friend from the other world! It's time to conquer the kingdom, boys; the best game has begun!"

(Moving to an unknown future is better than settling in a paralyzed present)

Archie always used to repeat it to himself whenever he remembered what happened to him so that he would never despair.

www.ingramcontent.com/pod-product-compliance
Ingram Content Group UK Ltd.
Pitfield, Milton Keynes, MK11 3LW, UK
UKHW041339070325
4899UKWH00039B/1289